Tingle

Bonnie Brunish

An Infernal Museum Book

To Corey

1

"Wﾍat's wrong with you—you used to be ugly!" Ix shoved a naked blue-skinned slave girl out of the way and glowered at Puflet.

Puflet shrugged. "Got tired of being ugly. How do you like the new me?" She struck a pose, sticking out her bum and tossing her hair in a parody of Ix's own posturing, though Ix wouldn't be quick enough to catch it.

Puflet was about to take over the planet. Her custom-engineered glowworms had infiltrated Ix's systems, disabling the slave mistress' control devices. She had kicked over a glowworm vat in her basement lab to garner a disciplinary summons to the apex. Her lips curved in anticipation as she stared over Ix's head through the clear dome of the apex.

Slave training—and torture—centers, breeding farms, food factories, warehouses, sample habitats mimicking various planets of the empire, and wonderdomes lay in the blue distance below, knit together by whizzing air traffic, forming a grid that flowed outward in all directions, details ever tinier, until it blended into the shore of the black sea or the curve of the planet.

"I didn't choose for you to look like that!" Rising to her feet to look down from imperious height, Ix stomped a red boot on the marble and sent a peal of thunder rolling across the floor. The sound effect had impressed Puflet when she had been a little girl. But that was long ago.

"You are my lab worm, not a courtesan." Ix huffed, sticking out her bum and tossing her hair. "After your punishment, you will return to the wonderdome and put your ugly face back on."

"I think not."

"How dare you!"

Puflet's internal link told her that Ix had directed the slave collar to zap her. If her glowworms hadn't worked she would be rolling and twitching on the floor. She laughed in Ix's face.

Ix's eyes flared. "Bring my whip!"

Puflet smiled at her fellow slaves. At her mental signal her glowworms simultaneously blocked every slaver's link and sent a message to every slave's link. "Control devices have ceased to function. Celebrate our freedom!"

Staring out across the planet, she pictured slaves defying their overseers in every building across the continent, and even on the smaller continent on the night side of Puztak. She expected to see some sign, some change in the traffic flow, but there was nothing. No, wait—a small eddy appeared near the silvery bubble of a wonderdome. Slaves being sent there for odious alterations—roots were the latest fad among the slavers' clientele—had realized that they didn't have to endure any more dehumanization.

With a mischievous grin, the blue-skinned girl handed Ix her whip—or what once had been her whip. Puflet's glowworms had devoured the fine mechanisms, and it dissolved into black goo in Ix's hands. Grunting in disgust, she hurled the thing at Puflet, but it barely came free from her hands and splotted across the rose marble floor between them.

"What have you done?" Ix gasped.

"Only what you directed me to do. I learned to command the glowworm technology you were too lazy to master, and now my programs have taken over all the systems on this planet."

Ix rolled her eyes. Perhaps she was trying to access her link and finding it blocked. She turned sharply toward the blue girl who had brought the whip. "Seize her!"

Neither that girl nor her companions—a male, a neuter, and a hermaphrodite, also blue—moved. Ix jittered about for a second or two, probably trying to activate their collars.

"Seize her." Puflet spoke softly, but the naked slaves sprang instantly to take hold of Ix's arms and legs and hold her outspread facing Puflet.

"You can't do this! You can't defy me!" Ix tried to kick, to claw, but the slaves were far stronger than she was, and held her still. "I am the empress! Do you understand!"

Puflet snorted. "Empress is a meaningless word when you don't have the power to back it up."

"You're mad! My forces will come to rescue me in a moment, and your suffering—"

"Puh! You have a few thousand free employees on this planet, and my glowworms have rendered their weapons useless. There are millions of slaves. Who is going to save you?"

"Other slaves aren't as foolish as you, or these ones. They know the value of obedience."

Puflet laughed. More eddies, knots, and jams had sprung up in the traffic around the tower. Air lifter riders flew free, spinning in crazy circles like flies. A few of them swirled around the tower on a level with the apex, waving their arms, mouths agape with cries that couldn't be heard through the dome.

Ix's voice rose. "All right, you may have subverted the systems on this planet, but you can't block my deep-level communications. I've already sent a call for help across the galaxy, and a fleet of my ships is on its way."

Fear wormed into Puflet's belly. She hadn't been able to penetrate Ix's deep-level system. Schematics showed only a single point, unconnected to any other system. There had to be untold complexities within that point.

Puflet was an expert glowworm engineer, but deep-level engineering lay beyond her scope. Observation had told her that Ix had a very good deep-level communications system. Her call to her fleet had undoubtedly gone through. How quickly the ships could reach Puztak was another matter. Puflet squared her shoulders. "You'll be long dead before your minions get here, Ix."

Ix strained against the slaves' muscles. "No! Kicce is just docking now!"

Puflet sent a message to the slaves on spaceport, instructing them to give Kicce a warm welcome, if Ix happened to be telling the truth. "No one is going to save you. I've made sure your mind-files were destroyed too. You are going to die."

"Nooo!" The spasm of Ix's muscles sent her spurting forward, but the slaves hauled her back again. "Puflet, this is ridiculous! This will all be yours anyway, you don't have to kill me. I've been training you to be my successor! I see you as my daughter!"

"I don't have time for this." Puflet looked at the blue slaves. "We are free! I'll leave her fate in your hands. You were closest to her and know best what she deserves."

The four blue faces grinned, revenge in their eyes.

Ix writhed, screaming. "Puflet, wait! I can tell you whose genes I used to make you—you really want to know who your parents are, don't you?"

Puflet did, in fact, long to know. "Well?"

"I used my own genes, and ... and...." Ix's eyes roamed. It was obvious that she was trying to make something up on the fly, but she didn't have the wits to do so.

"You've lied to me for the last time!" Once again Puflet looked at the blue slaves. "I must gain control of the deep-level system and make sure that none of Ix's ships gets here. If I fail, we will have a battle on our hands, so be prepared."

She crossed the circular room to a blue-shadowed alcove she had never before entered. Her schematics told her this was the way to the deep-level system. Her glowworms unlocked an airshift, and she dropped down into a chamber directly below the apex. Thumps and scufflings and Ix's screams followed her from the room above.

In the dimness she had entered, Puflet found that she carried a luminous envelope. In her surreptitious wonderdome float, she'd had her own genes expressed—Ix had never allowed her to see her true face—and her new, ice-white hair glowed. She laughed. But when she had called on another cloud of fireflies to increase the illumination, her mirth faded. She stood in a space as big as the chamber above, but it was totally empty except for a pillar rising in the very center. She walked to the pillar, her steps reverberating through the emptiness (the sounds from above had ceased). The pillar, made of a crystalline material, was half-again as tall as she was. A blue humanoid head rested on its top, long black hair flowing down the sides of the pillar. Inside the pillar, a blue liquid circulated through tubes running to and from the head.

When Puflet was a couple of steps away, the head opened its eyes, eyes as blue as sapphires, and looked at her. A voice deep as thunder rolled in her ears. "Greetings, Puflet."

She tingled with fear. The head knew her, though her fireflies told her it had no link to any of Ix's other systems. She gazed upon the deep-level communications device, and she knew what it was —who it was.

It was said that Quintillion had perished in a duel with Thermeon, the only mindsea who could rival him, their mindpowers cracking an enormous rift in the crust of the planet Lal and shaking the empire's capital. It appeared now that part of Quintillion had lived on.

"All right," Puflet tried to banish any quaver from her voice. "Send a new message out and tell those ships not to come. The crisis is averted."

"It is too late," the head told her.

"What do you mean?" Puflet yelled. At the same moment she realized the head hadn't moved its lips. The voice just sounded in her mind. It was said that mindseas could do far more than make you hear their thoughts. They could make you feel pain, see illusions, do anything, be anything they willed.

"You are the real power on this planet, aren't you?" she whispered.

"No," the head replied.

She giggled, then clasped her hands over her mouth. Fear was making her foolish. She had to master herself, or how could she hope to fight off the head's influence? "Why won't you tell those ships not to come?"

"I showed them Ix's last thoughts. It was her wish. They know she is dead, and Valri has declared herself the new Empress of the Unknown. She is coming to regain control of this world."

"How far out is she?"

"Three tenthyears."

Puflet took a deep breath. She had a little time, at least. "So, you're still transmitting messages for the slavers?"

"It is their wish."

"You wouldn't do it unless you wanted to. They could hardly make you do anything. You're a mindsea."

"I deplore their line of work," the head said.

"Then why don't you exert your powers over them and make them see the error of their ways?"

"I have never exerted my powers over a human."

Puflet blinked as she absorbed this. The head regarded her with its mournful blue eyes.

"Why not?" she finally asked.

"It would be wrong."

"Isn't raising millions to lives of torment and despair wrong?"

"It is not as terrible as the alternative."

A frisson went down her spine. "What alternative?"

"The destruction of everything."

She gasped, then clenched her fists. "How would your failure to obey the commands of a bunch of power-hungry slavers cause the destruction of everything?"

"They are only human. They only follow the prompting of their instincts. They cannot feel it."

"Feel what?"

The voice did not sound again in her head, but she heard its echo rolling around. "Destruction ... destruction ... everything ... everything." She tossed her head and took another deep breath, trying to clear her mind.

"Now see here, if you merely wish a mistress, then obey me! I command you to stop sending the slavers' messages! Transmit my messages to them. Tell them the game is up! Oh, and if you have a node in the empire, tell them about this planet. A few warships stationed here will put an end to Valri's plans. Ha!"

"I can't obey you," the head said.

Puflet ground her teeth. "Why the hell not?"

"You are not human. You are his daughter, aren't you?"

Her fingers stole to the tips of her fangs. "Whose? Thermeon's?" Ix had boasted more than once about having an illegal son by Thermeon, though Puflet had never seen him. "I suppose you hate all of Thermeon's descendants."

"I hate no one. But your mindsize is too great. You would feel it."

Puflet shut her eyes and concentrated on breathing in and breathing out. The head was messing with her, making her flinch at shadows, like a child.

She opened her eyes again. "You're lying to me, you self-mapped head, Quintillion, whatever you are! I don't know anything about deep-level stuff. Valri has been to the mindsea academy, so she does know about it, but you're obeying her."

"Yes," the head acknowledged. "She learned a few tricks there, and that is why the others fear her and have ceded preeminence to her. She has no real mindsize."

"But you're saying I do?"

"Yes."

Puflet thought it over. "So, you couldn't overpower my mind, even if you tried?"

"I have never tried to overpower anyone's mind."

She chuckled. "So you weren't trying to overpower Thermeon's mind when you two cracked the desert open?"

"No. We weren't fighting each other."

Her jaw dropped. "What? Then what the hell were you doing?"

"I had asked him to help me," the head told her.

"Help you? That's not what the historical memories say."

"They don't understand. I had hoped that the two of us together might be able to master it, so I relaxed my hold for a moment."

"'It' tore the desert apart and both of your bodies?" Puflet asked. "Then why didn't everything end right then and there?"

"I resumed my containment of it. I can hold it back, but I can't overcome it." The voice in her head reverberated with infinite sorrow.

"But I don't see why you need to work for slavers to hold it back."

"I merely need to suffer."

"What if I kill—uh, destroy you—you're sort of dead, already aren't you? That will stop your helping Valri."

"Then you will inherit my burden."

She snorted. "I don't think so."

The head smiled sadly.

Puflet ordered her glowworms to penetrate the head and burn out a vital spot, but the moment they touched the blue skin they ceased to transmit.

She glared at the head, wondering how to attack. It was

reasonable to suppose it could only destroy glowworms that penetrated its flesh. If so, she could blow up the pillar and cut off its blood supply. Of course, if it had lied, if it would and could seize her mind, she would die in worse agony than Ix had.

The head continued to smile at her and hummed a soft, sorrowful tune.

"Oblivion would be a release for you, wouldn't it," she suggested. "That can't be much of a life stuck on top of that pole in the dark."

"It's no different than the rest of my life."

"Because of 'it?'"

"Yes."

"Where did 'it' come from?"

"I inherited it from my father."

"And he got it from?"

"It was passed down from the time of the dinosaurs. An imperial flunky returned 'it' to the world when she created my grandmother from some gene specs she discovered in a museum."

"But she never noticed 'it?'"

"No, power is enough for imperial flunkies. But it isn't enough for you."

"So ... if not power, what is it I really want?"

"The truth."

Fear sliced through her, stronger than before, the jolt racing from her scalp to her toes like a lightning flash, illuminating something vast and terrible that was gone again so quickly she couldn't make it out. As she drew a ragged breath she realized what the mindsea was doing. If she kept talking to him, he'd have her so terrified of this formless 'it' she'd be rolling around the floor peeing herself.

With a scream she launched herself at the pillar. She leaped, seized the head by its trailing hair, and ripped it down. The tubes popped free, and the blue blood spurted in the pool of light shed by her hovering cloud of fireflies. She hurled the head over the pillar toward the darkness.

And then time stopped.

The head hung in the air above her, one eye in shadow, the other staring down at her with awful blue intensity.

In a silent thunderclap, an unseen force parted the world around her, hurling her into another universe. The eye's blaze had become a star. She stood on the surface of an unknown world and watched the star hurl down its bolts. The world burned, and all its creatures died. She felt their deaths, felt each life being snuffed out—it was the destruction of everything.

Then the star doubled, reddened, became the fiery eyes of a dinosaur that loomed from the smoking darkness. Puflet knew this was the being that had started the terrible chain of events. It was a monster, a mindsea, something beyond comprehension. The eyes touched hers and the force of their will crackled like electricity, making all of her muscles jerk.

"You must become me," the monster told her.

A tenthyear later, Puflet boarded a ship bound for the imperial capital. A few of Ix's ships had made port, but without the head to coordinate their efforts, the pilots were unprepared to fight the freed slaves who seized them when they left their ships.

Piloting a tetrascoping ship—one that transformed to mesh with the stuff of up to four patternistic levels deeper than the scum where humanity dwelt—required mindsize. Folks who didn't have the perceptions of those levels became inert when the ship transformed. If the head had told Puflet true, she would be able to act in the Deep. But she still couldn't pilot herself, because she didn't know how. That meant she had to depend on one of the captured pilots.

After interviewing all of them, she picked Kicce. One of Ix's erstwhile consorts, he was pretty much a laughing stock among the slavers. He had offered no resistance when the slaves seized him. He told Puflet he'd be glad to take her to the empire, on the condition that she let him pretend that he'd only just discovered Puztak, so he wouldn't be in trouble with the authorities.

The authorities would have to be blind to believe him, but Puflet just shrugged. It was nothing to her.

Although the majority of the freed slaves had entrenched themselves as the new owners of Puztak, the only home they'd known, a few among them wanted to seek the "great, free empire" along with her. Puflet told them to wait. She expected that she would have her hands full with Kicce once the ship downleveled.

She didn't need the voyage complicated by inert passengers he could take hostage.

Armed with glowworms and an inanimate knife and garbed in a deep-level whaleskin suit confiscated from another pilot, Puflet settled into the copilot's niche so that she could watch Kicce perform. The ship's bridge was a circular chamber lined by viewscreens. A floating control column housed the four level-detection disks that gave the ship its name. The column had a glowworm system for communications with spaceports and control of the home-level engines. Once they downleveled, this system, and Puflet's glowworms, would cease to function.

Kicce was a small man who didn't seem to care that he was ugly. Like Puflet, he wore a Mednean whaleskin—his was tinted red and marked with subtle designs a shade paler—equipped with the trademark rings on shoulders, hips, and ankles, and displaying the Pilots Guild logo on the chest. He gave her a nervous smile as they slipped free from their spaceport berth and slid among the stars, blue eyes leaping from his pale, sweat-beaded face. "You really think you can watch me the whole way?"

"Yes."

"Whatcha got that big knife for? You think you can use that in the Deep?"

"Yes, I do. It's a simple weapon, not glowworm powered."

He cackled. "You got a lot to learn, bit."

"I want to learn."

"Oh, do you now. Well, I can tell you think you got mindsize, but you better wish you don't."

"Why is that?"

"Ever heard of a thing called patternistic integrity?"

"No."

Kicce's belly shook as he savored his private joke. Puflet gripped the hilt of her knife. "Explain yourself!"

He clutched his nose and collected himself. "Going down ain't dangerous. It's coming back up that's the rub. The ship, when she's deep, is a fine, core thing, fused with all her ever-could-be's along as many axes as you went down. When you come up, she's gotta shed all of these to end up as just the home-level tissue she started out. In the old days, before the blasted fanged emperor"—he meant

Thermeon—"smashed them, the transways reckoned all of this stuff for you. Nowadays, every pilot is the chooser of his own history. But if you got two actives on a ship, and they pull different ways, then the ship comes apart, unfuses, and you end up with parts in this history, and parts in that history. And everyone is dead. See what I mean?"

Puflet tossed her head. "No."

"Then I'll make it simple. If you got the mindsize to see the Deep, you better mind what I want, echo everything I wish for, or the patternistic integrity will go whoosh."

"Or maybe you better echo what I wish for."

He shook his head. "That ain't happening."

She settled back in her niche, its straps tightening to snug her in. "We'll see."

Her eyes traveled about the bridge, noting the intricate convolutions on the curving metallic-sheened wall. It was like the inside of one of those Lalian decapod shells Ix had used for candy dishes.

A feeling of oppression grew as the ship jetted onward—though it hardly felt like that were moving at all, and the stars hung motionless in the viewscreens.

"Why do I feel so heavy?" she groaned.

"We're bound for Lal, so I thought I'd better turn the grav up so's you can start to feel accustomed."

"Everyone on Lal feels like this? It's like being crushed!"

His mirth echoed from the convoluted wall. "Only people that ain't used to it. People from low-grav planets like you."

"It won't affect my glowworms, of course," she said to remind him not to try anything while he had her at this disadvantage.

His laughter ceased. They sat for a long time among the silent, unmoving stars.

"I thought we were supposed to downlevel," she ventured at length.

He grunted. "Contain yourself, bit. I gotta find transaxis. It ain't like the old days when we had the ways. Everyone's gotta hunt around home-level until the right pattern of stuff just happens to show up on the disk so's the ship can go down. You ain't helpin' my concentration, so just go to sleep, will ya?"

Instead, Puflet stared at the four disks on the control column, wondering what pattern he was looking for. Random bursts of colors flitted across all of the disks. There weren't any patterns she could see, just noise.

To her chagrin, she had drifted into a semi-sleep when a movement in the corner of her eye startled her into full awareness. Kicce had reached out to grasp a lever protruding from his side of the control column. He pulled the lever.

The universe exploded with sensations too myriad and too intense for her to fathom. Kicce's body odor, which before had hovered in the background of her awareness, became a suffocating reek. The sensations of her own body were excruciating. Out of control, her gurgling, twitching organs sought to tear her in different directions. Another force shoved her from the outside. The smell told her the force came from Kicce.

His voice blasted her with a foul wind. "Off my ship, ya loopin' bitch! I won't unfuse for the likes of you!"

She tried to resist, but her body was out of control, and the overripe sensations the Deep had disoriented her so, she could neither see nor feel the ship. And the stars—what had become of them?

When she'd been sitting half-asleep, their brilliant white pinpricks against the blackness in the viewscreens had formed patterns. Suddenly she realized that those patterns were being repeated by sensations of weight that tapped against her skin, but unlike before, the patterns changed, the gentler, languid taps of more distant stars like soulful melodies riding on the swift, strong beats of the nearer stars.

She still couldn't untangle the sensations of the ship from the rest, and she feared it would soon be too late, for Kicce's shoving grew fiercer, the wind-song of his thoughts more triumphant.

Her rage and frustration erupted, not in a human voice, but with a white-hot blast. Amazed, she watched it blossom into twin fires —the eyes of the monster. Its voice thundered through the universe. "You are me! I am you!"

The molten rivers of its fury became her blood. Heated to incandescence, her mind sharpened, sorted through the sensations hurtling at it to form a picture:

She stood on the rim of an extremely high, extremely small circular mesa rising from a black fog. Other mesas, similar to hers, could be seen in the distance. Drumbeats sounded from the mesas, as if some person sat on each of them pounding out his own rhythm. Puflet recognized the rhythms and knew that the other mesas were the stars. Kicce, who looked and smelled like an overgrown stinkbug, was shoving her toward the precipice. A few more steps, and she would fall forever into the black fog.

"Treacherous insect!" she roared. The monster's power flowed through her, and when she shoved back, Kicce flew from the mesa with a tiny squeak. He plunged into the void.

Puflet fell as well, collapsing into herself, her senses all suddenly muffled. She fell through a world of absolute silence.

And then she realized that she was not falling. She sat in the copilot's niche of the ship's bridge, still strapped in, the control column with its winking patterns in front of her, and beyond it the viewscreens and the convoluted metallic walls. The ship had upleveled again. The glowworm lighting seemed dim and colorless after the searing sensations of the Deep.

Breathing hard, she turned her head very slowly to check the pilot's niche. Though the straps remained in place, Kicce was not there. A glimpse of the void leaped back at her, making her stomach knot. He was gone. How had she managed to push him out through the walls of the ship, not even disturbing the straps? For that matter, how was it that she had felt him shoving her, yet not moved?

Had the Deep opened other directions to push in, other dimensions? She shook her head. They said no one could really understand it.

Now that they were back on home-level, her glowworms worked again, though she had lost her internal link. She fashioned a new one, and meshed with the ship's glowworms. She inquired as to how close they were to their destination.

Her stomach dropped at the answer. Lal was a hundred light years away.

"What is the nearest imperial world?" she asked.

"Ulona," came the answer. "Fifty light years away. Hee hee." The shipvoice sounded like Ix—a drunken Ix. Puflet commanded her glowworms to render it impersonal.

Ulona was the location of the mindsea academy, perhaps a better goal than Lal. Puflet would have to learn to employ her mindsize. Questioning the ship, she found that it did not carry supplies enough to keep her alive for as long as it would take to reach Ulona on home-level. She had to downlevel again.

If only she hadn't been dozing when Kicce had found that crucial pattern.

She commanded the ship to head toward Ulona, then stared at the meaningless flashes of color in the four disks. Even if she did manage to downlevel, how could she navigate? She wouldn't recognize the characteristic pulsations of Ulona's star. But maybe if she studied the patterns of the stars in that part of the galaxy, she could find the way by their relative positions. She had the viewscreens run her through what she would see.

"How long will the trip take once I downlevel?" she asked.

"In Deep Four, the trip will take seven hours imperial time," the ship told her. "Perceived time will be two seconds."

"What? I'll have to uplevel again in two seconds?"

"Yes."

Puflet bit her lip. "How do I uplevel?"

"Release the lever."

There was no way she'd be able to examine the star patterns in two seconds. She'd just have to hope she was still pointed the right way, count to two, and release the lever. If she could identify the lever and her hand holding it.

"Was Kicce flying Deep Four?"

"Yes."

"What if I find the right pattern in the first disk instead of the fourth disk, and pull the lever then?"

"On Deep One, the trip to Ulona will take three imperial years. Perceived time, two tenthyears."

"I think I would prefer Deep Two or Deep Three. Can you tell me what patterns to look for?"

"Recognizing the patterns requires mindsize. The patterns cannot be categorized."

She sighed. "Then I'll just have to guess." She watched the flashes for a while, then gave the lever an experimental tug. It

16

didn't budge.

Hours and many tugs later, she flopped back in exhaustion, sweat rolling down her forehead. She realized she hadn't reset the grav.

"Make ship's grav match Ulona's," she commanded.

If anything it was worse. She gasped for breath.

"Set the grav halfway between Puztak and Ulona."

That was better. She could breathe again. She ordered snacks and a drink, and set her mind to the pattern problem.

A serving bioid popped out from an irising wall tube, bearing a tray with beer and a bowl of puffy triangles that tasted like lard. The beer was vile as well. The bioid was a knee-high copy of Ix in the nude with a grotesquely swollen red vulva.

"Disgusting!" Puflet spat. She tossed the tray into a recycle tube beside her niche, then grabbed for the bioid to throw it in too, but it skittered back into the wall.

Puflet sat back, gasping and tapping her fingers against the niche's metallic-sheened armrests. "What is the frequency of the right patterns appearing in the disks?"

"No data available. It is said that transaxes to lesser Deeps are easier than transaxes to greater Deeps, but the pilot shifts probabilities by his actions."

"Actions? I don't remember him doing anything except sitting there watching the disks. Was he sending commands to the engines?"

"Yes."

"Twistor it!" Puflet clenched her fists and gnawed on her lip until she tasted salty blood. "What do those ditbitted patterns mean, anyhow?"

"They show particles and energies around the ship."

"Same ship, same space around it—how can there be four different readings?"

"There is a different sampling area for each level, the greatest area being for the deepest level."

Puflet sighed and thought for awhile. Her stomach grumbled. She kicked her feet to get the blood flowing again. "What if I just grab the lever and keep hold of it until the right pattern comes along?"

"You may try," the ship-voice said with an almost-perceptible shrug. "It is my understanding that the force-worms react to the total grabbing configuration rather than to any linear pressure on lever."

"Force-worms!" Puflet muttered.

She was twistored.

Hours and much discussion later, she formed a plan. She left the ship on its heading toward Ulona, with the glowworms instructed to repeatedly broadcast her message to that planet at lightspeed until an acknowledgment was received. Then she had a firefly guide her through the ship's convoluted corridors to its wonderdome. Puflet stripped and laid herself down in the gelatinous prep nook. With a gurgle she was squirted through the intake tube into the warm, wet darkness of the pool. Wonderwater filled her mouth and nostrils. It infused her tissues with oxygen, and with other chemicals that made her limbs buzz and her mind grow foggy. Soon she would be in a state of hibernation, in which the ship could sustain her until it reached Ulona.

As her awareness plunged toward the void, a pair of fiery eyes ignited in the blackness above her, and a roar of fury shook the universe.

3

Puflet became aware of a dimly glowing wall, the gelatinous hug of a self-nook around her. She had returned to the human world.

With a gasp she sat up. She was in a little egg-shaped room, probably a wonderdome recovery cell. The glowworm link in her brain was still intact. She queried it for news. It was Imperial Year 104,397, some hundred years since she'd left Puztak. Emperor Gawoi and Head of the Circle Raolin ruled; the empire was at peace. Puflet's heart gave a little jump when she learned that Puztak had been admitted to the empire as a member world and all its inhabitants accorded citizenship. Her coup had succeeded.

She checked to see if the names of the pilots she had mentioned in her message had been arrested. Only a few of them had been detained for wonderdome guidance, but all had been thrown out of the Pilots Guild. Most had vanished to worlds unknown.

Her jaw clenched when she learned that Valri had been cleared of wrongdoing and restored to the guild. "She had been placed among the slavers as a government spy," the official statement went, "and would have brought all of the offending pilots to justice if Ix's deep-level comm system hadn't been destroyed."

That was a load of crap. Puflet had seen slaves after Valri had used her mind-tricks to discipline them. She hadn't been any government spy. The end of the news file indicated that Valri was the granddaughter of Member of the Circle Sagi Gidark Veance. That explained it. Puflet could have kicked herself for failing to notice that tie. She vowed not to make such a stupid mistake again.

With that in mind, she had the names and faces of government people flashed before her, and added them to her internal glowworm files. She had gone through the imperial family and members of the Circle, and was starting on notables at the mindsea academy when a door irised in the egg's wall. A beautiful, tall, pale woman with rippling wine-red hair bustled in, swishing her green robe.

"I'm sorry I didn't notice that you were awake sooner," she smiled. "I am Fanala Nefusen Aisoy, and I'm here to help your transition to citizenship. Now, we can count you as a citizen already, but you should really study for your niche."

"I'd like to be a deep-level engineer."

"That's a very difficult job, you know."

"I know," Puflet said.

"Maybe you'd like to try something easier?"

"No. I'd like to transmit my application to the mindsea academy so that I can study deep-level forces."

"Most people who try that fail," Fanala said.

Puflet sat up straighter and the gel nook conformed to her new posture. This little twerp was getting on her nerves. She found herself glaring at the girl with another set of eyes, the eyes that had been hers during hibernation. "She's just an empty shell," the ancient voice told her. "Hardly even alive."

Puflet had felt power flowing through her, charging her cells in preparation for profound action. Quintillion had been a fool to see the monster as a curse. It was a source of strength; it had saved her from Kicce. Even now, she could use its strength and flick out a mind-finger to dazzle the fool in front of her. Even though she was no longer on a downleveled ship, the extra dimensions of the Deep were still there, and the monster could help her find them. She already knew the tricks Valri had learned, and she hadn't even been to the academy yet.

Caution made her hold back. She was a stranger on this planet, and it wouldn't do to alarm the natives. She simply said, "I've already been preadmitted, so just see that my application reaches Headmistress Katora, all right?"

"Oh, of course!" Fanala smiled. "Now, what would you like to eat? You can order from the system, of course, but I thought you might appreciate a personal touch, after being on board that ship for so long. That must have been terrible!"

"I was asleep," Puflet said. "In hibernation."

"Oh. I didn't know that ships had a hibernation on them."

Puflet rolled her eyes.

Fanala tittered. "I guess they have all sorts of things I don't know about. My grandfather is head of the Pilots Guild. He knows all about those ships."

Puflet narrowed her eyes. Was that connection what had garnered Fanala her niche? She didn't seem to possess brains enough to shovel dirt for slime molds. Puflet had thought Ix stupid, but if this was an example of an ordinary citizen's intelligence, the empire was worse off than she had supposed. The Pilots Guild head, Orgmorgan, was an astute man. He could have made life hard for the slavers, but for a sufficient bribe he would look the other way. Member Sagi had probably given him a private moon, or something, for reinstating Valri. Orgmorgan was the cleverest man in the galaxy, if you measured brains by credits on command, but a couple generations of easeful living had produced the beauty in front of her.

She forced herself to smile at Fanala. She would have to be gentle. Getting Orgmorgan mad at her would probably lead to worse repercussions than having crossed Member Sagi. "I'd love some Saqufean fire dragons!" As a little girl she'd tasted the dregs in Ix's cups and savored their sting.

"Oh, that's much too strong for rising meal," Fanala giggled. "I'll get you some fern juice." She turned and bustled out.

"Thank you." Puflet stared at the wall that had closed behind her, then heaved a sigh and addressed her glowworm link. She started working on her application to the mindsea academy.

Fanala returned with a vile-tasting green liquid in a graceful yellow-tinted crystal goblet. Puflet sipped and went on with her work, hoping to be left alone. Fanala summoned a nook facing hers and flopped into it. "How old are you?"

"I think I was forty-six when I went into hibernation." In fact, Puflet had spent many, many years perfecting her glowworms, but she preferred to appear younger. There were ways to trace a person's metabolic footprints despite the antiaging process, but after the downleveling/upleveling transformations it got much trickier, and she doubted that anyone would be that interested in her.

"I'm not yet a hundred," Fanala gushed. "But I think you're younger than me! Who are your parents?"

"I don't have parents. I was a slave. I was created from random genetic bits."

Fanala leaned forward to peer at her. "You look human."

"I'm mostly human." Puflet sighed and plugged away at the application through her link.

"Oh." Fanala sat in perfect silence for a while, her face slightly tensed, as if she were attempting to think. Puflet sighed. Such a lovely container for bilge, like the crystal goblet perched on the arm of her nook. She made progress with the application.

Fanala gave a start. She smiled at Puflet. "I have a son. He's ... uh ... not yet twenty. He wants to be a pahmak herder. Would you like to meet him? Maybe you two could...." She bent her head, blushing and tittering.

"I'd. Love. That." Please get me out of the clutches of these morons, Puflet prayed to the forces of destiny.

Fanala beamed at her. "I'll call him right now." Her eyes went unfocused.

Puflet answered the final questions on the application, reviewed the whole thing, then transmitted it. *Please admit me quickly,* she prayed.

Fanala winced, reddened. She gave her head a shake. "Sometimes he doesn't listen to me." She let out a long, dramatic sigh. "Children are like that! Do you have any children?"

"No," said Puflet. "Uh ... Fanala, you know, I'm really tired out. Would it be all right if I went to sleep?"

"Go right ahead. I'll watch you."

"You know, I'm really not used to people watching me while I sleep."

"Don't worry, you'll get used to it."

Puflet shut her eyes and worked on her reviews of important figures at the academy and general information about the planet Ulona. From time to time she listened for Fanala's breathing.

Hearing it, and sensing the warmth of her body and the fragrance of her skin and hair, she cursed silently and got back to her work.

Ulona circled its distant star once every fifty imperial years—much of its heat came from its molten core. Its axial tilt was about ninety degrees, so that each pole in turn received twenty-five years of daylight. Native fauna, including the pahmaks, a species resembling Earth's dinosaurs, migrated from pole to pole, following the sun.

No native humans survived on Ulona when it was admitted to the Empire, though they had left some signs of colonization, as well as the plants and animals they had brought from Earth. It was believed that a terrible cataclysm had wiped them out about a hundred millennia before the planet's rediscovery.

Puflet was virtually touring a scene of pahmaks hunting zebra-crabs in a cycad grove when Fanala's outburst sent her clutching the arms of her nook. "Oh no, there's another patient! I'll have to go, but I promise I'll be back as soon as I can."

"Don't twist yourself," Puflet muttered.

As soon as she was alone, she shut her eyes and slept. In her dream she was a pahmak and Fanala was a crab burbling mindless pleasantries as it scooted across the black lava rocks. Puflet was about to seize the crab and feel the satisfying crunch between her fangs when her link flickered to alert her to an awaited message.

Crabs and cycads spinning away, she roused herself to receive the message. It was from Headmistress Katora.

"I appreciate your situation and all you've gone through, and I understand that you believe that you may have an aptitude for Patternistics. However, at the academy we believe that attitude is more important than aptitude. Do you have the attitude it takes to use the knowledge the academy will impart in a way that benefits humanity?

"As you have just undergone an long ordeal, you will need time to get settled and to think about this. You will also need to learn to conduct yourself in the new world in which you have found yourself. When you have successfully completed a course of introduction to modern imperial culture under the guidance of your wonderdome aide, please contact me again."

Puflet threw back her head and let a scream rip from her throat.

She had struggled for two centuries for ... this?

Fanala swept in. "Oh, my, what's the matter!"

"Uh ... a nightmare. I was having a nightmare."

Fanala stepped closer and patted her arm. "Everything's all right now. I'm here. Go back to sleep, and I'll watch you."

Fanala's smile was bigger than usual as she brought Puflet her rising meal fern juice. "My son has agreed to meet you! Isn't that wonderful?"

"I'll say," Puflet managed between clenched lips. She had spent much of the previous several days feigning sleep.

"He invited you to come see the herd he's watching. You'll have a wonderful time!"

"Oh." The prospect was suddenly less onerous. Puflet had remained enclosed in her eggshell room with only an occasional foray to the indoor garden a short, curving corridor away. She had yet to get any sense of the planet she was on, except for its miserable gravity. Outdoor exercise would do her good.

"He sent a programmed air lifter to pick you up. It's waiting. Come on!"

Puflet pulled herself up and struggled behind the graceful flow of Fanala's robe as she led the way through a much longer curving corridor. Staggering and gasping for breath, Puflet felt like an infant.

The corridor debouched into a golden-lit foyer. Puflet paused to look around. A black wall curved up to become the ceiling. A band of water circulated along the foyer's outer rim, against this wall, emerging and vanishing through archways, a quaint wooden bridge crossing it to reach the outer portals. Behind her, an inner curving wall was lined with rugged piles of the native black rock, planted with ferns and orchids and watered by trickling fountains. The ferny smell she had come to associate with Ulona flooded her nostrils. It reminded her of the vile juice she had to down each day, and her stomach flinched in response. Above the fountains, golden letters spelled out "Wonderdome of Alonaton."

Alonaton, the city Katora had built to support her academy, was located on Ulona's south pole. It was the planet's only large settlement.

"Your air lifter is over here," Fanala called. "You're probably having trouble finding it."

It wasn't like Puflet was a primitive who'd never seen an air lifter—she was a glowworm-engineer, blip it! Fixing a smile to her face, she dragged herself over, slippers scraping across the rough-hewn stones of the lobby floor. She hurled herself into the machine's airy embrace, sent it a "go" thought, and it rose from the floor and swept across the bridge and out through the lobby's parting portals into ...

Darkness.

It wasn't a black wall she had seen, but a clear wall with nothing beyond it.

It had never struck Puflet that Katora would allow her city to endure twenty-five years of night when the south pole faced away from the sun. Why didn't they move their habitats to follow the sun? A pahmak with a brain the size of a credit button could figure that one out, but apparently not the headmistress of the mindsea academy.

Lights of the city appeared ahead, the only color in all-enfolding darkness. A cluster of golden domes were quite attractive, but they fell below and behind quickly as the air lifter accelerated. The weatherscreen protected Puflet from the wind. After the initial acceleration, she might have been floating somewhere between space and land. The golden domes shrank to tiny points of light, then vanished. All was dark around her; there were no stars. She peered in all directions, but even the sky-glow of the city had been swallowed up. She made out a dull greenish tint to the blackness directly ahead, and guessed that it was the dawn that wouldn't turn into morning for a year or more. From time to time a reddish light illuminated clouds to one side—lightning, or an eruption. She thought there was a low growling sound following the flashes after an interval. But perhaps she was flying over herds of pahmaks, and it was they who made the growls. She could see nothing below her.

She floated on, through the unchanging darkness, for hours. She wished she'd peed before leaving the wonderdome. She wished she'd had something to eat. She began to wonder if the air lifter had been mis-programmed. If the son was anything like the mother, it certainly had been. She reminded herself that Ulona was a huge planet—all of Puztak would fit into one of its mid-sized lava flows. She would give it just a while longer before directing the air lifter to turn back.

The air lifter decelerated, wafted downward. Puflet peered into the darkness below. At last a small pool of light appeared. The air lifter landed in the light. A man wearing an ochre windbreaker, the hood pulled up to shadow his face, stomped up. "Yo!"

Puflet stepped from the machine into a blast of cold wind that took her breath away. Tepi threw back his hood, revealing a dark face beneath wind-tossed black hair, pale eyes glinting like pebbles. He stumbled against her, grabbing one breast and twisting it hard. Gasping, Puflet pushed him away. She tripped over a rock and almost went down. There was nothing but blackness beyond the light; so sign of Ulona's magnificent dinosaurs.

Tepi laughed. "So you're my mother's little friend. You're not as ugly as I thought you would be. But I bet you're stupid!"

She was stupid to have come. She took a step toward the air lifter, but Tepi interposed himself, and she wobbled backwards away from him. The wind whipped her hair about and stung her eyes. It was cold. She'd thought that Ulona was a hot planet, but here on the dark pole at the tail end of winter it was more frigid than anything she had experienced before. Her wonderdome robe had minimal response; it warmed a little, but it didn't cover her arms or her legs below the knees. Goosebumps popped up all over her skin. She started to shiver.

Tepi grinned. "Enjoying the dawn wind, love?"

"I-I-I—" Her chattering teeth made it hard to talk.

"Aw, poor little baby is cold!" Tepi laughed. "Let me warm you up!"

He flung his arms around her and bore her to the ground

beneath him. Bruised by the rocks and crushed by his weight on top of her, she could hardly think for a couple of seconds. Then she noticed rough hands working at her robe, pulling it up to expose her thighs to the wind.

"G-g-g-et oooff!" she managed to gasp.

He laughed. His pants split to reveal a swollen red cock.

Puflet cursed unintelligibly. She had been assaulted many times on Puztak. If the brute had been a slave she'd fought back. If it had been a citizen, she'd had to endure it, at least until she achieved her ultimate revenge. But she didn't have to put up with such things any more.

She tried to bring up a foot to kick him off, but the unaccustomed gravity made her so weak that she managed only a feeble wriggling. Pain lanced up through her body. Despite her resolve to remain stoic, a breathy scream escaped her lips.

"Gettin' warmer?" he grunted and thrust again, harder.

Her mind cast about wildly. Call for help—no, Ulona didn't have discipline-dispensing watch-eyes, and from the length of the air lifter flight she was in the middle of nowhere. Her glowworms had been left aboard Kicce's ship. She hadn't even thought to bring a knife.

There was nothing to be done. She would get the bastard later.

"Getting warmer? Ha ha!"

Puflet tried to distance her mind. Then Tepi's fat red lips descended on hers, his putrid, ferny breath choking her as he bit and sucked on her mouth.

A barrier inside her gave way. She didn't even recall putting it up—or perhaps she did. It had happened when she'd decided not to toy with Fanala. She'd been holding the monster back, just as Quintillion had.

She released the monster, and it rose in a satisfying rush of fire and fury. Gravity didn't matter any more; it didn't reach the deep dimensions. Tepi's body didn't restrict her in those dimensions, either. Becoming the monster, she slid free from him.

"Huh?" He lurched to his feet, goggling.

"HEEEEERE!" she roared, and kicked him into the darkness.

He fell just like Kicce, only there came a thud as he struck the lava plain.

Her laughter floated over the vast dark world. The monster submerged again as the echoes faded, and she found herself kneeling, bruised and shaking, in Tepi's circle of light. She started at the sight of his boots on the edge of the circle. She thought she'd thrown him some distance, but it looked like he'd just fallen over backwards. As she stared, the boots twitched. A hollow moan rose from the shadowed form, crescendoed, and faded into a gargle.

She spat in his direction. "Bastard!"

She staggered to the embrace of the air lifter, and sent it aloft with the thought "return."

She slept the whole way back.

Fanala met her in the lobby. "Ooh, you look like you had a wonderful time!"

"I fell, I don't remember anything," Puflet muttered, keeping her eyes on the floor. "Could I have a hot bath, please?"

"Not now, it's mid mealtime."

"I'm not hungry, just a bath and sleep, please."

"After your meal."

Fanala grabbed her arm to pull her across the lobby. One of Puflet's slippers caught on an irregular stone, and she fell to her knees. Pain stabbed her chest.

"My, aren't we clumsy." Fanala yanked on her arm.

Another wave of pain, tinged by nausea, crashed through her. She subsided into darkness.

5

When Puflet came to, she was back in the eggshell room. The stabbing pain in her chest had faded to a vague soreness. She must have been floated again. She flexed her fingers. Her first order of business would be to cook up a batch of defensive glowworms. She queried system and listed the supplies she needed.

"Amateur glowworm-breeding is not permitted on Ulona," system told her.

She bit her lip. She hadn't felt so defenseless since she'd been a little girl. Her glowworms had been her companions through all of her long, hard years of struggle and planning. What was she going to do now—rely on the monster?

She cringed when an opening irised in the wall, then gasped in surprise and relief. It wasn't Fanala.

The woman wore the same wonderdome-green robe, but her hair was gold. "Hi, Puflet. I'm Cidi. Fanala can't be with you today. Her son is very sick."

"I'm sorry to hear that," Puflet said, trying to keep her face from curling up into a smirk. "She always spoke so fondly of him. What's wrong with him?"

Cidi shook her head. "They don't know. He didn't report to his herding class yesterday, so they looked for him, and found him collapsed out in the wilderness. There wasn't anything outwardly wrong with him, but it was—" Frowning, she gave her head another shake—"like he was gone. And the exams have found nothing, except for a very small-scale disruption, like unfusing damage. It can happen anywhere, of course, but just because the academy is nearby, Headmistress Katora is questioning all of her students."

Cidi leaned over her. "How are you feeling today? Fanala told me that you stumbled in the lobby and cracked three ribs. Your bones aren't strong enough yet to be doing anything strenuous. Maybe some hydrotherapy would help, if you like to feel active."

"I think I would like that!" Puflet declared. "And no more fern juice, please. I think it disagrees with my stomach."

Cidi smiled. "Has Fanala been trying to fill you up with her cure-all? Just tell her no."

Puflet frowned. "I do, but she—"

"Doesn't listen?" Cidi laughed.

Puflet huffed. What had she been doing wrong, anyhow? Fanala didn't seem like someone who'd listen to anything short of a whack across the mouth. Or was there some other way to manage her, some secret known to citizens that Puflet hadn't discovered yet because she'd spent all her life in a glowworm lab?

"Do you have any tips about getting into the mindsea academy?" she asked. "I really want to study Patternistics."

Cidi shook her head. "I know that Headmistress Katora interviews all of the applicants. It depends on whether she likes you or not."

"What can I do to make sure she likes me?"

"Well...." Cidi summoned a nook and sat down facing her. "Just be yourself. Talk about your enthusiasm. She'll sense anything false—she's a mindsea."

"I thought all the mindseas were dead!"

"Katora doesn't like to talk about her mindsize, but ... my grandmother was her friend way back in Quintillion's reign, even though she was just a Lalian peasant, and she knew that Katora could engulf people's minds, if she wanted to. Katora chooses not to hold a mind-net like Thermeon or Quintillion. She felt that they had warped themselves by using their powers that way."

Puflet pictured the head, and wrinkled her nose.

Cidi's round face dimpled as she smiled. "How much imperial history do you know? I guess I should be helping you get oriented since Fanala was called away."

"I'd really appreciate that." Puflet tried to fill her voice with sincerity. Cidi clearly had brains, and Puflet suddenly wanted very much to spend the coming days chatting with someone she could regard as an equal. By necessity, she had never been able to confide in anyone on Puztak, and she regretted the gaping void in her life where friendship and love should have been. "I have the feeling you could give me the help I need to adjust. Couldn't you be my permanent aide instead of Fanala?" *Please don't let that bit-brain back into my life—it isn't healthy for either of us.* "If you just changed the assignment, she wouldn't even remember me, would she?"

"I'm sure she'd remember you! She's done nothing but talk about how you fell down and broke your ribs."

No, her bit-brained son broke my ribs trying to rape me. Puflet smiled grimly. "I think I'll kill myself if I have to deal with her again."

Cidi waved a finger at her. "You mustn't let the bad association with your accident make you afraid of Fanala."

"It's not just that," Puflet said. "I really feel a resonance with you. You've already told me things about Katora I didn't know, things that probably aren't in the memories, from the way you put it."

Cidi smiled. "All right, I can reassign you. Fanala is too worried about her son right now to think about anything else, anyhow. She doesn't have a husband to help her. She got Tepi through a time-orphan adoption service.

That didn't surprise Puflet. Fanala didn't have the brains for a lasting relationship. It amazed her that no one, not even Cidi, seemed to realize the vast difference in quality between the two aides. Probably because Fanala got her niche through patronage, and Cidi came from hard-working peasant stock.

"Is there any possibility you could use your grandmother's friendship with the headmistress to influence her decision about my application?"

Cidi shook her head with a sad smile. "Please don't bring it up, Puflet. Katora feels that my genes are tainted. You see, my grandmother's husband—my grandfather—was Thermeon."

Puflet started. "Well, then! But she has a lot of nerve to condemn you, seeing as she's a secret mindsea herself."

Cidi shrugged. "I'm sure that she will appreciate having someone so enthusiastic at the academy." She didn't sound very sure. "Your background will help too—I mean, not having any prominent ancestors." She lowered her voice. "You see, the whole problem is that Katora witnessed the mind-duel between Thermeon and Quintillion—in mind-link, because anyone near them would've been killed—and it was so horrible, she still hasn't gotten over it. One of her students is a nice young man named Kaanu, but because he happens to be a grandson of Quintillion, she's trying to blame what happened to Tepi on him." Her eyes moistened.

Puflet clenched a small fist. "That's really unfair!"

Cidi nodded. "My grandmother Galena was a very compassionate person. When the Fissure happened, she went out into the desert to see if anything could be done for Thermeon and Quintillion, even though Katora told her that she knew for a fact they both were dead.

"Galena found Thermeon. He was horribly mutilated, but she had him brought to her dro ranch, and she nursed him, though not much could be done for the deep-level wounds. But he had great powers of recuperation. Everyone thought that his mindpowers were destroyed, but he had to use them to keep his body alive.

"He was just like a normal person in those days, because his mindpowers were tied up. He and Galena married and lived happily on her ranch, which was a lot like the habitat where he'd grown up—he was raised as a slave, but not in a modern habitat like the one you came from, but a savage place."

Puflet nodded.

"Galena couldn't win reproductive rights. It's really hard for ordinary people to get a position in the mating flights, and Thermeon couldn't ride. But he had connections, and credits, so he paid to use someone else's repro rights, and that's how my family began. I got my green eyes from Galena!"

Puflet nodded and smiled at her.

"But, I can't help you with the headmistress. Members of my family speak out against Genetic Algorithms' unfair manipulations of the mating flights, so Katora has decided that we're tainted."

Puflet tsked. "She sounds like a difficult person."

"She sees herself as a warrior for the light against the darkness. But I don't think she goes about it in the right way—trying to rid the galaxy of the mindseas' genes. Unless they're mingled with her own, of course—she's married to one of Thermeon's sons."

Puflet shook her head. "Yes, it sounds ludicrous. Uh ... excuse my bluntness. She doesn't spy on us here, I hope."

"If she wanted to, she'd use her mindpowers." Cidi shrugged. "Since Thermeon recovered his mindpowers after a journey through Deep Five, she's decided that he's still evil and won't let him visit Ulona. But for some reason she believes that his son Dino isn't evil. They've had six kids already, and they're going to race again in the next mating flight. They're always given positions."

Puflet pursed her lips. "Sounds like Katora has one set of rules for herself, and another for everyone else."

"She always talks about an age of illumination that will come with the birth of a mindsea as powerful as the old ones, but free from their evil. Everyone knows that she expects her next child with Dino to be this mindsea."

"Uh," said Puflet. "The slavers are sure there isn't any genetic formula for producing mindseas. They think you have to subject children to pain and hardship to awaken their mindpowers."

"I know," Cidi said. "But Katora also believes that she can use her mindpowers to choose a future where things fall out the way she wants them to. It's part of what she teaches at the academy."

"Fascinating," Puflet breathed, curling her fingers around the edges of her nook. "It will certainly put a lot of pressure on that child."

Cidi nodded. They sat in silence for a couple seconds. Then Puflet said softly, "I think you're a very decent person, Cidi. The best wonderdome aide I could have. I hope we can be friends, too."

Cidi blinked tearing eyes. "I realize that you don't have anyone, Puflet. But at least you know that the one thing that makes life worth living is love. In my family, we don't measure each other by mindsize. Parents love their children, children love their parents, and spouses respect one another. Of course, Thermeon was different, but he always treated Galena with respect. He never once thought of divorcing her, even toward the end of her life, when she was crystallized."

Puflet seemed to recall that Thermeon had been crippled at the time, and not in any position to divorce the woman who cared for his needs, even if she had become an automation. She tactfully remained silent.

"All I hope for in life is to find my someone to love," Cidi said with vehemence. "I hope you find someone too, Puflet."

"So do I," Puflet said.

"I can give you a tip about Katora, though. Never question when she talks about her perfect love with Dino. She really sees him as a stud horse—something you replace if it doesn't perform optimally. And he knows it. If the next child isn't the special one she wants, he'll be out on his ear, and he's worried, of course, that she'll go after his father then."

Puflet blinked. "But doesn't she think Thermeon's uh ... evil?"

"She thinks that now, because it helps her to paint a rosier picture of Dino—pure son of the tainted father. But if she changes her mind about him, she'll change her mind about his father as well."

"Oh." Puflet's head whirled.

"It's absolutely ridiculous, of course." Cidi's ire had grown more apparent the longer she spoke. These last words were practically spat out.

Puflet stared at her, feeling a bit empty inside. She had offered her friendship, but Cidi hadn't responded. She seemed too wrapped up in her own family's saga to care about an outsider. Finally Puflet gathered herself. "When I finally meet—" *that harridan, the dictator of Ulona*—"the headmistress, how should I approach her? The brochure says that everything is informal at the academy, and everyone is to be addressed as an equal, even the headmistress. But I can't just walk in and call her 'Katora,' can I? Should I address her as Headmistress? Or Daughter? Her father is Head of the Circle, isn't he?"

"Don't bring up that connection. She's still mad at him for not taking up her call to purge mindsea genes. Call her 'Headmistress,' until she begs you to stop at least twice."

"All right." Puflet let out a long sigh. Someone who lied to herself about her deepest beliefs would be extremely tricky to deal with. That sort of person insisted that you lie to them too, that you reinforce whatever ditbitted illusion they had fed themselves. If you told them the truth, they'd fly into a rage because you attacked the cherished illusion. Eventually, in most cases, they woke up and realized they'd been deceiving themselves, and then they got mad at you for having lied to them. You could never win.

She sighed again. Someone of Katora's mindsize could warp another person's mind and make them believe whatever she wished them to. Did that mean she could warp her own mind as well?

Puflet let out a bitter laugh.

The day had come at last. Puflet stood before the Headmistress of the Mindsea Academy of Ulona. Upon entering Katora's space, she had been given a view through a series of archways of the headmistress seated in her nook in the distance. On either side of the path leading through the archways, objects had been arranged in spare and tasteful patterns within vast spaces where white sand floors blended into rounded pale walls—a stone here, a carved porphyry basin filled with water there, and to balance them a pole-trained vine whose tendrils carved green spirals against whiteness. Each softly-glowing archway was a bit lower and narrower than the one before it, and as their tones shifted from violet through blues and into greens, they drew all of spacetime into focus on a single point, the point where Katora sat in a pool of golden light.

Her nook was crimson with golden tassels, and her gown shades of blue like a cascade of water flowing down to the crest of the white sand eminence upon which the nook rested. Puflet trudged to the foot of the eminence, a supplicant before the mount of wisdom. She straightened herself against the gravity, then bowed low as if she were back before Ix once again. "Headmistress."

Katora gazed down her long green nose. Her features were symmetrical and strongly sculpted, her hands long and narrow—traits of the same old aristocracy that had produced Ix. Her blue slippers glittered with diamond dust, and earrings like droplets of burning water swung beneath copper-highlighted waves of chocolate-brown hair. "Greetings, Puflet." The warm and melodious flow of her voice urged Puflet to believe that she had reached the source of knowledge and comfort. "Here at the mindsea academy, we consider ourselves to be beyond the politics of the world. We do not use titles here."

"Yes, Headmistress."

The blue-gray eyes sharpened, and an edge of steel entered the voice. "You did hear what I said, didn't you?"

"Yes, uh ... ma'am." Puflet bowed again, eyes fixed on the curled tips of her own slippers. She had so longed to make herself beautiful. Ever since she was a little girl, she had wanted to flounce about in a red dress like the one Ix always wore, and her new coloring—produced by her own genes—pale skin and hair and deep blue eyes, would make it perfect. But knowing that any sign of pride would be unwelcome, she had forced herself to come to the interview in wonderdome issue. Emotions she thought she'd left behind on Puztak flooded her. Katora was too much like Ix in every way. Every bit of her shouted, "I am all-powerful, and you are a bug to be stomped at my whim."

Puflet clenched her teeth and breathed slowly and deeply. Her spirit raged against restriction, forced subservience, the divisions that gave some privilege and made others their playthings. Katora's domain was divided along a different axis than Ix's—instead of masters and slaves, here were the pure and the tainted—but whatever the excuse behind the division, it still gave those on the right side of the line the power to torment those on the wrong side. Puflet hated it, hated it with all her soul, and she vowed that she would be free, even if it took another two centuries.

Some day she would have that red dress.

Katora's voice rang out above her, warm and beguiling once again. "Don't be afraid, Puflet. There are no slaves here. You do not need to grovel. We are all equals before the universe."

Until you decide someone's tainted, Puflet thought.

"Please stand up straight," Katora said. "I can't have students who look as if they are ashamed of themselves."

Puflet straightened her back. "It's the gravity, ma'am. I'm still not used to it."

"That's quite understandable. There will be enough time during daily cycles for you to return to the wonderdome for therapy."

"I appreciate that, ma'am."

Katora peered down at her. "I appreciate the troubles you have been through." She paused for a moment. "That is, if you are what you have said you are."

Puflet blinked. "What else would I be, ma'am?"

Katora lifted a long, slender green finger to lips that pinched together like a rosebud. "The story that you singlehandedly destroyed Ix's empire is difficult to credit, I'm sure you understand."

Puflet lifted her chin. "But it is true." *Look into my eyes, bitch. If you want to know if I'm lying, the truth is right here for you to see.*

"You may believe that you destroyed Ix, but I think it's more likely that she set you up to inherit her business when she was ready to step down."

The old harpy was delusional, Puflet thought. "What makes you say that?"

"Your skin, your hair, and your teeth. They resemble Thermeon's. If Ix used his genes to breed you, she must have intended big things for you. For obvious reasons, it is illegal to keep mindseas' genes on record, but Ix had no respect for the law."

Puflet blinked. "You're going to reject me because of my teeth?"

Katora clucked her tongue. "I'm not rejecting you. I think you are very much in need of guidance right now. If I let you out into the world, you could fall prey to newsers or cultists, or even to the slavers if they planned to take you back."

Puflet frowned. She had thought the scattered slavers would be too busy worrying about their own survival to plan revenge on her. Still, it would be best if she could get hold of some glowworms.

"I don't believe that Ix is dead," Katora said. "She probably left a bioid copy for you to kill, having first traveled to another planet."

Fear lanced Puflet. Could that be true? But the head—the head would've known. It had told her that it had felt Ix die. She smiled up at Katora. "I assure you that she is quite dead."

The corners of Katora's mouth drooped slightly. "You seem very sure of that. What makes you so certain?"

Puflet clamped her lips together and continued to meet her eyes.

She wasn't going to bring up the subject of Quintillion—that was too likely to lead to questions about evil and tainting—but let Katora probe her thoughts if she dared.

The headmistress did not take up the challenge. "Then perhaps she made a miscalculation. But I can't help find it suspicious that you picked Valri to name as Ix's second-in-command and successor—the person I and the authorities in Lal had placed in Ix's organization in order to destroy it from the inside. Who pointed the finger at Valri?"

Puflet winced. "I got her name from Ix's deep-level communications system."

"And what was that system? We always knew she had something, but we couldn't believe that her level-engineers were so much better than ours."

"I-I don't know much about level-engineering, either, ma'am. That's why I came here. I want to learn."

Katora learned forward, her dark-ringed blue-gray eyes boring into Puflet. "How did her system appear to you? Was it a soul-gem? We guessed that her father might have had an extra one hidden away somewhere where Ix could find it."

"Uh ... well, it was about so big." Puflet moved her hands around in the air. "It was a self-contained system, not connected to any of the glowworm systems."

"You are aware, aren't you, that deep-level objects have no quantifiable appearance because they exist simultaneously in so many states?"

"No, ma'am, I didn't know."

"Still, it should have appeared to you as a crystal at least some of the time."

"Well ... parts of it looked ... sapphire."

Katora nodded. "You seem confused. That is normal for an untrained human confronted by deep-level phenomena. You probably misunderstood the message. Valri was one of my students. There is no way she went over to the slavers."

She was deceiving herself, of course, and asking Puflet to lie to her to support her delusion. Whatever Puflet said, Katora would find cause to despise her. But better defer her wrath to an indefinite tomorrow than face it today. "Whatever you say, ma'am."

Katora shook a finger at her. "I sense your suspicion and hostility. These are not characteristics that will aid in your studies. You need to open your mind, Puflet. You need to learn how to trust. Have you ever heard of the expression 'patternistic integrity'?'"

Puflet started. "Yes, ma'am."

Katora smiled, all loftiness and wisdom. "It is an important concept in shipboard safety, and also here at the academy. Unless all of us here work together, all train our minds on the same future, unfortunate accidents could occur." Her dark eyebrows drew downward. "Like the accident that struck Fanala's son. Do you know about that?"

"Yes, ma'am. Cidi told me what had happened."

Katora's eyes narrowed slightly. "Yes. It was an unfortunate result of that accident that you were exposed to Cidi. She is a failed student, and very bitter. I hope that she didn't take advantage of your naivety and try to fill you with misapprehensions about the academy."

"She just told me her family history, ma'am."

Katora snorted softly. "It's a very sad story, but I think that the lesson to be learned from it is that sometimes do-gooders should mind their own business."

"I don't follow, ma'am."

Katora smiled. "Then I will explain to you—if you promise to stop calling me 'ma'am.'"

"Yes, m—uh, yes."

Katora regarded her thoughtfully for a moment. "I can see that the gravity here is a strain on you. Please be seated."

A nook formed at the base of eminence and joined with Katora's to form a 2-nook. Puflet slid into it and found that the slope had her tilting backwards to gaze up at Katora. The tilt gave her the helpless feeling of being held by a giant hand that was about to fling her somewhere.

"More comfortable now?" Katora asked with a sweetness that felt too cloying to be sincere.

"Yes," Puflet said.

A softness crept over Katora's eyes—the mist of memory—and she began her tale in a low voice. "I considered Cidi's grandmother

Galena to be my best friend, even though she was an uneducated dro-rancher, and I was Daughter of the Circle. Galena had a very simple, yet powerful philosophy. She believed that Goodness was the most potent force in the universe, and she believed that everyone had Goodness in them. She didn't believe in the existence of Evil.

"But I have seen Evil, Puflet. I saw it at the Fissure."

Her voice quivered. Puflet felt the fear pouring off her. It was the same fear the head had conjured with its formless "it." Fear of the entity Puflet harbored within herself.

So why wasn't Puflet as frightened as they were? When she had released the monster against Tepi, it had felt hot and powerful. It had felt ... comforting.

She remembered the scene with the star and the dying world that the monster had shown her when it first came to her from Quintillion. That had been terrible, but Puflet believed it was the story of the monster's origins, something that had happened long ago, in the time when dinosaurs had roamed the Earth. It had seemed neither threatening nor evil.

Katora talked on. "Thermeon and Quintillion were probably the most powerful mindseas to arise since Attequol founded the empire. Each of them had a very different vision for the empire, and, to make matters worse, they were both in love with me. It was a very dangerous situation. Two such powerful minds, each exerting deep-level forces to bring about the future he wanted, could have torn the galaxy apart. The empire itself must have its patternistic integrity, Puflet.

"There was no way that both of them could exist in the same history. They went far out into the desert to resolve the matter, to let a future be chosen." Katora pressed her hands together and brought them to her lips. Her half-lidded eyes stared into the past. "I mind-linked with Quintillion. I loved him then. I had chosen him over Thermeon, whose powers were so violent. I thought that I would find Thermeon raging against my lover like a wild beast, and I hoped that I could help." She shook her head, a helpless look in her eyes. "But that wasn't what happened at all. Quintillion said to Thermeon, 'I have never been able to love anyone. No one is real to me.' I loved Quintillion, but my love meant nothing to him.

I was just a shadow. He told Thermeon, 'You are the only one who can help me.'" Katora clasped her hands, squeezing so hard the knuckles whitened. "He didn't turn to me. He turned to his enemy. And then—" she grimaced, and her voice suddenly deepened with a sound almost like retching—"these *things* started to pour out of their bodies. Shiny black things, like seeds. They were evil, Puflet. Seeds of evil. More and more of them poured out, from both of them, each one leaving a hole in their bodies. Quintillion had more inside of him—when they all had come out there was nothing left of him at all." She paused with a half-gasp, half-sob.

Seeds? Puflet thought. That was nothing like the dinosaur she had seen. But the horror and disgust in Katora's voice left no doubt that she had seen the same thing the head had been talking about.

Deep-level things have no quantifiable appearance. They exist in too many states. So perhaps the same thing could look like a dinosaur at one time, and a bunch of seeds at another. What if Katora mind-linked with her—would she see those same seeds inside Puflet? Puflet wrinkled her nose.

"Galena believed in the power of Goodness." Katora leaned down toward her with raptor-bright eyes. "She went out and saved Thermeon. She didn't believe me about the seeds. They were deep-level things, and no one saw them but me. Nothing was more important to Galena than family, the passing on of her traditions and her love. But she turned her back on her people when she married Thermeon, and now her descendants are tainted and ruined."

"Oh," Puflet said.

"They're infected, Puflet. They can't love. Power is the only thing important to them. Cidi's mother and older siblings scramble to mate with important people and grab prestigious posts so they can force their views on the galaxy. Cidi talks as if she still has a tradition, but I've seen the desperation of her family. Galena would weep if she were alive to see it! She would have been better off letting the mindsea die in the desert!"

The last words were delivered with a snarl. Puflet gripped the sides of her nook to counter the sensation that she was about to slide backwards.

Katora glared down at her. "No one believes me about the

seeds. They think I'm deranged, hysterical. But I know what I saw. And I know that their descendants can carry the taint." She narrowed her eyes, her voice dropping to a whisper. "You can tell the tainted ones, because they always seek power. They have no control over themselves, really. Only the shell of a human being remains. The evil controls all their actions."

Puflet gripped her throat. Was the monster a parasite that would eventually destroy her as well?

Katora laughed grimly. "Thermeon thinks that he's free of it now, that it all bled out of him in the desert. But he's living in a fool's paradise. The next time he loses his temper, it will come out, and who knows what cataclysm will result?"

Puflet swallowed. "I-I think it might be a good thing to try to understand these deep-level forces better."

Katora's dry chuckle turned into a hearty laugh. "That's why we are here, Puflet. I just hope that you don't think what you need is power so that you can avenge yourself on anyone who's done you wrong. Power and revenge are the goals of evil."

"I don't want power," Puflet said, remembering what the head had told her. "I just want truth."

Katora's eyes widened. Astonishment filled her voice. "Then perhaps we can work together. The one thing you must believe is that the danger is real, very real. Thermeon's loss of control once killed a planet. Humanity will not be safe until the taint is washed from our genes!"

"I think I understand the danger," Puflet said. Not that she agreed with Katora's solution. She had to learn more. Katora's relating of the battle, which matched in terror the head's wailing, had set her own heart pounding.

"Good." Katora gave her a dismissive nod. "I will have Eadin show you to your cell."

The head thought that wanting truth was worse than wanting power, Puflet mused as she rose to follow a pink-haired woman who appeared beneath the innermost green archway. *But Katora doesn't know that. I wonder if that's because she's seen the monster, but she's never felt it inside her.*

7

Eadin had a starfish-shaped yellow flower growing in her hair. Its perfume was very strong.

"Welcome to the academy, Puflet!" Her amber eyes glowed.

"Thank you, Eadin. Your flower—what is it?"

"Ylang-ylang. Isn't it amazing?"

"Uh ... yes."

Eadin's green gown wound around her body like a broad, tissue-thin vine, trailing tendrils around her feet and leaflets fluttering over her shoulders. With her dark complexion, she looked like an overgrown wood carving. Puflet peered, but she didn't think the gown had actual vegetation like the thing in her hair. Eadin's feet were bare, the toenails painted pearlescent pink to match her fingernails and hair, and she stood no taller than Puflet.

"I'll be your student mentor until you get settled in," Eadin said, leading the way back through the archways.

"This is such a wonderful adventure," Puflet said. "I'm so happy to be here!"

Eadin grinned over her shoulder. "Isn't it, though? And you haven't seen anything yet!"

Her warmth felt genuine, and Puflet couldn't help but smile.

"Katora is such a wonderful teacher," Eadin went on. "If I only understood a tenth of what she knows about the universe, I'd be satisfied!"

Puflet's smile slid away, but Eadin didn't see as she minced her way along the path beneath the archways. Puflet panted as she followed. Between the last two archways, Eadin paused and waved to a tall, dark-skinned woman with black velvet ribbons woven through her long golden hair. A blue-green gown flowed down to puddle on the sand as she adjusted a vase on a marble pedestal. She waved back at Eadin, then returned to her task.

"That's Sianne," Eadin explained as they walked on. "She's a new student too. She doesn't want to do any chores except care for the plants. Whenever she gets the lake assignment, she tries to trade with someone else, because she's scared of the water. She expects us to go along because she's the great-granddaughter of Empress Zupa."

Puflet frowned. "Which empress was she?"

Eadin tittered. "Query your history module."

Puflet wasn't sure what a history module was. She asked her glowworm link to snap to the nearest system, but it told her that no systems were available. Her steps faltered. "I'm afraid I don't have ... I don't know...."

"Oh, I forgot you grew up outside the empire. Well, Zupa was the last empress of the really ancient times, before the Decadent Epoch—before Horl, you know?"

Puflet knew about Ix's father, Riemis Ginarn Horl, who had run the empire for a number of emperors and empresses. He had championed human slavery so that he could experiment with genetic modifications and tortures to create mindseas. "That old empress' descendants are still around?"

"Because of her granddaughter Sagi, who's a member of the Circle."

"I see." Puflet frowned. That made Sianne and Valri relatives. She'd have to watch her step.

Eadin chattered on as they followed a serpentine path across an indoor lake afloat with giant lotus blossoms and abuzz with big, jewel-toned dragonflies. "Sagi's over ten thousand years old, but she's not the oldest Member. Ietipa is—everyone calls him Hube. I'm sure he's the oldest non-crystallized person alive. He only mates with emperors. Katora says that his genes are good and pure. Sagi's too."

Puflet repressed a shudder. Katora wanted such ancients to

stamp future generations in their insipid mold?

Eadin paused to watch a man and a women far out in a boat doing something with the lotuses. She lowered her voice. "Yusun and Hinomia are brother and sister, and they're a little too close, if you know what I mean."

Puflet shrugged.

Eadin spun to eye her. "No, you probably don't know what I mean. I mean, they take wonderdome floats together, and they're exchanging genetic material, or brain cells, or both." She pantomimed things flowing. "For instance, Hinomia used to be black, and Yusun was white, but now it's the opposite. And they both used to be fairly smart, but now Hinomia has brains enough for both of them, and Yusun has none. And his nose got all weird."

Prickling, Puflet stared hard at the distant figures, but she couldn't make out the man's nose. "What does your headmistress have to say about it?"

"She says that adjusting to the deep-level forces we study here can have weird effects on the human mind, and we should be patient with Yusun and Hinomia. Personally, I suggest you give them a wide berth. I think they would have been expelled if they weren't related to Sagi—more distantly than Sianne, but still...."

Puflet nodded. "Do you have a lot of these connected students?" She wanted to make sure to give them all a wide berth.

"Of course!" As they walked on, Eadin sketched the genealogy of several others, whose names immediately slipped from Puflet's mind. Her attention wandered. She gasped when Eadin belted out a laugh. "You can't blame him, can you? Quintillion was emperor!"

Puflet smiled warily. She really should pay attention, or she'd make more blunders. What had Eadin been telling her? Someone here was Hube's offspring?

"Right. Aren't there any non-pedigreed students?" Like me, Puflet thought.

Eadin shrugged her leafy shoulders. "Welia—we call her Pea-Pach, because it's her ridiculous last name—is a little nothing from Icrune, and Oakiza is a Coder—you can tell by their red eyes."

Eadin had lowered her voice again, peering back over her leaves as if a Coder were something that might fall on you like a panther. "And there are probably some people here who are descended from

Quintillion and not telling us. I can understand that, can't you?"

Puflet said nothing.

Eadin slowed her pace until they were side by side, then whispered. "Then there's Golen. He has fangs, can you imagine? He's descended from Thermeon, of course. But why advertise it? A sensible person would have had them removed."

Puflet kept her lips firmly closed over her own fangs.

"Most of these charity cases don't do very well, like that dropout Cidi who works at the wonderdome."

Puflet was liking Eadin less and less.

Eadin smiled and tossed her ylang-ylang. "We call Golen 'Serpenlino.'"

Puflet hoped she would not be saddled with a nickname. When she had received her citizenship, system had assigned her the name Hemita Wuner Doom. She would have thought it a joke if Genetic Algorithms had any sense of humor. But the letters corresponding to her genotypes just happened to form a word, and if she wanted it changed, she'd have to pay. Luckily, the option to retain the first name she was used to had been free.

Eadin thrust out her chest as she strutted on. "Some of us are planetary royalty—like me. My mom is Queen of Yohorb. Kael's father is King of Gilkay. We're practically neighbors on our homeworlds—planets 1312 and 1311, in case you don't know your list. That must portend something, don't you think?"

"I wouldn't know," Puflet murmured, still feeling self-conscious about her fangs.

Eadin gave her a wide-eyed stare, then laughed. "You certainly are a strange one." She walked on.

What was strange about wanting facts before you formed an opinion, Puflet wondered.

"Oh!" Eadin cried. "I didn't mention Kaanu. But he'll probably be out anyhow. He's one of Quintillion's loathsome spawn. Katora only admitted him because that sick seed woman had been making such a fuss before the Wall about her policies."

"Sick seed woman?"

"Guluda Mumoli Sik-Seed. The mother of that dropout Cidi."

"Oh." The woman had an even more unfortunate name—from Katora's perspective—than Puflet. And Cidi ... she hadn't given her full name; was she going by a nickname? Not Cidi, but Seedy?

"That interfering bitch claimed that there wasn't any danger," Eadin babbled on. "But I guess she knows better now. I'll feel a lot safer with him gone, won't you?"

"Why would I?"

Eadin stopped short with a gasp. She whirled toward Puflet in a leafy ripple. "You don't know about the taint?"

Puflet gaped at her, then remembered her teeth and snapped her mouth shut.

Eadin launched into a second-hand version of Katora's story of the seeds of evil. Puflet's mind wandered again. She thought she understood why Eadin found her strange. Eadin didn't need facts to form opinions. She got them ready-made from Katora.

"Doesn't your skin just crawl when you think about something so vile?" Eadin asked, hugging herself.

Puflet wrinkled her nose. She was trying to picture Ix finding the head in the newly-formed Fissure and taking it home with her. But a severed head could only stay alive for a few seconds without life support, so how would that have been possible?

"Katora hoped for the best from Kaanu," Eadin said. "She's always so positive and generous! But he betrayed us all." She shook her head sadly.

"How?" Puflet asked.

Another gasp. "Haven't you heard about what happened to that wonderdome aide's son?"

"I heard about it, but what does it have to do with Kaanu?"

"He was the one who did it to him. Katora examined his injuries, and she recognized the marks of the taint."

Puflet felt a sudden draining of blood. This was not good.

"It was jealousy, of course." Eadin nodded sagely. "Pea-Pach messes with all of the male students, but that Nander-brain took her seriously. And when he found out she was meeting Tepi in the wilderness, his control snapped."

The totally baseless accusation was delivered with such conviction it took Puflet's breath away. Kaanu was suffering for her sins. She vowed to make it up to him someday, if she ever got the chance.

"Come on," Eadin called.

After they crossed the lake, the path led through a softly-lit blue tunnel that ended in vaulted circular chamber of translucent green stone with a floor of black and white marble squares. Many other tunnels led to the chamber, and after she had turned around a couple of times, Puflet could no longer tell by which tunnel they come.

"This is the nexus," Eadin explained. "You can tell which archway to take by the symbols above them. The lotus is for the lake, of course. The beehive is for student cells. The checkerboard is for the free-form exercise hall. The night sky is for the meditation chambers. The goblet is for the dining hall, and the sun is for the lecture hall. The Academy looks like a giant snowflake when you see it from above. Dino helped Katora design it. He's a builder."

"Beautiful!" Puflet murmured.

Eadin beamed at her. "Isn't it wonderful what two people can do when they work together?"

Puflet nodded.

"Katora believes that if all of us work together, we can change the galaxy! Those seeds of evil are what make people hurt each other and start wars. They don't realize that these things are in them, taking over their minds, because most people don't have the ability to see deep-level things, even when they're being controlled by them. If we work on weeding out the evil, we can bring about an age without war or crime. Wouldn't that be wonderful?"

"An age of peace and freedom would be wonderful," Puflet agreed.

Eadin eyed her for a moment. She pointed to a glowing blue and green sphere at the apex of the vault above them. "If you ever get disoriented after a meditation session, the amount of green in the sphere shows you how much of the cycle is left."

Puflet nodded. It would be a new experience not having a system to tell the time.

Eadin led on beneath the beehive archway. The tunnel branched, and branched again, the lighting changing with each branch. Finally they reached a large chamber that opened onto a violet tunnel. It was bare except for shower and relief alcoves.

"This is yours. You can style it any way you like."

"Can I use breeder glowworms?"

Eadin blinked twice. "Why would you want breeder glowworms? Every student cell comes with perfectly good habitat-styling glowworms. You can make the surfaces and the lighting however you like, and sprout whatever furniture and accent pieces strike your fancy. And you can get some more attractive clothes."

Puflet sighed.

"I suppose it's normal to miss your old life when you first arrive here, but you'll soon feel right at home. We're one big family here, Puflet. It's a wonderful family. Katora is like a second mother to me, and I'm sure you'll feel the same way about her, once you get over your strangeness." Eadin flashed her a smile, and for a moment Puflet had the sensation that the academy and all its students were an extension of Katora's mind, a mind that was trying to engulf her.

Was that really any different than the monster engulfing its hosts? She was sure Katora would argue that her goals were beneficent, and the monster's weren't, but Puflet found the idea of making everyone like the living fossils Sagi and Hube repugnant.

Puflet wanted to be herself. She had fought long and hard for her independence, and she wasn't about to give it up now. She would fight Katora's engulfment. Whether she had to fight the monster as well, she did not as yet know.

Shutting her wall on Eadin's smile, she turned on a breeze to dissipate the scent of ylang-ylang.

8

Puflet created a large circular hot tub sunk into the floor as the center of her living space. Behind it was a spacious walk-in closet where she could contemplate her wardrobe. The styling glowworms spun gowns with enormous fish-finny sleeves or mushroom-cap hoods or pangolin-scaled bodices. Since there was no system to update the glowworms, those styles were probably all passé.

She stroked the silky fabric of her gowns and tried them on in front of her closet mirror, but for everyday wear she had simpler garments spun in pinks and pale blues.

Tiring of the closet, she soaked in her hot tub for a while beneath the golden glow of her ceiling and walls. She was so weary of living in underground labs and other enclosed places. But there was no view from her cell. The walls abutted other students' cells, and a skylight, which might be pleasant in the daytime, would now show only the starless Ulonan night sky. If she'd had her own glowworms, she could have imported or manufactured a view, but Katora's didn't provide that option.

So she had to be content with the color of the sun around her. When she had soaked enough, she decided to go straight to bed, even though it meant missing the setting meal. She was just more exhausted than hungry. She had created an expansive sleeping nook, piled with soft pillows and downy blankets where she could toss around in her sleep, if she wanted to. No more slave drawers or wonderdome nooks for her.

She slept peacefully and woke hungry, her wall-glow coming up crimson like a sun. She took a quick shower and put on a tunic-style pink dress. Leaving her cell, she hurried through the tunnels, hoping she wouldn't take a wrong turn.

She had just stepped into a green tunnel when someone seized her from her behind. His roar echoed through the tunnels. "Ha! I have you now! I am Thermeon, and I will kidnap every one of Katora's students!"

Puflet's heart raced, but she forced herself to be still. Powerful arms encircled her chest, pinioning her arms to her sides. If she struggled, she was sure to break some more ribs. Could he really be Thermeon? More likely, some student was playing games with her. She stared at the silvery hands clasped beneath her breasts. "Doesn't Thermeon have claws?"

The hands released her. Turning around, she faced a tall, broad-shouldered, red-eyed man with bristling white hair that glowed in the subdued tunnel lighting. The hair explained why slavers referred to Thermeon's progeny "lamp-heads." He wore a stiff white suit with crimson deco. A white-tufted tail curled and uncurled around his flanks.

"You're Dino," she said. *What an obnoxious man,* she thought. *If I were Katora, I'd kick him out in a second.*

He flung up his chin. "I might be Thermeon disguised as Dino."

"I don't think so."

He grinned. She noted that he had no fangs. "You're right. My father would never change his appearance. I'll show you the way to the dining hall." He offered his arm.

Reluctantly, Puflet slid her hand into the crook of his elbow. "Please don't try to walk me off my feet. I haven't adjusted to the gravity yet."

"Have no fear." He proceeded at a slow and stately pace, his head upflung, a solemn expression on his face, as if they were taking part in a memorial procession, all the while his tail tickled her bare legs and flipped up the bottom of her dress.

She gritted her teeth.

Bending his head down toward hers, Dino whispered, "My father and Orgmorgan and I have been following up on the names you mentioned in your message. We've managed to shut down some slave markets by tracing the stops their ships had made over the past centuries. They will be staying clear of our spaceports for some time."

A wave of surprise and delight rushed through her. "That's good news. I didn't think anyone was taking my message seriously."

"We take it very seriously! You are a hero to the empire, Puflet. If you were on any planet other than Ulona, newsers would be flocking around for your story."

"It still bothers me that Valri is going free."

Dino grinned. "She's hardly free. While her ship was impounded, Orgmorgan put a tracker aboard. If she makes any wrong move she'll be caught."

Puflet smiled and nodded. "At least you believe me about her. Katora refuses to admit that Valri could possibly be a slaver."

"My beloved is blind to the failings of those she cares about. Which is good for me."

Puflet sighed. "I think it would be better for everyone around her if she realized that real people weren't divided into pure and perfect heroes of light and agents of total evil."

"Katora is an idealist," he said. "She wants the world to be more meaningful than it sometimes is."

They walked in silence for a while. The murmuring of voices grew in the distance, like an ocean.

"I was told you built the academy," Puflet said. "I think it's beautiful." *Just a bit too inward-facing for my taste.*

"Katora and I rediscovered Ulona," he said. "When we arrived, we had to battle pahmaks that were still under the control of the long-dead last mindsea of Ulona."

They stepped into the dining hall, a vast, mist-gray chamber filled with wheel nooks where students sat eating and producing the chatter that formed an unvarying background noise.

Puflet sniffed the food odors on the air. "I hope there's no fern juice."

"I'm sure they have it if you want it," Dino said.

"I don't want it. How do we order if the academy doesn't have a system?"

"Students push carts past the nooks," Dino said. "I'm sure you'll get your chance to push once your bones get stronger."

He opened an empty nook and invited her with a wave of his hand to precede him inside. When they were seated, he said, "Katora got the idea for a systemless design from the Mindsea Academy of Eltien. Just be thankful that she doesn't have you grow all your own food and weave your clothing by hand, the way they do it there."

Puflet stared at her weak white digits. "By hand?"

"I'm told it's quite a revelation."

Puflet snorted. "We created systems to do our chores, why not make use of them?"

"Katora doesn't want her students to be helpless if they should someday find themselves in a place where the system is broken or never was built."

"That makes some sense, I suppose. Of course I'm a glowworm-engineer, and I could make my own system. As long as I could get some breeder glowworms. Any chance, Dino, that you could get me a batch?"

He smiled. "I can manage that."

Suffused by good feelings, she invited him to tell the story of Ulona's rediscovery, and he obliged.

A curvaceous blue-haired, brown-skinned woman and a slender blue-skinned man with wine-red hair and violet eyes joined their nook, introducing themselves as Pea-Pach and Kael. Both of them wore long, undecorated robes, belted at the waist. A tall, solemn-faced, brown-skinned man pushed a three-tiered cart laden with food and drinks into their nook. His red eyes fell on Puflet, and he spoke in a stern baritone. "You must be new. I'm Oakiza."

"Greetings, Oakiza. I'm Puflet." She picked out a goblet of water and some seeded muffins.

Oakiza stood staring at her until Dino waved him and his cart away.

"Is he a Coder?" Puflet asked. "Do they all have red eyes? Is everyone with red eyes a Coder?" She looked hard at Dino.

He grinned. "My mother was a Coder. For a time, my father was obsessed with bedding their empress, so they hid her and sent him substitutes."

A dozen more questions sprang into her mind, but he forestalled them by plunging back into his tale. When it was concluded, he began to tease. "Was there kale in the pea patch this morning?"

He repeated this inanity several times, but Pea-Pach and Kael seemed to think it as funny as he did. The three of them quivered with laughter. Puflet couldn't help but smile herself, just because their high spirits were so contagious.

When they could contain themselves, they discussed a game called Rebounders. Pea-Pach boasted that her mindpowers would make the balls drop for her.

"You can't beat me!" Dino crowed. "My mindpowers and my balls are much bigger than yours!"

The three of them cracked up again.

Wiping tears from her eyes, Pea-Pach turned to Puflet. "Why don't you join us for Rebounders after setting meal?"

"I'd love to," Puflet said. "But I have to go to the wonderdome for therapy."

Dimming lights signaled the end to mealtime. Dino bade them farewell as they exited the nook.

"It's time for free-form exercises," Pea-Pach told Puflet. "You may as well come along with us, and we'll try to orient you."

"What kinds of exercises do you do?" Puflet asked as they passed through the nexus.

"We get a tiny amount of deep-level material—Dino collects it on his ship—and then we use our mindpowers to try to shape it into useful artifacts."

Puflet buzzed with excitement. "That sounds fantastic!"

A quick tattoo of steps overtook them from behind, accompanied by a flowery perfume. "Kael! Where were you this morning! I was waiting at your door so we could go to rising meal together."

"Oh, hi, Eadin. Sorry, I must have been deep asleep. I almost missed mealtime."

Eadin pushed between Kael and Pea-Pach. Puflet fell back a couple of steps so the jostling students wouldn't collide with her.

"You couldn't have been later than I was!" Eadin challenged.

Kael's voice remained laconic. "Guess I was."

Eadin linked her arm through his. "Guess I need to see that you get your proper sleep. Don't I?"

"Uh huh."

"Oh!" Eadin stopped dead, dragging him to a halt beside her. Puflet stopped because they were blocking her way.

Pea-Pach took a few more steps, then swung around. "What is it?"

"Puflet can't go to free-form. She doesn't know anything. You go ahead, Pea-Pach. Kael and I will fill her in."

Pea-Pach shrugged and walked on, her gray robe swirling behind her.

Kael squirmed in Eadin's grasp. "I'm sure you can manage without me."

"Nonsense. We planetary royalty need to stick together, don't we?" She turned him around and headed back toward the nexus, Puflet falling into step beside them.

"I suppose it's just as well if I miss free-form," Kael drawled. "It will spare me from humiliating myself again."

"You have never humiliated yourself," Eadin soothed. "Some people just need a little more time to get in touch with their mindsize."

He sighed. "It's depressing when your father could do this stuff without any problem and you can't."

"Please don't feel sad, honey. Whatever else, you're a very clever glowworm engineer." She snuggled close to him, her ylang-ylang right under his nostrils. Puflet understood the pain in his face.

"Are you really a glowworm engineer, Kael?" she asked. "I'm one myself."

"No she's not!" Eadin snapped. "She just worked for the slavers. That's a different kind of glowworm."

"I didn't realize you were an expert," Puflet said.

"Kael taught me everything I know."

"I never taught you that slavers had different glowworms," Kael said. "All the glowworms originating from the empire are the same. There are other kinds—like the sort Dino and Katora found in the Ulonan ruins—"

"That's enough," Eadin muttered.

"—and the really, really archaic imperial ones that they think are in the Judgment Wall—"

"I said, enough!"

"—and they have what they call X-worms in Andromeda—"

"No one wants—"

"—and of course there are the force-worms we're trying to make in free-form—"

"—to hear about this."

"I think it's fascinating!" Puflet said.

"—but I don't have the touch for those."

"I'd like to hear more about them," Puflet said.

Kael opened his mouth, but Eadin jumped in first. "If you're so interested in force-worms, then go to free-form!" She released his arm and pushed him away. With a sigh, he turned and plodded off around the curve in the tunnel.

Eadin glared at Puflet. "You can play with any of the male students you want. But Kael is mine."

"I thought slavery was outlawed in the empire."

Eadin gasped and drew herself up. With a short, sharp squeal, she slapped Puflet's face, spinning her backwards into the wall. Puflet clutched the smooth tunnel curve and glared at her. *Just wait until I get my glowworms, bitch.*

Eadin placed herself in front of her, arms akimbo, eyes flaring. "You're stupid to antagonize me when you depend on me to teach you the basics. I was going to do it because Katora gave me the job, but I'm not going to bother with a nasty little vixen like you! You can just—"

Her voice ringing through the tunnel had covered the sound of approaching steps. Without warning a black man in a white robe and a white woman in a black robe were upon them. They had to be the brother and sister—Yusun and Hinomia—Eadin had warned Puflet about.

"Oh, if it isn't Miss High-and-Mighty Planetary Royalty," Hinomia sneered. She had a peaches-and-cream complexion and light brown hair.

"And Little Miss Free-Me!" honked Yusun, who resembled an elephant seal in coloring, shape, and in the bulbous nose bobbling over his lips. Little blue eyes glittered between rolls of flesh. A creature that looked like a winged rat perched on his shoulder. It glared at Puflet with orange, grape-sized eyes that bulged from the sides of its head, and hissed, baring rodent incisors.

Eadin fled. Puflet started to push herself away from the wall, but the woman's hand was around her throat, pushing her back. "Look at me, you little loser. I am Horl! You can't defeat me! You can't kill me! My body was destroyed thousands of years ago, but I willed my genes to regather so that I could live again and stomp on the likes of you! You think that you can persecute my family, but you will die on your knees before me!"

Puflet fought for breath, clawing ineffectually at the strong fingers clamped around her windpipe and arteries. *Oh, my monster,* she thought, *save me!*

No fire ignited within her. She hoped it was because this "Horl" only intended to make her black out, that it wasn't Puflet's death she wished, but rather to institute a reign of terror over her.

Once I have my glowworms, you'll be the one who's scared.

Black clouds swirled around her. Jabs of pain shot from her knuckles. Was that winged rat gnawing on them? Then a deep voice sounded from somewhere. "What'sss going on?" The "S" dragged out into a hiss.

The pressure on her throat stopped, and Puflet slid to the floor in a nerveless heap. She lay gasping and staring up at the three robed figures above her, two of them now in black. The newcomer hunched over, hood shadowing his eyes, the hem of his robe dragging on the floor.

"None of your business," Hinomia growled.

"Yeah!" honked Yusun. "Go on!"

The bat-rat fluttered at the hunched figure, but when he showed his fangs, it squeaked and darted away. He must be the one they called Serpenlino.

"You're an animal!" Hinomia spat.

"Better a live animal than a dead man."

"My resemblance to Horl is a miracle!" Hinomia posed with hands aloft, Yusun honking agreement.

"In your dreamssss."

"You don't understand deep-level forces, Serpenlino. You think that you can use your animal strength to win your battles, but in the end, no weapon is as powerful as a mind."

"Sssso, run along and hone your mindssss."

"C'mon, Yusun. Forget these animals. We're the future." The two swept off around the tunnel curve with rustling robes, the bat-rat looking back from its perch on Yusun's white-clad shoulder and hissing.

Serpenlino bent lower and examined Puflet with a glimmering of gray-green eyes. A hand slithered from his robe, and she allowed him to pull her to her feet.

"Hi, I'm Puflet." She peered down the tunnel where the other two had vanished. "Ditbittted vultures! What did she mean, anyhow, about being Horl? Is she delusional?"

He smiled. "She believes that she's been turning into him. That's what she focuses on during free-form—changing her body."

"You're not hissing your 'S's any more," Puflet noted.

"I only do that with people I don't respect."

"Huh. But you say Hinomia wants to change herself into Horl?" Puflet scowled and stomped her foot. "Why in all the permutations would she want to do that? He was an evil man!"

"He was a powerful mindsea, and her family traces their origins to him."

Her scowl deepened. "Through Ix?"

He inclined his head.

"So. Has her body really changed?"

"Her skin has lightened, but I think it's because of float sessions rather than Horl's disembodied mind coming home to roost in her. Certainly wonderdome floats are responsible for Yusun's nose."

"He infused elephant seal genes? What a pair of idiots! And Katora really puts up with such nonsense?"

"Oh, she teaches that dead mindseas can subsume the living. She encountered one during the early days on Ulona. So she believes that Hinomia can fuse with Horl, and she approves of her devotion to family."

Puflet thought it over. Wasn't the monster also the mind of a being that had died long ago? "Maybe she really has felt Horl's mind."

He snorted. "The line between self-delusion and possession by a dead mindsea is pretty wavery."

"I suppose. And if she really was Horl, she'd be able to bring back his lost technology for building transways to cross the galaxy, and she'd know where he'd hidden soul-gems, wouldn't she?"

"Of course." He smiled from the shadow of his hood. "So we have nothing to worry about."

Puflet grinned back at him. "I take it you also disapprove of slavery and torture."

"To be sure. Ah—you're the liberator of Puztak!"

She laughed.

"Were you on your way to free-form?"

She shook her head. "This is my first day of studies. Eadin was supposed to be instructing me. She said I couldn't go to free-form, because I didn't know anything. I'm not sure where she was taking me instead."

"You don't know anything about Patternistics?

"I know that ships and academies and empires all need patternistic integrity, but other than that...." She shrugged.

"Have you heard of the Four Tenets?"

"No."

"She was probably taking you to a meditation chamber to tell you about them. May I take over her duties?"

She nodded. He turned and led her the way she had been heading, his robe dragging behind him with a whisper, and soon they passed through the nexus.

Her mind kept going back to Hinomia's attack. "Hinomia accused me of persecuting her family. I guess she's related to Valri through Sagi. But are they related through Ix as well?"

Serpenlino's eyes glinted a deeper green with reflections from the tunnel glow. "All those ancient, aristocratic families are intertwined. To be frank, I don't like any of them. Katora's from one of them too, and she can't see beyond their noses. I'm sure you're right in fingering Valri as Ix's successor. Even if the government planted her there, she was playing a double cross, or something."

Puflet nodded her head so vigorously she felt dizzy.

"How did you catch on to her?" Serpenlino asked.

"Ix's deep-level system told me."

"How did you get into the system?"

"I knew where it was located, and my glowworms unlocked the chamber for me."

"Ah. But what was in the chamber, really? We knew she had a good system, but we couldn't imagine how she had gotten hold of it. And how did you destroy it? Usually deep-level objects cast a fusion field, and riddle you with unfusing damage if you mess with them."

Puflet's skin prickled. "What do you mean, 'we'? Who have you discussed me with?"

He smiled. "Orgmorgan. He's my great-grandfather. And my Aunt Eria, who's also a pilot."

"I see." Her sense of unease grew. "I guess you're related to that wonderdome aide—Fanala."

"Right. She's a cousin."

Puflet sighed. The slavers had boasted about how they got around Orgmorgan with pay-offs, but Serpenlino would probably bridle if she mentioned it. What a hypocrite! He might disapprove of Katora, but he was just as wrapped up in family tentacles.

"So, what was the deep-level system?" he asked.

She tightened her lips. Quintillion had sought Thermeon for help. She wanted someone to help her too. She needed someone to confide in, someone to work out with her what the monster was, whether it was good or evil, or both, and what she should do about it. But she'd just met Serpenlino, and she didn't much care for his relatives, or his grilling of her. She couldn't risk trust yet.

"Nothing that made any sense," she said. "And I'm not sure why I was able to destroy it. It scared me, and I knocked it off its pedestal, and it broke."

"A soul-gem doesn't just break," he said. "Are you sure you didn't use mindpowers?"

Her laugh rang against the tunnel walls.

"You were scared," he reminded her. "Thermeon says he can only access his mindpowers when he feels some powerful emotion."

"Oh! You've talked to him?"

"Of course. He's another great-grandfather of mine."

Puflet swallowed. "I suppose he knows more about deep-level stuff than anyone. Maybe he could help me sort out my experience. Do you think it would be possible for me to talk to him?"

"He'd be happy to help. But of course, Katora has banned him from Ulona."

They walked on in silence. Tunnels branched toward the different meditation chambers, their colors indicating whether they led to warm or cold, dark or bright chambers. Puflet chose warm and bright. She and Serpenlino seated themselves on a sand dune overlooking a virtual tropical ocean. She savored the warm, salty breeze.

"Valri reported on her experience with the deep-level system," Serpenlino told her. "She said that Ix took her into a dark chamber and made her touch something—fine fibers, like hair. After that, the system was able to contact her."

"Oh." Quintillion's hair, Puflet thought. She bit her lip, tracing a circle in the sand with a fingertip. Quintillion must have had vast mindpowers, to be able to sense the mind of someone who merely touched his hair. Should she tell Serpenlino what she knew about the head? But maybe she should wait until she made contact with Thermeon, who would have a better understanding of a fellow mindsea. She stared out across the ocean. Waves washed the sand below their feet. She looked at Serpenlino. The breeze rippled the hood around his face, the simulated sun casting its shadow over his eyes.

"How can I contact Thermeon?"

He smiled, fangs winking. "You're a member of his family too?"

She touched a fingertip to one of her own fangs. "I doubt it. Ix brewed me in her lab. She might have used genes from fifty different individuals. The fangs might have been something left over from one of her father's experiments."

His head fell forward, and he mumbled, "That's too bad. Humans aren't meant to be bondless."

A spurt of anger sent heat to her face. "Not having a family doesn't mean I can't form bonds. It just means I get to choose whom I get close to instead of having to kowtow to the wishes of a million relatives and pretend that they're all wonderful people even if they're not."

"That's not what family means." He sounded angry too. "Family are people who share your memories of the past and hopes for the future."

"I can do that with friends," she said, burning from the awareness that she didn't have any friends. "And I won't have to make up lies about them, like pretending that Orgmorgan won't do anything for credits."

His head jerked up, eyes emerging from shadow to drill her. "He will not do anything for credits! I'm sure the slavers believe so, but he just fools them into thinking that so he can get into their confidence."

She laughed. He was so predictable. "I suppose Katora's calling Thermeon evil upsets you too."

"Katora and the slavers call him evil," Serpenlino said. "To most of the empire he is a beneficent elder statesman."

"Ix told me he destroyed a planet with his mindpowers. That's not true?"

Serpenlino heaved a sigh, head dropping forward again. "He flashed Wamatu to end the Great War his son Maxuas began. Most people think that he had no other option. Of course, it was a terrible thing. The force-wind he unleashed ignited Wamatu's atmosphere and boiled its oceans."

The unknown planet burning, its creatures dying, every death throe her own, hurtled back into Puflet's mind. She yelped in pain, gripping her cheeks.

Once-again shadowed eyes studied her face. "We at the academy are learning about the forces he used, learning to wield those forces ourselves, as much as our mindsize will allow. Deep-level forces hold the empire together, but they could also destroy it. That's why we students especially need the guidance of our forebears."

She let her hands drop into the sand, taking deep breaths to calm herself. "And what about people like me who don't have forebears? What's wrong with my seeking out individuals whose wisdom and sense of right I admire and asking them to guide me?"

"There's nothing wrong," he said. "And if you want to talk to Thermeon, I can mention you to him next time he mind-links me. But he won't be able to mind-link you; he can only reach people he knows."

"All right," she said. "Any contact would be a start. Thank you, Serpenlino."

"And now, I suppose it's time to begin your own journey to the mastery of the Deep." His voice swelled and deepened. "These are the Four Tenets of Patternistics."

There is nowhere but here. There is no time but now. There is no one but you. There is no volition, only affirmation.

Puflet could hardly recall any longer what her world had been like before she knew the Four Tenets. They seemed so integral to her understanding of the Deep she could not imagine how she had ever lived without them.

It was free-form hour. The students sat spread out across a checkerboard of black and white marble that covered the entire area beneath one of the Academy's seven golden domes—one in the center over the nexus and the others capping the six arms of the snowflake. Each student chose one of the Tenets to work with.

There is nowhere but here. If you understood that with all of your being, if you knew that you stood in the center of existence that was all places simultaneously, then you could step from one planet to another as easily as you stepped from one of the white squares on the floor to one of the black squares. Puflet was sure that she had felt a quiver of this truth aboard the ship and in the struggle with Tepi, when she had found a dimension that was not one of the three spatial dimensions of the ordinary world. But somehow she'd done the opposite of what was intended in the academy exercises. She had moved in that other dimension while remaining fixed in ordinary space. She could not get the feel for how to move herself out of ordinary space, into this other dimension, and then back into ordinary space. Nor could any other student of the academy, past or present. They said that the empire's founder, Attequol, had been able to teleport himself, but that was a myth.

There is no time but now. The Second Tenet was like the First, only for the temporal dimension. Again the students sought a center of existence, wherein every moment in time lay superimposed. All that had happened, all that would ever happen, along every branching history of every possible universe, was happening now in the center. You had merely to focus your attention on a particular moment, and it would happen for you. Puflet had no idea how to go about practicing this skill, nor had anyone else. Not even Attequol had the aura of a time-traveler attached to his name. Strangely enough, a rumor whispered from student to student claimed that Quintillion had had this ability.

Puflet thought maybe it was true. It would explain how the head had survived in the desert until Ix found it. A spike of dread had hit her when she first worked this out. She'd had to reassure herself that she had disposed of the head; it could not still be alive. She recalled its peaceful expression as it had rolled down the waste chute.

There is no one but you. The Third Tenet was the mindseas' tenet. Once again, a student had to picture a center of existence and all points of view residing there, superimposed. There were no special points of identity, just as there were no special points in space or time. A student should be able to step out of his awareness into someone else's, or into an awareness that contained both at once.

This was, of course, something mindseas could do. Katora offered one-to-one sessions on the Third Tenet in a meditation chamber for anyone who requested it. Puflet did not request a session. The only other identity she had felt was the monster's, and she did not want that coming out in front of Katora.

Sianne had been to a few personal sessions. One setting meal, Puflet had sat in a nook with her and some others while she talked about them.

"She advises a dark, warm chamber. She holds your hand and tells you to imagine leaving space, time, and self, and plunging into the center, through the center, to become someone else. It's a naturally frightening experience, like falling off a cliff, but she has your hand so that she can bring you back. Only I didn't go anywhere."

None of the Academy's current students could mind-link, though several graduates from the past had mastered the art.

There is no volition, only affirmation. The student was again told to realize that everything that had ever existed, would ever exist, lay in the center. All the patterns that made up space, time, matter, and awareness were there. Nothing could be created and nothing could be destroyed. All anyone ever could do was to affirm the pattern that caught their attention; but depending on the pattern you chose, you could meaningfully change the arrangement of matter in universes of spacetime.

Puflet was working on the Fourth Tenet, the one several students had had some success with. On entering the hall she had taken some tiny, iridescent Mednean snails from the holding tank near the archway and placed them in a bucket. She plucked one snail from the bottom of the bucket and set it upside down on a black square, then backed ten paces away. The snails had evolved in an ocean with natural deep-level upwellings, and could contain deep-level stuff within their shells. When placed upside down on land, the snail would open its shell to release the stuff.

Even the tiny amount of stuff escaping the shell had a fusion field—the phenomenon that caused everything in a ship to downlevel along with the ship itself. Molecules of air would downlevel, then uplevel again, with sparks and crackles, as they lost patternistic integrity with the deep stuff, which passed beyond the world of spacetime.

Puflet was trying to resolve molecules of ordinary matter and bits of deep-level matter into a system that had patternistic integrity and wouldn't break apart. She couldn't will it into being—according to the Tenet, will was an illusion. Somehow she had to picture it, picture the pattern. It was something akin to picking out the right pattern in a ship's level-detecting disks.

She tried, but with crackles, pops, and whistles, the stuff was gone.

With a sigh she set a second snail beside the first.

A moment later a third snail followed, then a fourth. By the time the sixth snail was on the square, the first snail had righted itself. Puflet wondered whether the snails ever recaptured stuff released by their fellows.

As she contemplated the tenth snail, an image sprang into her mind. A small amethyst gem winked out from the bend in a hallway, and from a floor, and from a habitat; everywhere she turned she came across the same gem.

Seconds later, realizing that she had not heard any crackling, Puflet let out a long-held breath and ran to look for the gem she had created. She found nothing but the snails. She scooped them back into their bucket, then searched the floor again. She was on her hands and knees when a glint caught her eye. She bent closer. It was her jewel—it must be—but it was far tinier than what she had seen in her mind's eye.

Yet, if she was right, she had created a deep-level artifact that erupted into spacetime in several locations. Like a tiny soul-gem. Only soul-gems had relayed messages, and her jewel didn't have a function. She'd forgotten to choose it with a purpose in mind.

Sighing, she laid the eleventh snail on the floor and backed ten paces.

She created nothing else during the session. When a dimming of the dome-glow signaled mid mealtime, she gathered the snails back into the bucket, and set the bucket on the cart near the exit so that they could be returned to the lake. Pea-Pach was on snail duty. She stood by the cart chatting with everyone who came by.

"I made a pinprick gem today," Puflet boasted.

"I knew you'd catch the drift," Pea-Pach smiled. "I made some sort of rocks once, but they weren't good for anything."

"Mine's not good for anything either," Puflet admitted.

Serpenlino dragged up. "You touched the Deep today, Puflet?"

"Sort of."

"Hmm. Tell me about it over dragonfly fritters."

As they started through the archway to the tunnel, Pea-Pach called after them, "Aw, Serpie, don't you want some variety to your meals? Let Puflet sit with someone else today, and wait here with me. I'll show you my rocks if you show me yours!"

Serpenlino just hunched down deeper, and they escaped. Pea-Pach was a happy, bubbly person, but sometimes she got on

Puflet's nerves.

When Puflet and Serpenlino had found an unoccupied nook, she told about her tiny gem.

His nodded thoughtfully. "I've felt sure you had mindpowers ever since you told me about destroying Ix's soul-gem."

"Well, this was nothing spectacular," she murmured, picking at her fritters. All the local dishes disagreed with her, but Serpenlino kept urging her to experiment. If she was to be an imperial woman she had to know the tastes of the galaxy, didn't she? But her old life of bland and unvarying slave gruel had probably destroyed any chance for her to become a gourmet.

Sianne slid into the booth on her other side. "I'd like to request a private session with you on the Third Tenet."

Puflet let a forkful of crinkly wings fall back onto her plate. "Who, me?"

"Of course, you," drawled the elegant woman, looking down a long nose that strongly resembled Katora's.

"But I haven't had any success with Three!"

"Everyone is saying that you're the most gifted student here, and I need some help fast, Puflet. I've had bad news from Lal. My mother is crystallizing. I want to be able to contact her before it's too late. Travelling to the capital would probably take too long, and memory buttons are so one-way, and LZ-nodes just garble things. Can you meet with me tonight?"

The hours between mid meal and setting meal were used for meditation chamber exercises on most days, but once every tenthday Katora gave a lecture at that time, and it happened to be lecture day. It was also the day of Puflet's last scheduled wonderdome session. Afterward she would be free to join Dino and Pea-Pach—and Kael if he could get free from Eadin—for Rebounders, or play sidewalk golf in town with Serpenlino. She would also have to take her turn at the various housekeeping duties students performed.

"How about when I get back from Wonderdome?" she asked.

"Thank you," Sianne said, looking relieved.

After the meal the three of them sauntered together toward the lecture hall. Other students filled the tunnel in front of them and behind them. Swooshing their robes, Hinomia and Yusun cut past.

Hinomia looked back over her shoulder, pale blue eyes drilling Sianne. "I'm surprised at you—consorting with animals!"

"You're a sham, Hinomia," the taller woman shot back. "You were absolutely no help to me with the Third Tenet. So you can't be Horl, can you? He was a master."

"Maybe Horl is glad your stupid mother is crystallizing."

Sianne's dark face paled. "She's your grandmother!"

"I'm purging her genes from my body!" Hinomia's chin shot up, and she swept ahead.

"Ha ha!" Yusun laughed, nose bobbling. His pet glared with its popping eyes and hissed. Then he hurried after Hinomia.

Puflet wondered if Hinomia enjoyed the contrast between her beauty and Yusun's ugliness. Ix had enjoyed that sort of thing.

"Horl was a vile man," Sianne said softly. "He was cruel to my mother. I'm glad I'm not related to him."

Puflet nodded. "He caused a great deal of misery in the galaxy. Anyone who wants to emulate him is warped."

The three of them continued at their leisurely pace. The scent of flowers overtook them as Eadin steered Kael past. Her voice rang brightly against the tunnel wall. "Isn't it wonderful how we bring out the best in each other, Kael? Some people can only drag each other down." Her eyes were on the trailing end of Serpenlino's robe.

"Huh?" came Kael's baffled response.

Eadin pulled him on before he could say anything to embarrass her.

The tunnel ended at the lecture hall, a vaulted chamber with semi-circular rows of self-nooks stacked one above and behind the other as they wrapped around the stage. Vault and walls glowed with golden light. The nooks were velvety and maroon. Puflet, Sianne, and Serpenlino walked halfway down the sloping aisle before entering a row of nooks and seating themselves. Students continued to trickle in. Voices babbled around them, then hushed as Katora stepped onto the stage and walked up to the podium that sprouted from the tree-fern wood stage floor in the form of a pahmak's neck and head sculpted from translucent quartzite.

Her voice, clear and melodic, flew out across the hall. "Today I want to tell you about the history of the mindsea academy."

Since students were constantly entering and graduating, the lectures had to be of interest to those at different levels. So far Puflet had always learned something from them.

"The original concept of a mindsea academy came from Attequol," Katora began. "He founded the first academy along with the Circle of Experts so that the empire would never lose the technology he developed. While the Circle was given care of home-level sciences, Patternistics and level-engineering were the purview of the ancient mindsea academy.

"Unfortunately, the academy failed in its purpose with Aturon."

Katora spoke as if everyone knew why this would have happened. Puflet queried her link. She'd found that the academy's walls and domes were shielded against glowworm signals— whatever for?—so she'd run her siphon to the outside through the front portals, which usually stood open as a sign of welcome—for whom? Not for the tainted, or for ordinary, untalented citizens like Cidi. Perhaps the welcome was meant for certain special students whose coming Katora awaited.

Aturon was Attequol's son and heir apparent. Historians now believe that he had no desire to rule and so fled to a distant galaxy on his father's death.

An emperor fleeing to a distant galaxy to escape his duties struck Puflet as so comical that she almost laughed aloud. Sianne felt her shaking and darted her a look. She subsided.

Katora described the languishing of the academy under Rathax, again assuming that everyone understood that emperor's agenda. Puflet queried her link.

Rathax wanted to rule an empire of many world-lines and destroyed all the technology Attequol had emplaced to unify imperial history.

Puflet was aware of Sianne's erect figure beside her, her soft breathing and her subtle fragrance. Why had the great-granddaughter of a famous empress sought her out, after pretty much ignoring her up until then, other than begging her to trade assignments when she got the lake? Did she really think Puflet talented? Did she see her as a potential friend? Or was she just so desperate, she was willing to ask anyone for help? Obviously she had already asked Katora and Hinomia for sessions on Three.

Perhaps there had been others as well. She had nothing to lose by trying with Puflet, except an hour or two. But Puflet had nothing to lose either, so she would do her best to help, even though she hadn't an inkling of what it took to mind-link.

The monster knows, whispered in the back of her mind. Her scalp prickled.

Katora had gone through several millennia of history while her mind ranged. "Then Horl closed the doors of the mindsea academy and ransacked its memories," she was saying. "The keys to Patternistics, which had been safeguarded through many tumultuous times by a few dedicated men and women, now became Horl's private property. As far as we know, all of the deep-level technology of the earliest times was replicated or exceeded by Horl. The transways he built, the soul-gem-powered farfling towers and multi-level architecture were the wonders of the Decadent Epoch. There were extravagances never seen before and never seen since—like the gameboard for human players on Wamatu. The squares downleveled or upleveled at verbal commands. Horl even experimented with the Second Tenet, sacrificing entire cities to test his theories. The Decadent Epoch was both the glory and the shame of our species.

"Then Thermeon came, and the Empire's knowledge of Patternistics was all lost."

Thermeon, Puflet thought. *He has a monster too.*

She had heard the story of the Fissure from Quintillion and from Katora, but she had yet to hear Thermeon's view of the event. Quintillion had asked Thermeon to help him, and it seemed natural for Puflet to do so as well.

The new citizen gift she had been granted was not enough for her to travel to Lal, and she wouldn't have an income until she graduated—unless she decided to do some glowworm-engineering on the side—so it looked like she would have to wait. Sometimes it galled her that Serpenlino was in contact with Thermeon, and she couldn't be. But even a powerful mindsea needed some kind of exchange with a person before he could swallow their minds. That was why Ix had made Valri touch Quintillion's hair.

She sighed. More waiting. Almost all of her life so far had been spent waiting.

Katora had been telling about the rediscovery of Ulona and her capture by a pahmak that thought it was an ancient mindsea. "It was while I was in that dungeon, searching for the freedom within my own mind, that I discovered the key that opened Horl's encrypted memory files. That was the beginning of the resurgence of Patternistics. The Four Tenets, which had not been repeated aloud for eleven millennia, became the property of every citizen in the Empire. Mindseas, once thought to be extinct, walk among us once again. As we continue our work of decryption and experimentation, all of the wonders of the past will rise once again, and more. We truly will live in an age of illumination!"

As the last glorious echoes of her voice trilled round the ribs of the vault, students burst into wild applause. Katora acknowledged their enthusiasm with a graceful dip of her head, then left the stage, her copper-tipped hair rippling and long blue gown, slippers, and earrings sparkling beneath the vault-glow.

She was very good at making herself appear like a goddess, Puflet had to acknowledge. Better than Ix had ever been. Perhaps because Ix had been stupid and lazy, while Katora worked hard for the goal she believed in, using her intelligence and mindsize both as tools.

She really believed in the age of illumination she kept talking about.

After the lecture, Puflet went back to her cell and soaked in her hot tub for a while. Leaning her head over the foam rim, she stared up at the skylight, which provided the view she was importing from Ulona's north pole. The sun was about to set there, and the clouds were drenched in wild purples and crimsons.

"If you are illuminated does it mean you have seen the truth?" she mused at the clouds.

She dried and dressed and was ready when Serpenlino came to her door to escort her to setting meal. Kael and Eadin met them in the nexus.

"Serpenlino, I need to talk to you," Kael said. "Just you and me. You girls can chat together, all right?"

Eadin glared at Puflet and tossed her ylang-ylang.

They split up in the dining hall and went to separate nooks. Eadin craned her neck to keep an eye on the men. Her lips curled in a smug smile. "Kael's probably asking advice about how to please a woman sexually. Serpenlino would know, because he's had lots of partners." She looked at Puflet. "You know that, don't you?"

Puflet pushed back a strand of her still damp hair. "I don't know half as much as you do, I'm sure."

"I'm just trying to warn you because I don't want you to be hurt. Serpenlino is just playing with you. A man like him has too much of an animal appetite to ever settle for one woman."

"Thank you, Eadin."

"I know you don't believe me, but—"

As Eadin blabbed on, Puflet directed a firefly to hover over the men's nook to transmit their conversation to her link.

"I don't know how long to keep trying!" Kael's voice was anguished.

"Time makessss no difference." Serpenlino didn't usually use his snake voice with Kael. Maybe he was annoyed at him for whining. "Massstery is alwayssss one insssight away."

"The way my father talks about it," Kael said, "it was like something inside him he was always aware of in a way. But I don't know, maybe fathers just like to sound superior, or he doesn't remember how it really was. But then, when I look around, and everyone can do stuff except me."

"But in reality, mossst of usss are not very talented."

"Do you honestly know of anyone who had to work a really long time before their powers developed?"

"Dino tells me that he a has a ssssecret for increasing mindsize. He used it on Emperor Ressssuvilussss right before he died."

"I don't know if I'd want to try that," Kael said. "If he died right afterwards."

Serpenlino hiss-chuckled. "Ssssianne wanted him to try it on her, but he would not."

After a brief silence, Kael said, "Yeah, I've heard that she's pretty desperate to learn the mastery of mind-linking. It's sad about her mother. Over ten thousand years of good health, and suddenly ... it's over. Oh, I suppose you can't expect anyone to live forever. But I'm glad I don't have that sort of pressure. My father is still going strong. But still, how long do I want to beat my head against a wall? Maybe I should just quit and go home."

"How isss it when you travel?" Serpenlino asked. "Can you ssssensssse the Deep?"

"I don't really remember the trip here," Kael said.

Puflet tsked. That wasn't a good sign.

Eadin's voice rose to a querulous whine. "Are you listening to what I'm telling you?"

"Of course," Puflet said, concentrating on her link.

"You could ask Puflet to do Three with you. I'm sure she has a great deal of mindpower locked insssside her."

"Eadin's very talented too," Kael said. "She says she's going to be able to mind-link me soon, and I keep smelling her ylang-ylang, even when she's not around."

Serpenlino snorted.

"I feel like I'm letting her down," Kael said. "She expects me to be able to mind-link her too. She has some idea about forming a union of our planets, but I'm not the man she thinks I am. What should I do?"

"Level with her," Serpenlino said.

There followed a couple minutes of silence, and then Puflet heard them talking to Sianne about meal selections. She looked at Eadin and smiled. Eadin evidently had just finished communicating what should have been a devastating revelation. Her face fell at Puflet's lack of response.

Soon Sianne arrived with the cart, and Puflet picked out a palm heart loaf and a local date wine. She checked the men's nook from time to time, but they got to discussing sports, and whether mindsize really could affect a ball's trajectory.

After the meal, she picked up her air lifter on the front steps of the academy and headed for the wonderdome. As she started off, she admired the seven golden domes of the academy, their glow bathing nearby clumps of cycads in a soft pool of light. She passed over lighted parks, habitats, and a ring of shops, then descended toward the wonderdome with its single green dome. As she had every night for the past two tenthyears, she swam in the channel of water that circulated just inside the descending curve of the dome, staring through its transparent wall at ferns and cycads dimly-illuminated by dome-glow.

The water had a salt smell. It was infused with some of the healing and strengthening mixture of the float tanks, a diluted wonderwater. Puflet enjoyed the sense of accomplishment she got from churning through the water on her muscle power. Its slow curve made the channel seem endless, except when she passed under the archway into the well-lit lobby with its golden letters and ferny grottoes.

Puflet swam her five laps in personal best time. Then she showered and dressed and went to Cidi's office to check out.

She found Kaanu in the office with Cidi. Since his expulsion, Kaanu had been working Tepi's niche as a pahmak herder, but he made frequent visits to Alonaton. He was a big man, as Quintillion must once have been. His gaze radiated force, and Puflet imagined his grandfather appearing that way—the same blue skin, the same black hair flowing over his shoulders. But Kaanu's eyes were amber. As usual, he had a fiddlehead jammed between his lips. He called them nutritious, but Puflet still found the smell of fern revolting.

Cidi's eyes sparkled. "We have big news, Puflet! Would you like to join us for a little celebration?"

"Of course," Puflet said. "What's the news?"

At once the data charts and health polygons blinked out, and a view of some world with golden sands—Lal, Puflet guessed—replaced the shaded green tones of the hemispherical ceiling/wall, and the bi-level wondermaster-patient nook reformed itself into a 3-nook. When they had settled into the nook's three arms, Cidi said, "First of all, Katora's had to give up her persecutions! She thought she could have Kaanu exiled from Ulona, or worse, for hurting Tepi, but he was about half a planet away when the attack happened, and he doesn't have the mindpowers to unfuse someone. Anyhow, Kaanu's father works in the capital, and he talked to Katora's father, and he finally made her see reason."

"I'm very relieved to hear that," Puflet said truthfully.

Cidi grinned at Kaanu, and he grinned back as well as he could while continuing to chomp on the fiddlehead.

A serving bioid fashioned like an enormous dragonfly with a shimmering green-blue body and bulbous red eyes whirred in, carrying a crystalline tray with three goblets and a bottle. The bioid hovered by each of them until they had taken their goblets. Then it set the tray on the nook's center point and opened the bottle with the human hands on the ends of its insect legs. It served them all, replaced the bottle on the tray, then whirred off through an irising opening in the wall.

"To the future!" Cidi toasted. They raised their goblets in unison, then drank.

"Ooh!" Puflet cried. "Different. Is it imported?"

Cidi and Kaanu laughed.

"Imported from Andromeda," he said. "My great-aunt is an intergalactic trader."

"Ah, Andromeda!" Puflet took another long gulp, her mind spinning with the possibilities. There were so many wonders out there, adventures she thirsted for. Once she had her mindpowers under her control, nothing was going to stop her.

Her goblet was empty. She directed a sheepish smile at Cidi.

The green eyes twinkled. "I have another piece of news to celebrate. If you would like to offer the toast, Puflet."

Puflet extended her goblet to signal her willingness. The dragonfly returned to refill it and to top off Cidi's and Kaanu's goblets.

Cidi beamed. "Kaanu and I are going to be married. Next year we'll join the race for reproductive rights. My grandmother has made sure that Katora can't stop us from getting positions."

"Ah!" Puflet gurgled. "Long life and happiness to you both! Any many children!" She raised her goblet, then brought it to her lips and drew deeply of the mysterious amber liquid. Her mind swam in some distant ocean of stars and events. A shape rose before her. "Generations will pass," she said, "then, in the Hundred Tenth Millennium, one of your descendants will come in joy to bring justice to the beings of the galaxies. She will be called 'New Voice.' She will have your hair, Cidi, and your complexion, Kaanu. Her Genetic Algorithms assigned name will link her to Lal's native queens. And she will be a singer, of course."

Why a singer, a detached part of her mind asked. Then she recalled that Quintillion had been a singer. The head had hummed to her while waiting for her to make up her mind about killing it.

Cidi and Kaanu sat gaping at her. She took another sip, smiling at them across the goblet rim—the shore of the amber sea. "The New Voice will sing beautiful songs of freedom and fair play, the songs of an age of splendor we can not yet fathom. And she will bring love."

There, you see, you mean old bitch? her detached part flung at Katora. *Galena's Goodness will prevail; love in the desert will have its rewards.*

Then she realized that she was working the Second Tenet, and the goblet nearly slid out of her hand.

10

By the time Puflet met Sianne outside her door, she'd taken a sober-up, changed into a soft, clingy, and comforting white skinsuit, and tried to calm herself. She wasn't sure what had happened. Perhaps she really had stepped through the center to merge with another mind—or perhaps her own mind—in a distant future. But maybe she had just hallucinated while under the effects of whatever was in that Andromedean vintage. The only way to know for sure would be to wait several generations and see if her vision had come to pass.

Somehow, she felt confident that it would.

"Are you ready?" Sianne asked as the door irised open and Puflet stepped out. Sianne wore a black skinsuit rather than her usual flowing robe, her face tensed.

"As a freak at a free-for-all," Puflet said.

"Pardon?"

"Sorry—slaver expression. I'm ready."

They walked side by side through the tunnel, Sianne's dark face taking on hues of the glow around them, highlights accentuated by the thin layer of sweat on her forehead. Puflet wondered if most citizens felt so strongly about their mothers. She tried to put herself in Sianne's situation, but nothing she had experienced in her life informed her. After a moment she realized that she was making faces and directed her thoughts to mindseas and the Third Tenet.

Sianne led her through the tunnels to the warm and dark

meditation chambers, then paused at the branching between arid and moist. The arid tunnel glowed crimson like a dying ember, and the moist had a deep green glow.

"Which will it be?" Sianne asked.

Puflet hesitated for a moment, then chose the crimson. They entered the chamber, and warm darkness folded around them, softened only by the glow emanating from her hair.

"You're a Luminary!" Sianne exclaimed.

Puflet tried to brush the waves of light away from her face, but they kept springing back. "Sorry. Forgot that I was a lamp-head!" She laughed. "Ix must've put more of Thermeon into my mixture than was wise for her. I never realized it until I escaped, because she kept giving me floats to uglify me."

"She robbed you of your face?" Sianne's voice was shocked.

"Slaves own nothing, least of all themselves."

"I'm sorry you went through all of that. Ix was as vile as her father! I'm glad you put an end to her. I don't care what Hinomia and those other fools think."

Puflet gave herself over to soaking in the caring, the empathy in Sianne's words. She was bound for a distant shore she had never before seen, racing through the darkness, borne by a mysterious force of deeper-dimensions. Was this what friendship felt like?

"Well," Sianne said. "Why don't we get started."

The sensation of flight dissolved suddenly. Puflet became aware of the sand molding to the pressure of her knees, the still form of Sianne beside her, staring at her with yearning, and the close, heavy air around them.

Sianne didn't really care about her. She just wanted her touch of the Deep, if she could get it. But what else could human bonds be based on, except for need? Everyone wanted to be loved just for themselves, but the feeling that there was something intrinsic about one's own point of view, something setting self apart from the rest, was an illusion, as the Third Tenet showed. You could only be loved for the things you did, the gifts you offered.

Puflet reached out to take Sianne's warm hands in hers. She shut her eyes, concentrating on their handclasp. But her heartbeat shook her body, and her head whirled. She had to calm herself. She swallowed, and spoke. "The Third Tenet tells us that we are all the same self, divided by the illusions that our senses weave. Behold the truth now, Sianne, as we see it when we fly on a deep-level ship: Each of us is a tiny plateau of self rising from the black fog of the universe. But down there, beneath the fog where we can't see, we are all one, all joined together."

She gently squeezed Sianne's fingers. "See the truth," she urged. "Feel it. Know it."

She let a few heartbeats pass. "Now you must leave your tiny plateau and seek another plateau. Fly, Sianne. Fly over here to my plateau, and learn what it's like to be me. You can do it. I know you can. Because we all can do it. We all have the power to visit other pieces of ourselves. It's just that we're afraid."

She squeezed her eyes tighter. "It's scary to fly, to have nothing below you for support. You have to give up everything that makes you you—all of your convictions, all your precious family memories. They become nothing when you fly, when you leave your tiny plateau behind. But you have to risk it. You have to leave your most most cherished images of love behind, snapping the defining bonds of your life. You have to trust that those bonds will reappear when you land on the farther shore—which is another's point of view. You have to trust that the people you love really do love you in the way you think they do."

Puflet had no idea where these ideas about family bonds and love were springing from, since she had no personal knowledge of the matter. But she let her words flow on. "Do it now, Sianne. Free yourself. Take the plunge."

Sianne's fingers trembled.

"Of course you're afraid. We're all afraid. And we have good reason." Puflet lowered her voice to a whisper. "There's a monster out there in the black fog, waiting to take us. But don't be afraid, Sianne. The monster doesn't want you. It has me, and I will protect you."

"No!" Sianne jerked her hands away. "Why are you talking about monsters?" Her voice changed from the modulated tones Puflet had always heard into a screech, reverberating in the enclosed space and hurting Puflet's ears. "That's as bad as Hinomia, always telling me that Horl is out there!"

Opening her eyes, Puflet saw Sianne by the light of her hair, kneeling on the dune and twisting slowly from side to side. Her eyes looked as black as her face.

"If mind-linking was pleasant, Sianne, everyone would do it."

"But you don't have to talk about monsters."

Puflet sighed. "It just slipped out." She needed someone to confide in, someone to help her understand and deal with the monster. It wasn't going to be Sianne.

"Do you want to try it again?" she asked.

"No." Sianne scrambled to her feet.

Puflet rose too. Dizziness spun her head. Something was wrong with the meditation chamber. Sianne's profile against the dim light of the Ulonan false dawn had turned monstrous. Dinosaur horns spitted the night. Blood trickled down fangs and dried on the gums —Puflet's blood.

"Make your choice!" the monster roared at her.

"What do you mean?" she gasped.

"Upward, or downward? Make your choice!"

Bursting from the meditation chamber, Puflet raced through the tunnels until she found her cell. Sobbing, she cast off her clothes and eased herself into her hot tub. She still felt off-kilter, as if she had slipped halfway from the ordinary world into some other place, some deeper dimension where the monster dwelt. Slowly, slowly the heat worked through the spell that had slimed her body, until at last she felt resolidified, normal. She laid her head back over the edge of the tub and stared up at the blood-red clouds of Ulonan sunset.

If she'd ever turned off her view, she wouldn't have forgotten her glowing hair. The darkness brought memories of slavery, but she needed to get over it. She turned the view off, and floated in the near darkness, water lapping softly at her sides, her heartbeat slowing.

What had happened? Twice in one night she had dipped into deep-level experiences.

"Control slipped," she mused aloud.

The first time it had been the wine, of course. The second time.... She must have put so much effort into helping Sianne mind-link, that she had ripped herself open, or something. The blood on the monster's fangs had indicated a wound. And Sianne would probably hate her for it. If she hadn't in fact been swallowed by the monster.

Maybe Puflet should have realized that despite her apparent desperation, Sianne had never been willing to take the steps necessary to master the Third Tenet; if she had, she would've achieved her goal on her own. Instead, she'd been looking for an easier way, a way that didn't ask her to question her deepest beliefs, and of course there wasn't one. Puflet had been a fool to take her words at face value. She wouldn't make that mistake again.

Slipping deeper into the water, she blew out a stream of bubbles and watched them float away.

She'd tried to establish human bonds—first with Cidi, then with Sianne—but something kept getting in the way. Maybe something always would. Maybe that something was the monster.

It seemed as if she could never experience anything exhilarating or wonderful without it thundering out. The head had warned her, of course. It had told her it had to suffer constantly to keep the monster from taking over and destroying everything.

But Thermeon harbored a monster too, didn't he? Serpenlino had said his powers erupted whenever he was gripped by strong emotions. And it was common knowledge that every woman he'd ever had sex with had died smoldering with unfusing damage. Puflet wondered if that was true even for Cidi's grandmother. Or had Thermeon found sex with Galena non-lethal, when his powers —his monster—had been engaged elsewhere? Would Cidi think it intrusive if Puflet asked her?

She wondered if Thermeon had seen his lovers in dinosaur form, the way Sianne had looked to her. Had that only been her illusion, or had the entity actually seized Sianne's mind and body? However he saw his monster, what did Thermeon do about it? How did he coexist with it?

She had to talk to him.

Rising from the tub, she noticed a faint glow on one of her walls. She crossed the room, wondering what it was. It wasn't coming from glowworms. Crouching down, she made out a tiny gleam in the center of the glow.

Footsteps approached. They sounded like they issued from the gleam, but clearly it was someone walking through a tunnel. She thought she recognized Sianne's slow and measured steps. Thankfully, she seemed back to normal. Her shadow crossed the glow, then the steps faded.

The gleam was the tiny jewel she had placed in the floor of the free-form hall, and in a tunnel, and in the wall of her cell. Puflet fingered her chin. "Very curious."

Was that how soul-gems had worked?

She found herself musing on one of Katora's lectures. "Is There Such a Thing as the Past?" had been the title of the talk. Katora had opened it with the question, "If there are countless versions of the past going back from any moment in time, as well as countless versions of the future going forward from that point, can we truthfully speak about one past and one future?"

She had answered her own question with, "No, we cannot. Past and future are forever fluid. They exist only as constructs that help us to define ourselves as a progression of memories, and as a consensus among people who need a common past to frame their communal identity. In the Contested Era—" that included the reigns of Thermeon and Quintillion—"mindseas did battle to determine what the past would be, as well as the future.

"The archaic name of our empire, the Empire of the Common Mind, reflects Attequol's knowledge that imperial history is determined by the mutual consent of the Empire's citizens. The past can always be changed, but it can only be changed if all of its citizens remember the new past rather than the old. If citizens lived in different histories, the empire's patternistic integrity would shatter, and it would cease to be. Indeed, the Lost Planets came to be so called because their pasts diverged from the rest of the Empire's, and their people slipped into an alternate universe, beyond the reach of our ships or messages."

Puflet thought about her tiny gem that was all over the academy, saw it winking at her, much bigger in her mind's eye, just as it had been when she first pictured it. She felt more certain that it did have a purpose, a function. As soon as she recognized that function—she didn't need to will it into being, but simply to acknowledge it—it would always have been so, for no other minds would recall her gem differently. The other students believed that she had mindsize and could create wonders. By believing it, they helped her to make it so.

Katora's Sunrise Ball would be the talk of Alonaton for the next Ulonan year. Everyone—well, short of the emperor; but he was only a figurehead, anyhow—was there. Puflet had hoped that Katora would bend a little and let Thermeon come; unfortunately, he was still on her list of the tainted.

Still, it was a splendid gathering. The free-form hall, where the event took place, glittered with men, women, individuals of uncertain or dual gender, and a smattering of intelligent animals, artifacts that had won citizenship, and even a few aliens, all in the most gorgeous fashions of their worlds.

Katora and Dino stood in the very center of the hall, along with their youngest child, a girl of fourteen named Dilora, to welcome the guests as they arrived, while townspeople dressed up in white pawn outfits circulated, pushing carts with drinks and snacks, and another called out the names of the guests in a loud voice as they entered the hall. In a full-length red gown of her own styling, Puflet craned her neck to see past the press of other students. She'd left her glowworms in her cell, just in case some of the guests had brought glowworm nets to detect spy-eyes.

Katora's half-sister, Mind-River of Lal Cevana Niwarr Violole, swept in, her amber gown trimmed with silver ribbons that twirled behind her, more ribbons woven into her silvery black hair. Katora met her with an embrace and Puflet snorted, figuring that they must hate each other's guts.

Cevana's bright voice rang across the hall. "What a darling little place you've thrown together out here!" It went without saying that her own place in the imperial palace in the galactic capital was far grander.

As Cevana spun around to take everything in—or to show off her splendid person—a large oval ornament on her bosom flashed.

Next to make an appearance was the empire's oldest man, Member of the Circle Ietipa "Hube" Huberimton Siger, tall and spare in a smoky gray suit with cream lapels. His face, the color of tarnished silver, bore a quiet smile when the daughter accompanying him was announced and she flounced forward, her purplish complexion a clear sign of descent from Quintillion, and shocked the vast hall into silence. Even Katora seemed uncertain what to do, hesitating for a second before offering the pair a stiff, formal greeting.

Puflet decided that Hube was not such a bad sort, after all.

The guests kept pouring in—Members, Inheritors, Sages, Navigators, Patternists, Mind-Rivers. By ones and twos, students rushed forward to greet their relatives.

Puflet stiffened when Valri Sinart Vinu was announced. The Empress of the Unknown stalked in with the menacing undulation of a patrolling shark, cascades of pale golden hair wafting over her shoulders, eyes cutting like shards of blue-green ice as they scanned for potential prey. She embraced Katora with a shark's smile, then moved on regally, attended by a cloud of her sisters, some white, others with the tarnished silver complexion Valri herself and so many of the empire's elite shared. The sisters had black hair, yellow-green hair, pink hair. Valri alone was golden.

Hinomia and Yusun greeted Valri respectfully, then hovered about a pink-haired sister. Valri must be an aunt, or great-aunt. Sianne was out there too, embracing Valri, tears shining on her tarnished silver cheeks as her lips moved, asking no doubt for words about her mother. Her hair was golden as Valri's, spoiling its effect. Valri quickly slithered away from her.

Liaison to the Code Lelin Spashoob Weapoa arrived. The proud red-eyed woman wore a golden helix atop intricately braided black hair. The lines of her gold-trimmed red suit looked severe, almost military. The silence greeting her was nearly as profound as the one that had met Hube's purply daughter. Puflet wasn't sure why Coders were hated. Maybe the old aristocracy just hated anyone different. Oakiza stepped forward, and an odd series of formal gestures were exchanged.

Oakiza and the liaison—except for the red eyes, he didn't look anything like her—moved off. More guests flooded in. Planetary royalty was represented by Priestess of the Pentagon, Queen Ona Oozed Aataml of Niom, a dark purple woman in a topaz gown that trailed a salty spray; by Eadin's mother, blue-haired Queen Niti Mnihecaa Aniv of Yohorb, and Kael's father, King Quinofil Biari Fusen of Gilkay. Eadin's mother wore no flowers, but her hair streamed and fizzed about like a comet's tail. King Quinofil looked sterner than his son, his rigid face a deeper blue.

Head of the Pilots Guild Orgmorgan came wearing the pilot's traditional whaleskin suit, but with more colors splashed across it than were worn by all of the other guests combined, including colors Puflet didn't think human eyes were designed to perceive. A pale, red-haired woman accompanied him, and behind them trundled a potato-shaped little alien that was announced as Turpo of Xopeo.

The arrivals and announcements went on until the vast hall seethed and crackled with people. They clumped into inward-centered groups, all yammering and gesticulating at once. The students, who had massed by the archway at first, had broken apart, each seeking his or her own family members among the guests. It seemed to Puflet she was the only one who didn't have someone.

That was just fine, she thought. She would circulate and meet the empire's celebrities.

She headed toward toward the fiery heads of Orgmorgan and his companion. Happily, Hube and his shocking daughter had joined their group, along with the student who was related to Hube. Puflet would ask her for an introduction.

All at once she found herself staring at the broad shoulders and back of a tall man she didn't recognize. He'd slid in from somewhere to block her way. Seeing his long black hair, she wondered if Kaanu had been allowed to return for the ball.

"Excuse me," she said, and he turned with a fangy grin.

"Ah, Serpenlino." She frowned up at him. He'd always slunk about hunched over with his hood pulled up and his robe trailing snakelike behind him. It had made him seem shorter and more slender than he really was. The suit he'd donned for the ball revealed his real physique. He wasn't blue or purply. He might have been cast from bronze, and his eyes looked gray now beneath the glow spheres, but still....

"Yes," he said, reading her mind, "I am Quintillion's son."

She clapped a hand over her mouth. Good thing she hadn't mentioned the head to him. A wave of annoyance followed as she realized that he hadn't trusted her, either.

"I vouched for 'im," drawled a gruff voice. Orgmorgan, squat and orange-bearded, parked his garish colors beside them. "Tol' her he was my gritty-grandson, so the great green head o' lettuce let 'im be."

Puflet blinked. Did all pilots talk in that weird way? She hoped that Kicce hadn't been any relation.

"Had to vouch for you too," Orgmorgan went on.

She met his eyes. "Me? Why?"

"Guess she don't care much for where your finger points."

She exhaled with vehemence. "Well, I saw the slaves who'd been through—" her eyes darted for Valri—"her correction sessions. She enjoyed torture! Why hasn't she been called to task?"

Orgmorgan spread his stubby fingers. "Some pebbles need convincing. But we're on it."

Scowling, Puflet lifted her eyes and found Hube bending treelike over Orgmorgan and his party. Was he one of the ones who needed convincing? With a stab of guilt she recalled that she'd hardly given her fellow ex-slaves a thought since she'd arrived at the academy; she'd been so wrapped up in her own concerns.

"Patience," Serpenlino said at her side. He introduced her to his red-haired Aunt Eria.

A buttery voice issued from Hube. "Things work out. Today's tidal waves are but little ripples of history."

Puflet felt like grinding her fangs. "It's very hard to be patient when you know slaves somewhere are screaming in agony. Their pain might be little ripples to us, but it's sure tidal waves to them."

Hube merely smiled down at her. "The universe cannot be

hurried, my dear."

"The universe!" She fumed. "That's no excuse for inaction."

Orgmorgan laughed. "The filly's champin' at the bit, ain't she?"
Hube chuckled.

Their condescension stung. Puflet glared at Hube. "I suppose you've seen it all."

"Actually," said Serpenlino. "My aunt is older than he is."

Puflet's gaze shifted to Eria, who stood no taller than herself.

"I was born earlier," Eria admitted, "but as I spend most of my time in Deep Five, I'm probably not older."

"Just like a female to figger that," said Orgmorgan.

"Oh, so you're a pilot too?" Puflet asked.

Eria wasn't wearing whaleskin. A simple, yet graceful umber gown made her skin look very pale and her hair bright. "I'm just back from the Andromeda run."

"Oh!" Memories of the Andromedean wine almost brought a smile. Puflet forced her mind back to serious matters. "The two of you—" She looked at Eria, then Hube—"lived through the entire Horl period. What did you do to fight him?"

Eria's blue eyes shone. "I remained free."

"Outlived him," said Hube.

Puflet opened her mouth for another sally, but a sudden clatter drowned out her words. All the pawns had started to beat on the little drums slung around their chests. Guests fell silent. Katora's voice rose. "Let us drink a toast to the new dawn!"

Puflet's group broke apart as everyone moved toward the carts bearing goblets and bottles. Determined to toast the dawn with Saqufean fire dragons, Puflet had to run past a few carts before she found what she was looking for. She picked up a goblet. It had a gilded, many-rayed starburst foot that sent gleams of gold up through the stem. While she was examining the goblet, someone else had taken the fire dragons bottle, and she had to wait. Katora replaced the bottle on the cart, and Puflet took it.

"You like fire dragons too!" she said, pouring. "Who would have thought you and I had something in common!"

Katora inclined her head with the barest hint of acknowledgment. Her eyes remained cold. Orgmorgan's words rushed back at Puflet. The headmistress must already have decided to hate her, before they'd even met.

Katora turned her attention to the view beyond the clarified dome. The glowing spheres that floated overhead to light the hall dimmed, but the darkness was not complete. A faint green radiance could be seen on the horizon.

"Dawn approaches," Katora said.

Puflet and everyone else stared. A brighter pulse of green went through the clouds.

"Morning has broken," Katora announced.

Cheers rang against the dome. Some guests clinked their goblets together. Then everyone drank. Puflet shut her eyes and swallowed a dragon. It burned her tongue and raged down her throat. Wonderful. She took another sip.

Someone tapped her shoulder. She turned to see Dilora, green as her mother, but with Dino's glowing white hair.

"Would you hold my goblet for a moment, I have to adjust my trailer."

The girl smiled at Puflet the way Eadin smiled when she was about to say something cruel, red eyes agleam.

Puflet smiled back. "Just put it down on the cart, honey. Excuse me."

She headed off in search of Eria, but the small woman was lost among towering figures in the crowd. Puflet noticed Serpenlino and Kael's father, King Quinofil, in the center of a gaggle of students and guests. She moved to the outskirts of the clump, her eyes on the two men, who were engaged in a lively debate about water-chess.

A wet explosion toward the center of the hall made everyone's head turn. There were screams, laughter, and an unhappy honking. Yusun had fallen victim to Dilora's exploding goblet.

The sports debate had paused. Pea-Pach stood at Quinofil's elbow, stroking the golden epaulettes on his silken black uniform. "I'm sure you could beat him, King!"

"It takes finessssse more than power," Serpenlino warned.

The pawns started drumming again.

"One more announcement!" Katora called from the center of the hall. "And then there will be dance music composed by my daughter Dilora."

Everyone turned to face the center. The spheres dimmed again, except for one that shone directly down on Katora and Dino. Dino's suit—white, trimmed in red—shone. The couple raised their glasses to toast one another. Then Katora faced her guests. "We have won reproductive rights for this imperial year. Our son is in the incubator, and he will be born with the new day. Another toast to the new day! May it bring the dawn of illumination!"

Everyone cheered and raised their glasses. Puflet swallowed a third fire dragon. She wondered how Dilora felt about the announcement. It was like a kick in the teeth for her, wasn't it? Her mother saying, "You're a failure, so we're having another, better child."

The spheres glowed again and poured out music with their light. After a few quick shrills of excitement it subsided into a sensuous crooning.

Pea-Pach stroked Quinofil's arm. "Let's dance!"

Puflet looked around for a partner as couples whirled past her. Serpenlino was dancing with his aunt, and Orgmorgan spun about with Dilora. Oakiza had the Code liaison in his arms, and Hube had paired up with Sianne. She appeared to be weeping out her concerns to him, her face aglitter with tears. No one asked Puflet to dance. She directed her attention to her fire dragons.

Her goblet was empty. She'd felt good swallowing the dragons, felt like someone who could get the things she wanted. She wanted more. But if she got drunk, the monster might come. Sighing, she walked toward the periphery of the hall, where the carts had been withdrawn to make room for the dancers, and set down her goblet.

She watched the couples glide across the floor, casting multiple shadows beneath the glow spheres. Katora's blue gown trailed stars as she orbited around Dino. Eadin danced entwined with Kael.

Puflet noticed the little alien standing by itself, and headed for it. Its potato form was covered with curling strips of tissue-thin material—she wasn't sure if it was skin or clothing. A pleasant, cinnamon fragrance exuded. Dark green spots that she took to be eyes peeped from folds in its body. Pale filaments emerged from other folds, waving like the tentacles of a sea anemone.

"Greetings," she said. "I am Puflet Wuner Doom."

As she expected, it had a glowworm translator. "Greetings,

Puflet." The voice was mild, androgynous. "I am Turpo."

"I'd love to dance with you," she said.

"I am not very good."

"Neither am I," she said. "I've never even tried it before."

"I will endeavor to help." Filaments stretched out to curl around her fingers. They tingled. Turpo pivoted back on its stubby feet, and she followed. They shuffled around the floor, the slowest of all the couples, but she didn't care. Ix had never entertained clients on Puztak, and even if she had, Puflet would not have been invited. This was her first ball.

She felt glorious in her red gown, showing herself off for all the world to see, fire dragons in her belly. She grinned at the other couples as they swooshed past.

"What is it like on your planet?" she asked her partner.

"I find it pleasant," it replied. "My people stroke the wind. Since your people came, many new strokings. Orgmorgan is the your-species who first came. He and I are brother-friends."

"That's nice," Puflet murmured.

Hinomia glared as she swirled past in Yusun's arms. Puflet wondered if Turpo found Yusun's nose beautiful. The nose and the alien's body had almost the same shape.

The music trailed away into silence. Thanking Turpo for the dance, Puflet set out to find Serpenlino before it started up again.

Someone grabbed her arm. "Come!"

The urgency in the voice sent a charge of adrenaline through Puflet's body. She turned to run the way the hand on her arm guided her, across the hall, through the archway, along the tunnels.

Finally she stopped, panting. The sense of urgency was replaced by confusion as she turned around to face the person who had brought her.

Valri laughed in her face. "Just a little mind-trick, my dear."

It wouldn't do to show fear. Puflet stood tall. "What do you want?"

Valri's nostrils flared. Her frothy white gown rippled and rustled as she clenched a fist and shook it at Puflet. "You have a lot to answer for, you little piece of shit! And look at the airs you're putting on, dressed up like Ix!"

She grabbed a handful of ruffle and ripped the dress from Puflet's body. Puflet clutched at the remnants, then let them fall. She clashed her fangs together to hold back the tears. "I was right about you, wasn't I? Your heart was always with the slavers, wasn't it?"

Valri thrust out her jaw. "You don't know the first thing about me, bit-brain! But I'm going to make sure you learn a thing or two before you die."

Puflet drew in a deep breath and prepared to spring. She wasn't weak any more, and she had fangs. She'd rip out Valri's throat.

Instead, she found herself sprawled prone across the tunnel floor.

"I don't think so." Valri kicked her in the gut, hard. The fire dragons burned again as they came back up and pooled on the floor beneath Puflet's mouth and nostrils.

"I could have been empress!" Valri screamed. "Except for you!" She kicked Puflet in the ribs, flipping her onto her back. Then she stomped on Puflet's chest—once, twice, then a third time. Something cracked. Pain ripped through her body. She twisted and whimpered, then choked as blood filled her throat.

The monster, she thought. The monster will rise and destroy her.

Valri spat on her. "Think again!"

A cold, dark wave of despair swept through Puflet. The monster wasn't coming. Nothing could save her. She would die.

"It's another trick," the detached part of her mind told her. "You can fight it."

But the pain and despair kept coming in gigantic waves of red and black, tossing her mind about, never giving her a moment to gather herself. Beyond the red and black, Valri ranted on.

"Saving your wretched life was the biggest mistake I ever made. Well, here and now is where I start undoing that mistake."

Puflet struggled to roll onto her side, away from Valri. "Saved m-m-me?" she choked.

"That's right, you wretched little ingrate!" She kicked Puflet in the spine and sent her skidding and flopping onto her stomach. "When I was sent to ingratiate myself with Ix, I had to bring her an offering to prove my sincerity. I had to bring her an imperial child to enslave. She was going to use you up in the fights, but I told her you had great genes and ought to be put to work in a glowworm lab."

A wave of surprise crashed through Puflet, numbing her pain for an instant. "Good genes? You know who my parents are? What Ix said, about making me in her lab ... a lie."

"You're surprised that Ix lied?" Valri's laughter howled through the tunnel.

"I ... who...." Puflet sobbed.

"I've told you enough!" Valri shrieked, at full fury again. "You'll die without knowing who your parents were, or even if I know who they were! I saved you, and you repaid the favor by denouncing me to the galaxy. I could have been the next one on the Brain-Throne if it wasn't for you!"

Another wave of astonishment. When Valri had said she could've been empress, she hadn't meant Empress of the Unknown, she'd meant empress of the galaxy. She thought she could've beaten out Gawoi's relatives and all the other contenders for the throne. Who was she kidding? Puflet would've laughed if the pain hadn't been so terrible.

"Don't you dare sneer at me!" A slithering metallic sound made Puflet turn her head. Valri held a sword. "Now you're going to die."

She couldn't have really had a sword under her skirts. It was an illusion.

"It's real," Valri said. "I planned this all very carefully, knowing that Katora doesn't use glowworm scans. Not that it matters what you think, anyhow." She chuckled, anticipating pleasure.

Puflet tried to pull herself up, but it was no use. She flopped back, gagging at the fresh stab of pain, and stared dully at the curving wall in front of her.

She saw a tiny gleam.

In her mind's eye, the jewel was larger. It winked from the tunnel and from the hall and from her cell and from other mysterious places. She knew its purpose now, and she smiled. And spoke a single word.

"Switch."

The jewel's fusion field activated, and the mindsea academy downleveled. Puflet had rediscovered the technology Horl had used for his Wamatuan gameboard.

She sprang to her feet. She understood far better than when she had flown to Ulona how downleveling worked. She had fused with her other selves in alternate histories to become a higher-dimensional being of the Deep. But she was more than just a compendium of human selves from different histories. A unifying soul wrapped around those selves, a part of her native to the Deep. She had to exert this aspect of herself, her mind's eye, to make sense of the impressions racing at her, to weed them out and force them into a recognizable pattern. She had to choose what to perceive, and by choosing, bring her vision into hyper-solid reality.

Choosing to be a proud, free Puflet wearing a red dress, she faced Valri with a snort.

Valri had downleveled as well. She still held a sword, a deep-level sword that sparkled and sang along its cruel length. "Your naivety astounds me!" Valri sneered. "Do you think you can beat me on this level? I have been at home here far longer than you, pathetic worm!"

Puflet smiled. "That's what you think." She snapped her fingers. Each step rolling thunder across the universe, the monster came to her side. He was made of bones, burning bones, like one of the creatures in the world that had died. He nodded a great bony head fringed by spikes and spewed out fiery gusts of breath. Puflet flung herself onto his back. Though his spine was a series of jabbing bones, she seated herself comfortably on the cushion of flame that followed the contours where his flesh would have been. For a moment she had the sensation that something was missing, but as she gestured with her right hand, a shining lance coalesced there, and she couched it against Valri. She laughed. "We'll see who is going to die."

Valri's mouth had been hanging open. As Puflet surged forward on her skeletal charger, she turned and fled.

Whooping with delight, Puflet pounded after her. The monster covered ground like a wildfire. In two strides it burst out of the dimness of the tunnel.

The great hall with the black and white checkered floor stretched as if to infinity. Guests scrambled about in surprise. At least, those who were active in the Deep did.

Hube stood there like a black-barked tree, a quiet smile etched in the wood, blue eyes watching from a pair of knotholes. The Deep-blind looked like paper cutouts with painted on eyes. Puflet recognized Sianne and Kael among those.

A few of the students flopped and flailed with rapidly changing forms that might resemble a worm one moment and a butterfly the next. They must be experiencing the disorientation Puflet had felt on her first journey into the Deep. They hadn't yet mastered the art of forming themselves. More advanced students and graduates resembled the people she had known on home level.

"Help me!" Valri screamed as she fled the point of Puflet's lance. "For the love of Horl, help me!"

In the mist of the distance, two armored figures swung onto the backs of burning skeletal mounts and charged forward, lances couched. With a whinny of relief, Valri dove between them.

Puflet hesitated for a moment, then swung her lance toward the larger of the two charging riders. "If you ride for Horl, you are the enemy of freedom!" she shouted.

Laughing, he lifted his visor to reveal a handsome white face with pale blue eyes. "You think you can take me on, little Puflet?" He must be Hinomia, as she saw herself, as Horl.

"I am taking you on!"

Given the speed of their mounts, Puflet thought they would cover the distance between them in an instant and smash together, but though she thundered forward and Hinomia and her companion, who must be Yusun, galloped at full tilt against her, the number of black and white squares separating them didn't seem to diminish.

Spacetime in the Deep wasn't like anything like it was on home level.

The mounts of Hinomia and Yusun looked almost identical to Puflet's mount, except that the horns on their heads were arranged differently. By merely thinking about it, Puflet got a side view of the horns, which were the same on the two beasts. Each had a long, forward-curving horn that sprouted from the forehead, and a long, backward curving horn sprouting from the nose. Between the two big horns were two smaller, atrophied-looking horns. One curled over into a circle, and the other was zig-zag crumpled. The horns spelled out "Horl" in Lalian script.

Katora's guests—those who could—gathered alongside the chargers' course to watch. As Hinomia pounded past Sianne, her Horl-steed snorted a fireball at the wispy paper figure. Puflet cried out in concern, but Pea-Pach leaped forward and batted the fireball away with the sleeve of her robe, which dissolved into billows of steam.

Puflet charged on against the Horl riders. A flash of light came from somewhere, blinding her. Her lance wavered. Affected by her confusion, the monster's gallop went ragged. She blinked and turned her head, but the annoying light kept coming. Finally, squinting into the crowd, she saw Katora's half-sister Cevana holding a mirror.

Somehow, in the Deep, Puflet couldn't shade her eyes. The light, or whatever it was, shone through her body. As she waved her free hand in annoyance, she discovered that she could flick the beam aside. She faced forward again, flicking her fingers to keep the mirror-shine from her eyes. "You're such a coward, Hinomia!"

she shouted. "You don't think two-on-one is enough to beat me, do you?"

"Don't be a hypocrite, Puflet!" Hinomia shouted back in her masculine voice.

That was when Puflet realized that another rider galloped at her side, borne by a burning skeletal steed with the wide-spread horns of a bull. It was Serpenlino. In the Deep his hair hummed like the wind as it rippled over his back. He saluted her.

With a grin, Puflet sang out to her steed. "Surge! Surge, and we'll transfix them!"

The space separating her and the foe shrank. At last they would clash.

Then an imperious voice rang out across the endless chessboard. "Stop! There will be no fighting here!"

Katora stepped midway between the charging riders, her gown aglitter with constellations, and stretched out her hands to either side. An invisible force emanated from her fingertips, holding back the charging skeletons, so that once again they galloped in place.

The thrill was gone. "Switchback," Puflet said.

The academy upleveled.

The glowing spheres overhead seemed dull and colorless, the gowns and suits tawdry, and faces so much meat concealing the spirit. Puflet gasped and reeled for a moment, missing the powerful smoking beast she had ridden. A strong hand caught her arm. She looked up at Serpenlino. "I must talk to you about what happened."

He nodded.

Katora swept forward. "What is the meaning of this, Puflet? What excuse do you have for attacking Valri?"

"She attacked me first, ma'am. She—" Puflet looked down at herself. Her red gown glowed in all its glory. Nothing hurt when she breathed. Had her wound been an illusion? Or had she mended herself or changed the past when she was in the Deep?

"You little liar!" Valri screamed. "You know what that little harpy hates me, Katora, she was just waiting—"

Shrill screeches of protest rose from Dilora. The girl pushed through the knot of people surrounding Katora, Puflet, and Valri.

"I heard voices before the downleveling." Dilora thrust her chin importantly. "Valri threatened to kill Puflet. It was quite clear."

"Liar!" Valri screamed at her. "Hinomia and Yusun made sure that no one could follow us when we left the hall."

"The voices came from the floor," Dilora said.

Katora scowled at Puflet. "Have you tried to plant glowworms in the academy?"

"It wasn't glowworms that transmitted the voices, ma'am. My jewel—the one I used to make the fusion field—is in this hall and also in the tunnels where Valri and I were standing. You can hear and see what comes through from its other locations."

Katora's eyebrows twisted. "Where exactly did you learn this technology?"

"From you, ma'am. I was inspired by your talk about the history of the academy. You told us how Horl had built a gameboard with squares that would downlevel and uplevel at verbal commands, so I knew it could be done."

Katora nodded, eyebrows relaxing as a smug look crept into her eyes. She turned to face Valri. "I'm shocked by your behavior! What excuse do you have for attacking Puflet?"

Valri clenched her fists. "All she did is ruin my life! If it wasn't for her baseless accusations I could have enjoyed the confidence of the citizens of the empire."

"Your role in as a government agent in Ix's organization was explained," Katora said. "And you were reinstated in the Pilots Guild. What more do you want?"

"I want my reputation spotless, like it was before!"

"I don't understand," Katora began. Then she did understand. "I'm afraid I have no sympathy for your political ambitions, Valri. I thought the academy had taught you that there are things more important than that."

"Try giving up your position, and see how you like it," Valri snarled.

Hinomia stepped up behind her and laid a hand on her shoulder. "I'm sure that I can get you into a good position, when the time comes."

Valri whirled. "I don't care to be under you."

Hinomia folded her arms. "If I had known that's the way it was, I wouldn't have tried to help you."

"Yes," Katora said. "Why did you involve yourself, and you and you?" She pointed at Yusun and Serpenlino.

Hinomia glowered at Puflet. "Valri asked us to help. She was in trouble."

"I was just trying to even things up." Serpenlino grinned.

"So everyone thought joining the fight was the way to solve the problem?" Katora lectured. "No one thought to try to stop it?"

Silence.

Puflet smelled cinnamon and ylang-ylang. Orgmorgan and his alien companion pushed through the crowd to join Serpenlino, closely followed by Sianne and Eadin.

Katora humphed. She pointed a finger at Valri and at her sisters who hovered, a few steps back in the crowd. "You will all leave now. You will not be welcome here again."

Valri stomped her foot. Suddenly she was out of control, hurling curses and threats at Katora. Her sisters formed a ring about her and led her away.

Katora blinked. When Valri's shrieks had faded, she said, "I believe we have all been given an example of the ugliness that ensues when an ego is granted central stage in one's life. I apologize for the inconvenience."

Floating spheres resumed their music. The crowd started to disperse.

Katora pointed a finger at Puflet. "I want you in my office tomorrow morning to explain how you constructed this downleveling gem."

"Yes, ma'am."

"And stop 'ma'am'ing me."

"Sorry."

As soon as Katora had turned her attention elsewhere, Puflet looked for Serpenlino. He leaned toward her with a whisper. "I'll see you when the headmistress is finished with you tomorrow. If there's anything left." He grinned.

Buoyed by the flash of his fangs, Puflet went on to enjoy the rest of the ball. She had some more fire dragons. She danced with Serpenlino and Kael, and as many of the male guests as she could get her hands on—Orgmorgan, Quinofil, even Hube, who moved about the floor like a puck on ice.

"I saw you when we downleveled," she told him. "You're not

Deep-blind. Surely you're close enough to Sianne's mother to mind-link her. Then you could give Sianne the news."

He smiled his tree smile. "I eschew needless motion. Most of it, believe me, is needless."

13

Serpenlino awaited Puflet in the first sand room when she emerged from Katora's office. He rose and met her on the path beneath the archways, wearing his too-long black robe once again. To her annoyance, Oakiza and Kael were there as well.

"We all need to understand what happened," Serpenlino explained. "And to prepare for what lies ahead."

She tightened her lips, then nodded. He was probably right.

"Let's go to one of the meditation chambers." Serpenlino led the way, trailing his robe, and Puflet and the others followed.

"How'd it go in there?" Kael jerked his head back toward the office.

"You look like you're in one piece," Oakiza said. She didn't like the way his red eyes traveled down the form-hugging lines of her pink dress.

She sped her steps to come alongside Serpenlino, and the other two pressed close behind. "Well, she did put me on the spot, of course. 'What thoughts did you use to form the jewel,' and all that. I really didn't have any thoughts. The jewel just appeared in my mind's eye, and I had to figure out what it meant little by little. But she insists that there were thoughts in my head, thoughts from my deep-level self, and I just wasn't in touch with them. She actually wanted to mind-link me to bring those buried thoughts to the surface. It's a good thing that unwelcome mind-links are illegal, even on Ulona."

"Ah," Serpenlino said. "You know, she might have had a point. I'm sure there were deep-level thoughts associated with the creation of your jewel. Not like thoughts on our level. Not verbal."

"Hmm. Well, perhaps. I envisioned the jewel, and the vision had meaning. I just couldn't understand it."

"Then perhaps a mind-link could help you to winkle out that meaning, to anchor it on home-level—not with her, of course. It really is possible to do better than hit or miss in deep-level engineering."

"Oh? What sort of deep-level engineering have you done?"

"Haven't done any," he admitted. "My father did."

Puflet stole a glance at the serious faces following them. Did Oakiza and Kael know about his parentage?

Oakiza spoke. "I'm a Coder, Puflet. We've always been outside the pale. Ulona was once our home world, you know, and you imperials drove us out. We liked Quintillion because he traced his ancestry to our blue race. We don't care what Katora saw in the desert—Quintillion never flashed any planets or launched any genocides."

"I have an admission to make too," Kael said. "After the assassination of the old king, the people of my planet decided that they needed more impressive genes for their royalty, so they secured Thermeon's and Quintillion's to make my father—not that he has their kind of mindsize. So my family doesn't hold with the headmistress' party line either."

They walked in silence for a while. In a brighter voice, Kael said, "The way you answered the headmistress' question last night, I thought that you might have imported some glowworms here."

"I do have glowworms. Dino gave them to me."

"Good old Dino, the student's friend!"

"But that's not what I'm worried about," she said. "There's something else I need to discuss."

The three men pressed closer about her, radiating their warmth.

Serpenlino spoke for them. "You have our attention."

When they had passed the nexus, she said, "I usually like a hot, bright, arid chamber, but why don't we go to one that's most like Gilkay—as long as it isn't cold."

Kael laughed. "We have cold places and hot places on Gilkay—

night and day too. But like Ulona, it's overcast most of the time. How about hot, dark, and moist?"

"It sounds fine," she said.

They settled on a virtual hilltop in the warm, near-darkness— her hair providing the lighting. Puffs of fog rolled past, depositing tiny droplets on their faces which the warm winds dried again.

"Serpenlino." Puflet dug her fingers into the sand. "You have a monster."

"Monster?"

"The flaming bull skeleton you rode in the deep."

"Ah. Eria lent me her aurochs. One of her deep-level companions. She told me that she recognized your dinosaur companion, too. It used to be her father's."

Puflet had pulled her knees up to her chest and nestled her chin between them as she let the deep timbre of his voice and the heat and scents of the men's bodies and breaths flow around her. She stiffened at his final words, a thrill racing along her spine. "Her father's?"

"Eria's father was Quintillion's father as well."

"Ahhhh." Her voice trailed off into a long sigh, and she pressed her chin into her knees, thinking hard.

"Eria had control over the aurochs, and so did you," she said.

"I wouldn't say that exactly. You know the Third Tenet tells us that there are no barriers between identities. We are one with our companion animals. And the ties of blood, which are strong in our family, allow me also to feel the oneness with my aunt and benefit from the energies of her charger. Someday I will choose my own, but...."

"Why doesn't Katora teach about this?" Kael murmured.

Oakiza's laugh rippled around them.

"But I didn't choose my charger," Puflet said. "It was given to me."

"I know. My aunt was very surprised to see it with you. She felt there must be a reason."

Again Puflet felt a chill, as if the monster breathed down her neck and waited for her awakening. She swallowed. "Does Thermeon have one of these chargers too?"

"I've never seen it unleashed, but my aunt says that his is a dinosaur too, a winged dinosaur."

"And he doesn't have control of it, and it's powerful enough to flash planets?"

"Yes."

They all breathed softly for a while.

Finally, Kael broke the silence. "Excuse me if I sound naive, but ... are these like ... flesh-and-blood animals we're talking about?"

"No," said Serpenlino. "They're deep-level beings. What the ancients used to call spirits. But they're also us, in a way. I guess you could almost say they are our mindpowers personified."

"I guess that means I'll never have one."

"All living things have a connection to the Deep. You have to become aware of the part of yourself that stretches beyond what thoughts and words or even Mathematics can frame."

"It's hard," Kael whispered. "Eadin keeps telling me to focus on her, but it doesn't work for me, even though she says focusing on me works for her."

"I don't think it does," Puflet said. "I think she went flat when we downleveled."

Kael groaned softly.

"You have to let your deep-level companion come to you," Serpenlino said. "In a way, I misspoke before. We don't choose them. They choose us."

"So I don't understand," Puflet said. "It sounds like I have someone else's charger."

"And you don't feel at peace with it?"

"No."

"I think it was the same for Hinomia and Yusun. Their horses belonged to Horl. They put themselves into the power of a mind outside of their own. That isn't good."

"What should I do?"

"You have to make peace with your charger, tame it. You can't allow it to run away with you in directions you don't want to go."

She sighed. "But how can I tame it? Quintillion and Thermeon together weren't powerful enough to tame this beast!"

She heard the sharp intake of breath around her. Serpenlino asked, "What makes you say that?"

She froze. She couldn't tell him about the head. If he had all the family feeling he said, he'd hate her for killing his father. She settled back as she thought of another way. "Katora told me about the duel in the desert. Even though she saw it as seeds, that was the monster, wasn't it? It got loose and destroyed them both."

Once again they all sat silence. Since her eyes had adjusted to the dim light cast by her hair, she could just make out three faces hanging in the fog of the chamber.

Kael gave his head a shake. "Ugh! If that's what one of these deep-level things does to you, I don't want one!"

"I don't think Thermeon and Quintillion are good examples to follow," Serpenlino said. "They both got their chargers when they were too young and unformed to handle them."

Puflet gripped her knees. "Age is a factor? But—" she winced before admitting it—"I wasn't all that young when I got the monster."

"But you were raised as a slave, weren't you? You had no experience in determining your own life course. It's self-knowledge, not age, that determines a good working relationship. You have to know all of yourself, even the part of you that is your charger."

Puflet flexed her toes to create little waves of sand. She stifled a laugh. "You're saying if Quintillion had known himself better, he wouldn't have spent a life of misery and terror? And Thermeon wouldn't have flashed Wamatu?"

"How do you know about Quintillion?"

The sharpness in Serpenlino's voice made her go still for another moment. "I sensed it from Katora's tale. He told Thermeon he couldn't feel anyone, couldn't love. How well did you know him?"

"I didn't know him at all."

A silence like mourning fell over them again. Serpenlino continued in a low voice. "He never wanted children—at least, that's what he said. He did nothing to prevent Genetic Algorithms from awarding his genes to whomever they saw as fit to breed with him. I don't think anyone knew him. He was isolated as emperor. He refused to use glowworm communications, and mind-linked only with his mind-rivers, who grew so addicted to his touch that they died en masse after the Fissure."

"Like flies," Kael added. "At least, that's what they say."

Puflet dug a little hole in the sand with one finger. "And to think that this was all needless suffering!"

Suddenly, in her mind, she heard Hube's silken voice. "Isn't it always?"

She gave her head a shake to clear it. "I don't want to be like him. I need help, Serpenlino. I need someone who understands the forces of the Deep to help me tame the monster. You seem to know so much more than I do. Please help me!"

Her voice trailed away in the mist, and for a couple minutes she sat there listening to all of them breathe.

"I'll try," Serpenlino said. He too was scratching at the sand. "Understand, I have no personal knowledge. My charger hasn't chosen me yet. What I've told you is all second hand from Eria and Orgmorgan."

Oakiza spoke, his voice a lighter baritone. "He's told you his family religion. We people of the Code have our own beliefs. We look to the Goddess of the Code, the creator of all, for guidance. All things in existence are snowflakes crystallizing from the fog of her breath. The Goddess will help you, if you trust in her."

Puflet felt quite sure she wanted no part of the Coders' religion, but she said nothing.

"There are many ways in which we humans try to explain the Deep to ourselves," Serpenlino said. "All of them have some aspect of the truth. The Deep combines so many possibilities, so many alternate universes, it has dimensions far beyond what we can know."

Kael's bright tenor broke over them. "I want to help you too, Puflet. Not that I know anything about these chargers. But I'm sympathetic."

"Thank you," Puflet said.

"Do you suppose the headmistress would—" Kael stopped himself. "Oh. If this charger is the same thing that she saw in the desert and thinks is evil...."

"Yes," Puflet said.

"What about the other mindsea academies?" Kael asked. "Haven't you been to Eltien, Serpenlino?"

"Briefly. My grandmother Quixa is headmistress there. Her

motto is 'You Alone,' and she means it. She has all her students busy making everything they need to live on by hand, from basic ingredients. She'd make them each create their own universe out of nothing, if it was possible. If she knew anything about chargers, she wouldn't tell you; you'd have to figure it out for yourself. Anyhow—" He flicked away a spray of sand. "—she and I don't get along."

"Some of my people go there," Oakiza said. "Since it's in the Code capital. But the liaison—who would be Code Empress if we were still independent—advised me to come here. This was our original home world, after all. And, of course, we all hate Quixa."

"Why 'of course?'" Puflet asked.

"Because she's Thermeon's daughter."

Puflet sighed. Here was another piece of history she should have known. She tried to piece it together, but before she could figure anything out, Kael explained.

"Thermeon had a son by the Code Empress as part of his campaign to annex her empire."

"Maxuas Gedri Creasex," Oakiza said.

"He sided with his mother against his father," Kael went on. "That started the Great War. Maxuas made his capital on Wamatu, and you know...."

"Yes."

"So we Coders hate Thermeon like Katora hates Quintillion," Oakiza said. "But I think carrying it to all of his grandchildren and beyond is going a bit too far."

"A good thing for me," Serpenlino chuckled.

"But wait," Puflet said. "Serpenlino, if you're descended from Quixa, that's your connection to Thermeon. That's why you have fangs."

"Right."

"I have fangs too. I wonder if we could be relatives."

"You told me that Ix made you from bits and pieces."

"I know. But I've gotten new information." She squirmed in the sand. "Valri knows who my parents are, but she wouldn't tell me, the bitch! She claimed that she'd stolen my incubator and given it to Ix. I wonder...."

"I think I know who we could turn to," Serpenlino said.

"Who?"

Before he could answer, Kael let out a scream. "What's that?"

Puflet and Serpenlino and Oakiza turned to follow his pointing finger, but they saw nothing.

"It's on fire! No, it has yellow leaves fluttering from its antlers! I think, oh gods, I think it's one of those chargers!"

Puflet heard and felt hoofbeats then. Something mighty approached. The wind of its passage bowled her over. As she lay on her back, she looked up to find her own monster burning against the darkness. The thunderous voice rocked her. "Upward or downward?"

She stared into the fiery eye sockets and felt the heat rippling toward her from the center of time and space. She felt tiny and lost, a mouse in the talons of an eagle. Why didn't the monster go to Serpenlino and leave her alone? But the molten eye sockets burned steadily down on her. "You made the jewel for me, didn't you? And you let me see Cidi's future. You can work all the Tenets. I suppose you can flash worlds too. And you're giving me a choice. You will let me direct this ... magnificent power. And it's not hard to gather that upward is using the power for good things, and downward is pure ... destruction.

"So if I have a choice, why didn't Quintillion have a choice? Why did he see you as the end of everything?"

Katora's voice reached from her memory. "He couldn't love."

Love was the key, then. She pulled herself up as the monster whirled back into dimensions of the Deep. Serpenlino and Oakiza were on their feet as well, and Kael was screaming, "Something terrible has happened to my father!"

The revolving sphere in the nexus said it was still free-form time, so the four of them raced along the path through the archways to Katora's office.

Katora awaited them with an air of lofty solemnity at the top of her eminence. No doubt she'd heard their pounding steps and adjusted herself. "My father!" Kael yelled. "Something terrible happened to him!"

Katora arose and stepped down from her nook. "Where is he?"

"I don't know! I just saw ... I mean...."

Katora's lips bunched. "You seem confused. Compose yourself, and try to explain clearly what you think is wrong."

Yes, you stupid bitch, Puflet thought. *Your glowworm ban is really wonderful when you need to locate someone or call for help, isn't it?*

"I don't know." Kael milled his arms in frustration, his eyes flaring. "It was a mind-link, or something!"

Katora shut her eyes. Her face relaxed, and she wavered slightly, like a tall tree in the wind. She was mind-linking. The blue-gray eyes opened again. "It's too late," she said in a flat voice.

"Father!" Kael cried out. Tears ran down his face.

"I'm very sorry." Katora smoothed back her hair. "It's all over, I'm afraid. There's nothing we can do."

"Where is he?" Kael yelled.

She shook her head.

Serpenlino and Oakiza took him by either arm and led him away bent over and sobbing. Puflet fled to her own cell.

She soaked in her hot tub, trying to soothe the screaming of her nerves. Her monster had nothing to do with whatever had happened to King Quinofil. Maybe it was that other monster, the one Kael had seen with the trees growing from its head. Yet not knowing her monster's deep-level thoughts made her very nervous. If it indeed had thoughts, non-verbal, inhuman thoughts as Serpenlino had suggested, she needed to know what they were.

She changed into her most forgettable outfit, a pale blue tunic, and walked to the dining hall for midmeal. The happy buzz of voices told her that the students hadn't learned about the disaster yet. She searched the nooks until she found Serpenlino, who was sitting with Oakiza and Dino. She joined them.

"Where is Kael?" she asked.

"Resting in his cell," Serpenlino said.

"What happened to his father?"

Serpenlino pressed his lips together.

"My wife wants to be the one to break the news," Dino said.

Puflet put her head down and concentrated on eating.

Toward the end of mealtime, the lights unexpectedly went out, then came on to find Katora standing in the center of the hall. "Your afternoon meditations are canceled. Instead, there will be a special lecture."

As they rose, students rushed into the nook, eyes seeking Dino. "Tell us what it's about!" Pea-Pach coaxed him.

"I have no idea," he said.

More students piled into the nook, babbling the same question and receiving the same answer. Finally someone said, "We'll find out faster if we just go there," and they all ran off.

When the lecture hall had filled, Katora took her accustomed place at the podium. "A tragedy occurred today."

The hall gasped as one.

"A talented young man with a life of promise ahead of him died a few hours ago in Alonaton."

"Who? Who?" the crowd murmured.

"He was Quinofil, King of Gilkay, a former student of the academy and father of your fellow student Kael Biari Moot."

A cacophony of moans, sobs, and cries whirled about the hall.

Katora leaned forward, gripping the crystalline brow-ridges of the pahmak podium. The crowd hushed as she started to speak. "Quinofil's death is a tragedy because it could have been prevented. It could have been prevented if all of you would follow just one simple rule—do not engage in mind-duels."

Fresh exclamations swept across the hall. Even Puflet added to the noise. Mind-dueling? Whom had Quinofil been fighting?

"I know that you are young," Katora went on, "and the sensation of deep-level power can be very heady. Even I was not immune to its enchantment when I was young and foolish." She passed her eyes over all of them with a sad, wise smile. "Historical dramatizations and popular entertainments have painted mind-dueling as something glorious and meaningful—proof of one's mindsize and greatness."

Her brows drew down in a scowl, and she gave her head a slight shake that made her earrings flash blue and red. "The dramas lie. They lie because they are directed toward that class of citizen that never questions the dictates of ego—the class of citizen that will never sense the wonders of the Deep.

"We at the academy do not have the luxury of letting our egos dictate. We must look beyond the egocentric universe, beyond pettiness and ambition. We carry the light of the future in our studies. That must always be remembered."

She paused, using her eyes to push her words into the minds of those before her. The hall was quiet. They all were probably thinking, as Puflet was, tell us about the mind-duel already!

Katora clearly intended to draw it out for a while longer. "Mind-duels are not glorious. They are very foolish. They do not measure mindsize. They destroy indiscriminately. That's right. Thermeon and Quintillion were known by all as the most powerful mindseas of their era, but neither proved himself superior in their duel—they were both losers. And for those of you who consider Horl the model of everything a mindsea should be, I'd like to remind you that he died in a duel too.

"The rule is very simple: do not engage in mind-duels. If someone challenges you, walk away. If they attack you, you are still safer if you try to disengage and remove yourself from the situation rather than fighting back. If someone attacks you on the premises of the academy, you will of course come to me." Her eyes sought Puflet in the sea of faces. "If you have sufficient mindsize to engage your opponent, you will probably also find yourself able to mind-link me and call for help."

She tossed back her head and continued. "Mind-duels are ugly. There are two styles of dueling, and they are equally ugly. One is the mind-link attack. This is when the aggressor subsumes a victim's mind and transmits images of pain and bodily harm. This can kill if the victim believes those images to be real, but there is no reason any of you should ever be fooled. If you are ever subjected to a mind-link attack, use your own mindsize to shield you with the knowledge that nothing of what you experience is real, and walk away."

"The second style of mind-duel is much more dangerous. Talented people like yourselves, able to perceive and manipulate deep-level stuff, may attempt to use deep-level weapons, either pre-forged or envisioned on the spot, to do each other harm. Once a duel has escalated to this stage, it becomes unfortunately very likely that one or both combatants will die."

Once again her eyes sought Puflet and rained disapproval on her. "The events that transpired at the ball yesterday were an example of a mind-duel escalating to such a dangerous scale. A duel taking place within a fusion field by definition makes use of deep-level weapons, and it poses the additional danger of patternistic dissolution. There can be no patternistic integrity when two minds are in battle, can there? If I had not halted the fools who were trying to destroy each other and regathered the assembly into my vision, there would have been many deaths yesterday. Remember that copy insurance is of no avail to those of us with mindpowers, because it only guarantees restoration of home-level portions of the mind. A copy would be Deep-blind, not the person we are."

She paused to give her audience time to think over what she had said. Puflet frowned. Was that true? What would have happened had she and Hinomia smashed together? Katora was probably right about them each choosing a different universe to return to when the Academy upleveled again. They would each choose a history in which they had won. Hinomia would have died in her history, and she in Hinomia's. But what about the onlookers? If most of them saw your opponent winning, you'd kill off your audience. She gripped her chin.

Katora had started talking again, the hall going dead-still when she mentioned Quinofil's name. "He and Queen Niti had decided to see the city before they left Ulona. They encountered Valri in a little shop on the outer perimeter. Taunts were exchanged. Juvenile taunts. The queen told me that Valri said something like, 'So you're the big coward who won't admit where his genes come from?'"

Puflet gnawed her nails. How had Valri found out about Quinofil's origins? "Those are not the words a man should have died for." Tears glittered like diamonds on Katora's cheeks. Puflet lowered her hands from her mouth and clasped them on her lap. She'd imagined that Katora had a heart of ice. Did she really care about her students? It must be that she cared about those whose purity caused her no doubts. Puflet tried to imagine what it would be like not to be given the second-class treatment. Tears sprang to her own eyes, and she didn't bother to wipe them away. They were all supposed to be unhappy right now.

Katora went on, her voice catching. "Quinofil told Valri to step out onto the street. Niti begged him to let it be, but he wouldn't listen. It started as a style-one duel. They both grimaced and clawed at invisible things. But neither found a clear advantage, so the battle moved to style two." Katora bowed her head and heaved a sigh as she approached the inevitable end to her tale.

"Niti could not give me an accurate report of what happened next. There might have been flashes, or distortions in the air. Deep-level weapons had been unleashed. Quinofil died from unfusing damage, with no hope of refloating."

A vast, cold melancholy descended on the hall. Puflet clenched her fists. Why wasn't she experiencing the history where Quinofil lived and Valri died? A spasm of anger raced through her when she thought about Valri. The bitch deserved to die. It was more like murder than a duel if she'd had a deep-level weapon and Quinofil hadn't.

But maybe she hadn't had such an advantage. Maybe they'd both been envisioning stuff, and she'd gotten lucky.

And supposing she had told the truth about stealing Puflet's incubator and even about saving her from Ix's battle arenas? Puflet bit her lip, not certain whether that obliged her in some way. But it would mean she didn't want Valri to die until she could get the names of her parents out of her.

"I have two small announcements," Katora said. "And then I'll let you go to take comfort in your own thoughts. First, Ona will lead a memorial service for Quinofil by the lake this end of cycle. Second, Kael will no longer be with us. He must assume his duties as king of Gilkay."

A scream rent the air, and Katora glared at Eadin—who else could it be but Eadin?

"May the light of true illumination guide and protect you all," Katora gushed. Then she turned sharply and left the podium. Students started filing out.

Puflet was halfway up the aisle when the scent of ylang-ylang directly ahead snapped her from an amorphous reverie about the monster. Eadin was pushing her way down through the crowd. She stopped, blocking Puflet's way, and flung back her flower-twined pink hair. Her amber eyes shone with tears.

"It's all your fault, you—you evil thing! If you hadn't started the fight with Valri, none of this horror would have happened!"

Puflet placed her hands on her hips. "So I should have just flopped over and let her kill me?"

"No one would be sad if you were the one who was dead!"

The words bit deeper than Ix's whip ever had. Puflet fought hard to keep her stance steady and her eyes free from tears, but she felt tears creeping into them despite herself.

Eadin was too wound up in her own misery to notice. "You wanted this to happen! You used your stupid jewel to choose a future to hurt other people! You were so jealous of my love, so bitter because all the good men here reject you—"

"I don't want your type of man!" Puflet shouted.

"Liar!" Eadin shrieked, her cheeks suffused with scarlet, eyes rolling in their sockets. She slapped Puflet.

The blow rocked Puflet backwards because she was standing on an incline. But she wasn't a weak-boned foam-worlder any more. "Bitch!" she growled, driving her fist into Eadin's solar plexus.

Ylang-ylang girl doubled over, and Puflet marched past her and out of the hall.

Everyone was very subdued at setting meal. Puflet sat with Serpenlino and Oakiza, but they didn't say much. She wanted to ask Serpenlino how he thought they could learn the names of her parents, but dwelling on her own problems at this time would seem selfish, so she said nothing.

"It must have been his father's charger," Serpenlino said once after a long silence.

"Uh huh," grunted Oakiza.

They fell silent again.

It was a few nights later when she finally brought up the subject, and maddeningly, Serpenlino didn't seem to recall what he'd been talking about.

A few seconds later he slapped his forehead and said. "Oh, of course."

"Well, what?"

Instead of answering, he peered all about, to see who might overhear their conversation. Oakiza was the only one sharing their nook, and students in adjacent nooks all chattered about their own concerns.

Puflet rocked with impatience. "Do you want to go to a meditation chamber?"

"No, it's all right."

"Then tell me your plan."

"So, out of Thermeon's myriad children," he began, "only two of them are mindseas. One of these is Quixa, headmistress of the Mindsea Academy of Eltien, and the other is Vedina—or Dee as she likes to be called—headmistress of the Mindsea Academy of Lal."

Puflet suppressed a weary sigh. Everything with this man was about family. If he ever found out that she had killed his father....

"Dee and I have met at family gatherings. I'm planning to complete my studies in Lal."

"That's nice," Puflet said, trying not to grind her fangs.

"Her approach to the Deep is through history. She's been working long and hard to unlock all of the secrets that Horl knew. She acts as our family archivist as well, so if anyone's egg had been stolen, she would have records of it."

Puflet felt suddenly lighter. "Ahhh!"

He grinned at her. "So what I propose to do, is to send her a message with your story—all the details you have—and a sample with your gene specs to match against those of any child that went missing."

"Yes!"

As they grinned at each other, she saw both Quintillion and Kaanu in his features. He didn't have Quintillion's arched nose, but a trace of his primeval projecting brow ridge suggested the ancient wisdom he often referred to.

"You know," he said, "that data complex as gene specs never cross the time-lines totally intact, but they should still be close enough to tell."

"Yes. Please do it."

Using her glowworms, they prepared a memory button, which Serpenlino dispatched by way of Dino, and Puflet began to count the days until she could expect an answer.

No answer to Puflet's query had come by the time Katora and Dino's child was expelled from his incubator. By then, the view of the north pole in Puflet's fake skylight had become so dismal that she switched it for a view of the academy's real environs, where the horizon-riding sun had spread a pale green glow through the clouds. Sometimes a sun ray would even pierce the clouds like a lance of light.

Waking up to her new view for the first time, Puflet lay in her sleeping nook for a few extra moments and savored it, imagining that she could feel the heat creeping into her chilled, love-deprived bones.

Then she sprang out of the nook, chiding herself for giving way to self-pity. But it had been very difficult to watch Katora's joy the day before and not feel there was something wrong with a world where some children were welcomed into it as if they were the light of dawn itself, while others went missing and no one bothered to search for them.

Katora had been all smiles when she'd made the special announcement at rising meal. "Genetic Algorithms has assigned him the name 'Habel Chadrav Wandro,'" she'd said. "Dino and I have agreed to keep it."

Puflet muttered to herself as she stepped into her closet to find something appropriate for enduring Katora's celebration of her son. "If she's undertaking a breeding program for mindseas, why doesn't she just admit it to herself instead of pretending that she's raising a family? The slavers sent the scrubs to their battle arenas or sold them off at a discount. It almost seems kinder than torturing someone with parental scorn for however many years a citizen lives."

She chose a drab little gray tunic and marched off to rising meal. She expected to see Katora bubbling her joy at her favorite students, Eadin and Sianne, but everything seemed quiet as she slid into a nook with Serpenlino and Oakiza.

The three of them seemed to be spending more and more time together. Maybe it was just because the other students were keeping their distance from Puflet. Dino told her that they believed Eadin's theory that Puflet could use her jewel to choose the future that would make them the unhappiest. The good thing about her new reputation as a patternistic timeweaver was that Hinomia and Yusun had stopped trying to intimidate her.

She brooded as she chewed her date loaf. There wasn't a single female at the academy she could call a friend. Katora hated her because she refused to tell the lies she found comfortable. Eadin spewed poison words like she spewed the reek of ylang-ylang. As Puflet had expected after the meditation on Three, Sianne acted as if they'd never met. If she had to speak to Puflet, she dressed non-thoughts in a flow of graceful words to form a soft, but impenetrable barrier.

After the meal, Puflet and her two companions trailed the press of students over to the free-form hall. Katora wanted her to extract her jewel and place it somewhere where it couldn't downlevel the academy. Dino had told them the headmistress had been searching the galaxy for a deep-level engineer who would come to Ulona and perform the extraction.

"Quixa told her that she would only grow if she discovered how to do it herself. Orgmorgan's price was rather high. Dee is still studying the records."

Seating herself cross-legged on a black square, Puflet thought about her gem, which winked at her from its various locations, looking, as always, much bigger in her mind's eye. Her thoughts drifted to what Serpenlino had said about the gem speaking to her, giving her complex and detailed information in some deep-level form she couldn't comprehend. Could it tell her how to extract it and place it elsewhere if she wished to?

Too bad she couldn't ask him to try a mind-link and help to capture that information. He'd find out about his father. She wondered if she should ask Oakiza. But Serpenlino would wonder why he was being left out.

Free-form session ended before she had found any new insight, and Puflet went to her cell for her cloak, then took a walk outside. The grounds around the academy had become pleasant since sunrise, though a chill lingered in the air. She wandered through fern grottoes and clumps of cycads by pools and rivulets.

Mid meal was as quiet as breakfast had been. Again Puflet sat in a nook with Serpenlino and Oakiza. Suddenly the lights went out. It stayed dark so long the students started to murmur in anxious voices. Finally a single glowing sphere picked out the figure of Dino. He raised his hands for attention, red eyes glinting.

"An announcement. Katora will not be giving the lecture this afternoon. Habel had a setback that required floating. She is attending him."

Gasps and cries of "No!" came from the shadowed nooks. Puflet clutched her throat. If anything happened to the kid, Katora would go on a rampage looking for someone to blame. And what more likely target than Puflet, who was accused of engineering the future to hurt people?

Dino lifted his hands. "No need for worry, I'm sure he'll be fine. And now, I have a treat for you. I managed to get my father in to give the lecture in Katora's place."

Stunned silence. A few students, knowing Dino's penchant for joking, chuckled. But instead of saying, "just kidding," and telling them what really was going on, Dino smiled and walked out of the dining hall as the normal lighting resumed, his tufted tail waving behind him in a way that looked very self-satisfied to Puflet.

What was he up to?

She hurried to her cell to change, just in case Thermeon really was coming. She couldn't repress a grin as she flicked through her choices, settling on a pale blue robe that would give her a studious look as well as accentuating her eyes. She'd ask him about the Fissure. She'd ask him to help her with the monster.

If Dino was just playing another one of his stupid tricks, she was going to punch him.

It had to be a trick, though. Thermeon could not possibly have arrived from offworld at such short notice, even if he did have a vessel that fused to Deep Five.

A cacophony of voices grew as she approached the nexus. It was filled with students, all gesticulating and arguing. Puflet pushed through them. When she reached the archway to the lecture hall, she found it blocked by Eadin and Sianne, who stood shoulder to shoulder. Eadin came off worse by their proximity, Sianne being so much taller and more regal.

"We're boycotting the lecture," Eadin said.

Puflet snorted. "That's stupid!"

"I don't care if he warps you," Eadin said. "You're already beyond hope."

"Thank you." Puflet looked at Sianne. "What's your excuse?"

She glowered down her long nose. "He fired my mother." It was the most unadorned statement Puflet had heard from her since their contretemps.

"Huh?"

"She was his first mind-River of Lal. He was an ignorant savage, and he never could have ruled the empire without her help. As a reward, he fired her."

"That's sad," Puflet said.

"And now he'll never be able to tell her he was wrong." The corners of her lips curled, ever so slightly, and her eyes brightened.

"Oh." News of Sagi's crystallization hearing and subsequent euthanasia had just reached them. But why should Sianne deserve all the sympathy? Puflet had never even had a mother, and no one felt sorry for her.

Sianne lifted her chin. "If he had appointed my father as major, as she advised, the Great War would not have come about."

"Oh?" Puflet's imperial history was still weak.

She saw Yusun and Hinomia glaring at her from the other side of Sianne's elbow. "You're scared of Thermeon?" she called to them.

Hinomia narrowed her eyes. "We're not scared of him, we hate him. All of Horl's descendants hate Thermeon, and he hates us."

Yusun nodded, making his nose waggle, his blue eyes shiny and blank. His scruffy pet mirrored his expression.

Puflet turned around to look at the students massed behind her. Serpenlino was doing his slouching snake impression, feigning disinterest, and Oakiza was nowhere to be seen. She remembered that Coders also hated Thermeon. "I think Dino was joking about Thermeon being here. There's no way he could reach Ulona on such short notice, unless he was already here, hiding from Katora, or something. But I'm going to find out. What about you?"

The crowd recoiled from her with nervous giggles.

"Why don't you report back to us?" Pea-Pach suggested.

Puflet glowered. "If he's there, I'm not coming back. So you can just remain in your ignorance if you don't have the guts to check for yourself. But if he isn't there, I'm going to kick Dino through the tunnel, and you'll hear his screams."

Sianne chuckled. She disliked Dino, who always threatened her dignity.

Puflet headed for the archway. Eadin, who had been shy of physical confrontations since Puflet had punched her, flinched aside to let her pass. Puflet heard the rustle of Serpenlino's dragging robe behind her. Then came a thump and a soft grunt. She stopped and looked back.

Eadin had Pea-Pach by the arm, trying to keep her from following Puflet.

"Let me go!" Pea-Pach huffed.

"This is for your own good."

"You never cared about my good before, Eadin. I was always 'that little tramp.' Kael told me what you called me."

"He did not!"

When Pea-Pach smirked at her, Eadin released her arm and slapped her.

"Thissss isssss ridiculousssss," Serpenlino said. "Thermeon is one of my great-grandfathersss. No plant persssson tellssss me I can't sssssee him."

He slithered around Eadin and Pea-Pach, who were screaming, kicking, and pulling each other's hair, releasing the stench of crushed ylang-ylang petals.

Two of Pea-Pach's admirers pulled her free from Eadin, and

they followed Serpenlino into the lecture hall.

The lecture hall was nearly empty when Puflet and her companions arrived. A few small clusters of students, who must have come before Eadin could set up her blockade, sat in the back rows. Puflet spotted Dino sitting in the middle of the front row, so she marched down and seated herself in the nook just past his. Serpenlino took the nook on her other side, and the others fell into place on the other side of Dino.

Puflet glared at Dino. "This had better not be a trick."

"It's not." He looked smug. "I knew how much you wanted to see my father."

"And you know how much Katora doesn't want to see him."

"That's why I waited for a day when she wouldn't be here."

"I'm sure Eadin and Sianne will fill her in."

Dino laid a hand on his heart. "She can hardly begrudge me a chance to see my own father."

"I think it's more her impressionable students seeing your father she'll begrudge," Puflet said.

Serpenlino snorted. "He's my great-grandfather, and she can't stop me from seeing him either!"

"I think he might be my future husband," cried Pea-Pach.

Her admirers both shouted, "No!"

"She will see this as a betrayal," Puflet said. "How do you plan to explain it to her?"

"My beloved knows that I would never betray her!" Dino said. "I am a paragon of faith and loyalty. All right, maybe I do have stray thoughts sometimes, but who could resist my giant clam?"

"Clam? You're just trying to change the subject."

"Never!" said Dino.

"What clam?" Pea-Pach asked.

"I doubt there is a clam," said Serpenlino.

"Oh, my clam is very real. She lives at the bottom of the center of the lake. I visit her whenever I have underwater gardening to do. Ach, when she takes me between her cold blue lips...." He arched back in his nook, eyes shut, his face blissful.

Puflet grimaced.

"Ew," said Pea-Pach.

Then the lights in the hall dimmed, and Thermeon strode out

across the stage.

Puflet knew at once it was really him. There was no mistaking the power flowing from his figure, the deep-level radiance that wasn't quite visible to the human eye, though you knew it was there. He was tall and very slender, silver-white-skinned like Dino —and Puflet—his white mane of hair falling to the shoulders of his long white tunic, and he moved with a wild grace. When he reached the podium to stare down at his audience with violet eyes, the monster in Puflet awoke and rumbled in recognition. Puflet almost feared eye contact with the famous mindsea, though at the same time she thirsted for it.

Thermeon's eyes fell on Dino. "I thought your infant son was sick." His voice was soft and light, with a gentle twang. "Why aren't you home with him?"

"I seem to make the little fellow nervous, for some reason," Dino said. "I thought I'd best let Katora handle it."

Thermeon gave his head a slight shake, as if he didn't agree, but his gaze shifted to Serpenlino. "Greetings, Grandson."

"Greetings, Grandfather."

Thermeon looked at Pea-Pach, and she gasped. As his gaze passed from nook to nook, each student stiffened for an instant, as if Thermeon's eyes had stung them. Puflet's heart pounded. What was going on? And why was he overlooking her?

Just when she was certain she would be excluded from the ritual, Thermeon looked her way. When their eyes touched, something stabbed into her awareness, sharp and quick, like a brilliant shaft of light.

He probed me, she thought.

"Not probed," he said. "Just pinged." His lips hadn't moved. He was mind-linking her.

I'd like to talk to you, she thought. *Can we meet privately, after the lecture? In a meditation chamber?*

"Certainly." His mind-voice conveyed the image of a man loftily proceeding through the universe with all of eternity available in which to do anything he wished.

His attention shifted to the students in the far reaches of the hall. He gestured to them. "Come closer! I find it insulting when people sit so far away."

He wanted to "ping" them too, Puflet thought. She froze an instant after the thought had escaped, but he didn't get back in her mind to berate her. She relaxed and let her thoughts range.

Surely she had a good dose of Thermeon in her. His genes were common as hydrogen. In a few more millennia, probably only the people in the most isolated backwaters of the empire would be unable to count Thermeon as one of their ancestors.

At his repeated urging, the students in the back had left their nooks to troop towards the front. She should jump up to warn them that Thermeon would probe—"ping"—them. He apparently wanted all of them in his mind-net. Of course, they knew what a mindsea was, and they'd heard Katora's warnings about him, so it wasn't like it should come as a surprise. It had surprised Puflet, though. She'd thought Katora's warnings were nonsense.

The other students seated themselves in the first couple of rows, and Puflet watched each of them start at Thermeon's "ping." She couldn't keep the smirk from her face.

"Well then," Thermeon said when he'd finished getting to know his audience. "My lecture today is titled 'The Fissure and What it Revealed about the Nature of Evil.'"

Puflet stretched her legs and settled herself deeper into her nook. She really wanted to hear this.

Before Thermeon could start, a commotion rose in the back of the hall. "Evil go away!" shrilled a voice.

More voices took up the chant, until it swelled into a roar. Puflet twisted around to see a crowd of students massed in the upper third of the aisle below the entrance archway. She caught a faint whiff of decaying ylang-ylang.

Thermeon surveyed the hecklers and smiled. Leaning toward his audience, he spoke in a stage whisper Puflet heard clearly despite the background noise. "Perhaps I have time for one anecdote and a brief demonstration before I begin my lecture."

He rubbed his claw-tipped fingers together. "When I was emperor, the Contamination Laws were in effect. These laws protected citizens from mindseas. Mindseas had to keep a certain distance away from citizens." He gestured. "About half the length of that aisle. A mindsea couldn't touch a citizen or exchange words with him. This was because people in those days believed that if a mindsea knew you, your soul belonged to him. I hated those laws, so I invented my own way of getting around them.

"It was called the Game. I had it announced that citizens brave enough to risk Contamination would receive a gift from the palace. Every morning a crowd formed around the palace steps to play the Game." He grinned, revealing his fangs. They were longer than Puflet's, but identical to Serpenlino's. Sexual dimorphism, no doubt. She sighed with envy.

"Like that crowd." He pointed to the hecklers. "I'd warm up by running up and down the steps a few times." He leaped down from the stage and walked to the bottom of the aisle. "And then—"

He charged up the aisle, fangs bared and claws extended. Shrieking and shoving, the hecklers fled back through the archway. There were too many of them to fit. They clumped, some rebounding into the aisle. When Thermeon slammed into them, shrieks crescendoed to the thudding of bodies.

Thermeon didn't pause to survey the damage he'd wrought, but turned around and trotted back down the aisle, chuckling. "Citizens in those days were a bit more fit and alert, I think."

Pea-Pach had a hand over her mouth. "On second thought, maybe I wouldn't want him for a husband."

Puflet leaped out of her nook and faced the back of the auditorium where small figures groaned and picked themselves up from the floor. "I say there's better protection in strength than in fear!" she shouted at them. Eadin's flower must really be a mess now, she reflected happily as she settled back into the nook.

Thermeon leaped to the stage again. Turning, he smoothed his hair. "Contamination is a thing of the past, of course."

He examined his audience. "I am a native Lalian, but I have lived on the galactic circuit for a while. If you are wondering how it is possible to arrive on a hi-grav world like this one without needing a period for adaptation, it is a simple enough thing for anyone with mindsize. You just need to adjust your body in the Deep."

He strolled to the podium and gripped the crystal pahmak's head. "Now I will begin my lecture."

The lecture hall was silent. Puflet fixed her eyes on the dazzling white figure on the stage and waited for him to answer questions that had plagued her since she'd heard Katora's version of the Fissure. He began to speak in a soft, languid tone, enunciating carefully around his big fangs.

"When Quintillion asked me to come out into the desert with him, I believed that he meant to do battle. I believed that he despised me for destroying his homeworld. His philosophy and mine were very far apart. He was a vegetarian and a total pacifist. I believed then, as I still do, that sometimes battles must be fought.

"Though Quintillion never fought, I still feared his wrath. We had met once, before the war, and he had easily mastered me and made me feel like a child, without any exertion of his mindsize at all, except to understand me better than I understood myself."

Closing her eyes, Puflet tried to imagine the scene. Had the head exuded power and grace when it had been united with a vital male body? She pictured Kaanu, and Serpenlino. Both of them carried an aura of strength and energy.

"It was with some trepidation that I accompanied him far out into a wild place," Thermeon said. "We were alone in the same desert landscape where I had grown up, though slaves no longer eked out an existence within its borders, having been freed and integrated into imperial society.

"Imagine my astoundment when, instead of attacking,

Quintillion begged me to help defeat this ... emptiness inside him. He called it the curse of his father."

Puflet nodded. That was what the head had told her.

"I was not entirely surprised by his condition," Thermeon said. "Once, while traveling through Deep Five in my pentascoper, I had sighted Quintillion's reign as a great wave of nothingness—of non being—spreading across the galaxy." With a wave of his hand, he conjured a tide of shadow sweeping inexorably to quench the stars, and a chill touched Puflet's bones. "I used to refer to Quintillion, and not entirely in jest, as the 'Great Nothingness.'

"I have always been a man of hopeful nature, believing that I could overcome whatever dangers assailed." He thumped his chest. "Ever since the night I was exposed in the wilderness as a newborn because of my inhuman features, and I reached out to the stars with my mind, and my plea for warmth and comfort was answered by the appearance of what seemed to me stars come down from the sky, but were in fact my inhuman relatives, the nurrs, I have felt protected by powers beyond myself."

What were nurrs, Puflet wondered. Instantly, Thermeon was in her mind, showing her the image of a large Lalian predator created by Horl from a mixture of human, baboon, and lion genes. They had luminescent white manes, and they could interbreed with humans.

"I offered my hope to Quintillion," Thermeon said. "I believed that it could overcome his emptiness. And so we stood toe to toe on the sand and called forth our deep-level natures to put the matter to the test. I believe that I won. I gave Quintillion hope."

He shook his head. "But he had never known hope. He couldn't reconcile it with the darkness. He lost patternistic integrity and unfused."

Puflet jerked up in her nook. How could a person lose patternistic integrity with himself?

Thermeon grimaced, baring fangs, as his hands described unseen things cascading outward and downward from his chest. "The seeds, the black seeds Katora talks about were the emptiness pouring out of his body, seeking a different universe than the rest of him. But there was very little of him beyond the emptiness.

"I had some of the blackness inside myself as well—it was

locked into the killing rages that ruled my life when I was a young man. But it poured out of me that night, and joined Quintillion's emptiness, leaving me damaged but free."

He paused, head lowered, as if watching the black seeds pop from his flesh. "It was a terrible experience, seeing those ugly things come out of your body."

He lifted his head and resumed in a stronger voice. "So what did this experience teach me about the nature of evil? I believe that the answer is clear. Evil is not people. Evil is nothing. It is the opposite of life. Living things may be selfish, but they are not destructive for destruction's sake. That is the emptiness within them.

"Perhaps you are thinking, if this emptiness is within a person, doesn't that make the person the emptiness? Of course not! This is the reasoning Katora follows. Eliminate the agents of emptiness, and you eliminate the problem, right? Wrong. The seeds of emptiness are released back into the Deep, where they wait to slide into the wounds of another soul.

"It is the blackness, the nothingness itself that we must fight, not the pathetic beings it parasitizes. But in order to make this clear, we need to give our enemy a name: I call it the 'monster of nothingness,' Monstronon."

Puflet nodded. Finally he was getting to the monster.

"Monstronon is a single entity," Thermeon said. "It is not a life-form. It is not alive. It is not dead, either; though it is Death. It enters living beings through wounds in their souls, that is, the deep-level part of them.

"Sometimes, regrettably, it is necessary for us to take up arms against those Monstronon is controlling, when their actions become a threat to those we love or to the fabric of our society. But this is the last resort. Much better to try to heal the afflicted. When Monstronon is filled with hope and meaning, it exists no longer, and the soul is freed. When this happens, everyone is the victor, because we are all on the side of Life; and no one loses, because Monstronon is no one."

Thermeon threw out his hands, grinning, as he imparted his final bit of wisdom. Puflet led the applause.

"I will take questions," Thermeon said.

"Is it true you killed a lot of your brides?" Pea-Pach asked him.

Thermeon curled his hands around the pahmak's neck. "Unfortunately, yes."

"Was it because of the monster of nothingness?"

"No. It was because I was searching for my goddess-star. She had guided me from my savage birth land in the form of a star, but she promised to take human form and be my wife. So, in the height of my passion, I called out to her, and she filled my bride's body. But they ... the match wasn't right, and the human body unfused. But I have found my goddess-star. She is Katora!"

"You'll unfuse her too."

"No." He gave his mane a vigorous shake, his eyes fixing on a distant splendor. "She truly is a goddess, the goddess of illumination—a star. Has she not said so herself?"

The students fell silent. A couple of them fidgeted in the nooks. Puflet could only blink in amazement. After a couple moments, he said, "If there are no more questions, you can go do whatever you do next." He waved them away.

Students rose and moved toward the aisle. Pea-Pach hesitated, looking at Thermeon, but her admirers pulled her after the others. Puflet remained where she was. Thermeon leaped down from the stage and stalked up to Dino. "Why are you still here? Why don't you go take care of your child?"

"I told you—"

"You don't make any sense, Dino. What did you do, yell at the baby? You must have had twenty or thirty children by now, and I'm sure you know how to care for a newborn. What's going on?"

Dino gave his father a strange look, something between a smirk and a sneer, his red eyes lit by ... emptiness. Puflet gripped the edge of her nook as the monster took shape, wavering out of the Deep's dimensions. It held a newborn boy in its arms, a little wrinkled baby with a thatch of white hair, who cried and cried.

The baby grew. He became a laughing brown-skinned boy with Katora's gray-blue eyes. Intelligence shone from his face; but there was more. That invisible radiance of the Deep poured from him, burning brighter as he grew.

He was a youth, a young man. His eyes sought Puflet's and he called out to her across the years. "Help me! Only you can help!"

She reached for him, but he was gone. She jerked up in the nook with a gasp, smelling ylang-ylang. Had Eadin dared venture back into the hall? She peered up the aisle, but no one was there.

Thermeon studied her, his head cocked. "Were you in mind-link with someone?"

"Yes. With Habel. From twenty years in the future. He will be a powerful mindsea."

Thermeon raised his brows.

Dino smirked. "That's obvious."

"Why obvious?" his father asked.

"The slavers are right—it's trauma that makes a mindsea. The more severe, and the earlier in life, the greater the mindsize it produces. Look at you—exposed to die in the wilderness when you were a babe. That's the source of your powers. And you?" He looked at Puflet. "What were your first days like?"

"I-I don't know." Stepping from the nook, she stood beside Thermeon. Her head came only to chest-level on him. "Valri told me that she stole me when I was still in the incubator and and gave me to Ix. It couldn't have been pleasant."

Thermeon met her eyes, surprise and sympathy in his gaze.

"Already you're a preeminent deep-level engineer," Dino said. "And now that Habel has suffered this trauma, he'll develop his deep-level personality too."

Puflet's jaw dropped as a terrible suspicion struck her. She checked Thermeon, but his mind was still on her story. "Who are your parents?" he asked.

She shook her head. "Valri wouldn't tell me. She just taunted me, saying maybe she knows and maybe she doesn't."

His lips tightened.

"Do you know Valri?" Puflet asked him.

"No. If I did, I'd probe her now and get some answers for you. As it is, I think I can arrange that she and I meet sometime soon. Orgmorgan has a tracker on her ship, so I can intercept her somewhere."

A warm rush of gratitude filled Puflet. "That would be wonderful!"

Thermeon smiled, dipping his head. "You look like you might be one of my progeny."

She started. "I'm pretty sure that I am."

"I think no one should be without a family," he said. "Until the time you find your real parents, would you allow me to act as your father?"

She stared at him, open-mouthed. She wanted to dance with joy. But a warning rumbled in the back of her mind.

"He wants you to love him, to become part of his story. But he will always be the central figure in his story. You will stand on the periphery, along with thousands of others, holding out your hand and waiting for him to help you. Why do you think Quixa emphasizes self-reliance, and why do you think Dino plays the fool? They have had to struggle hard to break free from the mighty grip of their father's mind."

Puflet swallowed and looked up into the mindsea's searing eyes. "It might be safer to call your grandfather, so as not to insult my real father, if I ever find him. You haven't had any children stolen, have you?"

"No. It would be unconscionable to allow such a thing."

He was jealous of her unknown father.

She continued to gaze into the violet eyes, feeling a surge of self-confidence. She would be the hero of her own story. In her own way, she would be greater than Thermeon. She would master her charger as he had not. Fighting the monster of emptiness, indeed! Thermeon had given them a version of the Fissure that exempted him from any blame or lingering taint of evil.

"Have you mastered the First Tenet?" she asked him. "Can you teleport?"

"No."

"What about the Second Tenet? Do you ever catch glimpses of the future?"

He was silent for a moment. "Not that I recall."

"How did you know that you would be needed to give this lecture?"

"Dino told me."

"And you were able to arrive in Ulona within a few hours?"

"He told me a few tenthyears ago."

Dino broke in. "There's nothing so strange about that, my sweet little adoptive niece. I knew that Katora would be occupied when Habel hatched."

She faced him, curling her lip to show fangs. Katora had planned to deliver her lecture until Habel's mishap. The bastard had nearly killed his own baby in order to make him a mindsea. He was as bad as the slavers.

The image of the beautiful young mindsea reaching out to her swept back. Dino had wounded his tender newborn soul, and something horrible had taken root in the wound. Suddenly, with a dark thrill, she understood what the monster of emptiness really was—lovelessness. Without love, the monster, or whatever you called your deep-level part, would take you down, down, endlessly. With love, the power lofted you gloriously. Habel was calling on her to heal him, as Quintillion had called on Thermeon. Thermeon had failed, but she must not.

She looked at Thermeon, wondering why he didn't probe her or Dino to find out what they had been talking about. It would be good to see Dino catch a blast of well-deserved parental wrath. But maybe Thermeon didn't want to know. He caught her look. "Didn't you want to discuss something with me?"

With a final glare at Dino, she motioned him to follow, and they left the lecture hall.

18

Thermeon had chosen a hot, dark, arid meditation chamber. They sat side by side on the slope of a simulated dune, sand flowing away from the glow of their hair to vanish into darkness.

"It looks a bit like Lal on an overcast night," he said. "Of course, there would be living creatures in the sand there. And the scents would be much richer. Actually, the museum planet does a pretty good job simulating all of the imperial worlds with its exhibit domes, if you ever want a quick tour of the galaxy." He shot her a glance. "But what did you want to ask me about?"

"Quintillion didn't quite die at the Fissure."

Thermeon gasped softly, an expression of doubt and confusion covering his face. He gave his head a shake.

"Ix was using his head for her deep-level communications system."

"No!" He sprang to his feet. "That's not possible. You must have...."

She rose to her feet as well. "Seen some other head? No. It was him."

"But ... but...." He was having a hard time getting his mind around the possibility. "If you saw him.... The Fissure was ... nearly four hundred years ago ... and I felt nothing, all that time. I should've known, should have felt his presence in the Deep. He couldn't have been ... used, for all that time."

"He told me that he felt it was necessary for him to suffer."

Thermeon gave an incoherent cry. He clutched his hair and ground his fangs, a loud rasp filling the chamber. "How could I not have been aware?"

"I don't suppose he wanted you to find him. You would have tried to end his suffering."

"But...."

"I also think I understand now what you didn't tell us about the Fissure."

Straightening, he cast her a baffled look.

"It wasn't hope he wanted from you, was it? He asked for love, didn't he?"

Thermeon shut his jaws with a click.

"You see," she said, "he passed his burden on to me, and now I own his monster. But it's not an emptiness—it's a potential. It can destroy, but it can be tamed with love. Can't it? I know who needs my love, and I'll give it to him. But you didn't give Quintillion what he needed, did you?"

"I offered my friendship."

"But it wasn't enough."

He just stood there, a glowing figure of white against the darkness, his expression resigned, waiting for whatever she had to say.

Thermeon might be five thousand years old, but he was a still a primitive at heart, not like the imperial sophisticates who considered gender inconsequential. "You considered it unmanly to love him, didn't you?"

He snorted. "He was not about to take the place of my goddess-star, if that is what you're asking."

"But that's what he wanted, wasn't it?"

He spoke very softly. "I don't think so. Quintillion was a very complex character. He outstripped me in many ways—in his mind-linking skills, as a builder, both in the Deep and on home-level, as an artist. He was also, I think, the most arrogant being who ever lived. More arrogant than Horl—remember, I knew both of them. Horl flaunted his abilities, but Quintillion hid his, convinced that humanity was unable to appreciate the fruits of his mind. And he wallowed in hopelessness. He believed that no one had reached a stage of development high enough to claim his friendship."

Puflet nodded.

Thermeon went on. "He believed that no one would love him if they understood what he really was. That is why I maintain that he was asking for hope, and that my friendship should have been enough for him."

Only, clearly, it hadn't been enough. Puflet sighed. "He told me that his monster was so terrible that you and he together weren't able to overcome it. Then he bestowed the monster on me."

"And you killed him?" Thermeon asked.

"I ... well, yes. I didn't think I had a choice. He seemed to want it, anyway."

"He must have seen you as his heir. You must be related to him."

"I don't see how that could be."

"Well," he grunted. "I will get the truth out of Valri."

"That would mean a lot to me."

Thermeon seated himself on the sand again and stared into the darkness. "When Quintillion's father died, his deep-level self became part of Quintillion. That was why his store of knowledge was so vast." He looked at her. "If you now posses these memories, perhaps they have given you the talent for deep-level engineering."

Her scalp prickled. "The monster looks like a dinosaur to me. What would a dinosaur know of deep-level engineering?"

"I don't know."

"I have one more question. Serpenlino told me that you have a monster yourself—a winged dinosaur."

"My spirit-dragon. My deep-level self."

"It has the power that killed your brides. And flashed Wamatu."

He inclined his head, his hair bristling with tension and whirring softly.

She took a deep breath. "Is it tamed now? Did what happened at the Fissure make a difference? You said that you expelled the seeds of emptiness. Those must have been the violent, destructive urges of your spirit-dragon. Can you love now? Would Katora truly be safe in your arms?"

"Of course. She is my goddess-star."

She was about to ask him if he could probe her memories of

forming the gem for hidden knowledge, when he cried out and sprang to his feet. "Katora is furious with me! Those whiny kids went to the wonderdome and bothered her. I really shouldn't have knocked them down. I didn't mean to. I thought they'd get out of the way, and by the time I realized they wouldn't, I was going too fast to stop."

Puflet rose. Hadn't he just given her a very different answer to her last question? She'd seen the force he'd used against the protestors. If they'd pushed back, he would have become fiercer still. He'd let no barrier stand in his way, no matter how monstrous he had to become.

"She's threatening to send planetary police after me! I ask you, is this the Hundred Fifth Millennium or the Ninety-eighth? I had best retreat."

"Yes, that's wise." She had no faith at all that he would avoid violence if cornered. The planetary police would be ashes.

Thermeon put his arms around her. "Farewell, granddaughter! I will keep in touch in mind-link. I always use a violet flash to signal the start and end of my touch, so you'll know it's me. Perhaps you'll learn to mind-link me as well. What signal will you use?"

"Signal?" she mumbled into his chest. "Uh ... what about a puff of wind?"

"They've tattled on you too, I'm afraid. She wants to see you in her office."

Puflet cursed.

He stroked her hair. "You say you know whose love will heal your emptiness. I wish you luck. Love isn't easy—I still wait for my goddess-star to accept my love—but it's worth everything."

He slipped away and left the meditation chamber. By the time Puflet stepped into the tunnel after him he was racing around the bend. She shook her head, hoping he wouldn't smash into anyone. She proceeded toward the headmistress' office.

Katora was probably right to keep her distance from Thermeon. It would be very hard having to continually fight off his insistence that you were his goddess-star. And Puflet guessed that he would unfuse her just as he had all his other lovers, because how could anyone align themselves perfectly with his view of the universe? Katora might see herself as bringer of the age of illumination, but she probably didn't see her highest calling as filling Thermeon's emptiness.

Puflet composed her face as she approached Katora's eminence. The headmistress gazed down on her with marble-like eyes, earrings swinging gently, flashing blue, then red. "You know my feelings about Thermeon. Why did you insist on leading students into his mind-net?"

"Um, ma'am—uh, sorry. Well, it's like this. You asked me to get my jewel out of your Academy, but I don't know how. I thought that Thermeon might know, since he's such a great mindsea, and all. I thought I would ask him for some pointers."

"Did you?"

"I was just about to ask him to probe me for hidden information about the jewel when he shouted that the guards were coming after him, and he ran off."

Katora's brow knotted. "I've already offered to probe you, Puflet. Why won't you let me?"

"Because you don't like me."

"What makes you say that?"

"Um, I guess it's because when you look at me, there's always a scowl on your face. You never smile at me."

Katora blinked and made her face go blank. She was probably thinking, "Crap, am I that obvious?" Finally she heaved a sigh, and said, "Are you planning to maintain contact with Thermeon through mind-link?"

Puflet heaved a sigh of her own. "I don't care much for having him in my mind, but I don't see how I can keep him out. Besides, I might still learn things from him."

"At least you don't try to lie to me," Katora said in a thoughtful tone. "When he contacts you, ask him to probe you for the hidden information about the jewel. He doesn't have to be in the same room with you."

"I will do that."

"Report to me afterward," Katora said. "You are dismissed."

Puflet bowed, spun around, and marched off through the archways. She should try to be nicer to the woman. After all, Katora would be her mother-in-law some day.

After setting meal she soaked in her hot tub and stared at the dawn-lit clouds in her skylight. She pondered love. Why couldn't Katora see how disgusting she was, treating romance like it was a shopping expedition where you aimed to get the biggest blast per credit and returned merchandise that didn't meet your expectations? And Dino—what could he see in her except a way to show the galaxy he'd gotten a bigger prize in the romance market than his father had? Puflet guessed that he must totally submerge his personality when he was with his wife, because Katora would never put up with his stupid jokes or salacious remarks. It must be all "Yes, dear," and "No, dear," in their habitat.

Thermeon was equally misguided. Imagine killing woman after woman trying to fuse them with your deep-level mind! It would be like Puflet trying to make a lover embody her monster.

Wait—had she done that with Sianne? She tried to think, clicking her fangs together.

But it didn't matter. It wouldn't happen again. She wasn't going to be like Quintillion or Thermeon. She was looking forward to a lifetime of caring caresses with a man who fit her needs as she fit his, a man whose soul had already touched hers.

All she had to do was wait twenty years.

19

Sianne had begged Puflet to take her turn on the lake, so she was on a little boat with Oakiza getting snails out of the lake so Dino could take them aboard his tetrascoping ship and fill with deep-level stuff for free-form exercises. They sat on small benches at either end of the boat, paddling through the clumps of lotuses and pulling the snails from lotus leaves. Puflet had decided to steal a peek at Dino's clam while she was out there. A firefly had located the clam, and she was trying to position the boat so she could take a quick dive. She had dressed in a pink skinsuit that would be easy to swim in, and she was barefoot. She was about to slip over the side when Oakiza paddled the boat away.

"I see some snails this way."

They gathered some more snails, then Puflet brought the boat back into position.

"There are no snails here," Oakiza said. "We already checked."

"But Dino's clam is here, and I want to grab a peek at it."

"Why?"

"I'm just curious." Sliding from the bench, she crouched in the bottom of the boat, her toes squeezed between snail buckets, and peered over the side. The water looked black and opaque. She dipped her hand in. It was cold.

"Dino is disgusting," Oakiza said. "I wouldn't put credence in anything he says."

Her guts tightened. Dino was disgusting. But that wasn't the clam's fault, was it?

"There are many things more interesting than a clam," Oakiza said. "I could show you some of them."

She didn't look up; it would only encourage him. Her skinsuit would warm her. It wasn't that far, it was just deeper than she'd ever swum before. She positioned herself and peered past her reflection. Was that a tiny glint from the blackness? She took a deep breath and prepared to plunge.

A honk came from behind.

Releasing her breath, Puflet whirled around, making the boat rock from side to side. Yusun and Hinomia slid slowly past in another boat on a course nearly perpendicular to their own. As the gap between boats widened, they grinned and held up a couple of snail buckets.

"What do you think you're doing?" Oakiza challenged.

The two didn't answer, their eyes full of malice. They were up to something, but what? Trying to prove that they were faster snail-gatherers? It wasn't their day to gather, so what was the point?

"Now!" Hinomia yelled. She and Yusun flung their snails at Puflet's boat.

In that instant she realized what was happening. Those weren't empty snails from the lake. They were full snails from the holding tank. Yusun and Hinomia were trying to unfuse them.

The snails clattered against the sides and bottom of the boat, against the arm Puflet had lifted to shield herself. Shells smashed. There came a whoosh of flame, and pain. It happened too quickly for her to dive to safety. She had only time to scream a single word.

"Switch!"

The lake turned smooth and solid as a gel-rock floor, lotuses swirling mosaic patterns embedded in its surface. Snails poked out deep-level eyes and glided about, creating a pervasive background purr. They would all be full. They must've been full after the ball, too, but no one had noticed. Pure luck there hadn't been an accident.

Puflet's arm was a smoking ruin, but strangely, it no longer hurt. Stepping to her side with thunderclap hooves, the monster breathed on the wound, and a new arm formed, glowing like molten silver.

She sprang onto the flaming back of her steed and couched her lance.

Yusun tried to escape, flopping and honking like an elephant seal, but the monster lunged, and Puflet skewered him. A final, woeful honk released a gust of sewage, then his body deflated to hang on the point of her lance like a shriveled balloon. She flung it backwards over her shoulder.

"For Horl!" Hinomia had secured her mount. She charged at Puflet, lance aimed for her heart.

Grinning, Puflet couched her oozing lance. "Surge!"

The monster hurtled forward with muscles of fire, hornless hooves thundering in a cadence that rocked the universe around them, the mighty skull nodding its crest of spikes and snorting flames. The glory of it made Puflet want to sing.

Hinomia rocketed toward her. Puflet screamed in jubilation as the impact shattered planes of spacetime. The monster tossed his head, catching Hinomia's lance between two spikes and wrenching it from her hands. Puflet's lance pierced Hinomia's heart, making her suck back in the name of Horl. The pressure popped her eyeballs out with a ghastly double "lroh" whisper, and her body deflated. The fire went out of her steed. It collapsed in a heap of dry bones. Puflet let the body slide from her lance and drop across the bones.

She swung her steed around, reality swirling beneath the prancing, booming hooves. She spied no more enemies, but the urge to gallop onward forever, proclaiming her freedom to the universe, swept through her with dizzying force.

"Stop!" Katora's voice stung like a shower of icy water. For an instant Puflet seethed with defiance, then she recalled that this was the mother of her beloved, and subsided.

"Switchback."

Pain and shock enveloped her body, and she thought that she was dying until she realized that she had fallen into the lake. Coughing and spitting curses, she began to swim. Luckily the practice at the wonderdome had made her a strong swimmer, but she was still thoroughly exhausted when she pulled herself from the water at Katora's feet.

"What have you done?"

Puflet shook her head to clear her ears, then squared her shoulders and faced the headmistress. "Hinomia and Yusun attacked without provocation. They threw full snails at us. They killed Oakiza."

"And that gave you the right to execute them? I told you to call for help if you were attacked."

"There wasn't any time!" Puflet yelled. "They burned off my twistored arm!" She jutted her elbow into Katora's face. The skinsuit was covered with strange smoke-colored squiggles where the arm had regrown, like tree-rings or tide-marks.

Katora gasped when she saw them, her face going a sickly yellow-green. She stumbled back. "The taint! You're tainted! Get away from me! Leave my academy this instant and never return!"

Puflet ran. When she had pounded down the steps from the academy portals she summoned an air lifter. She flew to the wonderdome and stood shivering in the lobby until Cidi came out and escorted her into a conference room. Unsoothed by the pale green curve of the wall, Puflet paced around the 2-nook where Cidi sat, spilling out all that had happened.

"And now I can't even go back and get my dresses!" She fell into the nook, sobbing and gnashing her fangs.

Cidi leaned over from the other curl of the nook to examine her "tainted" sleeve. "I don't know what that pattern means, but it seems to me that creature you were riding was encouraging you to kill. I mean, Yusun was just Hinomia's sidekick, wasn't he? He wasn't any real threat once you downleveled. He didn't have a steed or anything from the way you described it."

Puflet swallowed her tears. She had expected total sympathy from Cidi, not criticism. Didn't she have enough people against her? "I don't recall," she muttered. "He had one at the ball."

"What are you going to do now?" Cidi asked.

"I don't know."

"Why don't you stay here for a few days until you get yourself organized. After that horrible experience you could use a nice, relaxing float."

Puflet's hands curled and uncurled on the nook's rim, as if with volition of their own. "Thank you," she muttered. She kicked her feet, but she couldn't get comfortable.

Cidi spoke in a low voice. "It was you who injured Tepi, wasn't it? I kept wondering why Fanala said you were his girlfriend when I thought you'd never met him."

"He was trying to rape me," Puflet said. "He broke my ribs. All I want is to be free to live my life without anyone raping me or trying to kill me. Is that too much to ask?"

"Of course not," Cidi soothed. "Maybe the academy just wasn't a good place for you. Maybe you should think about settling on some other planet."

Puflet kicked her feet. "I can't leave Ulona. There's someone I care about here."

"I'm glad you have someone. Will that person be able to help you?"

"No. I have to take care of myself for awhile. But ... maybe ... Dino can help me." She smiled as a plan began to form. "Do you think you or Kaanu could ask him to come and see me when my float is done?"

"Of course," Cidi said. "Why don't I start to get you prepared now. And we'll get rid of the garment you're wearing, all right?"

"All right."

Cidi led her to an intake room, where she stripped and showered before lying down on the gel nook beneath the intake tube. The tube swung toward her, closing gently about her body like an elephant's trunk, and sucked her into the pool.

As darkness streamed and gurgled about her, stinging her skin with its chemicals, she began to work on her plan. Her thoughts soon became one with the flowing darkness, and yet, when a tube spat her out from the pool again, she found the plan fully formed.

Wearing her white wonderdome robe, Puflet reclined in an egg-like recovery chamber while Dino studied her, hands gripped behind his back.

"Now, listen to my plan," she said. "You are going to help. I know I'm asking a lot from you, but you can do it. You will do it, too, if you don't want what you did to Habel to become common knowledge."

He laid a hand on his heart. "It wounds me deeply that my dear niece feels it necessary to threaten, when she should know that I would gladly do anything she asks."

"This is my plan," she repeated. "I am going to found a new mindsea academy on the north pole of Ulona. It's going to be in the ruins of the ancient city that you and Katora found there. And do you know why?" She felt a wicked grin split her face. "My gem is there already. For many tenthyears now, I've seen it winking from mysterious places I didn't recognize, but at last I figured it out. The extent of the gem's fusion field, there in the north, will determine the outline of the new academy's walls. You will build it, you see?"

He bowed deeply. "I am at your command, my adoptive niece."

"You will see to it that the Ulonan government grants the charter for my academy."

He bowed again.

"And have them grant existence to the new city of ... what was it called, anyhow?"

"Tadruhemdron."

"Yes. Let Tadruhemdron rise again in this new age, so that my academy has habitats and shops and a wonderdome about it just as hers does."

"You do not plan in half-measures."

She laughed, a clear ringing sound of victory. "I know Katora thinks she has the planetary government in the palm of her hand, but I'm sure that your monetary gifts will prove to be of more moment than any respect she commands."

"No need to spell out distasteful details," he said. "O Mistress of the North Pole."

Puflet rather liked the sound of that.

20

"**Y**ou have visitors," Cidi said.

Puflet sat up straighter as two men entered her chamber. She recognized Serpenlino. The other looked and moved like Oakiza, but his skin was green as Katora's. So was his hair. Even his eyes had gone green.

He smiled. "Yes, it's me."

"I thought you were unfused!"

"My goddess saved me. She helped me to come into my own."

"Oh?" Puflet's monster had healed her by letting her choosing which among the many possibilities of reality she would bring back from the Deep. Perhaps his goddess did the same. "You wanted to be green?"

"There were four races living on ancient Ulona. The reds were our military, the golds our artisans, the blues our priests, and the greens our scientists. I have determined to become a deep-level engineer."

She offered the congratulations his proud stance and glowing green eyes seemed to desire.

"Katora wasn't born green either," he said. "She underwent the Ritual of Choosing when she was captive in Tadruhemdron. Before then, she was white as her father."

"Hard to imagine," Puflet murmured. Then she recalled that Katora's half-sister Cevana was white. Katora must once have looked a lot like her.

She turned her attention to Serpenlino. He too stood with out-thrust chest and gritted jaw, his eyes smoky with inner fires. "I have resigned from the academy. I am coming to Tadruhemdron with you."

"So am I," Oakiza said.

Her spirits rocketing, Puflet thrust her hands out to both of them. "What glorious times we shall have! What wonders we shall see!"

It felt so good to have friends.

They spent the rest of their waking hours eagerly discussing the details.

Within a matter of days, the three of them were camping out amid the ruins of the ancient underground city. Oakiza described wonders of the past, while Puflet described the future she envisioned.

"In my academy, there will be no talk of taints or evil," she told her friends. "All bloodlines will be welcomed. We will provide a haven for talented men and women who have suffered enslavement or other persecutions. Our course of study will center on acquiring and taming chargers. We'll have deep-level races and jousting tournaments." She pictured colorful banners rippling in deep-level winds while fiery steeds charged to the blast of higher-dimensional trumpets. "It will be splendid!"

Following her instructions, Dino raised spectator stands above what had once been the pahmak fighting arena of the ancient kings of Ulona. The arena and stands were built from rough-hewn basalt blocks that, along with the damp smells of the phosphorescent moss that had colonized the cracks between blocks, commanded an aura of ancient mystery. The original inhabitants' carvings of domesticated pahmaks performing sundry tasks could still be seen in many places, their crumbling edges adding to the mystique.

But Puflet was not so much into mystique that she let the Academy of Tadruhemdron be uncomfortable. The ancient system of drawing heat from the planet's depth was overhauled and augmented, excess heat going to provide a delightful series of hot baths in phosphorescent grottoes attached to the academy. She installed modern, glowworm-powered furniture in all the ancient halls, including the stands overlooking the arena. The academy had a system too—no false primitivism for Puflet.

She had her own series of meditation chambers, some in deep underground environments, or surrounded by the majestic rubble of parts of the city she had not redeveloped, or on the surface amid cycad groves or beside ponds and streams.

While the building took place, busy glowworms and bioid workers secreting materials or moving stones, Puflet and her comrades spent many an hour in the meditation chambers. They flew where Sianne had feared to go, and by the end of the construction phase, they all could work the Third Tenet.

Once the shell of the academy stood glistening in its dewed dark basalt walls beneath the phosphorescent ceiling of the enormous cavern that enclosed the ancient city, they sought students.

Puflet found that she had been very lucky to secure the assistance of Oakiza and Serpenlino. Both had connections, and with their growing mind-linking skills, they reached out to the galaxy.

Sons and daughters of the Code who had languished at Eltien came to Tadruhemdron. So did talented offspring of Quintillion who had felt unwanted by Alonaton. Puflet tried to reach out to former slaves she had known on Puztak, but here she encountered an obstacle. Every mind she touched recoiled in fear—no, in abject terror. While an unexpected mind-link could startle—Oakiza and Serpenlino had to deal with this—none of their contacts reacted as Puflet's did.

At last, when one mind spewed out a brief, clear image before dissolving into amorphous horror, Puflet discovered the source of the obstacle. It was the image of Katora, broadcasting a warning to the new citizens of Puztak that their so-called liberator, Puflet, had only dethroned Ix in order to take her place, and that she was honing her mindpowers to exert a domination even more complete and terrible. Naturally, every Puztakian Puflet touched believed that her attempts to subsume their minds had begun.

"Why does that bitch hate me so?" Puflet ground her fangs and paced the halls of ancient Ulonan kings. How she longed to let monstrous power surge through her and strike back and her tormentor. But she could do nothing, for Katora was the mother of her husband-to-be.

Fortunately, an unexpected arrival shook her from the morass of suppressed fury.

"I abdicated the throne," Kael told them. "Without my father or any other family member, the honor was really hollow. I told the people to find one of their own, and after I did, I discovered that it had only been one small, powerful group that wanted my father in the first place. The vast majority of people wanted a homegrown monarch."

"You're always welcome here," Puflet told him. "And your experience as king could be useful. How would you like an administrative post? Or perhaps you'd prefer to manage our glowworms."

"I'm at your beck and call." He smiled. "But I'm not as Deep-blind as you may think. My father's charger has never left me since the day he died."

Oakiza instructed the Code students in how to turn to the Goddess for deep-level power. Serpenlino guided sons and daughters of Quintillion in the traditional deep-level rituals of the Nander people, the ancient race from which the father of Quintillion and Eria had sprung. Kael helped the students who had trouble finding their deep-level selves, offering endless patience and encouragement. Puflet worked with the more advanced students, those who had felt the chilling brush of deep-level power. Each tenday, the academy held a tournament in which students of roughly equal level were paired in jousts. When students and instructors had gathered in the stands, Puflet set the gala in motion with a single word:

"Switch."

The ancient arena glittered in the Deep, its walls smooth once again, its size and perspectives distorted by fusion with deep dimensions. On home-level it was circular. Downleveling left it vastly elongated, broken by shadowed turnings from the depths of which strange cries echoed, and dark, putrid streams seeped. Long histories woven into the shapes of holding pens formed dank mazes where ghosts of pahmaks wailed.

The fires of their steeds sent weird shadows leaping as jousters intersected with dark memories from the twists and turns of stone walls. Black seepage smoked when hoof bones splashed through.

A chorus of haunted roars greeted them as they neared the holding pens. The heavy stone portals thumped ominously. They did not enter the pens. A student had been lost in one of them during the academy's first year. Only Puflet sometimes bade a portal rise so that she could search for him yet again, safe from the shadows aboard her monster. She thought the past had eaten the student.

Eyes from the spectator stands followed the contestants. There was no perspective in the Deep, although it took a bit of practice to send your point of view where you wished. Their armor shining, surcoats ablaze with colors and personal symbols, ribbons streaming from their helms, the contestants turned their steeds before the holding pens. Eye sockets flared. Skeletal hooves pawed at the shadow-crawling ground. Then, with a growing thunder, they charged.

Stones beneath the stands shook to the rhythm of the chargers' strides, telling Puflet wonderful things she could barely fathom. "Here lies the essential human story," the hoof beats whispered. "Here ride the heroes of ages past and future, those who have dared draw up from the Deep a gleam of something beautiful and extremely personal."

From the planet's other pole, Katora decried and deplored, predicting cataclysm. She strove in vain to keep her own high-spirited students from venturing north to take part in the jousts.

"We lead evolution here," Puflet told a newser who arrived at her pole to assess the danger. "The riders' spirit and dedication is solidifying a vibrant future from out of the ever-shifting possibilities of the Deep. My jousts draw youth because they resonate with an ancient and noble heritage of human prehistory. They bring structure and safety to mind-duels, which were contests in chaos before my academy.

"Katora claims she has initiated an Age of Illumination. But the future she envisions is limited by her feeble powers of imagination. All citizens would mirror her sensibilities and replicate the bloodlines of the Ninetieth Millennium. In contrast, my future is free and expansive—many minds joined by a single ethos, free citizens each pursuing his or her unique vision! Does mankind want to contract, or do we want to expand?"

It was setting mealtime after the close of another heart-pounding tournament. Puflet, Serpenlino, Oakiza, and Kael dined together in a little cupola that poked above the planet's surface, a sheltered walkway connecting their outpost to the stairway that led back down into the cavern. Kael gestured toward a glowing elliptical structure visible beyond the cupola's clear round wall.

"My father's memorial hall is completed and ready for dedication. Come with me tonight, Puflet, when I do the final walk-through."

She smiled and nodded.

Together they entered a new building. A broad dirt path led between rows of stately amber diamond trees with their black branches outspread and fluttering with yellow leaves. So thick were the leaves that their yellow glow felt like the caress of a myriad invisible hands. Their sweet, nutty fragrance filled the air. They weren't native to Ulona, and couldn't survive its long winter, but the dome enclosing them would provide light and warmth when all outside was cold and dark.

At the crossing of two pathways, Kael turned and faced Puflet. "I feel my father's presence here."

She inclined her head.

"It makes me realize how important such bonds are. Now I have no one. And you have no one. Puflet—" He took her hands in his. "I love you. I think I've always loved you, even when that silly Eadin was dragging me around. You swept into the academy like a fresh breeze, refusing to let anyone change you or douse your fire. You and I, Puflet. That's all it would take to create the bond that makes life what it should be. Marry me!"

She felt tears creeping into her eyes as she gazed into his earnest face. But she pulled her hands from his and took a step back. "I value your friendship, Kael. In a way, I do love you. But not in the way you want. My heart belongs to the young man who reached out to me from the future, to the son of Katora and Dino."

He shook his head. "How can you know—"

"The Second Tenet, remember?"

"I still think there's something wrong, something you're overlooking. I'll be here, Puflet, waiting patiently, when you realize you've been mistaken."

"That won't happen," she said.

A tenthyear later, Oakiza invited her to tour the Pool of Revelation he'd built for Code students who practiced the old religion. Side by side they descended a series of ramps that wound through underground tunnels shaped to suggest the interior of a living being. At the bottom of the last ramp, the pool awaited, warm waters exuding steam that beaded the low arched ceiling and exuded a briny odor.

"When a man and a woman decide to join, they shed their clothing and their old lives and discover one another fully in the pool. It is an ancient ritual more primal, more basic and necessary even than our tournaments. Enter the pool with me, Puflet, and let us pledge our lives to one another! I have waited so long for you, and it has been so hard holding back the tide of passion that longs to sweep you into my arms!"

Puflet gave him a sad smile and took a couple of steps back. "I'm sorry, Oakiza. I care very deeply for you, but I can't join with you. I'm not a Code woman. I'm probably one of Thermeon's grandchildren. I'm sure you can find—"

He lunged and swept her hand into his. "It doesn't matter!"

"But I know that genes are very important to your people, and I don't even know where mine come from." She'd waited in vain for an answer from Dee. Serpenlino kept urging her to wait a while longer, but she sensed that he no longer expected anything to come of it. Thermeon hadn't contacted her either, which she found strange. But perhaps he'd forgotten her. He did have thousands of others in his mind-net, after all.

"I don't care!" Oakiza pulled her toward him. "I can see what you are—beautiful and spirited—and that's all that matters!"

She braced her feet and bared her fangs. "No, Oakiza. I'm very sorry, but I will not join with you. I'm waiting for the son of Katora and Dino to grow up. I've already pledged myself to him."

He let her hand slip away, searching her face with troubled eyes. "But why? That child is the son of an obnoxious mother and a disgusting father! Why do you want to waste your beauty and intelligence on such a creature? It's a sin!"

"It's not!" She stamped her foot, and pathetic little sounds like those of a flopping fish echoed about the steamy chamber. "I saw his future self in a vision. He will be beautiful, and he needs me!"

Oakiza kept searching her eyes. "I think some enemy has attacked your mind with this illusion."

"That's ridiculous! Who would do such a thing?"

"Katora perhaps."

Puflet snorted.

"Someday you will free yourself from this snare, and you will come to me."

"Don't hold your breath." She whirled and stomped back up the ramp.

Four years later, Serpenlino invited her to come out to ride around the racetrack he'd laid out encircling Tadruhemdron. He gave her a whaleskin to wear against the chill of the Ulonan winter, and donned one himself. When they stepped onto the plaza in front of the ancient king's mansion, Puflet found pale gold and silver horses awaiting them.

"The mare is Planetary Secret," he said, indicating the pale gold. "And the stallion is Fused Shadow. They don't need saddles or bridles, we guide them with mind-link."

Puflet smiled. She'd never ridden a horse, but it couldn't be harder than riding the monster, could it? It took her a little while to develop a rapport with the mare, who would toss her head or sidestep or stop short and stamp at anything but the lightest mind-touch, but after a while, both horses moved smoothly. They proceeded along the ancient city's main thoroughfare, hooves clattering over stone, newly emplaced lanterns making their shadows shrink and fall behind as they passed.

The old street stones petered out, but Serpenlino had smoothed a new road leading up and out from the city's cavern and into the wilderness. Then the track stretched before them, bathed in the glow of floating orbs.

"My aunt has been telling me about an ancient imperial tradition," Serpenlino began.

Puflet relaxed, letting the rocking motion of the mare's canter lull her as she prepared to endure another interminable paean to the wisdom of his extremely elderly aunt. "Mating flights still involve a short, ceremonial race, but at one time, every ..."

Puflet let her gaze roam the darkness beyond the track, searching for any sign of the coming dawn, but she saw nothing.

She hadn't been listening to Serpenlino for several minutes when the words "... and when the horse chose someone else, she crystallized" snapped her attention back to him.

She wanted to cry out, "What? Say again?" but how could she admit that she hadn't heard most of the tale? Who was he referring to, anyhow? Sagi?

Before she could think of any politic comment, he went on. "So you can be sure that Hube takes good care of his horse."

"Yes, of course," she murmured.

"Let's race!" No sooner had he spoken than Fused Shadow surged away, spattering dirt behind him, silver tail whipping about like a banner in the wind.

Before Puflet could make up her mind what to do, Planetary Secret flung herself forward with such force that she nearly flew backwards over her hindquarters. She clutched the long mane with desperate fingers as the mare galloped faster and faster and the wind brought tears to her eyes.

She felt the mare's mind. "I love to race. What's wrong with you? Stop wobbling, sit tight, and let me catch him!"

Puflet tried to obey. This was not what she had imagined horseback riding would be like. Just when she thought they couldn't go any faster, the ground dropped away from beneath them, and they plunged downward like a comet.

Puflet's shriek turned into a whoop as she saw more and more planes of reality unfolding about them. They had gone Deep.

Planetary Secret and Fused Shadow raced side by side, elemental horses of molten gold and platinum who splashed through the sparkling waves of a sea of stars beneath spinning rainbow-hued nebulae.

"So this is what you've spent all your time on for the past four years!" Puflet shouted. "How does it work?"

"This is how the ancients built their tracks. Riding on one is like piloting a downleveling ship. There are certain patterns in which levels intersect, but as the track is more stable than space, they can be built in. And the horses do the downleveling."

"But all animals can't downlevel, can they?" Puflet still had very little experience with animals.

"No, of course not. These horses are the equine equivalent of human mindseas. They have horse senses and horse brains, but with mindpowers."

"How strange."

The star sea folded inwards around them, and they were back on the track.

"C'mon!" Serpenlino cried, and both horses put on a fresh surge of speed.

Soon they swept into another deep-level interface, this one a golden bridge leading across fractal canyons of intricate beauty.

"The track is actually more like the ancient transways than modern ships," Serpenlino told her. "Because the intersections mesh you directly with other spacetimes. And they're always different, depending, I suppose, on the changes to the universe every time you come through."

"Amazing," Puflet breathed, her eyes following the vast convolutions of reality about them. "Why don't I sense my monster?"

"I was wondering if you would." Serpenlino had not yet found his charger, so he could not compare his experience to hers. "I think that, somehow, Planetary Secret has taken the monster's place, that you can't ride both at once."

She frowned.

"The last time I spoke with my aunt about it—" This must've been in mind-link, Puflet supposed. Eria had not been at her academy—" she gave the impression that her chargers, Aurochs and Quagga, had once been living creatures, but after their species died out, only their deep-level parts, their spirits, remained. She said that it was possible, since extinct species can be recreated now, that her chargers might be reembodied, but she didn't think just any individual of their species would do. It would have to be a specific individual. Eria isn't sure whether her chargers are the aggregates of the the minds of many of their kind, or the deep-level parts of individuals that had mindpowers during their lives."

Puflet was glad this amazing aunt was unsure about something.

"But she thinks the latter."

"Hmmh!" Puflet snorted.

The next intersection point the track led them through provided a vista of strange conical hills that seemed too mathematically precise to be real, though grass and bushes with brush-like leaves clothed them.

"So you think that my monster is the mind of a once-living dinosaur, and the same for Thermeon's flying reptile."

"I think so," Serpenlino said.

"Then what about Kael's charger? I don't think there's ever been a species of deer that sprouts yellow-leafed trees for antlers."

"I'll wager there has, if you include all the alien worlds and all the alternate universes. But I don't think that's what his charger is. It's clear that his charger is his father."

When Puflet felt a chill in the deep, snakes of lightning raced across her skin.

"And the Horl horses," he said, "obviously, were Horl."

"Then what do you think Thermeon's goddess-star is? She can't be a star. Do you think she's some long-dead woman who could be reembodied if only the right gene specs were found?"

"That's what Thermeon has been trying to do all along. Don't you see? He's hoping to find the woman who embodies her. When he was emperor, women used to flock to him claiming to be his goddess-star, probably thinking the chance to become empress was worth the risk."

Puflet tossed her hair. "The fools! And now he thinks Katora embodies her, but Katora doesn't think so. Do you think if he actually found this woman he'd be satisfied?"

Serpenlino didn't answer until they entered the next intersection point, a labyrinth of shimmering planes that splashed and gurgled and exuded misty rainbows, yet never got them wet.

"Since this goddess-star has promised him eternal dominion as well as everlasting love—things that can only be found in the Deep —I think that maybe she can't be reembodied. She's grown too distant from our level of existence."

They passed through one more intersection point, galloped through ice caverns that rendered hoofbeats into exquisite musical echoes from multitudinous chambers, and then, after a cooling walk, brought the horses into a circular, slate-roofed stable complex that had been erected between the track and the city.

Serpenlino showed her how to brush the sweat from the mare's hide, how to provide her with feed and water in her stall. Then he led Puflet around the complex, introducing her to a dozen other horses of various colors.

"I hope that students who, like myself, have no charger can bond with one of these," Serpenlino said. "We could have races every tenday, staggered between the tournaments."

"Yes." Puflet nodded. "I think that would work."

He turned from the black mare whose forehead he'd been scratching, eyes fierce. "Puflet, I want you to ride beside me in a mating flight. Bond to one of these horses. Bond to me! Banish your monster, and start a new life with me!"

She shook her head and stepped back, but his arms swept out to enfold her. "My blood sings whenever I see you! Stop hiding behind your fears and let yourself go! We can work magic together!"

She wanted to tell him about her pledge to Habel, but his lips were on hers, hot and quivering. Their fangs clashed. Her heart raced. A pulse of lightning swept through her. Thoughts tumbling away, she pressed herself against his strong, tall body.

And then the walls between their minds came down.

He saw the whole scene with Quintillion's head, and flung her away with an anguished roar.

And she saw the equally horrible secret he'd been keeping from her.

21

Puflet climbed black basalt steps that wrapped around and around the inside of the shaft that penetrated the rocky vault above the underground nexus of Tadruhemdron. Dino had carved the shaft for her because she hated the idea of being enclosed. Tadruhemdron was warm and comfortable all year around, and bright enough with glowworm lighting as well as the natural phosphorescence of its caverns, but it wasn't the same for her as actually touching the sky.

The shaft's spiraling steps had been her one surrender to the primitive. She could have let an air cushion lift her through the shaft, but she thought the exercise did her good. She did have an air cushion to keep anyone from falling, but it didn't move.

Leaning into the air cushion, she stared down at the blackness in the center of the long twist of steps below her. It made her think of the monster's question: "Upward or downward?"

"I want to go upward. I thought I was going upward. What is pulling me down?"

She climbed on at a steady pace, her breathing even. She was strong now, and the frequent dips into the Deep, the caress of the monster's fiery forces, kept her vigorous. Yet she harbored an unpleasant suspicion that the monster did not serve her, that it was using her. On a day not long ago, she had suddenly understood that the monster did not want a dinosaur body to be resurrected for it to inhabit. It meant her to embody it. That had been the meaning of its first words to her.

"You must become me."

For some incomprehensible reason of its own, it had fixed on her. It didn't care about her genetic heritage at all.

At the thought of genetic heritage, furious tears spurted from her eyes, as they had every day since that horrible moment when she'd seen the truth in Serpenlino's mind.

She was the daughter of Ix.

The daughter of the person she most hated in all of the world. The daughter of a sadistic bitch who never once had given her a straight answer—except for that last day. She'd told Puflet the truth and Puflet hadn't believed her.

She'd killed her mother.

And Serpenlino's father.

Maybe that was why the monster loved her so. Knew that she could never be close to any human being. The deeds she'd committed on that first day of freedom condemned her.

Serpenlino had heard back from Dee right away, but knowing how Puflet felt about Ix, he'd chosen to shield her from the truth. That had been admirable, she supposed, but of course she would have found out eventually anyhow, so maybe stupid was a better word for it. Thermeon had cornered Valri on the slavers' favorite imperial world, Morsamto, and reamed her mind. Puflet smirked, picturing that. He'd gotten only useless information, though. After he and Dee had compared notes, they'd decided that Ix must have lied to Valri about the fate of the incubator she'd stolen, because it hadn't been Puflet's.

Ix must have concocted Puflet in her lab, using her own genes, and Thermeon's. So Puflet was Thermeon's daughter, after all. But when Thermeon learned who her mother was, his taste for playing the role of father had evaporated. He hated Horl's descendants as intensely as they hated him.

Interactions between Puflet and Serpenlino had been cold and brittle as a sheet of ice since that day of dual revelation. He worked with his students on the track, and she avoided the track. Oakiza still lusted after her, but she wanted a relationship that went beyond what instinct provided. Kael still mooned after her too, but he would never understand her.

She was utterly alone. With her monster.

But no! She'd forgotten Habel. Only one more tenthyear remained before his majority. Smiling, she continued upward. It was hard to grasp that her long, lonely vigil was approaching its end, for this loveless life had become so much part of her. But she would have love. Oh, what love she would have!

She reached the top of the steps, then crossed on the enclosed walkway to the little cupola perched above the Ulonan surface. All was black around her. There might be ferns, cycads, sparkling streams and pools out there, but she saw nothing. Even the light in Quinofil's memorial hall was doused at this hour, and the cupola's walls kept out scents, sounds, the wind. It was somewhere near this spot that she had transmitted the view to her skylight when she had first entered Katora's academy. Then, as the sun had risen over the south pole, it had set in this place. Darkness had reigned here since then, through all the time Habel had been growing up, enjoying the sun and warmth on his mother's side of the planet.

Soon everything would change. Sunrise would come in another four imperial years, and she and Habel would watch it together. She grinned in anticipation.

Once again she let her head fall back and shut her eyes to contemplate the teachings of Patternistics. All possible combinations of patterns, everything that had been and everything that would be, existed already in the center, available for her mind's perusal. She could not create the pattern of her life or will it into being. She could only choose it from among the uncountable others and focus her awareness upon it. But that was everything.

She focused on the day of Habel's coming-of-age. She would downlevel the academies and meet him in the free-form hall. She would offer him her hand, pull him onto the back of the monster, and they would ride together into an endless dawning of love.

A smile flickered across her face. Yes, that was how it would be.

Her mind delved deeper into the patterns. It was the little details that made things real. Thoughts were generalities, but actual events always had a fine-grained structure. She became one with the patterns.

She was aware of sunlight on cycads, the chattering of a small rapids, the smell of ferns. A mind other than her own contemplated the scene.

Habel? she thought.

His mind-voice laughed. "Puflet?"

You should use a signal when you mind-link someone, she chided.

Again a laugh. "I would have, if I'd linked you. But this is your mind-link."

Oh! Sorry. This is my signal. She envisioned herself blowing on his cheek and thrilled at the double sensation—his and hers—that spread through her awareness like sets of rings rippling through a pool. His mind tasted so fresh and vibrant. What potential he had —the powers of Thermeon, but without the primitive mind-set. Only twenty years old, he must see everything as new and wonderful. So many possibilities to explore, and she would be at his side.

You will meet me in the free-form hall on the night of your majority?

"That may pose some problems," he thought. "The ball isn't being held at the academy. My parents are erecting an outdoor pavilion. My mother's really scared that you might downlevel the academy and wipe out all of our guests."

She giggled.

"Your mind-voice sounds the way she always described you," he thought. "Beautiful, powerful, and wicked."

That's how she describes me?

"She had a vision of you killing me."

No! she protested. *I love you, Habel. I love you more than anything in the universe.*

"I'd rather be killed with love." The focus of his mind shifted abruptly, and she felt something powerful and ugly welling up.

You're thinking about what your father did to you, aren't you?

"I hate him, Puflet! I hate him more than anything. But everyone ignores the crack he put in my soul. Everyone acts like I'm perfect, like I only have the happy, loving feelings they want me to have. I think maybe you're the only person in the universe who cares to understand the real me."

And you're the only one who can understand me. Because I

have a curse like yours. But together we can overcome the curse. We can tame the power it gives us. Instead of destructive power; with love, it can become creative power. You can I can build beautiful things!

"Then I will find a way to meet you in the free-form hall," he promised. "I think I have an idea. I'll tell my mother that I've envisioned a way to remove your gem from the Academy. You can't believe you obsessed she is with that thing."

Puflet heard herself tittering like a mischievous schoolgirl.

"She's consulted with my Aunt Quixa and Aunt Dee, with Orgmorgan, even with people like Hube and her half-sister Cevana, who don't have mindpowers. Hube told her that time would take care of it, and Cevana told her she needed to make a setting for the gem, but she couldn't tell her how."

Again her laughter rippled out.

"My mother thinks you are the most evil being in the universe."

Suddenly the conversation was heading in directions Puflet didn't want. *Just meet me in the free-form hall.*

"It's a promise."

She puffed her breath on his cheek twice to let him know she was going. Then, finding her way back to her body—it was a bit of a struggle—she gave herself a shake to restore her ordinary, home-level perceptions.

The light of the south pole gone, the darkness of the north fell over her like a thunderclap. But soon things would be reversed, she reminded herself.

Then she lay back again to think about the mind-link she had initiated. She had mastered the Third Tenet. She was a mindsea. She had also linked with someone she had never met—something even Thermeon couldn't do, or he wouldn't have had to chase Valri all around the galaxy. The surge of blood through her veins came with a whisper of power and the promise of marvels to come: She and Habel together, sweeping through the galaxy, upward, upward, the inferno of their love blasting away the slavers and inbred aristocrats who had tried to curb their freedom.

22

"Switch."

The hallways of the Academy of Tadruhemdron glowed in the light of deep-level force, dazzling with added dimensions and intensified realities. Puflet mounted her burning charger and turned into a hallway that led in a direction that didn't exist on home-level. A brief, thunderous romp brought her to the black-and-white checkered hall of Katora's academy on the other pole of the planet.

As he'd promised, Habel awaited her, alone in the vast, mystical hall. His beauty sped her heart—his white hair aglow like Thermeon's and Dino's and eyes gray as thunder. As she had dreamed, she extended her hand to clasp his, and guided him onto the back of her charger, behind her. When his arms encircled her waist, she urged the monster with a cry, and they rumbled back through the connecting hallway to Tadruhemdron.

"Switchback."

As much as she would miss the splendors of the Deep, it would be more private on home level. Even if the celebrants at Katora's ball found out Habel was gone and where to, they couldn't easily or quickly follow.

They stood in her office, formerly the throne room of the kings of Ulona, a stark rectangular chamber clad in dark stone. A panel of pahmak carvings at about eye-level went all around the room, the perimeter of which was cut into a number of shallow alcoves. There was no furniture except for the black velvet nook on the dais from which Puflet could peer to intimidate the uninitiated in much the same style as Ix or Katora.

Tonight, she wanted only to examine and admire her guest. Stepping back an arm's length from him, she brightened the lighting and looked him up and down.

Habel matched Thermeon in height, but his shoulders were broader, and his complexion was a rich brown. His hair was cut short in front, standing up in a thick brush—a bit like Dino's style, but he kept one long lock that curled between his shoulder blades. His face resembled his father's—handsome and square-jawed, but without those demonic red eyes. He had Katora's cool, intelligent eyes. Strangely enough, something in those eyes reminded her of Serpenlino. Even his body did, though Serpenlino might have been a bit taller. Habel wore a gray-blue tunic and slacks with fine iridescent deco, quiet and dignified as befit a young man who had just reached the age of responsible citizenship.

As she stepped around him he folded his arms on his chest and studied her in turn, his face slipping into a crooked half-smile, distressingly like his father's.

"You'll have to excuse me if I get right to the point," she said. "I've been waiting for twenty years—chaste as a babe—for you to grow up so I can have you."

His laugh rang from the stone ceiling. "You'll have to excuse me for not waiting for you."

"That's all right. I wouldn't want a man who didn't know what to do."

She went to him and entwined her arms around his neck, pulling his head down so she could kiss his lips. He responded with authority, and she tasted fire dragons from the ball.

"Yes!" Taking him by the hand, she led him onto the dais and across it to an alcove in the back wall. Granite steps took them up onto the roof of the circular building.

It was night in Tadruhemdron. Puflet had the city's lighting mimic a day-night cycle of thirty imperial hours, the official Lalian day. Ancient buildings and pahmak pens glinted in the shadows, phosphorescent patches on the roof of the enormous artificial cavern taking the place of stars.

"We're standing on the roof of what once was the king of

Ulona's palace," Puflet said.

His teeth winked in that crooked grin. "I know. My parents discovered this place. I had many virtual tours when I was a kid."

"Oh."

He wrinkled his nose. "It doesn't smell quite as bad as those tours, though. I guess you've cleaned it up some."

"I try." Locking her fingers around his wrist, she led him to her sleeping nook, a circle within a circle, which she had placed in the center of the roof. The cushioned rim parted to welcome them.

In a moment they were free of their clothes, sharing the warmth of their bodies as they lay beneath the pink and green shimmer of false stars. Pressing her face against his chest, she inhaled his wholesome scent. Tears slid from her eyes, splattering onto his skin. He wrapped his arms around her and softly kissed her moist cheeks and eyelids.

She sought his lips, and rolling him over beneath her, kissed them in a frenzy, her tears pouring faster. "You're so beautiful! So warm! I can't believe we're together at last! You mean everything to me—the truth, the hidden meanings, the way upward!" Images she wanted to express welled into her mind faster than she could find words to describe them.

He chuckled between her kisses.

"My monster," she gasped. "When I get aroused, it will rise."

Again he chuckled. "I've heard plenty about your monster from my mother. But I have a monster too, Puflet, and none of them will admit it. My father's tainted. My mother denies it, but he's evil, and he gave his evil to me. I'm wounded and infected deep in my soul, but they won't ever let that wound see the light of day. It just festers, festers."

"Love will tame the monster," she panted between kisses. "It has to be real love, the kind that blooms when two people really look at each other and see each other. Not the sort of love that substitutes what you want to see for what's really there. Look at me, Habel."

She lifted herself on elbows to stare down on him, and he gazed up into her eyes. A flash of deep-energy flew between them, and they both started from the shock of it. Then he seized her and rolled her beneath him and thrust himself deep into her. She arched her back, moaning.

The monster was there, pouring from her throat in a deep, hollow voice. "Love me! Love me! Love me, or blip you!"

Once again, she, the monster, was on the sands soon to be the Fissure, reaching out for Thermeon's power and screaming, "Love me, or I'll destroy everything!"

She was unloved, and Quintillion saw his mistake and tried to fold himself back in, but it was too late and the fault in his soul split wide open.

Habel thrust deeper. She arched and screamed, "Yes! Yes! Just a little farther!" If he could just reach the place where the troubles all had began, his molten passion would fuse and heal the fault line, and their ascent would begin.

The rhythm of his thrusts became the rhythm of hoofbeats. A fiery charger pounded closer and closer, the rider's lance couched to penetrate her soul.

"Impact!" she screamed.

She came, shuddering, in his arms, as he spurted deep inside her.

They drifted for a long time afterward. Lights glimmering around them might have been the cavern's phosphorescence, or something behind her eyes, or upwellings from the Deep. Finally Habel heaved a long sigh and rolled himself off. He flopped beside her, sending ripples through the gelatinous core of the nook.

"I'll have to get back. Before they get worried. But I don't think I can move."

She laid her head on his chest, soaking in the comforting thud of his heart. "When will we meet again? There's so much we have to talk about, so much we have to do."

She lifted her head and scooted forward to look into his eyes. "Marry me, Habel! I don't want to ever be parted from you again!"

He swallowed. "My mother will think I've been warped."

The words were like a slap in the face. She blinked. "What do you care what she thinks? As of today you're your own man. You can do what you like."

"I can't just shed my life, Puflet. What would I do, live in this pile with your acolytes, until we all kill each other in mind-duels?" He slid from beneath her and stepped onto the roof.

Dazed, she scooted after him and swung her legs down through the gap in the parting rim of the nook. "Is that what you think this is about? I've just been passing the time here, waiting for you to grow up. I've only been thinking of you, Habel. I felt your call when you were first born. The day after your father ... did it to you."

His head jerked around. "I know. I felt you too. I've wondered what you were like since I was first able to think." He gave his head a shake. "Reality wasn't what I expected." He drew on his clothes and smoothed the front of the tunic. "I thought you would want me to join you indulging in Nander blood rituals."

She rose. "I don't know anything about Nander rituals. Your mother lied about me, Habel. She isn't interested in the truth. She just tries to fit things into her theory of life. The theory that she's the guiding light and I'm the evil shadow creature. She doesn't know about me. I'm a free person! That's the first thing you have to understand about me. I won't be bound by anyone's theories, or by Quintillion's accursed monster, either. I've always had the choice to use its power for creation or destruction, and I choose to be creative." She stepped closer and laid her hand on his shoulder. "But I need your help. Please don't desert me."

He gave her his crooked grin. "I'll come back. Or maybe we could meet somewhere else. I find this place a bit depressing. It's probably because of the scary stories my father always told me about it—the minds of the dead kings plotting revenge, you know."

She humphed. "No dead kings have bothered me."

He kissed her eyelids and the tip of her nose. "I still prefer my grove."

"The place I mind-linked you?"

"Yes."

"I'd love to meet you there. But I'm sure your mother will harass me if she catches me in Alonaton." She queried her link to see if there were any legal measures Katora could bring against someone she deemed to be "tainted."

There still was a death penalty for those who engaged in Nander blood rituals. Puflet frowned.

Habel stroked her brow with a fingertip. "Don't worry about it. I don't plan to stay on this forsaken planet much longer. Do you think I like having my mother fluttering around me all the time? Or my father? Or Eadin?"

She started. "She's still a student at your mother's academy?"

"No, she's an instructor. A very annoying one."

Puflet suddenly smelled ylang-ylang, and realized that he was mind-linking her. They laughed together.

"I don't plan to stay here either," she told him. "I've been wrestling with a decision, ever since...." She sighed. The knowledge of her parentage had destroyed whatever hope she'd once had for her academy. "I think it may be time to turn over this academy to my successors." The three men could do fine without her.

She looked up at Habel. "You and I could settle anywhere in the empire. Maybe on Medne, where they have those natural deep-level upwellings. There's so much we could build with the power I got from Quintillion, so much potential we could tap once the monster is tamed."

His gray eyes sharpening, he swung toward her and took her hands in his. "That sounds like a real plan, Puflet. What kinds of building do you envision?"

"Deep-level architecture with home-level components. I think, with your help, I could finally uncover the instructions the monster whispered to me when I fashioned the gem. Plans for a new kind of living space, for a new kind of people, free from the cruel ways of the past. If we knew those details, then we could make other gems with the same or slightly different purposes. You and I could return in mind-link to the moment when the gem appeared to my mind's eye and find those instructions, I'm sure of it!"

"Yes," he whispered, squeezing her hands. "That's what we'll do. Come to me at the grove. I'll mind-link you when I'm free from encumbrances." He winked.

She laughed, giddy, and drew him closer for another flurry of kisses. She needed to fortify herself for their separation. Finally she allowed him to disengage himself.

"My mind-link signal will be this:" He sang a few notes in his vibrant young baritone. "And now, my beautiful, powerful, and wicked one, you must return me to my captors."

"But only for a short while."

23

Puflet hadn't come down from the palace roof since she'd taken Habel back to the south pole. She lolled in her nook, watching the light of artificial dawning submerge the night's phosphorescent stars in a sea of pink-orange light. A bioid shaped like a small, winged pahmak brought her breakfast on a chalcedony tray. A newly-sprouted hot tub waited a few steps away, along with shower and relief booths, should she require them. Kael, Oakiza, and Serpenlino daily climbed to the roof to try to talk her into resuming her duties, but they were the past. She hardly heard their voices.

The exertion of her mindsize had become as natural to Puflet as using a glowworm link. She prepared herself by envisioning the center, the superposition of all possibilities and points of view, then narrowing her focus to the awareness of the person she wished to contact. It pleased her to think that she could never again —well, not easily—be isolated from human society. Like the ancient mindseas, she could instantly reach out to anyone she knew.

She had become familiar with the different flavors of minds— Kael's was crisp and clean as his yellow-leafed trees, Oakiza's the interplay of rock and brine, Serpenlino's the memory of distant grasslands. She knew from the first taste whether she liked someone, and whether they'd been lying to her.

Having learned how mind-linking worked, she was more

amazed than ever that Quintillion could have known someone just by having them touch his hair in the darkness, but her own powers were satisfying enough.

Less satisfying were other thoughts and feelings that swarmed through her head. Since the night with Habel, the monster never fully submerged. Its roar and rumble remained the background to all of her thoughts.

"Impact! Impact!" it groaned.

She was almost afraid to exert her mindsize, sometimes, especially if she would touch the mind of anyone she felt the least dislike for. The monster would surge into focus, commanding her to direct his fury through her mind.

She had almost began to feel that Katora made sense, calling it a "taint." If the monster was not her own deep-level self, but some long-dead dinosaur mindsea trying to inhabit her body and quench her own mind, she had to fight it.

She had to defeat it, take its power and expel its bitter-flavored personality. The battle had begun already, without her realizing. Its craving for "impact" rose with every beat of her heart, never giving her a chance to rest. It was maddening, wearing, like a headache that wouldn't go away.

"You told me I had a choice!" she argued at the monster. "Upward or downward. I chose to go upward. Why are you dragging me down?"

You have made your choice! Magma leaped skyward somewhere, somewhen, spelling doom for countless small lives.

Puflet rolled into a ball, clutching her ears. What was happening, what choice had she made?

Then she understood—Habel. Their lovemaking had opened a gateway in her mind, and she couldn't close it again. It was like the moment when Quintillion had reached out for Thermeon, asking for his love. She'd thought that Habel had said yes, because they'd touched so deeply. But he really hadn't made a commitment.

She forced herself to uncurl and lie on her back, facing up into the fake morning sky that now glowed in hazy blueness from the cavern roof. She shut her eyes, breathed deeply, and extended her mind to Habel.

He started at her touch, other voices spilling a cascade of words over their joined awareness. Through his eyes she glimpsed golden sandstone planes and burbling fountains of Katora's private habitat. Katora and Dino were there, Eadin as well.

"Shush," Habel thought. "Not now, my love."

Puflet savored his scent. Then she wanted to cry out in despair. On first impression he had seemed so wholesome and abrim with vitality. She had been mistaken. A slight off odor came from somewhere. He was like a newly-killed animal, still fresh and edible, though the decay had begun and would eventually consume all of his beauty. Dino had done this, had taken a perfect baby boy and killed his joy in life.

Her soul wept. *I'm sorry if I've interrupted, but you can't keep ignoring your wound. It must be healed, or the rest of your life will be for naught.*

"I know," he thought. "That's why I called out to you in the first place."

Stop delaying. We have to meet and make plans. Tell me when and where.

"I don't know if I'll have time. They've decided to send me off to pilot school."

Fear roared like flames around her. *Don't leave without seeing me! Commit yourself to our plans! I have an idea—why don't we just get married? Please, Habel. Trust my love!*

"I do. But not here. Meet me on Bri."

Before she could think of a response, Katora's search beam eyes swung toward her. "Habel? What's wrong?"

On Bri, she thought, withdrawing her mind.

She lay shuddering on her bed, hating the artificial sky above her. Why was she always closed in? Maybe going to Bri was a good idea. They'd be away from Katora, Dino, and Eadin. She refreshed her knowledge of the planet.

It was a small world, location for the Pilot Training School since the Decadent Epoch. Quintillion had built an amusement park there called "Take Care" which featured a Mini Milky Way.

When she told her three assistants that she was going away, that they would have to run the academy without her, they came up to the roof to argue.

"You're the heart and soul of this academy!" Kael whined.

"Puh!" she said.

"Your love for this vile man is a sin," muttered Oakiza.

"And you're blinded by jealousy."

"My colleagues are right," Serpenlino said.

She stomped her bare feet on the weathered granite of the roof. "Why must you all conspire to keep me from the man I love?"

"We're only trying to help," said Kael.

Oakiza nodded. "We don't want you to ruin your life."

"My life is already ruined!" She rose with a sigh and had the flying pahmak bioid bring them a snack—homegrown honey cakes and pomegranate cider—it was her mid mealtime, anyway. Goblets in hand, they stood side by side at the rooftop balustrade and looked down on the city. Townsfolk, students in long robes, and tourists in their garish offworld styles thronged streets radiating outward from the central plaza where the palace stood. A few sinuous necks and tails could be seen in the distance where tamed pahmaks provided rides for the tourists.

Puflet had long since tired of such sights. Pahmaks were self-evolved beings, but to tourists they were no different than bioids. The artificial sky, though it provided light, seemed to make a mockery of everything beneath it.

Serpenlino laid a hand on her shoulder. "I know I haven't handled what I saw in your mind very well, but I want to make it up to you now."

"I love Habel," she said.

He frowned.

"And he loves me. He called out to me when he was a little child. There is a wound in his soul that only I can heal. And only he can help me to tame the monster. I will only be able to turn its hunger for destruction into a creative force when I know love."

"That is true," Serpenlino said. "But you can't love Habel. You're too closely related."

His words stunned her. "Too closely related! That's ... that's a primitive notion. Bah!"

"You're his aunt. You have to look for someone else."

Without warning, she found herself bawling like a baby, her tears splotching the granite balustrade with its carved pahmak-neck posts. The three men pushed and shoved as they all tried to hug her at the same time.

"We love you!" Kael cried.

"Choose one of us," begged Oakiza. "Even if it's not me."

"I have forgiven you for my father," Serpenlino said.

"But Habel called out to me, reached to my mind for help! How could that happen if we weren't meant to be together?"

"I don't know," said Kael. "It's one of those deep-level things beyond comprehension."

"But we see what it's doing to you," said Oakiza.

"It isn't love," Serpenlino agreed. "Love doesn't destroy."

She straightened with a gasp. "What do you sense from me? Tell me! Do you smell something decaying?"

The three fell back.

"No, nothing like that," Kael assured her. "But if you were a tree, you'd be dropping all your leaves."

"You're staring into yourself," Oakiza said. "And you don't seem able to see what's around you any more."

"Yes," Serpenlino agreed. "This obsession—that's the right word for it—is twisting you tighter and tighter! You're not the bold, free woman we knew in Alonaton. You must fight it and free yourself!"

"There's something really wrong with me, isn't there?"

The three men nodded, the three pairs of eyes intense with concern.

"But why? He called to me for help, and I'm trying to help. Why is everything so wrong?"

"I don't know," Kael repeated. "But I don't think we need to know. You don't need to understand how a poison works before you spit it out!"

"Real love does not cause the unhappiness we see in you," Oakiza said. "This is something evil disguising itself as love."

She stared at him, wondering what he would know about real love. All he knew about were the formulas set down in the Book of the Code.

"You can find real love, Puflet." Serpenlino laid a hand over his heart. "Don't settle for anything less."

"I promised Habel that I would meet him in Bri." She hung her head. "I asked him to marry me."

"You can't!" the three cried as one.

"It's the only solution," she said. "Genetic Algorithms doesn't consider our kinship too close."

The men were silent for a moment. Then Serpenlino asked, "He's going to the pilot school?"

"Yes."

"That is good for him," Oakiza said. "Getting away from his parents could solve some of his problems. But those problems aren't you responsibility."

"But I promised to meet him on Bri. I can't break my word."

"If you must go, let one of us go with you," Kael pleaded. "I'm the most expendable one here."

"No. I go alone."

"Then let me contact one of my pilot relatives and ask them to take you there," said Serpenlino. "Orgmorgan and Eria have pentascopers. They can get you there way ahead of any commercial flight."

She stared at him, flaring her nostrils. What was he expecting to gain from this? Did he think his all-wise aunt could talk her out of her plan? But Puflet wasn't afraid to face the maven. She threw back her head and laughed.

Two tenthyears later, Eria shuttled down from her ship, the *Serious*, and toured the academy with her nephew before meeting Puflet on the rooftop. On this occasion she wore a pale green whaleskin, her hair falling in a rusty cascade around the big gold rings on her shoulders. She fished something small out of the whaleskin carryall on her belt and held it out to Puflet. "I think you could use this. It used to be my grandmother's."

Puflet took the object and examined it. It was a ring of some silvery material. It bore no gem, but a dinosaur skull in profile, sculpted from the same silvery material. The nose horn pointed forward while six spikes on the skull's crest angled back. Puflet clutched the ring and glared at Eria. "It's my monster! Your grandmother, did she have the monster before your father?"

"It was a part of her that she neither questioned nor fought."

Puflet gripped the ring. "I suppose that could be good or bad. But Katora never mentions your grandmother. She calls your father the source of the taint."

Eria made a dismissive sound. "Katora has seen a single scene in a tale from time's beginning."

"But you know the whole tale?"

"No."

"Hmm." Puflet uncurled her fingers and looked at the ring. She slipped it onto the little finger of her left hand. It fit perfectly. "It's animated, isn't it? Force-worms?"

"It comes from the time of Empress Besi. Not even Horl understood all about their science."

Puflet frowned. She thought she recalled Katora mentioning Empress Besi as someone who had inspired her to bring forth an age of illumination.

"Quintillion was not troubled during his early years," Eria said. "It was only at the end of Thermeon's reign, when Wamatu died and the farfling towers Thermeon had powered with his soul-gem tumbled down, that the darkness entered my brother."

"You mean it's not inherited? I suspected as much." Puflet tried to imagine Quintillion without his gloom. Would he have been like Kaanu, or Serpenlino?

She met Eria's blue eyes. "Do you understand my gem? When it first appeared, it seemed to me that it had always been there, and of course it had, if I remember my Second Tenet." She sank into mumbling, half to herself, as she studied the ring again. "But were there other things, other details, I missed in that instant of insight, that someone else could catch? Do you think you could—" The flow of words cut off. The empty eye socket of the tiny skull had been bothering her. Suddenly she knew why. She raced down the spiraling steps to the throne room.

Puflet sighed as she stepped into the shadowed space at the bottom, remembering how she'd made light fill the chamber when Habel had come. Now she needed only enough glow to catch the tiny glint in the wall behind her throne-like nook.

"Switch."

Downleveled, the pahmak carvings on the walls pranced and roared, and the monster, their king, thundered in answer.

"Insight!" Puflet cried.

Fire gouted from the monster's eye, slurried about her in warm, red-orange waves, carrying her upward through the cavern roof and through the roof of clouds toward the stars. When she upleveled again, her jewel glinted from the eye of the monster on the ring. There would be no more tilting from the backs of skeletal steeds in the mindsea academies of Ulona. Katora's fears could be laid to rest.

Kael, Oakiza, and Serpenlino stood on the dais beside the nook as Puflet made her farewell address to the students. She felt like one of the ancient empresses with a triumvirate of faithful majors beside her. But no longer would she be Mistress of the North Pole. Sorrow swept through her as she thought back on the past twenty years. She had endured the dark of the pole's winter waiting for the light to come, but she would not be there to see the dawn. She had tried to build a common perspective in the Deep, tried to share her love of courage and daring, but that convention, the tournament of the Deep, would fade without her gem to provide its backdrop. Perhaps Serpenlino's racetrack would carry on some of the tradition. And perhaps, once she tamed the monster, she could return, to reopen deep-level lists. But how would she tame him? With whom could she find love, now that her faith in the vision of Habel had been shattered?

She didn't know, could only cling to vague hopes that something would come to her.

Eria took her up through Ulona's clouds in her shuttle, docking in the belly of her magnificent pentascoping ship, the *Serious*, without the need to set foot in spaceport. There was a two-second trip through Deep Five, which ate up about twenty imperial days. Puflet had a lightning-quick glimpse of Eria in her deep-level guise, with sapphire eyes and fiery hair, and the ship was not a ship, but a living steed. Her own monster bellowed and shook with fury.

"If the ship is Eria's monster, it's been tamed," she thought. "But how did she manage it?"

"You must tame yourself," Eria told her.

Serious slid into its assigned berth at Bri spaceport, and they descended in the ship's shuttle, once again avoiding spaceport itself. Puflet gazed out from the shuttle dome to see a mottled sphere sheathed in a dull yellow atmosphere that met the blackness of space with a line of green.

"It's an ugly world."

"It's one of the sulfur worlds," Eria said, "covered with swamps and fissures that vent noxious gases. The inhabited spots are weather-engineered, but no one much cares about the rest. The Pilot Training School is the only real draw to the planet, and that keeps other people away, for the most part. No one wants to live near untested pilots trying to downlevel their ships for the first time. Invariably, some of them nip the planet with their fusion fields."

She sniffed. "It's still ugly,"

"Maybe it's just different. Glowworms can protect you if you wish to go out and explore. You'll have plenty of time. Habel will be en route for a year, unless Katora can wrestle Orgmorgan into taking him on *Counting on Kindness*."

"Hmm." Puflet hadn't really thought that part through.

The planet's surface expanded beneath the shuttle, swirls of red and yellow mingling with the black. It wasn't until they were almost down that she saw patches of green and the shining sinuous blue of a river. Then the shuttle port's vast black plain filled the view, rows of parked shuttles shining in waves as they reflected the sun. Eria contacted the shuttle port system, and set down on a numbered square.

The thrum of the engines ceased, and they stepped down the ramp to the planet's still surface. Puflet felt light and springy; Bri's gravity was weaker than Ulona's. She sniffed the air. It seemed pleasant, even fresh. She hadn't realized how accustomed she'd grown to the moss and mildew of Ulona. The sky directly overhead looked blue, though it yellowed around the horizon, and a few amber clouds scudded by.

They stepped onto one of the walkways that divided the parking squares like shining rivers, and were whisked across the lot. Rows of shuttles of various sizes and shapes swept past. Finally a building resembling a white mushroom cap grew ahead.

"We can ride the walkways to our hotel," Eria said, her hair rippling in the walkway wind. "I've reserved some suites for us at Take Care. It's one of Quintillion's finest works."

Puflet dipped her head to show that she'd heard, though she had mixed feeling about viewing Quintillion's achievement. Her guilt about his death already drained her like an open sore.

The walkway slowed and curled, feeding into a broader walkway that led toward the building's portals. Golden letters spelling "Welcome to Bri" flashed in the sun.

Imperial guards in golden armor and red surcoats bearing the sun insignia of Emperor Gawoi stood at the portals. Puflet studied them as the walkway flowed toward the opening portals. She'd never seen any of the empire's armed force before, though they must have been present when she'd been taken off Kicce's ship. Tadruhemdron shuttle port was too small and underused to merit their attention, but Bri, though sparsely settled, claimed an important imperial resource in the pilot school. The guards were tall men, taller than Thermeon, and their nodding red plumes added to the impressive height.

The walkway stopped before she and Eria reached the portals, and the guards stepped onto it in front of them. A voice blared from a golden face plate.

"Puflet Wuner Doom, you are under arrest for the practice of Nander blood rituals."

24

Puflet was once again a prisoner. She paced around the self-nook in the center of the small gray cell, letting hatred consume her.

What else was there to do? She was allowed a system node that she couldn't send out on, and her body had been scoured for glowworms (though her link had already been slipped in the Deep, and they didn't find anything). At least they let her keep her ring. The furnishings in the cell were inanimate, and the self-nook had to serve as bed and bath as well as lounger. The only customization she was allowed were flat and inanimate wall decorations. Eria had flown off after blithely telling her not to worry; someone in her family would send a lawyer. Puflet had tried mind-linking with her, just to see what it would be like linking with someone in Deep Five, and this was how it was: she received a continuous stream of blinding, deafening, and suffocating sensation while Eria—if that stuff really was Eria—seemed not to notice her at all.

So around and around she paced, brooding, grinding her fangs, and beating her small fists on the rim of the nook.

The status of her case was displayed on one narrow wall of the rectangular cell.

"Charge: Practice of Nander blood rituals.

"Specifics: Accused is said to have arranged battles to the death at the Mindsea Academy of Tadruhemdron.

"Jurisdiction: Galactic crime. Trial to take place on Lal."

A few days later the bottom line changed to "Trial to take place on Ulona."

A few days after that, a new line appeared at the bottom. "Edict 101939.057.16.49: Pilots Guild will not transport subjects with mindpowers."

Still another line appeared a few days after that. "Remedy for Edict 101939.057.16.49: Subject can be transported in freezing chest."

Two more days passed, and yet another line appeared. "Inter-level freezing chest unavailable."

The next day Puflet awoke to find the fourth through sixth lines gone, while the third line read, "Jurisdiction: Trial to take place on Bri."

After that, nothing changed for many days. She paced and gnawed on her bitterness. "What did I ever do to her?" she declaimed to the walls. "I even took my blipping gem away! Why is my very existence such a threat to her?"

She paced in silence for a while, trying to answer her own question. What did Katora fear most? It wasn't really those black seeds in the desert, as much as they obviously had disgusted her.

"She fears that her son won't be the greatest mindsea in the galaxy," Puflet decided. "She's afraid that my mindsize is greater. Oh, what a selfish, hypocritical old hag she is!" She laughed wildly, whispery cascades of echoes goading her to near-hysteria, until the sounds finally choked off, and she could straighten and wipe the tears from her eyes.

She resumed pacing. Her own thoughts sickened her. They did nothing but go around and around, just like her feet. They were starting to fester. She had to break free somehow.

Maybe there was someone she could mind-link. She slid into the nook, shut her eyes, and went through the list again. Kael, Oakiza, and Serpenlino would all have different variations of "I told you so." Thermeon hated her. Dino would be playing with his giant clam. She'd wondered, when she used to contact him a lot, during the building of her academy, how she always happened to catch him at the bottom of the lake, until she figured out that he was projecting his fantasy at her.

Then there was Habel. She shivered. Too dangerous. Anyhow, he was probably also in transit by now.

She curled her fingers around the sides of the nook. She had to think of something to do. Ix's lab had had glowworms, but this place was utterly barren. Maybe it was time to complete her neglected historical studies ... and to work on the mastery of her monster and the solution to its upward/downward question.

Turning on the historical memories flooded the space around her with sights, sounds, scents and sensations that transported her, briefly, beyond the walls of her cell. The empire's earliest periods were mythical, so she skimmed through them, settling down to study Besi's era forty thousand years ago. As she reclined in the nook, soaking in memories recorded during the reign of the empress Katora claimed to emulate, Puflet found herself stroking the silvery spikes of the dinosaur skull on her ring.

The ancient empress spoke of the dream she had: love and beauty would triumph over hatred and evil. She would accomplish this goal through galaxy-wide examinations that promoted the finest minds of the empire to positions of power.

Puflet was not impressed by this idea. It felt too restrictive—a cage of rules and measures. The free individuals who had found ways different from whatever Besi could code into an exam were left out. The exams had failed, anyhow; undermined by cheaters of various sorts; though, for a time, art and science had flourished.

Letting the silence and darkness of her cell return, Puflet mulled over similarities between the ancient empress and Katora. They both practiced an enveloping kind of love. They wanted to guide and protect, but they also controlled and stifled. To Puflet, love had to be a bond between two equals, two spirited horses racing side by side, urging each other on. One person carrying or dragging the other was not love. And if you were a leader—an empress or a headmistress—love for your people meant giving them their freedom, even if they were going to do stupid things.

But how did this relate to Puflet's problem with Habel and the monster? Where had she gone wrong? He had called out to her; she had responded. She had waited until he had reached his majority, because only then could they meet as equals. Had the monster wanted her to somehow whisk him away from his parents when he was still a babe? She snorted. Katora would have had the entire galaxy's armed forces on her trail.

Then, should she have gone to Katora immediately and told her what Dino had done? Another snort. As if Katora would have believed a word of it.

Besides, Habel had appeared to her as an adult in that first mind-link. Surely that meant he expected to meet her as an adult.

So why did the monster roil and rumble so within her, giving her a sense of perpetual near nausea? Why did it roar that she'd made her choice, the downward choice? As she laid back her head and shut her eyes to think, she envisioned the wound within Habel, his darkness and emptiness, flowing into her monster, burning like acid. She had wanted her touch to heal Habel. Instead, his touch had wounded her.

She had wanted her love to heal, but suddenly she realized that she wasn't strong enough. She had no love to give. She didn't know what love was. She had failed to form the human bonds she needed.

She sighed. It was hopeless. She had murdered her mother and estranged her father. She couldn't respond to the men who pursued her. The academy students had been closer to Oakiza or Serpenlino than to her. She had wanted to reach out to her fellow ex-slaves, but Katora had come between them. She was an island mind, easy prey for Thermeon's "Monstronon."

Another realization swept in. That was why Thermeon had failed to heal Quintillion. He didn't know what love was, either. He thought he'd offered his friendship, but anyone looking at him could see that his giant ego recognized no equals. Inflated and ferocious on the outside, on the inside he remained the abandoned babe crying for his "goddess-star" to make everything right.

Quintillion had reached out to the wrong person. That had been his tragedy.

Puflet smiled grimly. So, she had solved a mystery of the ages. Little good it did her.

She was still plunged into gloom when system informed her that her lawyer had arrived. A firefly guided her into a small cubical chamber where a tall man with gray eyes and glowing white hair awaited her. He wore a quiet gray suit with conservative lines like the one Hube had worn at the ball, and he had Hube's tarnished silver complexion as well.

"I am Lakus Dooted Giren. My brother Dino asked me to take your case. I understand that I am also your brother."

She offered proof by grinning at him.

With a gesture, he suggested that they seat themselves in the colorless 2-nook that had formed.

"You are accused of forcing citizens to take part in a ritual of sacrifice in which there was a death. The victim's name is Zoron Corovica Caton."

She started. "That's the student who was lost!"

When she had explained everything to him, Lakus told her she had nothing to worry about.

"Katora is pursuing a vendetta against you and trying to stretch imperial law to match the severity of her hatred. She has no facts on which to base her case. She is counting on her prestige to win for her, but the court of Bri will not be swayed."

Puflet swallowed, hoping that he was right. "But why does she hate me so? What did I ever do to her?"

"I'm afraid no one knows. I have, of course, consulted with her husband, hoping to get some insight into the roots of this case, but he has no idea."

While the lawyers prepared for their day in court, Puflet returned to her ruminations. She read more historical files. They told her that trials like hers had evolved from the trials by combat engaged in by prehistoric humans. She pictured herself mounting her fiery steed to charge against Katora's perfidy. But, alas, her weapons were only to be words.

The day came at last.

"Puflet Wuner Doom," boomed the glowworm-enhanced voice from one of the tiny gray-clad figures in the high wall niches of the Judicial Building of Bri. "You are accused of practicing Nander blood rituals, which is a crime against the Galactic Mindsea Empire. Are you guilty of this crime?"

Wearing a prisoner's gray robe, Puflet stood alone in a circular pit facing the Judiciary Committee's wall. The judicial teams' nooks curved around the back of the stage like a pair of gray wings. Higher than the teams but lower than the committee, spectators' gray nooks were supported on thin, vaguely organic-looking extrusions of fake wood that glowed a warm red-brown.

"I have never practiced Nander blood rituals," Puflet declared.

"Who has accused this citizen?" the committee member demanded.

Katora's voice rang out from the right wing. "I have."

"What proof do you offer?"

Katora had taken her seat, and her lawyer, Fetina Sicard Viol, who bore a disgusting resemblance to Valri, rose. "Puflet Wuner Doom was headmistress of the Mindsea Academy of Tadruhemdron," she began in a high-pitched, nasal voice.

She went on for some time, describing a view of her academy that only Katora could have concocted. "Students were encouraged to clash in this ritual of death," she concluded.

The voice from the wall again asked for proof, and Fetina offered a deposition from Sianne Tafe Veance, who claimed that she had been accosted by someone she knew as Serpenlino during one of the times when the two academies down-leveled and fused.

Sianne's tarnished silver face appeared, much enlarged, on one side of the hall, while on the other side the patterns within her brain were displayed. She spoke, and the patterns seethed to her words. "He told us it was all for the glory of the Nander god."

Again it was a struggle for Puflet to keep a smirk from her face. Mindseas were not permitted to give depositions, as it was assumed their control over the cells of their body permitted them to fool analysis. If Sianne thought she had such powers, she was mistaken, for the truth rating displayed beneath the patterns hovered around thirteen percent.

Puflet winced when the next deposition played. It was Eadin, and the smell of her ylang-ylang filled the judicial hall. "She tried to involve us in her horrible rituals too. She took Sianne into a meditation chamber and told her there were monsters waiting to eat her if she tried to mind-link."

Puflet frowned, because Eadin's truth rating was eighty-seven percent.

"Has the defense any evidence to offer?" asked the committee.

Lakus rose. "I have proof that these charges are untrue," he said in a quiet, assured tone. He called his first witness.

Puflet gasped when Oakiza rose from her side of the court, splendidly green in the spotlight.

"Puflet wanted us to work together to strengthen our deep-level selves," he said. His displayed brain patterns showed a high truth rating. "We could maintain patternistic integrity even during fierce competition if we believed in the ideals of courage, honor and fair play."

Kael rose to his feet. "Our contests were modeled after a prehistoric human convention. Serpenlino worked with students who had Nander ancestry, but that had nothing to do with the tournaments, and Puflet didn't know anything about Nanders, anyhow. The jousting was about horsemen on ancient Earth. Something called Chivalry."

Serpenlino was there as well. "The student who died wasn't jousting. He got lost in the old king's catacombs. For all we know, he's still in there, downleveled."

Fetina cross-examined the witnesses. "Ancient Earth rituals and Nander rituals are one and the same, aren't they?"

"They are not," Kael maintained. "Nanders had a Stone Age technology, and jousting knights belonged to the Steel Age."

Fetina asked Serpenlino for more details about the missing student, and he went on at length about how hard Puflet had searched for him.

Fetina asked Oakiza if it wasn't true that Coders also practiced ritual sacrifice, and he responded with quotes from the Book of the Code that described rules for an idyllic and peaceful society.

When Fetina had finished, the committee spoke again. "Evidence has been received. Is there anything more that needs to be said about this case?"

Katora rose. "I have something to say."

Since she was a mindsea, the court didn't look at her brain patterns. She simply spoke when the committee had given her leave to do so. Her voice, amplified, pealed through the hall.

"The case is not about whether Puflet felt remorse about the dead student or about what sort of ritual she used to excuse the practice of mind-dueling. The issue is that Puflet is infected by an incurable deep-level disease that will force her to kill whether she wishes to or not. Puflet has no control over this disease. It controls her as it controls all those it infects. The damage she is capable of is directly proportional to her mindsize, which is already considerable. Though it is not genetically transferred, Puflet's close kinship with Horl and Thermeon, two of the most powerful mindseas in history, makes her doubly dangerous."

Her voice rose. "Perhaps the court needs to be reminded of the horrors of the Hundred Fourth Millennium when half a million interplanetary travelers had their throats slit by Nander pilots, or the Ninety-sixth Millennium, when Horl's madness wiped out entire cities. I hardly need remind you of the flashing of Wamatu. This disease is deadly. Those infected should be considered, as crystalloids are, to have ceased existence as human beings. Unlike crystallization, the course of this disease causes its host excruciating pain. Puflet's life will not be a happy one as she finds her human emotions and faculties warped by a will she cannot resist. She will only be the first victim. Many others will follow, I shudder to guess how many, if Puflet is not granted merciful release from her condition." Casting a look of false pity toward Puflet, Katora took her seat.

Puflet nodded to Lakus, who told that committee that his client had something to say.

A firefly hovered in front of Puflet to amplify her voice. Like Katora, she was not subjected to brain patterning. "I thank my accuser for her concern. I assure her it is not necessary. Whatever problems I have may be traced to spending my formative years in slavery, subjected to the cruel punishments of my owner's whims; and from traveling thence to the Mindsea Academy of Alonaton, where I hoped to be welcomed as a student, but instead found myself subjected to the headmistress' campaign to destroy me, a campaign which she continues with this trial." She threw back her head and smiled up at the tiny figures in the niches high overhead, wondering if it was coincidence that they were beyond the "Contamination" distance. "I assure the committee that having freed myself from my former owner's tyranny and from the deadly intrigues of the Mindsea Academy of Alonaton, I am not about to let any so-called 'infection' rob me of my freedom.

"I would also like to remind the committee of the nature of deep-level phenomena. As Headmistress Katora well knows, things of the Deep have many aspects. They cannot be fixed or defined in our human terms, but change according to the mind that perceives them. It is Katora alone who perceives this contagion within me. I myself perceive that I have potential, to use for good or ill, as I decide. It is my intention to use my potential for the benefit of the empire and mankind."

Lakus rose again, and indicated that he had one more view for the defense. The committee bade the view speak, and a number of students from Tadruhemdron gave their dispositions, all speaking glowingly of the camaraderie they shared in the tournaments and races at the north pole.

Katora rose. "The students are not mindseas, and see in Puflet only what she wishes them to see."

Lakus rose. "Do you feel then, Headmistress, that only mindseas are competent to judge in this matter? If you wish, I can subpena Quixa Pyen Soam or Vedina Iynoolit Woat to testify."

Katora huffed. "Your sisters cannot present an unbiased view. They suffer from the same taint!"

Murmurings of concern came from the spectators.

"There is another mindsea present," Katora said. "Habel Chadrav Wandro."

Puflet stiffened as her eyes darted to a glowing spot in the back of the hall.

"I doubt that your son can present an unbiased view, either," Lakus said.

"This is ridiculous," Katora said. "We do not need to examine Puflet. We only need to look at the trail of death she has already left behind her."

"All but one of those deaths occurred at your academy," Lakus said. "So I think we can lay most of the blame at your feet."

"All the killings centered around Puflet," Katora argued, her earrings flashing.

"If I may make one more observation. Headmistress Katora has told us of the extreme danger of those who are closely related to Thermeon."

"Only in proportion to their mindpowers," Katora said.

Lakus gave her a cold smile. "Indeed. Habel is just come of age, and already wielding such powers. Puflet was much older when she first became able to mind-link. Habel's mindsize is much greater than hers."

Katora gave her hair a swipe, rosy patches blooming beneath the green of her cheeks. "Habel is not on trial."

Lakus smiled meaningfully at her. Katora swallowed. She sat down and looked at her lawyer.

"The prosecution has completed its presentation," Fetina sniffed.

"The defense has completed its presentation," Lakus said.

Puflet alone remained standing, heart pounding, as she waited. She was concentrating so hard that the voice of the committee member made her jump when it shattered the silence.

"The Judicial Committee of Bri has weighed the evidence, and will recommend to Emperor Gawoi that Puflet Wuner Doom be found innocent of the charge of practicing Nander blood rituals."

Puflet let out a quiet gasp of relief and joy. The glowworms in her robe turned it from gray to white, indicating that she was a prisoner no longer. She wanted to dance over and spit in Katora's face, but it wouldn't suit the decorum of the place, so she just smiled at her lawyer, then climbed the ramp from the prisoner's pit and joined Lakus on the walkway that bore them from the Judicial Hall and out into the daylight. She lifted her hands toward the sun and laughed.

Eria, Serpenlino, Oakiza, and Kael joined them. The three men rushed at Puflet, grabbing her shoulders, her arms, her waist, laughing and swinging her about, and stumbling over each other's feet.

"Why don't we all go to Take Care and celebrate," Eria suggested.

"First I am going to have a hot bath and get rid of this dismal thing." Puflet tugged at the sleeves of her shapeless government-issue robe.

"I've rented us suites in the hotel section," Eria said. "You can bathe and change there."

They all stepped onto a shining walkway to make the long-delayed trip to Take Care.

The first sight of Take Care glittering across the river with its hundred gates and starburst lights sizzled in Puflet's mind as she made her preparations in the suite Eria had reserved for her. It might have been a sight she had dreamed of while locked in her sleeping drawer in Ix's stronghold.

Certainly it was not like anything she had seen in person or in memories of the rest of the empire.

The suite itself was charming, with gently sloping floors that made unexpected turns leading to surprising views of artwork or mini-gardens. The slopes of the pool beneath an arching bridge and its mossy, flower-dotted rim seemed more landscape than habitat, but the overhead view through skylights of vertical colonnades and more skylights told her it was no ordinary landscape, but rather some deep-level sensation singled out and slowed down enough so that a person could contemplate it.

The odd thing, she decided as she floated on her back staring up, was that it seemed the view had been created by artfully placed colonnades and mirrors up there rather than by glowworm projection.

Abruptly she recalled that people were waiting for her, and pulled herself out to dry in a storm-hued wind room beneath miniature wall grottoes where finger-wide streams trickled through forests of moss and tiny red-capped fungi. Dried and tingling, she donned the star-sprinkled purple whirlaround she had chosen to celebrate her return to freedom.

As she and her companions walked a serpentine path of small fitted-together stones leading from the hotel to the main exhibit hall, Lakus boasted about the time he had represented a sentient forest fighting greedy developers, Kael babbled about students at the north pole academy, Serpenlino broke in to describe the latest races they'd held before leaving, and Oakiza assured her that a committee of his brothers and sisters in the Code would keep everything running smoothly until they returned. He seemed to assume that Puflet would come back with them.

Puflet looked from one side to the other, trying to take in the view. There was always something to see: the way a gnarled black trunk cut across the grassy slope, or an alabaster post, delicately carved, held a shimmering wind chime. It reminded her of Katora's white sands rooms at the Academy, but more meaningful, somehow, with Bri's sun and wind providing light and motion, scents of grass and stone filling her nostrils.

Eria, walking ahead of the others, looked back over her shoulder. "Quintillion built all of this by hand, as much as possible. Katora lived here for a time and saw him working on it."

Puflet dropped her eyes to the stones beneath her purple slippers. She looked back at the stones they had already traversed, then ahead at those still to come. Fitted together by hand? The work must've taken years, while with glowworms it could have been done with a single thought. And the difference was barely noticeable, for Quintillion had done his work with great precision. "He did this while he was emperor?"

"That's right," Eria said. "He could do other things while he held the mind-net. He never dropped the mind-net at all, unless he was at the point of death."

Puflet brushed the hair back from her brow, and gave a little sigh. Was fitting these stones together, and other such labors, the penance Quintillion had done before he'd served the slavers? Suddenly the whole of Take Care seemed to possess the face of the monster. And what did that name mean, anyhow—"Watch Out? Beware?"

They entered another building with an arching facade that

flashed innumerable tiny lights like some frozen rainbow. Within, they traversed a series of interconnected halls, each one a different color of the spectrum. A ruby bridge spanned a red lake bordered by crimson rushes. Amber boulders overlooked an amber stream winding through amber grass while yellow birds sang from yellow-leafed trees. A green lake reflected boulders green with lichen, innumerable green frogs peeping and splashing in the scummy shallows. Blue deer waded in the surf that washed across cobalt blue sand. Mauve-barked trees dropped violet blossoms into an amethyst lake where barbeled purple fish swam and violet dragonflies whirred and swooped. There were black, white, pink, and silver halls as well.

"He didn't use glowworms for these, either, for the most part," Eria said. "He collected species and minerals of the desired color from the planets."

"Amazing," Puflet breathed. "He didn't like glowworms, then?"

"He said that his brain couldn't tolerate them. He never spoke to anyone except face to face or in mind-link."

Puflet gave her head a shake, the effort of trying to figure out such a convoluted mind stultifying. How could Katora have walked beside him and never noticed something very wrong, long before the Fissure? But she hadn't noticed anything wrong with a husband who tortured babies either.

"Quintillion couldn't love," she repeated to herself. But he had wanted to love. So were these exhibits, and all of his other penance, cries for love? Who were they directed at—Thermeon? Or anyone who could understand? But Thermeon had told her Quintillion believed no one could understand. She turned to Eria. "Was your father much like your brother?"

"Very much. My grandmother bore three children, and he was the youngest. Darkness filled his soul from the moment of birth— we always thought it was because his mother died birthing him in the primitive way of her people. She belonged to an ancient human race—some say subhuman. Horl created the Nander race from my father's genes, but his father was an ordinary imperial citizen."

"Birthing?" Puflet wrinkled her nose. "You mean the babies came out of her body, instead of being grown in incubators?"

Eria nodded.

They walked on to a golden building with wires radiating down from multiple spires to form a complex pattern and sighing in the wind.

"Not glowworm-powered, am I right?" Puflet said.

Eria nodded.

Within the building, a curving hallway led past darkened archways marked by golden letters: "Visit Other Histories," "Concoct Your Own Physics," "Fight Any War."

"These exhibits are very intense," Eria said as they paused in front of the third archway. "Sometimes visitors never return."

"Like the catacombs of the Ulonan king," Puflet whispered.

"Quintillion was a master level-engineer. No one knows where these portals lead. So I think it would be best if we forgo the exploration of them right now. But I wanted you to know they were here."

A complete circuit of the hall brought them back to the building lobby. They exited and walked on to yet another building, this one dominated by a tower of black stone into which were set minerals with gorgeous, phosphorescent hues.

The designs were beautiful, and yet they crawled over Puflet's skin like a many-legged creature. "Oh!" she gasped.

"It's Nander writing," Eria said. "It says, 'Welcome to the Mini Milky Way.'"

Stepping in through portals in the base of the black tower, they found themselves in an octagonal lobby of translucent aquamarine stone that drew light down from above. The floor was made from squares of black and white stone. Across from the portals by which they had entered, an alabaster archway opened onto darkness. Benches carved from alabaster rested against the other six walls. Archway and benches were ornamented with numerous curlicues that gave the impression of bursting waves. The faces of exotic beasts peered from amongst the waves. Puflet stared at the carvings for a long while.

"The nexus at Katora's academy is copied from this room," she said finally. "But I think this is more beautiful."

This room spoke to her, told her wonderful things. Dino's architecture was competent, but it wasn't inspired. Again she imagined how Katora must have felt, being rejected by the man who had made this room with his mind and his hands. Every day she must try to convince herself that what she had now was better, but that would never be true. If she were to eradicate every one of Quintillion's descendants, it still wouldn't make it true. She would only need to come to this place to know her life was a lie.

Puflet felt certain that Katora would never set foot in Take Care.

Eria led the way through the portal, and they followed her into a great darkness. Lakus's hair and Puflet's hair glowed, but the glow didn't reach anything in the room. It was as if they stood in the midst of space. Stars shone all around them, above their heads and below their feet as well.

"This is the Mini Milky Way," Eria said. "The pilot school uses it for training cadets, because it's a perfect replica of the galaxy. It downlevels so that cadets can experience the Deep before they get onboard a ship—or learn that they're Deep-blind. It's easy to get lost in here, since you can't see the doorway once you step through, and it's the charming custom of instructors at the school to make sure every cadet does get lost at least once. But don't worry—I won't get lost, because I'm a pilot." She chuckled.

"Bri is the planet closest to the door. Over this way we can find the neighboring planet of Allnici."

Everyone followed her, their steps silent. Unexpectedly a star flared into an enormous ball of light with fiery plasma streamers. As they filed past, it shrank quickly. A planet swelled into a gray sphere that hung in the air before them. Music filled the spaces between the stars, eerily beautiful.

Silhouetted by the planet, Lakus took Eria's hand. "May I have this dance?" As they whirled off among the stars, Kael, Serpenlino, and Oakiza converged on Puflet, eyes glinting by the light of the Allnici simulacrum.

"One at a time," she said. She stepped into Kael's arms, and they danced, the music drawing them across the galaxy in waves of wonder and lamentation.

She kept a lookout for Lakus's hair, worrying that they might get separated. Each time Kael whirled her around she felt dizzy. The others seemed to be above them or below them or along the axes of deep dimensions. When a pause came in the music, she slid her fingers from Kael's grasp. "Thank you for the dance."

She hurried over to Oakiza. "Your turn."

Oakiza took her hand. She looked around to make sure the others were still nearby. The glow from her hair barely caught their eyes and the planes of their faces. Serpenlino resembled a basalt statue in a false dawn, gazing into the distance with a solemn expression. The music rose again, like the morning breeze, and Puflet danced with Oakiza.

"This place disturbs me," she whispered. "It's so beautiful. All the carving he did, all the colors and the planets and the music. He could have built more places like this, and instead he chose to relay the slavers' messages for hundreds of years."

"He was lost," Oakiza said. "He had no belief, except for the greatness of his own mind, and that will lead a man into madness."

"How could the monster have been so terrible for him?" she asked, "that not even creating places as wonderful as this could give him relief?"

"To live in a state of unbelief is to dwell in infinite darkness."

"Don't you think that he would have overcome the monster if he had found love? Isn't this art a cry for love?"

"You know, Puflet, there is no monster."

She started. "But I've seen it, and Quintillion and Katora have."

"Yes. But it is made of shadow, not substance. It is the emptiness that fills the soul when you believe in nothing."

"Now you sound almost like Thermeon when he gave that lecture about the monster of emptiness. Do you think believing in nothing means that nothing feels real to you, that you can't love?"

"Yes, because the Goddess is love."

"Thermeon believes in his goddess-star."

Oakiza snorted. "But he does not surrender to her. Instead he tries to make her obey his will. He ravaged our empire trying to exert his will over our Goddess."

Puflet sighed. "Serpenlino thought my monster was the actual deep-level mind of a once-living dinosaur. But you think it doesn't exist?"

"Puflet, you don't believe either. That's why you are troubled. When you look at the universe, you will find something looking back at you. But it is the something your deep-level mind chooses from infinite possibilities. You yourself are creating this monster out of nothing, making it the things you named. Don't you see how you've already changed its nature? In the beginning, it was Quintillion's 'death of all things,' but you changed it into your burning charger, a force for heroic battle. Don't lose heart. You will find the truth."

The truth. Quintillion's voice echoed in her mind. *You want the truth.*

The music paused. "But you think the truth is your Code Goddess."

"I *know*."

Suddenly angry, Puflet pulled away from him. "It's Serpenlino's turn now."

She started toward where she thought she had last seen Serpenlino, but he wasn't there. The music started again. Puflet remained where she was, thinking Serpenlino would see her hair and find her, but he didn't come. The music sounded faint and distant, and she felt cold.

She couldn't see anyone any more. She began to walk, mostly because she felt cold. The stars seemed to slide farther away with each step she took.

She jumped when giant letters burst into flame right in front of her. "FIGHT ANY WAR." The heat almost seared her face.

She stumbled back. "No! I didn't want this. How did I get here?"

"Throughout the history of mankind," droned a voice—not Quintillion's—"wars have been fought for many reasons. For what reason do you fight your war? Is it for greed? For vengeance? For freedom?"

"I don't—" Her protest was cut short as the unseen floor tilted beneath her feet, hurling her forward. Somehow she landed on the back of her flaming skeletal charger, already thundering through the darkness. She found a lance in her hand.

As her thoughts struggled to make sense of what was happening, a fiery dot appeared ahead, and rapidly grew in size. Her challenger rode a skeletal steed with four enormous tusks sprouting from its upper jaw and curling back toward its skull. As the armored rider pounded closer, he flung up his visor, and Puflet cried out in anguish.

He was Habel.

26

"Sorry about the illusion," Habel said. "I wanted to draw you away without your alerting your friends."

They stood in the sunlight beneath the black tower of the Mini Milky Way. Puflet sputtered, wanting to slap his face and deliver a stern lecture about mind-linking without a signal, but he looked so tall and handsome in his blue-gray cadet uniform that she just goggled.

Laughing, he took her hand and led her along the path away from the tower. "I've had to use my mindpowers for self-defense since I got here. Some blipping trainer tried to get me lost in that galactic simulation chamber, but I linked to my father and got the star-orientation out of his mind. At least his wretched existence had some use, for once."

"Oh," Puflet gasped.

"Then I mixed up the stars in the trainer's mind and made him get lost. That was a laugh."

"Uh...."

The gold building with the singing wires loomed ahead, but he followed a branch of the path that went around it.

"Let's go someplace private. What about 'Amberland' or 'Rubyland?'"

"Whichever one you like best."

He chose "Rubyland," locking the hall behind them as they entered. Perhaps Quintillion had intended these places for assignations. They stood enfolded in shades of red, the scarlet sward beneath their feet, chattering leaves of a red willow on the hilltop above them, a flock of tiny red birds searching the grass around them for red ants. Habel doffed his uniform and stood nude and proud on the bank of the red lake.

"This is the beginning of time, Puflet, and we are the first man and the first woman. Nothing else matters."

Fear was a little worm beneath her breastbone, but how could she spoil this perfect moment? She cast her purple dress aside and went to him. He enfolded her in his strong arms and covered her eyelids, cheeks, lips with his warm breath and his kisses. She smelled nothing dead in him now. Maybe getting off of Ulona and away from his mother had healed his wound.

"I love you, Puflet! I haven't stopped thinking about you since that first time."

"You don't think I'm evil?"

He made a sound of disgust. "That's my mother. And your friends—they think I'm evil, don't they?"

"Not evil, exactly, but—"

"They want to keep us apart."

"Yes."

"They're the past. Forget them. Forget my parents! You and I are the future. We'll make a better world than they have, won't we?"

"We can try."

Taking both of her hands in his, he fixed her with solemn blue-gray eyes. "We can. We must! No matter how they've tried to whittle us down into a size they can understand. You and I are the two most talented young mindseas in the galaxy, aren't we?"

It was his mother talking—that emphasis on comparisons and the need to place oneself at the top. She had to moderate him. "I don't know about that, Habel. The galaxy could be filled with all sorts of minds we know nothing about."

He laughed. "The two most talented imperial citizens."

She shrugged.

He raised his white eyebrows. "You think maybe there's some very powerful mindsea out there somewhere who only uses his powers to clean his toenails or something?" He slid his finger down her nose and gave her nose tip a playful poke. "That's what I love about you. You're absolutely unique!"

His face went solemn again. "One thing I do promise you. I will build you a city—a wonderful city on the planet of your choice. After I get my pilot's license, of course. Until then, you will be my city." His voice grew husky with passion. "I love you so much!"

He seized her and threw her beneath him on the grass, then caressed and kissed every part of her, awakening a cascade of rapturous sensations, until she felt herself expanding, soaring through deep dimensions, becoming a city in fact.

"My beautiful one," he groaned. "My powerful one."

"I'm not evil," she whispered.

"My wonderment, my attractor," he murmured, fingertips spiraling around her nipples. "O, foundation of my universe and ornament of my realities."

He entered her city on his fiery charger, and its citizens gave him homage, dancing through the thoroughfares of her veins and arteries.

In the deepest chamber of her being there was a chest wherein her jewel lay stored, its gleam large and brilliant in her mind's eye.

"The truth is there," she whispered, caressing Habel's sweaty shoulders. "Find it. Find the truth."

He thrust deep, his burning steed snorting fireballs into her stronghold, clattering across the drawbridge, plunging through shadowed halls toward the secret chamber.

"Deeper," she whispered. "The truth is there."

Flames leaping from empty eye sockets, the four-tusked monster peered into her depths, and all the secrets of deep-level building spilled out.

Her eyelids were carved of stone. She was a statue, so there was no need to move, was there? No matter what the voices up there said. She'd had a perfect moment of love, and it was enough to last her for a lifetime.

"Puflet," came the voice again. "Return to us. We want you back."

She ignored the voice. It had nothing to do with her.

"Puflet." Now he was touching her hand. He had no right to do that. She was for Habel to touch, not for anyone else. But he wouldn't stop running his fingers up and down her arm. She should have been a statue, unfeeling stone. But for some reason the stone in her arm had turned into flesh. She could bear it no longer. She would have to move, at least long enough to tell him to go away.

It was more of a struggle than she had expected. Her eyelids and her lips remained stone, numbed and heavy. Her hand twitched first, then her arm. Finally her eyelids rose, as slow and ponderous as the portals of pahmak holding pens. Light stabbed her eyes. Her face scrunched as she struggled to blink the pain away. After a while her eyelids moved more easily, and she concentrated on the face that was staring at her through the light. The face was a green blur. Squeezing her eyes, she tried to bring it into focus. Green eyes stared back at her. It was Oakiza.

She tried to master her sluggish lips, finally croaking, "Go away."

Instead, Oakiza smiled at her. He grasped both of her hands and said, "Welcome back."

She tried to free herself, but her fingers quivered helplessly in his. How had she grown so weak? She kept opening and closing her eyes, trying to focus on more of her surroundings. The reds of "Rubyland" were gone. Pale indefinites curved around her.

"Why am I here?"

"Your mind was attacked. You've had a long course of floating."

She spasmed in his grasp. "Was not attacked. Where is Habel?"

"Gone to Lal. He's the one who attacked you, isn't he? We were all pretty sure about that."

"He didn't attack me. He's my lover. Let me go!" She wanted to say more, but she was out of breath.

He didn't let her go. "Eria had to make her Andromeda run, and Serpenlino and Kael returned to the academy. We drew lots, and I won, so I stayed here to watch over you."

"I need to get to Lal."

"No you don't."

"How dare you—" she paused to pant—"tell me what I need or don't need!" She struggled, and he finally released her hands. She flopped back against the gelatinous nook.

"Your mind, your body, and your spirit have suffered a terrible shock," he told her. "Now you must work to recover your strength."

"Why am I so weak?"

"Your mind withdrew. Over a year has passed since your trial."

She digested this.

"I don't suppose Habel meant for you to ever awaken," Oakiza said.

Her nostrils flared. Trembling, she tried to sit erect, until the nook pushed her into a more upright position. She glared at Oakiza, her eyes at least starting to behave normally. "You know nothing. Habel and I made love most exquisitely. It was an act of such sublimity I had to contemplate it for a while." She paused, not sure whether she was making any sense. She tried to toss her head, but managed only a little wobble. "Why has he gone to Lal?"

"They're making him emperor."

Something twirled in the pit of her stomach. "Habel ... emperor? Who's making him?"

"All the bigwigs got together and decided. Gawoi will step down."

"I thought one of his offspring would be the next emperor."

"Habel is a mindsea. No one else comes near to him in mindsize."

She let her eyes go unfocused, stared past the green face at the featureless wall. After a while she let out a sigh. "Katora wanted this. Now he'll never be free."

"No. So forget him."

"I can't. He loves me."

Oakiza shook his head. "You've been deceived. I'm sorry."

She curled her fingers, trying to make fists. "You know nothing."

"I know that he plans to march down the Way in his wedding procession after he takes the imperial oath."

She jerked up. "I must get to Lal!"

Oakiza placed his hands on her shoulders and gently pushed her back. "He's not going to marry you. He's marrying Eadin Trewa Cooldiem. I'm sorry."

Puflet howled and squirmed, unable to see again because of the tears flooding her eyes. Oakiza's unwelcome voice persisted like gurgling water in her ears. "You must continue your own quest for the truth, Puflet."

He began to talk about the Book of the Code, and what it meant to him, and how the profundities had slowly dawned on his developing mind as he grew from boy to man. Finally she gathered all of her strength and screamed, "Go away and leave me alone!"

Oakiza smiled at her. "If you have something to drink I'll let you rest for a while."

She gave a weak nod, and he pulled a squeeze bottle from a floating tray and handed it to her. After a few sips she murmured that she was exhausted, and he left her.

Now I can become a statue again, she thought.

But once made flesh, her body was filled with restless sensations of life, and she couldn't go back.

Every day she had to endure Oakiza's solicitude and perform

tasks for him—drinking, eating, climbing from the nook, using the shower and relief alcoves. A tenthyear of struggle later she had the strength to walk as far as the wonderdome lobby and look out at the walkways and grassy slopes and habitats of Sax, capital of Bri.

Oakiza stood at her elbow as she watched citizens in bright tunic suits and fluttering whirarounds stream past on the walkways. "You have worked hard, Puflet. You grow stronger. But today, according to the agreement I made with Kael and Serpenlino, I must take leave of you, and allow Kael to assume the duty of supervising your healing. His ship has made port."

She shrugged.

She sensed his disappointment as he hesitated before speaking again. "Puflet, I want you to know that, despite everything, my love for you remains strong. Far stronger than he is!"

He must mean Habel. She had to chuckle. Nothing would ever impact her as powerfully as Habel had.

"Do not mock me," he warned. "For you have not felt my love. In accordance to your wishes, I restrain myself. A man of the Code always respects his woman, for only she has the right to initiate joining. Know this—" His voice trembled with passion—"if you joined with me, if you surrendered yourself to my embrace and to the love of the Goddess, you would be at once restored to your full strength and glory!"

Puh, she thought. Aloud, she said, "I'm sure that my exercises and my studies will restore me."

"All right, then. I must bid you farewell for a time. If there were not students—sons and daughters of the Code—who needed me, I would remain at your side." He stretched his arms toward her.

Puflet let him embrace her, but gave him no kiss, though she felt his hopeful green lips breathing softly on her cheek.

The next morning, Kael showed up in her cell to go over her diet and exercises, bringing with him a dried yellow leaf from his father's memorial hall. It had a pleasant fragrance. They reviewed her schedule, and developed a new routine. This wonderdome, like its counterpart on Ulona, had a large, warm pool for toning the muscles. She and Kael swam side by side.

At the end of another tenthyear, she was assigned a singleton habitat a short walkway ride from the wonderdome, and given some glowworm work—all about walkway enhancement and expansion—to earn her keep. She returned to the wonderdome daily for her swim with Kael. After that, they climbed in the 3-D room.

Then came the day when it was Serpenlino's turn to relieve Kael as her keeper. She felt well enough to go out to meet his shuttle, so she and Kael spent the day before in town, shopping for something for her to wear. She chose a violet whirlaround with a border of narrow stripes—blue, salmon, orange, and blue again, and shoes with matching colors. She found the effect pleasing, reminiscent of rainbows.

The following evening, as Bri's noxious atmosphere blossomed into waves of fiery oranges and purples around the setting sun, they rode the walkway to the shuttle station. Imperial guards stood at the portals. They remained unmoving as Puflet and Kael approached, their scarlet plumes and surcoats looking almost the same as they had when Gawoi had been emperor.

Then Puflet saw the insignia each of them bore on his chest. It was a little red bird, wings outspread against a circle of yellow.

In a flash she was on her back again on the scarlet grass of Rubyland, looking up at the skylight, the little birds swooping overhead in a whir of wings. She felt the weight of Habel's body and drew in the scent of his flesh. The Second Tenet was correct—each moment could be an eternal now, and this was her eternal moment, celebrated by the new emperor in his insignia. He had bound her to him in that moment. She would never be free.

28

Puflet downed one goblet of Saqufean fire dragons after another, but she hardly felt them go down. Boisterous music throbbed through the Pilots Lounge as she danced with Serpenlino, or with Orgmorgan, who had brought them to the Lounge as his guests, but she hardly felt their hands in hers. As she and Serpenlino looped and whirled around the lounge's central pool with its water ferns and spiny frogs, he spoke to her. His voice splashed through her mind like the water in the pond. His eyes seemed to hold no more sentience than would a couple of fat raindrops floating in the air before her.

Finally some words broke through. "You have regained your physical strength, but your mind remains broken."

She sighed deeply. "I begin to understand how Quintillion felt. Nothing is real. Nothing except the moment I shared with Habel in Rubyland."

His thick black eyebrows bunched to overshadow his eyes. "You've sustained a deep-level wound. Like the one Dino inflicted on him. No doubt that's all he understands."

Orgmorgan cut in.

"Go to the Stairway of Ice," the burly pilot whispered in her ear, tickling her with his thick, curly orange beard. "Thass how ol' Fang-face finally cured hisself of the Fissure holes."

"What is this Stairway?"

"A stairway into th'Deep, over by Earth."

"Quintillion built it?"

Orgmorgan threw back his head and bellowed with laughter so loud and raucous it drowned out the music.

"Excuse my ignorance!" Puflet huffed.

He kept laughing as he swung her around, tears running into his beard. "Oh, thass a good one! I gotta tell everyone that one!"

It was odd, but things didn't feel so unreal when she was being mocked. "So tell me about the Stairway, already!"

He clasped her close as they swung around the pool, and whispered into her ear. "Th'Earth-God, Kokkiro, made it so's people could spread over the galaxy. The lowest steps, anyhow. The upper part's deeper than time, so it's always been there."

"Fascinating!" she whispered.

"Every step goes one level deeper. But the shallowest ones are gone now, 'cause they ain't eternal, and it's been a million years, give or take. Now you can only see the stairway if you got a pentascoper. Like me."

"I see," she murmured.

The three of them returned to her habitat and reclined in a 3-lounger in her unlit atrium, stars glimmering overhead.

"The human soul is like glass," Serpenlino said. "A deep-level attack makes the soul molten and stamps it with its mark. It is impossible to remove this mark, unless the soul is heated again. This is what the Stairway will do."

"So, Orgmorgan, you'll take me there?" Puflet asked.

"Nah, I ain't got the time to spare. A trip like that takes a hunnert years, at least. Not gettin' there, but once you step onto that deepness, the years whip past faster'n you can count 'em."

"So who has hundreds of years to spare?" Puflet demanded.

"What you need to do, Puf, is you an' your three buddies slip over to the pilot school and train up to a Deep Five rating. Then you can borrow Fang-face's stupid tub."

"The *Kiadox*," Serpenlino said.

"By 'Fang-face' you mean Thermeon, don't you? Why would he lend us his ship? He hates me!"

"He don' hate you," Orgmorgan said. "He's just sore 'cause you didn't want him to be your Daddy."

Serpenlino chuckled from the shadows. "This is a twistored

plan, Orgmorgan. The training itself will eat up a decade. Why, we might as well wait for Eria to get back from Andromeda and let her ferry us to the Stairway."

"You think she's got the time? She could make twenty Andromeda runs while she's messin' about with you."

"Frankly, I don't think a few centuries here or there would make much difference to someone her age."

"Look!" Puflet threw up a hand, which seemed to materialize from shadow as it caught the glow of her hair. "It's my problem, and I'd rather solve it myself. I'll go for the pilot training—I mean, as long as I can get a scholarship, or whatever pays for it. And then I'll worry about finding a ship." She took a deep breath of the night air. Just picturing a solution infused her with new energy.

"I'll train too," Serpenlino said. "I'm sure that Oakiza and Kael can run the academy without me."

As it turned out, Oakiza and Kael both insisted on taking part in the plan.

The four of them attended the pilot school together, donned blue-gray cadet uniforms, attended lectures in a great, acoustically sculpted auditorium, bunked in the barracks, and did exercises in the Mini Milky Way. They even partook in the famous tray wars in the mess hall—the students rode airborne serving trays as if they were ships and shot one another down with fruits and vegetables.

It was almost like being back in the Alonaton academy again, but without Katora or Eadin. The commandant, Qula Meon Miathog, was tough, but fair. He came from an unknown family, beyond Katora's sphere of influence.

Nearly two years of training passed before the cadets of their class were permitted aboard an actual ship, but after that, Puflet progressed rapidly.

Her first confrontation with the ship controls brought back the awful flight from Puztak. After a few training flights, she learned to relax, and trust in the monster. It recognized the deep-level patterns in the ship's scopes as a human would recognize memories of a homeworld.

"Now," it whispered. It was never mistaken.

Oakiza claimed that he received similar guidance from his Goddess, though sometimes, if his surrender was less than total, he botched a downleveling. He did not progress as rapidly as Puflet.

Kael claimed to see the leaves of his charger in the scopes when the pattern was right. He also did well.

Serpenlino struggled hardest. He had neither goddess nor charger to guide him, but only his own passion and will. His gray eyes grew fierce and bitter beneath his heavy brows, and once again he slunk about bent over like a question mark.

When Puflet was ready to be tested for her Deep Five rating, Kael and Oakiza were hoping to get their Deep Fours, and Serpenlino his Deep Three. Orgmorgan arrived to administer Puflet's test, as the school did not keep a pentascoper for the rare occasions when one was needed.

Like the *Serious*, his *Counting on Kindness* was a vast, labyrinthine ship that seemed more to have grown than been constructed. From the outside, it resembled a beautiful snowflake with too many planes, but within, it resembled a vast starfish or jellyfish with pulsating tunnels and burbling tubes filled with substances unknown to human science. Refuse from previous voyages littered the bridge, and small, hand-like alien creatures of various gelatinous colors peeked out from crevices in walls and ceiling. Puflet and Orgmorgan strapped themselves in.

"Now," he said, "once we're down, I know yer could have us to Andromeda an' back in no timatall to our 'spective, but that ain't no challenge. You can hardly miss that pinwheel. So take us across to Haslo."

Puflet nodded, and went through the now familiar routine of casting off from the spaceport and easing a safe distance away before looking to downlevel. Her heart pounded fiercely, but she felt the monster breathing over her shoulder, and listened for its whisper.

When she gave the button beneath the fifth dial a jab, the ship seemed to implode. This deep, one's mind was so powerful that each fleeting thought and every unexamined assumption took solid form. Puflet's years of training discipline directed her thoughts and assumptions to produce useful forms. Her mind would be the ship's steering assembly. Her monster was its motive force, its engine. The ship itself became a tiny snowflake agleam on the point of the monster's nose horn. Crisply, she turned the monster toward Haslo, picking the system's personality out from amid thousands of beaming, vibrating, singing, smoking, exuding, and tugging entities of the galaxy. The stars were alive on this level, and finding the one you sought was like picking a friend's face out of a crowd.

Two ponderous steps, and the monster reached the silver ribbon that was the Haslo system.

She upleveled, and breathed a sigh of relief to find the water-covered planet—now a grayish globe—on the viewscreen. Not too near and not too far.

Orgmorgan grunted. "All right. Now take us back to Bri."

Puflet turned the ship's nose and repeated the process, this time homing in on the sulfurous smell of Bri.

The Commandant had the whole school turn out to greet her upon her triumphant return, for it wasn't often that a Deep Five rating was granted. While she'd been gone—her test had taken two tenthyears—her three companions had all secured their Deep Four ratings.

"Wait for us to make Deep Five," Oakiza pleaded as the three sat around the table with Puflet and Orgmorgan at their victory dinner in the Pilots Lounge. "Then we will go to the Stairway of Ice."

"No," she told him. "All of you have been advancing more and more slowly, and one pilot is enough. We go now."

Serpenlino sighed and bowed his head. "She's right."

"I have to agree," Kael said.

"I'll take ya to Lal where you can pick up the *Kiadox*—that tub!" Orgmorgan growled. "Fang-face is off somewhere doin' some sorta detecting business, but he tol' me you could take her."

Puflet hoped this was true. She didn't want Thermeon raging at her.

"We may not be able to fly her that deep," said Oakiza, "but we are coming with you."

"Yes!" chorused Kael and Serpenlino.

She scowled at them. "What about the academy?"

"The Code Empress has sent a representative to take over as headmistress."

Puflet shrugged. "Well. It will have been reshaped into

whatever she wants by the time we get back."

Their eyes on her made it known that they didn't care in the least.

She gave another shrug.

Orgmorgan laughed into his beard.

29

Puflet's heart boomed as the four of them lifted off from Lal's surface after a brief stopover in the imperial capital. The decade of training and anticipation had coalesced into a conviction that she would find her answers at the Stairway of Ice, not only to cutting the tether Habel had attached to her soul, but to reshaping the monster into her deep-level self; in short, she would find her truth.

Would she find love as well? Ever since Quintillion had told her his story, she'd believed that she had to know real love before she could mold her monster into a creative force. It would have been so easy if Habel had been the one, for he was beautiful and powerful. But she couldn't forgive him for marrying Eadin. Not only that, but he had used the imperial insignia to play with her heart after his marriage. Was he a hypocrite like his mother? But Katora really believed the things she said about her age of illumination—she was self-deluded—while Habel must have known the effect his little red birds would have on Puflet.

The golden world of Lal shrank away behind their shuttle. Spaceport appeared ahead, a silver track twisting against the star-pricked blackness. It was easy to pick out the *Kiadox*. The pentascoper resembled an iridescent celestial whale with too many flukes and nasal bulges. It differed from the tetrascopers about it in size as well as in the complexity of its outline. If it was a whale among sharks, the moon-skippers and pleasure craft swarming about spaceport were minnows. As the shuttle neared it, a docking bay in the great ship's belly protruded its nozzle, and the shuttle slid inside.

Thermeon's scent lingered in the twisting corridors with their bioluminescent organic convolutions. Glowing eyeball-like shapes protruded from every plane around them. Orgmorgan's and and Eria's pentascopers had also resembled living things, but *Kiadox* looked like it hadn't known when to stop growing. The bridge too was festooned with eyeball-shaped lanterns, some of which twisted on their stems and hummed as Puflet and her companions pushed through a pulsating ribbed pink doorway. Four frilled niches had sprouted around the control column. Puflet chose the farthest niche from where they entered the circular chamber, and the men lined up behind her—Oakiza, Kael, Serpenlino.

Puflet couldn't help but smirk at them as she contacted spaceport system to commence their departure routine. She knew what they hoped: on the Stairway of Ice her passion would be unleashed, freed from Habel's devices and directed, instead, to one of them.

How wonderful that would be. She longed for real love, and if she could come to love one of the three the way they hoped for, all would be well.

She had her doubts.

Of the three, she felt the least attracted to Oakiza, despite the devotion he had shown when she lay prostrate in the Sax wonderdome. He was solid, dependable, perhaps too much so. Too predictable. And his endless proselytizing. How could she truly love someone who insisted that she worship his vision of reality?

Kael and Serpenlino both had their intriguing aspects.

Kael had the sweetest temperament of the three, overflowing with enthusiasm and boyish naivety. She knew he could love. His devotion to his dead father proved that. He didn't need any goddess to tell him what to do.

Serpenlino had a dark streak in him, and he was by far the most complex character among them. She suspected that he had not yet discovered whom he really wanted to be: the spawn of his great-grandmother's subhuman race, the brilliant son of Quintillion, or the rider of deep-level horses. He had shown his ability to love in his caring for the horses, but she did not feel she could love him until he defined himself and gave her an actual someone to love.

A strange thought struck her. Suppose she did discover a bond with one of the three while they were at the Stairway of Ice. Would that ruin their camaraderie, and along with it the shipboard patternistic integrity?

The sensation like the prickle of an approaching storm snapped her alert. "Now," whispered the monster.

She downleveled.

On Deep Five Kael's deep-level self flared beside her, spreading warmth and spice like a scented candle, Oakiza condensed into a pillar of greenstone, and Serpenlino became shadow, silent and quick within a wind that blew winter nights over frozen wastelands.

Puflet looked at herself and saw the same face she met in the mirror each morning, only her hair streamed like clouds in the wind and her eyes were patches of sky glowing from beyond. A chain fastened to one ankle rattled whenever she moved. She didn't have to look to know it linked her to the imperial palace on Lal.

The monster took two tremendous steps toward the hum of ancient life that was Earth, and then a geometric elegance of incomparable magnitude burst upon them, tier upon tier of it soaring, scintillating, singing, rainbow-hued fires burning within its planes. Blackness surrounding it made it burn brighter. Though it looked like one would imagine time to look if frozen, with all of its possibilities caught and sparkling along edges that ran in all of the infinite directions of the deepest Deep, it exuded warmth. They had reached the Stairway of Ice.

With tender care, the monster set the ship down upon its shining shore. Puflet threw out a mooring rope that gripped the Stairway with finger-like appendages, and they exited along one of those deep directions—one step brought them beyond the ship.

The blackness overhead hung in perfect stillness. Their steps crunched ever so softly on the frozen possibilities. That is, hers did. Oakiza remained a limbless green peg on the ship, blinking his glassy eyes and forming an "O" with carven lips. Kael flitted wildly about, like a flame in the wind, and Serpenlino swooped and slid. They couldn't yet control their forms on this level.

Puflet gazed upward along dizzying perspectives that seemed to propel her in different directions if she but caught sight of them.

Alternate histories lay along those axes, captured in the substance of the Stairway for her perusal.

Serpenlino screamed as if at a knife thrust. His shadow form rippled and went crimson. "No, no, no! Don't let it happen!" he howled.

Puflet snapped out her eyes, trying to see what had caused him such pain, but histories swirled about them like shoals of shining fish. To fix on the exact one he had gazed into would be impossible. She froze as she became aware of something massive looming over her. She looked up.

The monster stared down on her with empty eye sockets. His fires had gone out. His bones were all blue-white, clean and cold, a fine mist whirling off of them. His voice thundered deeper than ever. "Upward or downward!"

As the message reverberated about her, she heard it a thousand times more clearly than she had before.

She knew at once how muddled her thoughts had been—like those of a dreamer. The monster had never asked her to take a lover. He was much too ancient, too far-seeing to concern himself with such petty things. He had been asking if she loved her life— not her life as an individual, but her life as a species. Did she choose evolution, or extinction? Should mankind continue to develop new minds and climb the Stairway of Ice, or should they die off and let some other species try the ascent?

The monster knew all about extinction, for he was a dinosaur, or at least the deep-level mind of an entity that once had been a dinosaur.

Her mind hushed before the magnitude of the decision facing her in those empty eye sockets. Somehow, the monster saw her fleeting existence as pivotal in the story of her species. But how was she to know whether the descendants of her contemporaries had a greater potential than dinosaurs or some other species?

In the scintillations of the steps above her, she saw traced out the rise and fall of countless life-forms. They rose like rockets, burning their own substance in brilliant colors until they reached the apex of their flight, when some shadowy impediment stopped their ascent and caused them to fall back into oblivion. The goal of all was the same—to reach the center of space and time and connect with an eternal mind.

Thermeon must have witnessed these aspirations when he had visited this profound realm. But he had misunderstood, or forgotten, imagining the eternal mind to be a goddess for him alone. Oakiza's Code religion took a step closer to the truth, for his Goddess called to all of his people. But the authors of his Book fell short when they wrote that ascent could be maintained by following rules or believing in dogma.

No, only the essence of a life-form's being and perceptions mattered. The rays of possibility pierced her and held her suspended. What she must do was ... experience.

Another wave of enlightenment crashed through her. Quintillion had been posed the same question, and had seen the death of all things. He had hated humanity. He had seen only the downward possibility.

"Upward or downward?" snorted the monster, sending waves of hot and cold vertigo about her. The waves rippled through her mind with images of upward and downward events of varying severity. The downward might be a small setback, a war or plague. It might be the extinction of most life forms, as in his time. It might even be the end of a universe. The upward could be an awakening to a more compassionate understanding of life's web, the development of new technology that made all citizens as mindseas, or an evolutionary change that allowed them to freely enter the Deep. The members of an ascendant species would work all of the Tenets. They would understand their oneness, individuality becoming a matter of choice rather than necessity. They would have outgrown the need for hierarchies as well as any instinct to attack or enslave their fellows, knowing roles could always be reversed.

Puflet's insight gained another dimension. As her perceptions and actions added to the human experience, the monster would back her choice with all of his glorious power. He would lend his leverage to her life, allowing her to carve a molten path through history. She could be a destroyer beyond measure, or a leader surpassing all the mindseas of the past. It was so wonderful, so heady, her deep-level body erupted with shimmering fireworks of celebration.

What would she do? Downward would be easy. She had merely to exercise her wrath and hatred. Upward would be difficult. How could she increase the awareness concentrated in the whole of her species? How could she truly love all of wayward humanity?

The monster had tried to lead his people, the dinosaurs, and when his people had ceased to exist he had melded with one of Quintillion's ancestors, to be passed down his family line to Puflet. From the Stairway she could see all possible branches of history, past and future. For a moment she gazed along an axis of past Earths to see the dinosaurs dancing about the rock formation the monster had shaped with his feet and his horn. Cycads swayed about them and leather-winged reptiles circled overhead as they shook the earth with their ponderous feet, creating the patterns for a gateway to ascension, much as arrangements of particles scanned by the pentascope became transaxes to the Deep.

There was a deep-level empire, and the dinosaurs would enter it.

But in Puflet's history, there were no more dinosaurs. Humanity had come, and Kokkiro had built the Stairway of Ice for them—the lowest steps, at least. His work had been greater than that of Attequol, who had only built the human empire. That was why he was accorded the status of god.

What could Puflet do to rival such wonder? Could she repair the fifth step and rebuild the lower steps so that humanity would not lose touch with the eternal empire?

Something brushed the back of her head. Kael stood on the rim of the lowest step, fluttering like a yellow-leafed tree. He called to her, and the call became a leafy arm that pulled her to him.

"Oh! Oh! Oh!" he fluttered, smacking her with his soft leaves. He didn't know how to articulate yet on this level. Human words did not exist here. One had to fling pure concepts.

He flung a leaf, directing her attention. A vat lay empty in his mind.

She could not comprehend his loss, but slowly, as she took in her surroundings, it sank in. Serpenlino was gone. Even more surprising, the *Kiadox* and Oakiza were gone as well.

Her "oh's" joined Kael's as they stood on the shore of space, gazing outward, while the monster still rumbled, "Upward or downward!" at the back of her mind, unconcerned with her current perplexity.

Deep Four space had looked to her like a black mist dotted by pillar-like mesas, but on Deep Five, space solidified. It seemed to be made up of corridors that shot out along all dimensions, each one lined by rooms. She wanted to walk along a corridor and peer into those rooms.

She'd unfuse, of course, once she left the Stairway's fusion field. Or would she? How had humanity reached worlds all across the galaxy, and even galaxies beyond—as it was said had happened—if not by taking such a stroll?

A giant snowflake twirled through a corridor and settled onto the step beside them. A mooring line was flung out to grip the step, and a great, colorful being regarded them with guffaws that rippled the event-mists before it transmitted the image of a prehistoric train preparing for departure, the conductor calling, "All aboard!"

The colorful one was Orgmorgan. Cheering, Puflet and Kael tumbled aboard his ship.

Seconds later they were on home-level, Orgmorgan growling at Lal spaceport to prepare a berth for *Counting on Kindness*. Puflet looked about. The bridge was still littered with memory buttons and unidentifiable odds and ends, still crawling with the hand-like gelatinous alien life-forms. It smelled of spilled beer and alien effluvia. Yet beneath the detritus, its lines were clean and elegant, free from the organic frippery of *Kiadox*. Beyond the control column the bridge extended into a sleek curved viewport filled with stars and the twisting silver thread of spaceport.

Orgmorgan grunted. "You see it don't you? This ship is quality, not like Fang-face's creation. She was built by the Archtick himself."

"Who?" Puflet said.

"The Archtick. Whorl." Orgmorgan fixed his bright blue eyes on her and combed stubby fingers through his tightly-coiled orange beard, dislodging crumbs and a small alien. "Why are you sitting on my floor? Don't you know how to board a ship?"

He and Kael were strapped into niches behind the column. Puflet picked herself up and walked with all the dignity she could command to the empty niche on Orgmorgan's other side, and seated herself.

"I could beat that lumbering *Kiwiducks* three times before tomorrow," Orgmorgan boasted. "Matter of fact, I just did."

"Beat Thermeon?" she said. "He was coming to the Stairway too?"

Orgmorgan laughed. "He's a wracked pilot. Speaking of which, that green buddy of yours comes bleatin' to Taynax saying you dissolved, so he unmoored *Cuckooducts* and let her uplevel so he could go for help. I took his license and had him tried for mutiny."

"Mutiny! I hope he wasn't terminated, or anything."

"He got off with a warning, since he is so obviously ignorant. But he's not gettin' his license back."

"One of us did dissolve," Kael said.

Orgmorgan's eyes flashed at him. "You're ignorant too."

"Well, what did happen to Serpenlino?" Puflet demanded.

Orgmorgan gaped at her. Then he rolled forward in his niche and laughed, beating the armrests with orange-furred fists, until tears streamed from his eyes. Minutes passed before he could contain himself enough to speak. "Pretty partons, but you are a prize crew! I guess ol' Commandant Cooler didn't teach you nothin', and you can't figure out nothin' for yourselves, either."

Puflet scowled at him, but she didn't dare speak, fearing the quagmire of ignorance she'd somehow wandered into would just suck her down further.

Kael smiled at Orgmorgan. "Please enlighten us with your wisdom."

"Since you ask so nice, I will," Orgmorgan said. "Even though any four-year old could figure it out."

Kael and Puflet waited, and at length he said, "You're on the Stairway of Ice, right?"

They nodded.

"Each step takes you a level deeper, right?"

They nodded.

"So your friend goes up one step from you, and you can't see him any more. And you think he's dissolved. Ha ha ha!" He doubled over again.

Puflet and Kael exchanged a look.

"But we heard him scream," Puflet said.

"I'd scream too if I had the likes of you for a crew. Ha ha ha!"

Puflet compressed her lips. "Now what will happen to Serpenlino?"

"Let Fang-face deal with him," Orgmorgan said. "He loves to play the hero, an' all."

Puflet and Kael remained silent during most of the rest of the journey, while Orgmorgan discussed pilots whose ships he saw at spaceport, belittling them all, often with ridiculous names. He was gruff to spaceport personnel as well, growling when his berth wasn't instantly activated, behaving altogether like the master of the universe.

The Lalian sun was a few hours past its zenith when they set down on the spaceport landing field.

"I guess we should go to a hotel and wait for word on whether Thermeon finds Serpenlino," Puflet told Kael. "And catch up on the news."

He nodded.

Orgmorgan put the shuttle down in a parking place close to the spaceport building. As they stepped out, they found three air lifters awaiting them.

Puflet mounted one of them, and the weatherscreen closed about her. The machine rose, swung around, and headed south.

Kael and Orgmorgan headed north.

She tried to query the machine, but its comm node was closed, and she had no glowworms on her to override its program—they'd been slipped in the Deep. Dread grew in the pit of her stomach as the tall, thin banks of the capital's towers rose on the horizon. She swept over them, then descended toward a glittering golden edifice with many towers—the imperial palace.

Puflet's air lifter swept through an irising portal three-quarters of the way up on one of the towers. The portal closed behind her, and she corkscrewed down through the darkness. After three or four turns, she popped into the light once again. The air lifter deposited her in a perfect replica of Rubyland.

Habel awaited her. He wore a long cream-colored tunic that looked a lot like Thermeon's favorite style of dress and sparked an unflattering comparison in her mind. She wrinkled her nose. "So now you kidnap citizens!"

He drew himself up, laying a hand over his heart. "How can you, of all people, berate me for acting as my heart prompts?" His voice had lost its youthful timbre. "It was you who kidnapped me first, dear Puflet. Don't you recall the night of my majority, the swift ride to your pole of Ulona on your burning skeletal charger?"

"I asked you."

"I can't ask you," he said. "It seems your friends will go to any lengths to keep you away from me. Sending you to the Stairway of Ice! I don't think you can even begin to understand how much I suffered every day when I couldn't feel your mind."

"How long was I gone?" she asked.

"The year is 104,570."

It had been over a hundred years. She stared at him, amazed by how detached she felt. He would try to enslave her again, but she would never forget the bracing, frozen mind of her monster as he'd appeared on the Stairway. She was free from the aching need she'd experienced before that trip. The Stairway's vision had filled her. Maybe she still didn't have family or lovers, but she understood now that she was bonded to all of humanity.

Habel shook his head, and a wistful tone entered his voice. "You don't understand how much I love you, do you?"

"If you loved me so much, you would divorce her and marry me."

He swallowed and shook his head. "I wish I could, but I can't."

"You twistored liar," she sneered. Little red birds cheeped as they fluttered down to pick through scarlet blades of grass around their feet, but they were just birds.

His eyes flared. "You don't understand my position, Puflet. You've been off in the ethereal realms of the Deep, but I have the empire to deal with every day. Duties, responsibilities. People who depend on me. Unfortunately, she's part of the network that maintains the empire. I despise her, Puflet! She's an empty headed little nuisance. She's one of the burdens I bear. Can't you have mercy on me? You're the only one who really understands my soul. The rest of them are just using me."

"Stop letting them use you, Habel."

"I can't!" His voice twisted with anguish. "There are so many threads tying me in now. So many people depending on me."

"Do they depend on your being a liar and a hypocrite?"

His jaw went slack for a moment. Then he gritted his teeth. "Your father has really succeeded in freezing your heart, hasn't he? I guess I should have expected this. He's an ancient and experienced mindsea."

"Thermeon has nothing to do with it. I just grew up."

He shook his head.

"Let me explain, Habel."

He raised a hand as if to hold back her words, but she went on. "My deep-level mind was a gift from Quintillion. He bestowed it on me in the same way his father bestowed it on him, and he promised that it would ruin my life unless I found someone to help me control it. I believed him. The more I heard about the Fissure, the more frightened I became. If Quintillion and Thermeon together couldn't control the monster inside me, how could I ever hope to? So I searched for the strongest mindsea I could find to help me. And I found you."

He smiled at her, raising his brows as if to say, "What was so wrong in that?"

"I also believed that Quintillion's failure at the Fissure was a failure of love—Katora told me so. So I thought that I must find love with the powerful mindsea who would help me tame my monster, and our love would solve everything."

"It will," he whispered.

She shook her head. "I'm afraid that love is a very different thing from needing someone to solve your problems. You can't make them one."

"Needing someone's help isn't wrong!"

"I discovered something else when I was at the Stairway of Ice." Smiling, she tossed back her long, wild mane of hair. "I don't need anyone to help me tame my monster, Habel. It's mine—my mind, my soul, my universe. I decide whether it will climb toward a sublime life or sink into fury and despair. I don't know why Quintillion never figured that out, unless it was his penchant for avoiding any hint of responsibility. I'm free from my illusions now, and you need to be freed too."

His eyes shuttered. "I'm afraid I don't have a hundred years to spend on the Stairway of Ice. You have to help me." He reached for her.

She stepped back. "You have to help yourself, Habel."

"Why are you so hard?" he cried. "I'm begging you, Puflet. I may be emperor, but with you I'm just a slave. You enslaved me on that night you took me onto the back of your burning charger. You wanted me then. Is it right for you to toss me aside because you've had some second thoughts?"

"You tossed me aside when you married Eadin."

His lips twisted. "That was for political reasons. Can't you understand that? Do I have to spell everything out? You're the one I love, the one I've always loved."

"I think you're confusing love and need. You may want something from me, but it isn't love."

His chest heaved. "I'll prove how much I love you! I have repro rights, and I'm willing to bet that you threw off the curbs in the

Deep. We could have a child together."

He lunged, and she darted to one side. He spun around, and again they faced each other.

"I don't think you're in any state to become a father," she said.

He laughed. "An emperor has no problem at all winning repro rights. Eadin contributed to seven little darlings, and plenty other cits have vied for the right to mix their genes with mine. But my next child will be yours!"

He lunged again. Puflet avoided him until she found the lake at her back. Then they grappled. She had done well in conditioning her body in the Deep; he did not find her easy to overpower.

Then he used his mindpowers. Sensations and emotions not her own tried to insinuate themselves into her consciousness. She called upon the image of her monster in his blue-white splendor, and Habel's artifacts shriveled and dropped away. Finally he collapsed sobbing on the shore of the ruby lake and she scrambled away and smoothed the wrinkles in her travel suit.

The reek of his mindscape nauseated her. The hint of rot she'd sensed when he was young had spread, and now only the shell of a strong, healthy man remained. She found herself exhaling forcefully to clear her nasal passages, even though the stench was only in her mind's nose.

Habel beat the red rushes that grew along the lake's edge with his fists, cracking the thick leaves and releasing the pungent sap. "My mother and my wife can't see who I really am," he sobbed. "They believe I'm perfect. My perfection is so important to them! And imperial citizens! They think I'm perfect too. I'm a beneficent mindsea unlike any who went before. I build and I protect and I lead them into the Age of Illumination. My life must be so happy with my perfect family and all the honors bestowed upon me!" He lifted his head to stare at her through dripping eyes. "You're the only one I can show my true self."

Her lips curled from her fangs. "The only one you can treat with the real rottenness that's inside you?"

He was still for a moment, probably asking himself, "Is that what I just said?" Then he pulled himself to his feet. "I can't love, Puflet. And I think you're wrong about Quintillion. It has nothing to do with responsibility. I have plenty of responsibility and endless duties, and I try to discharge them faithfully. I want to be a good person. But I can't, because of this darkness inside me."

She nodded. "Yes."

"I think it's because I've never known love. My mother thinks she loves me, but she just expects things of me. She only grants her love in proportion to those expectations being met. That's how she forced me to marry Eadin. I knew that she would withhold her love if I didn't pick her favorite student for my wife. And Eadin doesn't love me. I'm a piece of furniture to her. She keeps me because she likes being the emperor's wife and feeling superior to everyone."

"Yes," Puflet murmured.

"And my father—" his face was a snarling mask—"my father mocks me because he sees my darkness and knows where it came from—from him." He shook his head. "I don't know if he meant for me to remember what he did to me. But when you take an infant's mind and force it into the Deep, you fix it in that moment forever. That moment, when my father betrayed my trust and forced me to reach for something beyond myself in space and time in order to survive, defined my personality."

Slowly she nodded. "The soul is like glass. When it's exposed to deep-level forces they mark it. The only way to remove that mark is to reheat the soul with deep-level forces again. That's why you have to go to the Stairway of Ice."

"I don't have time for that! I don't need the Stairway, anyhow. Just love me, Puflet. Love will heal."

She stared at him, the blood pounding in her ears. "Maybe you're right. Maybe love could heal you. But you have to find that love within yourself. No one can pour it into you. If you loved anyone—your children, your people—you'd be healed."

"I love you!"

"No you don't. You're just trying to find an easier way, trying to make me do all the work. But I've given up on you. I'm not going to twist myself any more for a pseudo love."

He snarled. I can't bear this—being betrayed again, by you of all people! You always loved me!"

"Even if I did love you, I wouldn't give myself to you until you divorced her. Do you think I'm a fool?"

He took a step forward, then stopped, his face uncertain.

"You can't get love from a slave, Habel, and you're trying to enslave me. Love has to be freely given, or it isn't real."

"You always loved me before," he choked.

"Maybe if you'd given me some devotion back then, I would still love you."

"Your stupid acolytes—those three stooges—kept us apart."

"There must be someone in the galaxy you can love. What about your children? Surely they crave your care?"

"The kids I had with Eadin belong to her and my mother, not to me. The rest—" He made a dismissive gesture—"belong to whatever lucky citizen won the mating race."

His tone was starting to remind her of the whiny brat his sister had been. "Your whole universe can't be sour, Habel. Look around you. There has to be someone you can confide in. Maybe you had a friend at the academy or pilot school."

He made a disgusted sound.

"I'm sure your mother does really love you, even if it's not always in the way you want. She must have worked hard to make you emperor, and I don't think she really likes politics. And your father. He didn't do what he did because he hated you. He convinced himself that—"

"No!" he yelled, his brown face flushed with blood. "He loved torturing me! And now I don't know the difference between love and torture!"

She backed from his fury until she felt the shivering branches of the red willow touching her back and her hair. The little birds flitted and chirped around them. "Maybe," she said. "Maybe you should ask one of the empire's ancient pillars to help you. Hube maybe. He struck me as a wise man."

Habel nearly choked. "Hube? Do you know how many emperors he's seen go past? We're like an evening's entertainment to him and his ancient buddies. I'd like to strangle every damn one of them with my bare hands!"

Puflet's lips twitched into a smile despite herself, picturing Hube's tree smile.

Habel glared at her. "You find that amusing, do you? You enjoy torturing me just like the rest of them!"

"It's not that, Habel. It's ... well, I know there are good and caring people out there. I don't know why you can't find them. Maybe—"

A firefly flared in the air before her. "What?"

His laugh sounded rotten as his mindscape. "Everyone else has claimed my children up until now. My next child will be all mine —and yours."

"No! Habel, this is evil!" Like an idiot, she tried batting at the firefly, before she bit her lip and desisted. Habel was tormenting her by making it visible.

"You're talking to me about evil!" He laughed again.

She realized that he never had stopped thinking of her as wicked. There never had been any hope for love between them. The firefly vanished into her body. She shut her eyes and tried to picture her cells snuffing it out, the way Quintillion's had snuffed the fireflies she'd tried to probe him with. She felt nothing, didn't know what she should have felt. It was no use. The ditbitted thing had probably already collected her genetic material and slipped away, invisible. Opening her eyes, she regarded Habel's smirking face as if from a vast distance.

"You can't protest, can you?" he chuckled. "They'd just terminate the child."

"You bastard!" What was he planning to do with this child? Torture it to punish her? Maybe it would be more merciful to terminate the poor thing rather than let that happen.

She tried to still the quivering of her face. "I have nothing more to say to you ... ever."

"Oh, but I'm sure I'll have more to say to you." Again the ugly laugh. "However, I'm done with you for the moment."

An air lifter put on its green ready glow in front of her, and she got onto it.

The vast expanse of Lal flashed before her. Brilliant city lights swept below, then shrank into tiny gleams and winked out. Above her, stars gleamed through rents in the clouds as a late rainy season storm blew across the horizon.

When she arrived at their hotel she found Kael in their suite's gathering space, still in his flying suit and on his feet in the sunken central area, where he'd probably been pacing. When he saw the expression on her face he ran to her. They held each other for a long time, and she felt as if she were in the embrace of a quiet, sweet-smelling forest where all the leaves glowed yellow.

Soaking in the wonderful heat of the irregularly shaped sandstone-rimmed pool, a gel cushion to buoy her head, Puflet stared up through the skylight until the stars came out. After a quick splash in the cool pool, she retired to the sleeping nook, her body tingling and primed.

Kael joined her, nude, his shoulder-length hair damp from the bath. She rolled over to welcome him with hands and lips and tongue. No need for words, the warm pressure of silken skin and the throb of their hearts said everything. He felt what she felt and she felt his sensing of it. With a groan, she experienced the exquisite agony of him entering her. Rocking gently, they let the waves of sensation rise and subside, rise again. His hair gently brushed her shoulders. In the skylight above them, a few stars burned, touched his hair and shoulders, gleamed from the deeps in his eyes. In her mind, she saw him clearly.

He walked through the yellow forest, looking much the same as he did beneath the home-level sun, only his hair was shaggier, and circles, drawn in ashes and chalk, decorated his body. He brought her something, held it in his outstretched hand, but he was too far away for her to make out what it was.

"Come closer, closer," she thought, drawing his body down on hers.

Every time they made love, he seemed to come one step nearer before the vision froze in their climax. Maybe tonight—

A flash of violet lightning shattered the scene.

Kael jerked up. "Wha'?"

Puflet cursed. "It's Thermeon! He waits until now, of all times, to contact me!"

Thermeon's voice sounded in her head. "I'm back in Lal, and I need to talk to you about Serpenlino. I hope you don't hate me. I hope you will accept me as your father."

I don't hate you, and I pretty much have to accept you as my father, since you are. What about Serpenlino?

"I'll explain when I see you."

Morning had broken by the time Thermeon arrived at the hotel. He stormed in like the first deluge of the rainy season, yelling, "No one dies on the Stairway of Ice!"

When Puflet and Kael stepped into the gathering space, he leaped up onto the rim of the sunken area and paced up and down above them. His flying suit exposed his tail, and it lashed his flanks. "It was unconscionable of you to leave him there!"

"We didn't know!" Kael protested.

It annoyed Puflet that Thermeon had taken the high ground, emphasizing his dominance over them, as if his height wasn't enough. "He screamed like he was dying."

"I think he saw his own death," said Kael.

Thermeon looked down on them, nostrils flaring. "Well, someone should have explained the Stairway to you before sending you off."

"Orgmorgan perhaps?" She jumped up onto the rim beside him. "He sent us off with no preparation, then laughed at our ignorance. He abandoned Serpenlino, even though he's his great-grandson too."

Thermeon scowled and ground his fangs. "Blipping Orgmorgan!"

"He insulted your ship," Kael said.

Thermeon snorted. "Of course. He could hardly boast about his character, so he boasts about his ship."

"He didn't help when Habel kidnapped Puflet," Kael said.

"What!"

Breathless, talking over each other, Puflet and Kael explained what had happened.

Thermeon made his fangs rasp impressively. "Habel must have let him bleed the mind-net, or something. Orgmorgan's all about credits. As for Habel, I'm beginning to think that Dino should have finished the job of suffocating him."

"You know about that!" Puflet cried.

"I found out when I probed him on Bri. That worthless Dino! What an idiot!" He shook his head repeatedly as he continued pacing, nearly knocking Puflet off the ledge with each pass, boots thudding against sandstone, and muttered under his breath.

"Do you think there ever was any hope for Habel?" Puflet asked.

Thermeon thought it over for a few steps. "Oh, I think he would have been fine if they had let him alone. Making him emperor when he was still unformed was deadly."

"Weren't you about Habel's age when you became emperor?" Kael asked.

"Perhaps," Thermeon said. "But I grew to manhood in a primitive land without antiaging. In that context, I was mature. You can't sit around in a place like that and do nothing for years and years. Each day is a struggle for existence."

"What about Serpenlino?" Puflet asked.

"We must return to the Stairway of Ice and call Serpenlino down. It's impossible to get back down by yourself to the spacetime you left, because of the infinite number of branching universes and histories. You need someone to call to you and guide you. Anyone who's close to him should go."

"We're going to try to mind-link him?" Puflet asked.

"No, you can't mind-link someone on the Stairway—they're outside of your universe. You just send up a beacon, a flare, so that they can find your universe. But it has to be a signal they can spot."

"How will we make this signal?"

Thermeon paced and turned, clawed hands gripped behind his back. "You call their name—or it will feel like that's what you're doing. You translate your feelings for them into deep-level force and radiate it outward."

"Have you done this before?" Kael asked.

"Of course not. This is just common knowledge."

Kael summoned a 3-nook and some refreshments, and Thermeon and Puflet left their ledge to join him.

"I think we should ask that ancient aunt of his to go," Puflet said. "Eria. He's always talking about her."

Thermeon shut his eyes and strummed his mind-net for a couple of minutes. He snapped back into focus. "She's out of reach. Probably in Andromeda. That's out of mind-link range too."

"What about bringing his favorite deep-level horse," Puflet suggested.

Thermeon nodded. "And I can ask his grandmother Quixa."

Puflet scowled. "He told me he doesn't have very good rapport with her, so I don't think she'd be any help. Besides, isn't her motto 'You Alone?' Wouldn't she expect him to navigate the infinities all by himself?"

"Oh?" Thermeon scratched his hair, making a sound like ripping fabric.

Kael turned to Puflet. "You and I should go. And Oakiza."

"And his mother," Thermeon said. "And his grandmother Fuerida and his two closest brothers."

"Wouldn't it be better just to bring one person, or the horse?" Puflet asked. "Won't all these people's signals together just create confusion?"

"No. We don't know who, if any, will create the right signal. That's why anyone with a connection to him should go."

It took several tenthyears to gather everyone on Lal. Two days before they were to depart, a message arrived for Puflet at Thermeon's desert mansion, where the expedition members had been staying. It consisted of nothing except a baby's cries.

Puflet's body went cold when she heard it. Had the child Habel threatened her with hatched? Truth or not, that was what the message implied.

Rushing outside, she saw the faint green glow of a ready air lifter. No one else was about. There was nothing anyone could do to help her, anyhow. The palace was the most secure building in the Empire, with force-worms as well as glowworms guarding its perimeter. Not even Thermeon could bull his way in there. She didn't see any point in calling Habel's bluff, either. She would have to deal with him eventually, and she preferred to have it done with, rather than delay it any longer.

She got onto the air lifter.

Instead of taking her to the Rubyland copy, the air lifter dropped her in a huge chamber with a floor of black and white squares—a recreation of the free-form hall of the Mindsea Academy of Alonaton. A knot of people awaited her there—two women and a bunch of imperial guards. She peered about in growing bafflement. Where was Habel?

The shorter of two women stepped forward, and the sudden sickly sweetness in the air identified her as Eadin. Her hair had been spun out and stiffened in a grotesque style that was, no doubt, very trendy. Puflet couldn't see the ylang-ylang in the tangle, though she could smell it. Eadin's gown spilled great quantities of semi-transparent red material around her body, and the stiff, circular collar reached up to her chin. Through the red crawled an intricate maze of golden thread that hurt the eyes. "Steal my repro rights, will you! Give me a baby with fangs!" She slapped Puflet's face. "I think this gene-thief should die, what do you think?"

She looked at the taller woman, who wore a blue sheath that complemented her creamy complexion and silvery black hair. A flashing oval pendant hung between her breasts. Puflet recognized Mind-river of Lal Cevana.

"I agree," Cevana said in a bored tone.

Eadin smiled. "Then do it."

Cevana turned toward the guards. "Kill her."

Puflet's heart pounded and her mind raced. She was about to die, and there was nothing she could do to save herself. She could mind-link Thermeon and tell him what had happened but there was no way he could prevent her murder. Then she remembered her ring.

"Out of sight!" she cried, and the jewel vanished from the dinosaur's eye, embedding itself into the floor of the great hall and other places. "Switch!"

The hall downleveled.

As she'd hoped, the guards went flat. Eadin and Cevana looked at her and laughed. Puflet had hoped the women would go flat as well. But no, Cevana had played some part in the battle at the Sunrise Ball, hadn't she? And Eadin must have awakened her own mindpowers since then.

Eadin's voice rang out with flourishes and overtones in the Deep. "Pathetic little Puflet! So predictable! You can't escape my justice with your old tricks. I am the empress!"

"You're not empress in the Deep," Puflet retorted. The monster stood by her side, blue-white as he'd been on the Stairway, mist swirling off his bones.

"So you think maybe you are?" Eadin laughed. "Well, your reign is about to end."

Her words reminded Puflet unpleasantly of what she'd said to Ix on the day of her coup.

Eadin mounted her skeletal steed, whose hornless skull was wreathed by flaming vines that blossomed into ylang-ylang flowers of fire. The gold thread on her gown turned into dancing lightning. With a triumphant yell she galloped to the indistinct distances of the hall, then turned to make her charge.

Puflet sprang onto the monster's back and couched her lance. His bones ignited with orange-red flame as they had in the days of her academy. She charged at Eadin. The little fool had no idea how powerful Puflet was in the Deep. She imagined that being empress would count for something here, but it wouldn't.

The monster's hoofbeats shook the universe with their thunder, and thunder echoed back from Eadin's side of the hall. Puflet and her rival flew toward each other.

Eadin's steed looked different than it had a moment before. It had the same nose horn and spiked frill on the back of its skull as Puflet's steed. Its hooves thundered in rhythm with the thunder of the monster's hooves.

Something was wrong.

The sensation of wrongness grew with each stride as Puflet's twin surged nearer and nearer on the back of her fireball-snorting monster. Her mind screamed, "Danger!" She had to turn aside.

It was too late. Puflet crashed into her mirror image.

Only there was no impact. Her lance slid into the other lance. One monster's horn met the other monster's horn, and they merged. Puflet fell.

32

Cevana's voice sounded in Puflet's ears. "Switchback."

"It worked!" Eadin trumpeted. "She's gone!"

"Naturally," Cevana sniffed. "She was just like her sire—fierce, but stupid."

"There's no way she can come back?"

"None. Remember your Patternistics, if you can." Cevana's tone was condescending.

"I remember! You remember that I was Katora's best pupil. But —"

"It's very simple, Eadin. Everyone wins in their own history. But since Puflet was battling herself, she both won and lost in every history. But you can't exist in two simultaneous states on home level. Hence, she can't exist in any home-level history. Hence—vanished."

"There's no body," Eadin whined.

"No. There's nothing left in a death by contradiction." Cevana sniggered.

The voices sounded as if they stood next to her, but all Puflet saw was a vague glow. She kept craning her neck and shifting her eyes, and suddenly the black and white checkered floor and the figures of Eadin and Cevana flashed into view. It seemed as if they were directly below her. Cevana fiddled with the shiny ornament that hung around her neck.

A mirror, Puflet thought. That mirror was a deep-level artifact, and Cevana had used it to ... do whatever she'd done. But she was wrong, Puflet wasn't dead. She was right above them.

At least, she thought she was. But when Cevana and Eadin started away and she tried to follow, she found herself beyond the walls of the palace, staring into Lal's blazing sun.

Puflet wasn't in the human world at all. She was merely watching it from dimensions of the Deep. A chill rippled through her. Didn't she have a body any more? She tried lifting her hand in front of her face to see if she still wore the ring.

Another shock. Instead of a hand she saw the monster's skeletal foot, blue-white bones exuding a swirl of sparkling mist.

She had become the monster.

She ran. There was joy in the sensation of flight, the surge of power following the resonance of thunder through corridors of the strange dimensions she now inhabited. She could have run forever, but she recalled the shallower world and desired to see it again.

It took much craning and twisting of her head before she found the direction she needed to look.

Trees. Dark trunks, thick and straight, standing in close rows to form deep shadows. The whisper of a warm breeze and scents of sap and leaves. She remembered Lakus boasting about a forest he had represented in court and saved from voracious developers, where trees embedded wonderful tales in the cells of their wood.

She ran again, and again paused to look. Potato-like life-forms like Orgmorgan's friend splashed in a lake, vibrating their tendrils in patterns that were taken up by one after another, with small variations. Puflet roared, and everyone's tendrils stretched upward for a moment, as if to test the air for signs of an approaching storm.

She ran again. For an instant beautiful horses raced alongside, and her heart surged, but then they were gone, leaving only the swirling eddies their hooves had brought forth.

On and on she roamed, trying to comprehend the landscape surrounding her when she wasn't watching the world of mortal beings. It was magnificent, rife with sweeping perspectives of great complexity and achingly-beautiful illumination. Somehow she realized that she wasn't seeing it properly, nor could she focus on the beings she vaguely sensed watching her.

She was immature. The development she should have followed,

building one skill upon another until she bloomed into full awareness, had been interrupted.

Had been interrupted more than once, this latest time with her expulsion from her human body and her identity as Puflet. As a dinosaur, she had sought the thrills of evolving from the murk of instinctual behavior into the clarity of meta-awareness. She had not ceded the vision to extinction, but had returned in human form to ride the waves of possibility once again.

She needed to return to complete her growth. She had enjoyed being Puflet. The realization of what "upward" or "downward" meant had been good, a little spurt in her awareness. That life had been far more useful than the one that had named itself "Quintillion," and she wanted it back.

She ran through the sublime but shadowed landscape, pausing every so often to root into a mortal world, but it was no use. There were infinitely many mortal worlds and she would never find the one she had left.

Then she recalled Thermeon's words about finding a way down the Stairway of Ice. The problem was the same, and it would have the same solution. She would listen for a call. Someone would project their voice into the Deep, wanting her back.

She moved among the shadows, senses tuned for a call. A haunting melody drew her, until she realized that it was just a memory of her life as Quintillion, and she herself had hummed it.

She paused, tossing her great, spiky head and snorting plumes of mist. All of Quintillion's memories belonged to her, including the tricks of deep-level engineering Puflet had sought. She would find them useful when she returned to her mortal life.

She continued her quest, stilled the noise of her own mind, the better to listen. At last it came—a tendril of longing that beseeched her return. She followed. It was not far, all mortal worlds equally near to where she walked. She merely turned, peered, and saw ...

Habel. He knelt in an alcove in a vaulted circular chamber that wasn't copied from any place Puflet recognized. The chamber was wrought from dark stone and carved with interlocking patterns for a solemn and elegant effect. It wasn't on Lal, for the air lacked the sandy smell pervading that planet. She was able to sense as well that the local gravity was less than Lal's.

Puflet roared and Habel started. His eyes cast all about, but he couldn't see her. Then he said, "Switch," and the chamber became part of her realm. They stood eye to eye.

He spoke first. "Puflet?"

She dipped her nose horn. "Where is this place?"

"It's Yohorb. Eadin's homeworld. We built a new city here. I used all the concepts you shared with me in Rubyland."

"I didn't share them," she growled, her voice deeper than thunder. "You ripped them from my mind."

"I did it to honor you!"

"Did Puflet receive any of the credit?"

"No, but I know—"

She cut him short with a roar, flame issuing from her throat.

Habel stepped back, hands raised defensively. "It wasn't me who banished you! It was all Eadin's plan, the little bit-brain! She boasted about it to me, later that night. The guards were just to scare you, you know. Cevana would never have had you shot. Thermeon knows her, and she knew he'd probe her mind when you went missing. He would've killed her. But because it was a duel, because you accepted the challenge—as they had planned—he couldn't do anything."

Puflet rumbled and tossed her head. She had been a fool.

"Kael went back to Gilkay," Habel said. "Oakiza is back on Ulona. And Thermeon's off at the Stairway of Ice. They've all given up and forgotten about you. I'm the only one who really needs you, who really wants you back."

"They think I died, don't they?"

"I'm sure Kael and Oakiza do. I don't know what Thermeon saw in Cevana's mind. But he's not praying for you to come back to him, is he?" Straightening, Habel gazed up at her. "Do you need to take that form? Can't you adopt a more ... human shape?"

Growling, she shook her massive head.

"You don't want to. You still hate me. I had to do it, Puflet. It was the only way I could think of to bind you to me after you'd become so hard. But it turned out well. Our daughter has become a fine young woman."

She snorted puffs of mist. "What year is it?"

"104,662."

Puflet went very still. Nearly a hundred years had passed while she'd roamed the Deep.

Habel went on talking. "We sent Mana to the Orphan School of Mosalno for her education, since Eadin couldn't stand the sight of her. But it was much better for her than being cosseted at home. She graduated with honors—as I told you, she's a fine young woman. She'll be here in a few days with the rest of the family. Eadin has to put up with her for public occasions, and we'll be celebrating the big Yohorban holiday—the Festival of Suffering— which comes around every thirteen imperial years." He chuckled. "Suffering—that's very apropos, isn't it? The average Yohorban, excepting Eadin, is a deep thinker."

Puflet stood silent, staring at him while mist gently wrapped around her forefeet and her horn. The stench of decay, seeping from his pores, hung about him in a gray cloud.

"I'd bring you back if I could," he said.

She released a blast of mist. "Only if you could keep me for yourself." Stomping a hind leg she rattled the broken chain that hung from her ankle.

Habel's gaze flicked to the floor for a moment. "Puflet, I'm sorry for all the trouble I caused you. But I really do care."

"I could have had a happy life, if it wasn't for you."

He gave a wry smile. "I could have had a happy life, if it wasn't for my father. So here we are—two ruined lives."

"If you abdicate now," she said, "you might still save yourself."

He shook his head. "You should hear the newsers. They love me, and Eadin, and our kids, and our city. This is the Age of Illumination."

"It's built on sewage."

"Nothing in this human world is perfect. You, on the other hand, are perfect." He stepped closer. "Will you burn me if I touch you?" She remained silent. He stretched out a hand and very gently touched her horn. The touch prickled her. He started, as if her chill tingled. Then he smiled and ran his hand down the length of her horn and onto the curve of her beak.

An expression of deep melancholy filled his face. He stepped back. "Don't leave. I'll come back." He upleveled the chamber and walked away.

She didn't move. She didn't want to lose the one connection to the world she had known. She willed her toes to meld to the floor of the alcove, and she became a statue. Habel came every day to talk to her, to tell her about the preparations for the Festival of Suffering.

"I'm afraid Mana won't be coming after all," he said a couple of days before the affair. "She's gotten herself involved in deep-level horse racing. 'I can't leave my horses right now,' her message says. But I think it's more than that. She believes that hurdling world-lines on horseback affects the empire's future. Takes after you, doesn't she? I think there's a man, too. Maybe your old buddy, Oakiza."

Puflet clacked her beak in annoyance.

"On the other hand, the royal family of Gilkay have arrived, their first appearance in thirty-nine years. Seems they've finally forgiven us for our part in the loss of the old king."

Puflet growled low in her throat.

"Isn't it better to forgive and go on with life?"

"I'll believe that when you forgive your father."

He stood silent, head bowed.

A quick tattoo of steps came through the chamber, followed by the scent of ylang-ylang. "What are you doing here? Oh, what is that thing?"

Habel turned to face his wife. She no longer wore her hair in tangles; now it rose in two horns that writhed and flamed in the Deep.

"This is my newest deep-level sculpture," Habel said.

Eadin eyed Puflet from various angles (she didn't need to move to do this in the Deep). "I find it perfectly hideous! It looks like Puflet's charger! I want you to get rid of it immediately."

"I like it," Habel said.

She huffed. "I don't care what you like. Just get rid of it."

Habel sighed and upleveled the chamber.

On the day of the festival the emperor and his family paraded through the main street of the city of Kodato, beacon for the Age of Illumination. Afterward, they were joined by their guests in the palace to which the downleveling chamber was attached. Unseen in her dimension, Puflet watched and listened to the party goers.

Waves of them rolled in and out of the chamber, glittering in fashions that were all new to her. Katora's voice pealed above all the rest, quelling even Eadin's. When the two women shared the room, Eadin became the same cooing sycophant she'd been at the academy. Out of Katora's earshot, her voice went lower by an octave and she hurled commands at lesser mortals. Dino was all shuffling feet and "yes, dear's" in the presence of his wife and daughter-in-law, but when he cornered Habel he mocked him with an excellent parody of Eadin—"You better have gotten rid of that ugly statue! Keep your eyes off of that slut!"—red eyes sparkling malevolently.

The two oldest children of the imperial couple, Jasal and Reselona, were present, behaving like well-programmed bioids beneath the eyes of their parents and grandparents. Members of the Circle abounded, as well as other government officials, including Mind-river of Lal Cevana. Katora's half-sister pronounced the Yohorbian palace "precious" and "quaint," her condescending laughter rebounding from its walls.

There were scads of lesser celebrities Puflet didn't recognize.

When Kael appeared in the group with the new king of Gilkay, something ached deep inside her monstrous body.

Groups of men and women formed and dispersed again in seemingly random patterns of color, sound, and scent. Habel's son drew a pair of women into Puflet's alcove and pawed them in the shadows. Katora swept into the chamber, star-strewn swirls of blue fabric following her, a tiara agleam on her head. "Jasal!" she blared.

Jasal and his women slunk off. When Katora turned to retire in majesty, he made a face at her back, and the girls giggled into their hands.

Eadin and Cevana entered the chamber in heavy, brocaded velvet gowns with enormous collars, Eadin's in green and Cevana's in purple. Cevana's mirror pendant glimmered against the bodice of her gown like a moon from a night sky. Eadin pointed at Puflet's alcove. "It was in there. You can't imagine the start it gave me."

"I'm sure." Cevana's voice dripped with contempt.

Kael strode up to the two women. He grabbed Cevana's mirror and gave it a yank. The chain snapped. He slapped her face. "I challenge you!"

"You dare!" she gasped.

"Who do you think you are?" Eadin screeched.

"Switch!" Kael cried.

All the men and women in the chamber except for the three of them went flat. Kael mounted a prancing charger with enormous antlers sprouting from its skull. The antlers were trees with yellow fire for their leaves. "Scared to fight without this?" He waggled the mirror on its broken chain.

"I'll squash you, puppy!" Cevana sneered. Snapping her fingers, she summoned a charger with an axe-blade sprouting from its forehead, the name Horl etched in its mirror-surface. Another one of his worshipers, was she? Flames ignited in Puflet's belly.

Eadin fluttered about. "I'll help you!"

Ignoring her, Cevana galloped off, the hoofbeats of her charger like thudding rocks, while Kael raced in the opposite direction. They turned as one and charged each other across the chamber.

Puflet roared as the combatants crashed together. Cevana's lance smashed into the antlers of Kael's steed, sending a spray of yellow flame across the chamber. His lance pierced her chest where the mirror had hung. With an eerie, too-high shriek, she deflated.

"Help!" Eadin screamed. "Save me! Katora, save me!"

Kael had heard Puflet's roar. He rode to her alcove and dismounted. He trembled as he looked up at her. His eyes gleamed with tears. "I'm sorry. I should have protected you better." He held the mirror out toward her.

She shuddered, sending forth slow ripples of deep-level force. This was the moment she'd always seen in their lovemaking, the mirror the gift he bore. The long-sought enlightenment had arrived at last, but it brought only sorrow, and all her memories of thrilling intimacy turned bittersweet, seeing that this had been their goal. He knotted the broken ends of the mirror's chain together and hung it over her horn.

Did he know that she could hear him, that she was alive but trapped in the Deep? She dared not speak and give him false hope.

Katora's voice rang out. "Switchback!"

Kael turned away from Puflet. Guests, rousing from their Deepinduced torpor, saw Cevana sprawled across the floor and screamed.

Katora pointed her finger at Kael. "Begone! And don't ever come back to this planet!"

"Not that I'd want to." He stalked from the chamber.

Eadin flung herself around Katora's waist, blubbering. "It was still there! He didn't get rid of that ugly statue like I told him to!"

Katora gave her a startled look, no doubt wondering how she could be worried about statues when one of the guests lay dead. She disengaged the clutching fingers and gently pushed her away. "Send the guests home, Eadin. I'll contact the wonderdome."

Eadin scurried out, the guests filing after her. Katora remained, staring dispassionately at the corpse.

A few minutes later, Habel walked in. "Everyone has left." He looked at Cevana and smiled. "She was a vile person. I would have dismissed her, except it would have made too many enemies. Now they can't blame me."

Katora drew her starry shawl around her shoulders, as if she felt a chill. "I wonder if it was wise to copy Puflet's battle arena in your city."

"You know why we did it, mother."

"Why?"

"To prove that we could do it better than her."

Katora's green lips curved in a smile. "So, who will be the new mind-river of Lal? I think that Reselona would be good for the job."

Habel nodded. "Oh, but Orgmorgan told me he had a granddaughter who would suit, if the niche opened up."

"You shouldn't be in that man's debt, Habel. He's very greedy."

He shrugged. "It couldn't be helped."

The two of them left the chamber. Not moving her feet, Puflet assumed a bipedal form and examined the mirror that had proved her undoing. She found no complexities within; it was a simple plane of reflection, though it reflected deep-level force as well as home-level radiation. Tilting it, she caught glimpses of parts of the city beyond her anchor point, delicate spires and covered walkways, snow-trimmed bridges and frozen ponds, an indigo sky graced by unfamiliar stars and three moons. She watched departing guests catching air lifters or buses, some heading for hotels, others bound for the nearest shuttle station.

She sighed. No part of her essence was trapped within the mirror. It could do nothing to free her from her dilemma.

The contradictory nature of her existence remained the problem. When she'd struck the mirror, the sensation—so different from impact with a rival—had confused her, sent her rebounding at a strange angle. As Cevana had pointed out, she hadn't known whether she had won or lost, so had lost contact with histories in the mortal realm.

She kept staring at the mirror, wondering whether another impact could twist her back into alignment, but no answer came to her.

The next morning, when Habel came to her alcove, Puflet stood in monster form once again.

"I have bad news for you," he said. "Your champion was found dead near the shuttle parking lot."

A roar of protest pouring from her throat, she sprouted fingers and tilted the mirror this way and that until the sight she sought flashed to her eyes. Kael lay prone on rimed grass, lines of frost ants crawling to and from his gaping mouth and eyes. She shuddered and let the mirror fall. It clattered on the stone and cracked.

"I'm sorry," Habel said. "I had nothing to do with it, of course."

Puflet bowed her massive head and mourned in silence, waves of mist rolling like tears down her snout.

"He must have sustained wounds in the duel last night," Habel said, "and succumbed to them."

A laugh sounded from across the chamber. "Actually, I helped him along just a little. I had a guard drop an ice crustacean into his air lifter." Eadin pranced nearer. "I thought I told you to get rid—"

Habel whirled on her. "If you must commit crimes, don't tell me about them!"

She tittered. "What are you afraid of? Thermeon's going to rip into your mind? If you were like me, you wouldn't have let the old lunatic know you." She stood grinning, arms akimbo, hair horns swaying and crackling with sparks of deep-level force.

The rottenness within Habel pulsed and expanded as he stared at her. Only a thin and brittle shell kept it from oozing out.

Eadin's ylang-ylang spewed out another cloying wave. "I think it's about time he died too, don't you agree?"

Habel choked. "Who? Thermeon?"

"Yes. He's been around for long enough. And now that I think of it, why must I put up with a fanged child? I'll—"

A shuddering groan had built within Puflet from the moment Eadin had mentioned her part in Kael's death. As she prattled about destroying the last thing in the world Puflet cared about, it exploded. "No! You will die!" Waves of fire erupting from her eye sockets, mouth, and nostrils, she charged from the alcove, knocked Habel aside, and drove her horn into Eadin's body. Eadin had time for only a tiny squeak before she ignited, and the reek of ylang-ylang turned into a pall of ashes.

An ancient mind within Puflet, the most ancient of those she had collected in her mortal lives, awakened. "Die! Die!" she shrieked, pounding the blackened thing that had been Eadin against the stone of the floor, then stomping on it, rocking the chamber with her wrath.

As Habel tried to scramble away a fireball caught him. He screamed and burned. His shell shriveled and cracked, releasing the putrefaction within. Flames sizzled around him until the bad odor was gone. It took only seconds, Puflet reflected, to purify what he had collected over a lifetime.

The ancient mind gave her no more time for thought. Knowledge that had somehow been locked away burst upon her with the violence and majesty of starbirth. Bellowing her triumph, she rose, expanded, smashed through the vault of the chamber. Its fusion field was gone, but she didn't need it. She overcame Cevana's contradiction on a tide of power.

"Die!" she thundered, and the city burned. Spires, bridges, walkways sent plumes of black-edged orange into the morning sky. "Kael is dead!" she roared. "And you will celebrate my suffering!"

Members of the Circle ran screaming from their fiery hotel suites, and she stomped on them. "Vile insects! It's time you paid for your crimes!"

"Calm yourself!" Hube admonished, but she shoved him into a

fountain that billowed into steam at her touch.

Her rage grew more excruciating with each death. There was no end to it. Expanding to still greater size, she looked down on the planet's indigo oceans and pale blue glaciers. She understood now how Thermeon had flashed Wamatu. She could flash Yohorb. The unending wrath pounding in her temples urged her to go ahead.

"Stop!" A sparkling figure rose on the horizon, tower tall, its eyes blazing blue stars—Katora.

Puflet faced her, roaring out fireballs.

Katora swept them aside with her airy sleeves. "Go back to your void, you evil monster!"

"Not until I destroy you, witch!" Puflet lunged to lodge her horn in Katora's heart, but Katora unleashed a gale that tumbled her back.

"I foresaw you killing my son." Katora's visage brooded like a stormy green sky. "And despite all of my efforts you've taken his life."

"It's all your own fault!" Puflet raged. "Why did you persecute me and encourage anyone else who wanted to kill me, starting with Valri? Why couldn't you have left me alone? I just wanted to be free. I just wanted to lead a quiet, happy life like anyone else."

"You're not normal, you twisted thing. You hunger for destruction."

"Yes, I do now, because you've taken away everything I cared about!"

"I saw this in you from the beginning."

Puflet snorted and tossed her head while the city continued to crackle about them. "I never was free, was I? The moment I escaped from Ix, I made an enemy of Valri. And just by being who I am, I made an enemy of you. There was never any escape."

"No," Katora said. "It would have been better for everyone had you never been born."

"No!" Puflet thundered. "I had good in me! I had beautiful dreams and aspirations. You're the one who made my life hell!"

"And now you've done the same for me."

Puflet jabbed her horn toward Katora. "Your 'Age of Illumination' was a farce, you bit-brained hypocrite! It was built on lies and hate, beginning with your son's hatred for his father."

Katora compressed her lips. She had no answer to that. Perplexity marked her brow. She still refused to think it through.

"Hah!" Puflet stomped a foot, and a burned out spire crashed into the rubble. "You got exactly what you deserved, bitch!"

It occurred to her, in a sudden burst of insight, that when Katora had foreseen her killing Habel, she had in fact chosen that history and made it happen. Because that was how one worked the Fourth Tenet. Will was an illusion. The act of envisioning a thing and focusing awareness on it brought it into your life.

But how could Puflet have avoided playing her role in the tragedy? She hadn't understood what was happening, the forces Katora had set in motion. Aside from giving up and dying, or fleeing to another galaxy, she still didn't see any way she could have escaped the pitfalls that had lain in wait for her.

Of course, she could have stayed away from Habel.

As she contemplated this truth, her fires died, and blue mists swirled across her bones once again.

Katora's voice pealed over the planet. "I refuse to accept this history! Knowledge of the Second Tenet will allow me to rechoose the past." Perspectives and dimensions shifted as she applied her mindsize to effect her choice. Flames sucked back into buildings. Rubble reassembled itself into a spire.

Puflet's fury reignited. "So you think you can have your rotten son back? What about my feelings? Are you going to bring Kael back too?"

"This time I will make sure that you are removed before the party," Katora said.

"Then Kael will still kill Cevana, and Eadin will still kill him. You despicable old hag! You care about no one except yourself, do you?"

Katora's words lanced down from the sky. "I care about all good people. Your friend was a killer just like you, and not entitled to my compassion. I can't use half-measures with evil. If given any quarter, it just grows. It must be eradicated."

"You've had your way long enough!" Puflet rumbled. "It's time you suffered like the rest of us!"

Katora smiled and pulled somewhere, somewhen with her mind. The planet shifted, air and land and ocean coming apart like pieces of a puzzle, the gaps behind spacetime shooting an intense repugnance through Puflet. It was horrible seeing this mortal world for what it was, a construct of arbitrary patterns rather than something essentially true.

Puflet stomped her feet and roared, but Katora went on disassembling the world. Puflet charged, but dimensions had been twisted around, and she couldn't get traction. She slid sideways, skidded upside down, ended facing every way except where Katora was.

Quintillion had mastered the Second Tenet. Puflet summoned his memories, but as she did, the will to fight left her. Katora cracked spacetime like a whip, and she tumbled through dizzying perspectives to land in her alcove.

34

It was the morning of the party. Puflet stared in horror as Habel crouched before her repeating the words she had heard, it seemed, the day before.

"First there will be a parade to the city plaza, where I will lead the populace in ritually plunging a dagger of ice into my heart. A larger icy dagger, sculpted from—"

Katora entered the chamber. She hadn't been there on the first enactment of this day. She paused for a moment, staring at her son, her face going radiant just to see him alive once again. Then her words snapped out. "Habel, you must get rid of that statue. I don't care what you do, but it must be gone by the time our guests arrive. It's an evil thing, and extremely dangerous."

He rose and turned to face her. "It's a deep-level artifact, mother. It can't easily be destroyed."

"Then banish it."

He threw out out his hands. "How?"

"This is no time for games. It's very dangerous! I foresee disaster if it's not gone."

Puflet understood her frustration. She had seen the future, but how to make him believe her?

Habel folded his arms across his chest with the air of a man very tired of having his mother dictate his life.

Puflet tried to come up with her own solution. If Katora would only work with her, and try to preserve Kael's life as well as

Habel's, there would be no problem. Why couldn't the old hag understand that Puflet was motivated by love for her friends and hatred for her enemies, and not by some amorphous impulse toward evil?

But maybe Habel would work with her.

If they had been on home-level she could have mind-linked him for a private channel, but in the Deep she couldn't speak to him without Katora overhearing. She waited.

Katora reached the end of her patience. "Very well. If that's how you want to be, I'm calling your father."

Habel sighed as she strode away, then turned back toward Puflet. "Maybe if you changed your form, so people wouldn't know who you are. You could do that, couldn't you?"

"I'm not giving up my form, Habel. It's about all I have left. Now, listen to me. I could go away now to make her happy, and you could call me back later. But you have to promise to do something for me."

"What?"

"Kael will fight a duel with Cevana at the party and kill her."

Habel squeezed his eyes. "How do you know this?"

"Your mother and I both had a vision of the future."

"So what did you do that has her so worried?"

She blew out a long whorl of mist. "Eadin will try to murder Kael with an ice crustacean after he leaves the palace. You have to save him, or I'll be very angry."

He smiled knowingly. "You'll go on a rampage?"

She tilted her ponderous head up, then down. "But I don't have to go on a rampage. I don't want to. I want to have some reason to hope for the human species. But if a good man like Kael is going to die because your blitted mother thinks he's evil, then maybe it's time for this species to give way to something else."

Habel cocked his head as he studied her. "So this Kael is more important to you than I am?"

She snapped her beak in annoyance. "You're just the man who robbed me of my life—with Eadin's help, of course. Kael is guileless, enthusiastic, and good-hearted. And if he's anywhere near as loyal to his wife as he is to his father, he'll never cheat on her."

Habel scowled. "Is that what you have against me?"

Puflet fell still, her monster face impassive as the statue she was supposed to be. She felt hope slipping away.

Dino sauntered up, dressed in a white tunic suit with a jaunty red scarf around his waist and his hair in a hedgehog cut, brilliantly aglow in the Deep. "So, son, this is the little lady you've been keeping on the side?"

"Shut up," Habel growled.

Dino pushed past him and ran his hand up Puflet's horn, grinning at the tingle. "Hm. I'll bet you've had some thrilling times with this thing up your ass."

Habel' face went crimson. "Shut up!"

Dino sank to his knees and kissed the tip of Puflet's beak. "Ach, my giant clam will have to worry with this beauty around!"

Habel's face twisted with revulsion. The decay inside him roiled. Suddenly he aimed a kick at his father's back, but Dino saw it coming. A wave of his hand summoned a swirl of deep-level wind that slid Habel beneath Puflet's skull and discharged him out into the chamber.

Cursing, Habel scrambled up. Again his darkness seethed, and this time his facade cracked, and a mass of slimy, maggoty stuff pushed out. He screamed at his father, his voice cracking. "I've had all I can take of your insults! I've had all I can take of your insulting existence! I challenge you!" With the speed of thought he was astride his burning skeletal charger with the four curling tusks, lance aimed for his father's heart.

Dino yelped and scrabbled crabwise on all fours, his tail sticking straight up into the air with its tuft bristled into a ball. Puflet had the impression he was still toying with his son. An instant before Habel's lance pierced him, he sat his own charger, a crazy-looking beast with water instead of fire dripping from its bones and clam shells for its head and hooves. The grotesque thing clattered and slid across the stones of the floor, always one step from collapse and always one step ahead of Habel's lance.

Habel screamed and urged his charger forward. He chased Dino around and around the perimeter of the chamber. Though it looked like he was racing four times as fast as the slip-sliding clam shell steed, he couldn't quite get close enough to jab Dino with his lance.

Katora rushed in with a swoosh of starry sleeves. "Stop! Stop!"

Father and son raced around her, Habel's face agonized, a plume of reeking darkness trailing from him.

"Stop!" Katora pleaded.

Screaming, Habel leaned out over his charger's neck as he thrust forward with his lance. He still failed to nail Dino.

Katora glowered at Puflet. "What did you do to them?"

Puflet blew rings of mist at her. "Exactly how do you imagine I am responsible for this? Or am I just your convenient scapegoat for all the evil in existence—the source of plagues, earthquakes, and evolutionary maladaptations? If you haven't noticed the dynamic between your son and his father before this, then maybe you've been living in some other universe."

Katora had stopped listening to her clever speech midway through, eyes once more on the combatants. "Stop!" she wailed. "Stop it this instant!"

It ended with the suddenness of a lightning stroke. Dino wheeled his steed, no longer clacking with clam shells, but wreathed in flame and possessed of the clawed feet and the skull of a Tyrannosaurus, and Habel rode onto his lance. Habel gave a small "urk" as lance point and spoiled flesh burst out from his back. Then he shriveled.

Katora's screams rang through all the dimensions of the Deep.

35

Puflet thought that Katora would try to rechoose the past again, but the tragic turn of her new history seemed to have unnerved her. She sobbed in Dino's arms and he murmured comforting words, his demeanor solemn, yet tender. The planes of his face looked different than when he had been teasing Habel, no longer mischievous but handsome and noble. Even the spikes had vanished from his hair.

Katora upleveled the chamber so that the wonderdome team could enter. Of course there was no hope of refloating Habel. The unfusing damage was extensive.

After they packed the body into a pod and took it away, Katora sobbed again. "My poor son! My beautiful, wonderful boy! There will never be another one like him!"

Dino clasped her to his chest and smoothed the rumpled curls of her dark brown hair. "We could have another one."

"But he wouldn't be a mindsea. Habel was one in a million."

"We could have another mindsea if you really want it. I made Habel a mindsea, and I can make the next one a mindsea too."

"You can't make a mindsea!" she wailed.

"Shhh, shhh," he soothed. "Of course I can. And hopefully, the next one will be a little more grateful for his gift."

Katora went quiet, thinking this over. A few minutes later, she said, "I chose a universe where our child would be a mindsea."

"Of course," Dino said. "I felt the pressure of your choice.

That's why I did it."

She stiffened. "You did something to Habel? But he had mindpowers from when he was very little. You.... No! Not.... You couldn't have...." Lifting her head, she stared up into his eyes. "You weren't responsible for what happened when he was an infant."

Dino kissed her. "Of course. There's only one way to make a mindsea."

She gasped. "But ... that's...."

"I know, I know." Dino smoothed the hair back from her brow. "It was so hard to do, but I felt your wishes. I had to steel myself."

"I didn't wish that!"

Dino kissed her. "There was no other way."

"No other way?" she murmured.

Invisible in her alcove, Puflet snorted softly. Katora certainly was taking the revelation without much show of spirit. No doubt Dino was exerting his mindpowers. He'd caught her at her weakest moment too, the clever bastard.

A wailing arose in the distance and swelled, accompanied by the smell of ylang-ylang. Eadin pelted in. "Where is he? Where is my husband?"

Katora and Dino broke apart.

"The body was removed," Katora said.

Eadin's mouth gulped, fish-like. "But ... he...." Her eyes widened as the ramifications of Habel's death sank in. She wouldn't be empress any more. A yowl ripped from her throat, and she pitched forward to throw herself into Katora's arms. Katora caught her by the elbow and gave her a shake.

"Contain yourself, Eadin! You have to contact the guests and tell them not to come. The festival will have to be canceled."

Eadin gulped. "You can't cancel the festival! Yohorb has always celebrated—"

"The emperor is dead!" Katora screamed. "This is a galactic tragedy!"

"Yes, yes." Eadin's head bobbed, horns and ylang-ylang waggling. "How do you think I feel? He was my—"

"Get to it!" Katora snapped.

"I ... yes." Eadin dragged herself out, wails echoing through the corridor beyond the chamber.

Puflet smiled in her alcove. The party was canceled. Kael would be safe. She sneered at Katora. *You wanted to sacrifice him and save your son, but things turned out exactly the opposite way.*

Katora looked at Dino. "We have to worry about the succession. I can have Orgmorgan impound that sick seed woman's ship for a few days, so she can't reach Lal until it's been settled. I think Jasal would make a good emperor."

"Of course," Dino agreed.

Katora fingered her lip. "No, wait. He washed out of pilot school. We can't have an emperor who's Deep-blind. But Reselona would do. She's a pilot, and she's been all around the galaxy. She has a certain air of majesty, I think." She smiled.

"Yes. Reselona will make a wonderful empress."

"Get her and take her to Lal immediately. We can't afford to ask for Orgmorgan's ship. It comes at too high a price."

"Of course," Dino said. "We don't need his help for delaying Sik-Seed, either. I'll persuade spaceport to lose her ship for a while."

"Very well. And tell Reselona to dismiss Cevana after she takes the oath. Dilora can be mind-river of Lal. We don't need vile people in the highest echelons."

"Of course not."

"Why don't you take them both with you," Katora said. "No, wait. Maybe Dilora should take her own ship. Yes, she might need it. But hurry and get Reselona over there."

Dino gave her a last quick hug and kiss, then strode away. Katora looked after him. When his steps had faded she clenched her fists and muttered, "I should have married Thermeon."

She must have forgotten, or not realized, that Puflet still watched her from the alcove's deep dimensions.

Katora remained silent and still for some minutes, reaching out with her mind, Puflet guessed. She started when heavy boot steps came through the corridor. Jasal burst in. He was a big, lion-like man with his mother's amber eyes and a swirling mane of golden-orange hair.

"Grandmother! Why does Reselona get to be emperor? I'm the eldest! It's not fair!"

Katora shook back her curls. "Your sister has seen more of the galaxy than you have."

"But look at all the work I've done on Toneos! My big convention hall with its famous restaurants and shallow-level tower!"

"That convention hall is where the ID-pooling Society meets every year, isn't it?"

"Yes. ID-pooling is a viable way to increase human brain-power without mindsize."

Katora gave him a chill smile. "Switch," she said, ending the argument.

Turning away from her flattened grandson, she glowered at Puflet. "Why are you still here?"

"I'm a family member too. I'm your sister-in-law! And I do have mindpowers."

"You're not human."

"I was. You could have been nice to me." She gave a misty sigh. "No one seems to please you."

"I was pleased with Habel. He was my perfect child! Everything about him was right! Why couldn't he have been happy?" Bright tears shone on her green cheeks.

"I don't suppose Dino gave him just a little dose of fear and pain," Puflet said. "It must have been an extended session."

The keen eyes flashed toward her. "Exactly how long have you known about that?"

Puflet thought back. "Since the day it happened. Habel reached out to me with his mind."

"To you?" The eyes flared like novas. "Why would he do that? He didn't know you! I'm his mother! He should have come to me." Sobs shook her. "He never did come to me. Why?"

Puflet remained silent.

With a shudder, Katora mastered herself. "Who else knew?"

"Kael, Oakiza, and Serpenlino. Orgmorgan. Eria. Thermeon. I was always discussing it with them, wondering if anything could be done to help him."

Katora gazed upon her in the eerie silence of the Deep—breathing and heartbeat were unnecessary there, and only affected by some as a dance of the spirit. At length she spoke again. "How long has Thermeon known?"

"Since Habel went to pilot school."

"And he never saw fit to tell me either!"

Puflet clacked her beak. "Exactly why would someone you constantly badmouth and ban from planets owe you any explanations?"

Katora tossed her hair, swirling out sparks and stars. "You don't understand what Thermeon and I have together. I am a lot closer to his ideal goddess-star than any of those shallow creatures who chased him when he was emperor."

"Yet you withheld your love from him!"

"I examined the possibilities. Thermeon and I never would have had a mindsea child."

Puflet stared at her, letting the echoes of her words cascade in small ripples across her flanks. "Of course not," she said finally. "He wouldn't treat a child the way Dino treated Habel."

"That can't be the only way!" Katora stared into distant vistas of the Deep. Her brow furrowed with concentration, and she slowly raised her hands, as if lifting a great weight. Sparkling planes took form around her, with crystals of time tinkling softly along their edges. The view along them reminded Puflet of the Stairway of Ice.

"Look!" Katora pointed. "Thermeon and I would have had a son named Uno, a talented musician."

Taking her human form, Puflet stepped from the alcove and stood by her sister-in-law's side. She sighted along the edge where Katora pointed, and glimpsed a copper-haired youth. Waves of music washed over her, invigorating as a cold shower.

"His life would've been tragically short," Katora said. "Unnecessarily so, but Thermeon is very strongly opposed to copy insurance."

"So you chose the history that gave you Habel rather than him," Puflet said. "You denied the world that amazing music."

"His life was too short," Katora said.

"Not too short to create something beautiful. And he looked happy."

"I could not have borne that life!" Katora snapped.

"Are you going to rechoose the past again?" Puflet asked.

"Bring Habel back?"

Katora shook her head, her eyes tragic. She swept out her hand, indicating a plane of glistening moments. "Look at his futures—all black! Always he challenges his father; if not on this day, soon afterward. And he always dies. I didn't look far enough when I aimed my life toward his birth. When I saw that he would be a mindsea, and emperor at a young age, I was so happy. I never imagined that it would all fall apart this way." She darted Puflet a look from the corner of her eye. "If only you hadn't been tangled up in his life. If only he hadn't hated his father so!"

"But that was the key to his being a mindsea, wasn't it?"

"There must be another way." Katora examined future histories, shifting them with solemn gestures. Each shift gave Puflet a fleeting sensation of pure emptiness.

Katora pointed along another edge. "If I divorced Dino and married Thermeon, I could still have a musician son, and a daughter who would be president of the galactic union, after the empire converts to democracy."

Puflet spewed out foggy laughter. "A galactic democracy? Impossible!"

Katora scowled at her. "It's right there."

Puflet looked where she pointed. Space battles sparkled like fireworks. Famous landmarks fell. Aliens swelled the ranks of citizens. It was a very different galaxy.

"I can't see Thermeon marrying you," Puflet said. "Not after you've rejected him for so long."

Katora smiled smugly. "As I told you, I fit his ideal."

"I think his ideal is someone who loves him. You don't."

Katora's brows drew down sharply. "What would you know about love? You're incapable of it."

The sting of her words made tongues of flame dance from Puflet's fingertips. "The Stairway of Ice showed me what love is. It's something that pours out of you when you say 'yes,' to life."

Katora continued to shift and study futures. "If I stay with Dino, we could have a pilot son and a musician daughter." She shook her head. "I don't see any mindseas, with either of them." She kept twisting her fingers, bringing that terrible lurch in reality, then peering into new vistas.

"Have you always had this ability?" Puflet asked.

Katora smiled, though her eyes remained on the planes of spacetime. "I don't have the communications or engineering skills of Quintillion, or the destructive power of Thermeon—the power you have as well. Seeing through time is my special skill."

"I suppose you had an unhappy childhood too."

Katora's eyes flitted from the futures. "Why do you say that? Oh, that's your theory—that mindsize develops in relation to early unhappiness." She smiled. "You're wrong, because I had a very happy childhood."

"Your parents both loved you?"

The green face went still. "I—I don't actually remember my childhood. My father erased my memories when he was trying to keep me away from Quintillion. I suppose it was that feeling that I could get them back if I concentrated really hard that began my explorations into time."

Puflet nodded and swirled out a thread of mist. "How come you never showed your students at the Academy how you can look at alternate futures?"

Katora's eyes flared and then her face went still again. Finally she said, "I've never been able to show them to anyone else this way. I've never been able to see them this clearly myself before, either." She looked at Puflet as if seeing her for the first time. "I don't think that you are really Puflet any more. You're not human, not even the deep-level part of a human being. I don't know what you are."

"I'm a deep-level being," Puflet said. "But I'm just a baby. I need to get back into the mortal world in order to continue my development. Help me!"

Katora shook her head. "You'll never be human again."

Gouts of flame erupted from Puflet's nostrils. "You're not looking!"

"Don't you think I checked the futures carefully when you arrived in Ulona? I saw there was no possibility for you to ever be happy."

Puflet felt the planes of the universe give way beneath her. "No chance?"

"I'm sorry. Everyone's lives would have been better if you had never been born."

"Everyone's?" A small tongue of flame returned to her index finger. "What about the people of the Hundred Tenth Millennium?"

Katora raised one eyebrow. "What do they have to do with you?"

"There's something very important I have to do for them. I have to repair the Stairway of Ice so that humanity can continue to evolve into deeper levels."

"I don't see how your life in the Hundred Fifth Millennium could have any bearing on that. The Age of Illumination will lead humanity forward. It doesn't involve you."

"Your Age of Illumination sputtered and died with Habel."

"There will be another mindsea in my family line. One nurtured in love and kindness."

"You said there was none."

"I will keep looking."

"What about me?" Puflet roared, the monster's voice and flame shooting from her mouth. "Why can't you get it through your ditted head that I am the Age of Illumination you're looking for."

"Your histories lead nowhere," Katora said with finality.

"Show me the point of my conception," Puflet said. "I will stand there and look for myself."

Katora pointed, and Puflet glided away.

36

Dizzying perspectives surrounded Puflet. Planes of possible history burst outward from the point where she stood. She turned herself along the endless axes of the Deep trying to follow them all. It was impossible. There were an infinite number of them.

Yet she quickly saw that most of the histories led to bad endings for herself. In most of them she died in Ix's lab. In most of the others she perished on the journey to Ulona. If she made it to the planet, she was killed half of the time by Tepi, and another third of the time by Fanala. If she made it to the academy, death from attacks by Hinomia and Yusun or Valri was the most likely outcome. If she had stayed in Tadruhemdron, arrest and termination would have followed, the Ulonan Judicial Committee more responsive to Katora's sensibilities than Bri's.

More times than not, she would have died after the mind-rape in Rubyland. More times than not, she never returned from the Stairway of Ice. If she had fled the palace rather than engaging in the duel with Cevana, Eadin would have murdered her.

Of all possible chains of events she might have followed, it seemed that she had chosen the best of them. But once she became trapped in the Deep, there were no more links to follow—her nature was no longer bound by the linear paths of mortal beings.

Perplexed, Puflet turned back toward Katora. The figure before her stretched upward as it gathered more distant memories. It held aloft a light, and its hair became burning rays that streamed outward from the light.

Katora thought of herself as a guiding light, but the light of her most intense focus burned with menace. Puflet's dinosaur memories roared out in recognition. "You are the star that cast your fire to Earth and first turned me into a blazing skeleton! You ignited my rage and hatred when you destroyed all of my people and our aspirations! I still do battle with you, O terror of the skies!"

In dinosaur form once again, Puflet charged her ancient foe. The goddess-star cast down her spears of light, ending a million species' lives. The fire engulfed Puflet. Once again she lived through that awful moment of pain, terror, and the bitterness of defeat. Once again she trapped the fire within her rib cage and turned defeat into victory. She spat fire back at the goddess. "You will never kill me!"

The goddess shifted again. She was Katora, twisting the radiant event-chains, trying to shut Puflet out of human history. Puflet leaped from glittering spacetime plane to glittering plane, searching for the one angle among trillions that would allow her to become human again.

"Begone, evil one!" Katora trumpeted. "Have you not seen for yourself that there is no future for you?" She tipped a sheaf of possibilities and sent Puflet plunging toward the void.

Snorting and leaping like a charger, Puflet soared across the chasm and dug her bony toes into a plane on the far side. "You don't understand the consequences of your actions!" she bellowed.

"On the contrary, my mind is clear, and yours clouded by animal passions. I am guiding light to the good and purifying fire to the wicked."

"You'll exterminate the human spirit with your purges. But you don't care what happens in the Hundred Tenth Millennium, do you?" Puflet challenged. "That must be after you yourself will depart the human world."

With blazing eyes, Katora lashed the time stream. "I will have my Age of Illumination!" A vortex of possibilities caught Puflet and spun her about, event-chains screeching past in a blur. She got her toes onto another plane and heaved herself clear of the time-storm. "I fight for life, Katora. You are the bringer of death."

"A garden requires weeding."

"Destroying is easy. But I say, let humanity grow wild and free, extending its histories as far as ever it can. Surge!" Puflet leaped over one majestic wheel of possibilities after another, her mind's eye alert for the tiny gleam that would mean the combination of patterns she sought.

A gleam, a scent, a call—she knew it was there.

"Stop!" Katora's voice tugged at her with its overtones of unassailable authority.

She shook her head and forged on.

The gleam swelled. Puflet narrowed her focus to a single axis of time, to one plane out of the infinitudes spinning around it, to one line among countless lines making up that plane. From somewhere along that line came the gleam. She plunged toward it.

Infinities whipped past her, spiraling upward against the blackness of the void. She recognized the perspective as she swooped down to it—the Stairway of Ice.

She might have known, for the higher steps, those that had always existed because they had no component of time, could only lie in the center where students of Patternistics always brought their mind's eye when they wanted to work on the Tenets. Puflet and Katora had fought their battle there, beyond time. As Puflet descended the Stairway, time would start for her again.

Taking human form, she landed with a gentle crunch on the sixth step, where a shadowy figure stood awaiting her.

Sparkles of surprise flitted across her bones. "You knew I would be up there?"

Serpenlino bowed.

"All the people in Thermeon's expedition must be calling you. We'd best get down to them before time passes us by."

He offered his arm and she took it. They poised on the edge of the precipice, the array of all possible fifth steps outspread below. Puflet heard only the whispering of time-streams against the silence of the Deep, but Serpenlino turned toward one of the fifth step's embodiments and nodded to her.

They leaped and landed on the shore of the corridor of space. A ship shaped like an iridescent many-finned whale bobbed there, and Thermeon stood before the ship, his form merged with that of his dragon-spirit, violet eyes ablaze in his reptile face and leathery wings outspread. Small jewel-like figures beside him must be members of Serpenlino's family.

Serpenlino and his grandmother, mother, and brothers blew toward each other and met in a song of shadow and light. Thermeon's eyes flashed fire when he saw Puflet. He threw back his head and roared. Taking her own dinosaur form for an instant, she let her roar mingle with his to shake the corridor of space with their triumphant joy. Then she showed him her plan for returning to the human world. It was simple, elegant, and only slightly illegal.

Puflet tried to open her eyes, but the eyelids were made of stone. She was a statue, numb and motionless. The only things that moved were inside her skull. There was much activity in there. She roamed the vaulted chambers with her mind's eye, moving thoughts and ideas and memories around, trying to get them arranged just so, the way one did when moving into a new home. Imagine finding this delightful mansion vacant. So of course she had swept in from....

She couldn't quite recall where she'd been before. Somewhere where everything sparkled, and the rooms were all at odd angles, piled up on each other very high.

No, that couldn't be right. She'd been in the mansion of her mind, but she'd felt very lonely because all of her chambers were empty and still. Then, in a flash from above, a flaming dinosaur had appeared, his eyes like stars and his voice like thunder. "You must become me!" he'd roared.

Wait.... She was the dinosaur, because the dinosaur had brought all of the memories she was trying to organize. She was also someone named Quintillion, and someone named Puflet. But mostly Puflet, because the voices up there called her that.

They were calling again.

Sometimes she wished they would go away. They were always asking her to do things she couldn't, like move the statue that was her body. They were touching her. She felt it, so she wasn't all numb.

She wasn't sure that she liked being touched. There was something special about touching, and she wanted someone special to touch her. Was it Habel?

Memories like little red birds flitted through her mind. Then she remembered that Habel was dead. She heard herself sigh.

For a while she just drifted, mourning Habel. He'd been beautiful and gifted, but his parents had done bad things to him, and all had been lost in a river of sewage.

But other things were happening now, and there were other people out there, the ones touching her. She wanted to find out who they were, so she struggled to lift her eyelids.

The stone doors over her eyes creaked and moved ponderously. She gave up the effort and went back to managing her memories. There had been doors like her eyelids in an underground city. Doors facing an arena where duels had been fought on flaming skeletal steeds like the dinosaur that had brought her memories.

Tadruhemdron. She thought about her academy for a while. Was it still in operation, or had the Coder headmistress closed its doors? She didn't have her deep-level jewel or her ring any more, but she could make new ones. The knowledge was stored away in one of the chambers of her mind.

They were still calling her.

She made another effort, and her eyes cracked open. Light stabbed into her mansion, so bright and shocking she slammed the doors shut again.

She'd get used to it, though. She'd gone through this before.

After a few more efforts she was able to keep her eyelids raised. She worked on making her eyes focus. A face loomed over her, offering encouragement. It surprised her that it wasn't green. Hadn't a green man always been bothering her—Oakiza?

It wasn't blue either. There had been a blue man named Kael. Was he dead? Memories flared—power like a million suns coursing through her, a city in ashes. She blinked.

The face remained, brown as a cliff ledge, pierced by two holes through which she saw the rainy sky. No. Those were eyes.

"Serpenlino?" Her voice creaked and rasped.

He grunted. "I'm here." His hand wormed out until the fingers could wrap around hers. She drifted pleasantly with that point of contact keeping her in the universe.

Sometime later, when she forced her eyelids up again, Serpenlino still leaned over her from a mushroom cup on the side of her gel-nook. She licked her lips. "Kael ... what happened to him ... the festival of Suffering ... Yohorb...."

He shook his head. "I don't think he ever attended one of those festivals. The last time the empire prepared to celebrate the occasion, Emperor Habel was killed in a mind-duel with his father, so the festival was canceled. After that we no longer had a Yohorban empress, so it ceased to be a galactic event. Kael married a princess from Gilkay some years ago. He sends his best."

She smiled. "Good for him. What year.... Who is emperor?"

"It's 104,805. Katora is emperor."

Puflet gasped.

"When her child with Thermeon was in the incubator, she took the throne in its name. That child didn't turn out well, but there was another on its way. And so on. We're still waiting...."

She tried not to laugh. It hurt to much. When the spasm subsided, she looked at Serpenlino. "You screamed when we were on the Stairway of Ice. What...."

"I saw what Cevana did to you."

"You saw it before it happened?"

Nodding, he took both of her hands in his. "There seemed no way to prevent it. It was like a boulder that had already dropped from the cliff. I could only try to undo the damage afterward."

"And my daughter, Mana?"

His smile broadened until the tips of his fangs winked out. "She still rides deep-level horses in Tadruhemdron. Come home with me, Puflet, and you'll see her."

The monster's roar rolled around inside her skull. She squeezed his hands. "I'll think about it. I need to rest now."

In the days that followed Serpenlino returned and made her work to regain control of her body, as Oakiza had done the last time this had happened to her. His eyes awaited her answer, but she continued to ponder in silence.

Once as she lay alone, thinking about Serpenlino and Mana and Tadruhemdron, a stealthy step made her look up. Dino's red eyes leered down at her. "You made Katora divorce me, and I'm going to kill you!"

As he lunged for her throat she jerked up and bared her fangs, planning to slash his wrist, but he jumped back again. "Just kidding! Ha ha ha!"

"I find it not amusing," she snarled at him. "What are you doing here, anyway?"

Drawing himself up, he placed a hand over his heart and gave her a wounded look. "What am I doing here? Just where do you think you are? Look at these walls!" He ran his hand over the striated dun curves around her. "This is water-sculpted sandstone. This is not your ordinary wonderdome. You're at Vuduna!"

"So?" she said.

"It's the resort I own, out in the midst of the Lalian desert. Where did you think they were going to float an illegal copy? I was the one who got your gene specs from the palace, too."

"Thank you, Dino. I guess I owe my new life to you."

"Yes, that and your complimentary vacation. How do you like the meals so far?"

"All they've given me so far is gel."

"I'll see that you get lobster tonight." He tapped his head as if to show that he was sending commands to the system. "I have one more question."

"Hm?"

"Will you marry me?"

"No!" she screamed. "It's bad enough being your sister."

He laughed.

"You're better off without her. Seriously. I think she warped your soul. I mean, I hope you weren't always the person I saw in that battle with Habel."

His face screwed up. "If anyone warped me, it was him. I never imagined that he would hate me so much, for his whole life! I never imagined that he could possibly remember! He was just an infant!"

"An infant with mindpowers."

He shook his head. "Infants are unreasonable. He couldn't get it through his head that I was just trying to help him." He gave his head another shake, then looked at her. "I'm surprised that you didn't tell on me."

"I promised not to in exchange for my academy."

"Well, after you didn't need me any more."

"It would have been better for everyone if I had, wouldn't it?" He sighed.

"Look," she said. "You've been a pretty good brother to me, on the whole. But you were a wracked husband to Katora."

He threw up his hands. "She won't be able to take my father for very long. He's always the primitive patriarchal male with his mates. I, on the other hand, can respect a strong woman."

Puflet sat up and yelled at him. "You didn't respect Katora! You groveled before her! What she needs is someone who won't take her shit!"

Laughing, Dino scampered out, and she fell back in exhaustion.

38

The lowest steps of the Stairway of Ice had once been anchored to the planet Mars, but between the time humans left their birth system and the foundation of the galactic empire, they had torn loose and crumbled. Puflet needed only to construct four steps, each on a successively deeper patternistic level, before they connected with the steps of the Stairway of Ice that were everywhere. She decided to base the lowest step on an extinct volcano near Tadruhemdron.

Mt. Knightbone rose in a decapitated black cone above lush greens of the jungle. Glowworm-powered construction equipment had already leveled the mountain's top and prepared the way for eventual pilgrims and tourists. Puflet climbed a thousand gleaming black lava-stone steps to the summit and paused, breathing deeply of the crisp air. She gazed down into the greenness far below; then, shading her eyes, peered upward into the sun's white blaze.

Imperial citizens who'd had a proper upbringing—not like her—grew up associating their suns with the empire's founder, Attequol. She winced at the sun's intensity. It was mid-summer. The jungle sweltered below her. This high, the air was less humid, though still hot.

"I am your protégé," she called into the light. "Guide my evolution." Her head whirled with glorious anticipation.

To begin work on the next step, she needed patternistic tools. On her finger gleamed the silvery ring forged during Besi's era.

Her jewel winked from the dinosaur's eye hole.

"Out of sight," she whispered, and the crystal embedded itself in the mountaintop. "Switch."

The crystal radiated its strange light, bringing forth the deeper shapes of things. Puflet began to work, using the larger, more powerful body she now commanded. Scooping up material from a nearby red cinder cone, she carried it to the top of Mt. Knightbone and spread it out to form the base of the next step. She worked without rest while the sun—somewhat shrunken from the deep perspective—began its downward swoop in compressed time that made years feel like hours.

It seemed as if she worked harder and harder, but moved less material with each return to the mountaintop. How could that be? Here, in the Deep, rays of light alone should inject her with energy. Yet she found herself scrabbling over the heap of red rocks she had created. Her feet slipped out from under her, and she was on her knees.

Then the sun went down, and the emanation of her crystal outlined rocks around her with a sickly glow. She tried to push herself up, only to fall back. To her horror, she saw that she had worn away her fingers. As she struggled for purchase on the mountaintop, more and more of her body disintegrated. Why was she failing to evolve?

The monster! It had driven her on this path, it would lend her its strength. But where was it? After thrashing about, scraping more of herself away, she finally spotted it halfway down the heap, inert and disarticulated, half-buried by red dust.

Something was very wrong. She had seen the monster burning with red-orange fury or wreathed by ice-blue mist, but now it looked dead, powerless. She called to it, but it just lay there.

Her fear swelled. She must have done something wrong, but she didn't know what it was, and she had no idea how to stem the erosion of everything she'd felt to be true and right. She had to escape from the mountaintop before she was ground down to nothing. She rolled over and let herself slide downward, faster and faster, toward the shadowy skeletons of the jungle trees. She landed with a thump on a large skeleton that gave slightly to soften the impact. It moved about her with a rhythmical swaying.

Puflet stretched out her hands—somehow restored—and laughed as she felt the ribcage of the monster enclosing her. All was well.

The sun rose, and the seemingly dead jungle burst into leaf around her. Green tendrils twined around the monster's bones and ripened into sagging fleshy sacs. Their stench nauseated her.

"Back to the mountain," she directed the monster, but it merely plodded along.

"We can't go upward," groaned a sepulchral voice. "We must suffer."

To her horror, she found Quintillion crouched inside the ribcage beside her.

"Get out!" she screamed. "The monster is mine now! You gave it to me!"

She kicked Quintillion, and he smiled as her feet stove in a couple ribs with a sickening crunch.

"My suffering is eternal," he chanted. "For my life is a day in the life of a dragon. I have roamed uncounted worlds. I have felt every blessing and every torment. I have loved countless times and I have been torn by every vile passion that is possible. Can you possibly have pity on me?"

Puflet gritted her teeth. "No. You've never helped anyone in your life—or lives."

"There are evils that pander to the naked soul that has been cast out from everything it's known to be born again alone and afraid, with no one to understand or show the way. Can you blame me for straying?"

"What evils?" she demanded.

"I share the feelings of everyone I know, everyone I touch, whether human or animal, and it tears me apart. On every side I see the wrongs that may result from any move I make. I try to avoid them, but it only makes more wrong things happen. Everything I do is a disaster!"

She shook with frustrated fury. "Then go away! Die! Just leave me alone!"

"Have you ever felt a world die?" he ranted. "Can you hear the screams that burst from the throats of animals and men when the sky above them blossoms with fire? Can you hear the hiss of an ocean turning to steam? It is like the roar of a vast crowd that is very far away. When your eyeballs boil and darkness falls, you have not long to live—all around you in the darkness you hear the thud of dying hearts, the flutter of convulsing limbs. Then the blackness becomes total—your world has died. Such was the gift Thermeon brought to my home planet Wamatu."

Puflet sat speechless.

"It was Monstronon," came Thermeon's voice. "We must fight that blackness, the nothingness."

"But wasn't Wamatu a planet?" Puflet sighed. "Full of people and animals?"

"Monstronon enters living beings through wounds in their souls, that is, the deep-level part of them, and sometimes, regrettably, it is necessary for us to take up arms against those Monstronon is controlling, when their actions become a threat to those we love or to the fabric of our society. But this is the last resort."

"But-but-" Puflet stammered. "Aren't you speaking of the monster? The same monster you yourself harbor?"

Thermeon lifted his chin. "I'm free of it now."

"Then what are you doing here?"

"This is not Monstronon. It is my goddess-star. She guided me from my savage birth land in the form of a star, but she promised to take human form and be my wife. In the height of my passion, I call out to her, and she fills my bride's body. But they ... when the match isn't right, the human body unfuses. But I found my goddess-star in Katora."

"You could have sex without unfusing her?"

"Yes." He gave his glowing white mane a vigorous nod, ethereal violet eyes fixed on a distant splendor. "She could not remain in the human world. She granted me one moment of perfect bliss, a light that brightens everything in my life, and then she returned to her homeland, where we will be joined in eternity someday. She left her human body behind so that our child could be incubated."

Puflet's stomach roiled. "So who is empress?"

"I am." A voice wafted down from above. A gleam of silver shone beyond the monster's ribs.

Puflet glared at Thermeon. "Your goddess-star is up there. Go to her!"

He smiled, but continued to caress a pus-oozing rib.

More and more figures rode entwined with the monster's bones, all telling their tales.

"I am Quazi," said a quavering female voice. "When the father of Eria and Quintillion emerged from my body, he took with him all the tales of the world's ending, the suffering of all the souls that ran and died when fire rained from the skies. The dinosaurs defied the fire, their mighty roars made tiny by its thunders. Countless lesser creatures were quenched with the barest hiss, their struggles forgotten by all but me."

"But this can't be right!" Puflet wailed. "The monster is mine! Mine alone!"

Katora's mocking laugh floated down from overhead, and Puflet craned her neck to find her perched atop the monster's skull.

"Have you forgotten the Second Tenet?" Katora sneered. "There is only now. Everything that ever happened is happening now."

Puflet slipped a finger into her mouth and worried it with her fangs. "You mean that anyone ever plagued by the monster is still part of it?"

Katora's laugh blended with the chorus of wails and groans and screams that trilled up and down the flesh-swathed bones.

"No!" Puflet yelled. "I won't be part of it! I'll get myself free!"

She wriggled and slashed and stomped at her fleshy enclosure, but it only squirted blood and pus all over her, until she dropped back in frustration.

A moment later she sat up straight and shook herself. One only saw the compression of time in the Deep. In the human world, time was neatly divided.

"Switchback," she said.

The flesh monster vanished, and she found herself sitting up in her cell at Vuduna, heart pounding and hair damp with sweat. She stared at her hand in the dim light from her hair. Of course, she wore no ring. She had lost it when she'd lost her body. Taking a long, deep breath she thanked all the stars that the agony she'd just been through had only been a dream.

39

Puflet had grown strong enough to leave her recovery cell and visit Vuduna's lake. Live fish and other harmless aquatic life forms swam through its waters, and in its deepest center lay the giant clam, which Dino had moved from the mindsea academy after his divorce, or so he claimed. Numerous small islands dotted the lake, each one beautifully landscaped and topped by a guest cottage. Some could be reached by bridges, others required one of the resort's boats. The wonderdome, as well as Vuduna's offices and main restaurants, were located on the mainland. Puflet and Serpenlino walked side by side along the path that followed the lakeshore. She breathed in the warm, moist air, then gazed up at her companion's solemn bronze face. His mind-flavor had changed since the Stairway of Ice. He no longer flitted, shadowy and amorphous. His core had solidified into a smooth gray monolith. An ancient scent clung to him, legacy of his forebears, yet he was newly shaped. He embraced the creativity and intelligence he shared with his father, but directed them toward his own goals, his newly-awakened vision.

"I know you want me to live with you in Tadruhemdron and ride your horses, but my monster says no."

His eyes met hers. She went on. "I can't just live my life and never think about what lies beyond. I've been given a power, and it needs to be used! Quintillion wasted it, for the most part, but I refuse to!"

"So what will you do?" he asked.

"I can't stop thinking about the people of the Hundred Tenth Millennium, and how the monster asked me if I chose upward or downward, and upward means evolving, awakening, new awareness...."

She took in another deep breath of the wet wind. "I thought about trying to re-engineer the crumbled steps of the Stairway of Ice, but then I had a nightmare. I was in the Deep, trying to carve out the steps, but all I accomplished was wearing away my own bones.

"And then I realized that I have to take smaller steps. It's a long term project. I can't make it all happen at once. If I give just a little push, maybe it will gather momentum, get bigger as time goes on."

"That sounds reasonable," he said.

"So I thought about the impediments that need to be removed before humanity can grow in awareness. And what do you suppose the biggest block is?"

"Hatred and bigotry?"

"I think it's slavery. Even though Ix is gone, there are still slavers hiding out on obscure planets, still slaves who suffer for their whole lives. I have a powerful monster, Serpenlino. I can look for these slaver rings and smash them!" She beat a fist against her palm.

He nodded. "But what about love, Puflet? I still love you! I want very much for you to live with me in Tadruhemdron. And what about your daughter? What about the children we might have together?"

She pursed her lips as they walked along. "Well, maybe there will be times between my raids on the slavers when I could live in Tadruhemdron. I could do some of the searching out in mind-link. And the planning." She shrugged. "What do you think?"

"I think it might work."

Hand in hand they walked on.

ACKNOWLEDGMENTS

This book would not have been possible without the inspiration of the museums that first introduced me to the mystery of monsters from the past, especially the American Museum of Natural History in New York City and the National Museum of Denmark in Copenhagen.

Thanks also to the my instructors and fellow graduates from Taos Toolbox 2007, who gave me the tools to start writing this story, and to the organizers of NaNoWriMo 2007, who shepherded me through the first draft.

Finally, thanks to my beta readers, especially May-Lin Iversen.

ABOUT THE EMPIRE

Information about the Mindsea Empire and other novels in this series may be found at www.bonniebrunish.com.